I0766915

RACING HEARTS
PINE VALLEY COLLEGE BOOK ONE
USA TODAY BESTSELLING AUTHOR
K. A KNIGHT

READER CONSIDERATIONS

This is a dark book not meant for anybody under the ages of 18.

Content includes: explicit sex, explicit violence, stalking, murder, torture, sexual assault, dubious consent, depression

PINE VALLEY COLLEGE
Kings Hall
Maven Hall
Bell Tower
Isaac Hall
Pool
Becker Hall
Library
Magnus Hall
Tomb

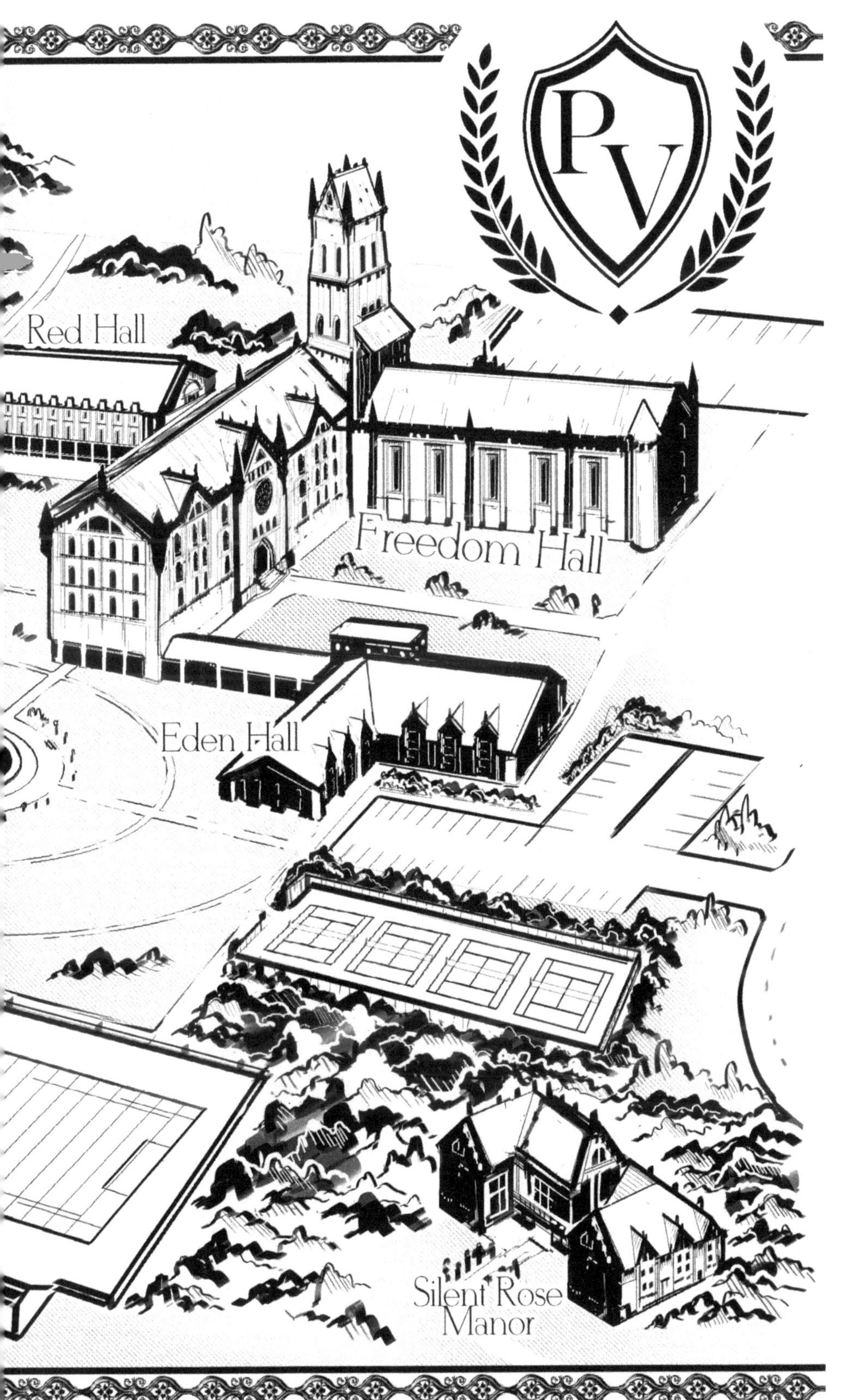

PV
Red Hall
Freedom Hall
Eden Hall
Silent Rose Manor

SHAW DRIVE
ANDERS AVE
ONE WAY
ACTIVE DRIVEWAY
STOP
SILENT ROSE
EVER
Drive Valley

ONE

The first time I saw Evan Shaw, he was walking with his preppy, rich friends, dressed in designer clothes from head to toe as he strolled toward the sprawling buildings that made up the university my sister had joined.

Pine Valley College.

I was dropping her off for her first day, and his laughter pierced my music-filled car. He didn't see me. Why would he?

It immediately pissed me off. Actually, all these pretty fuckers here annoy me. They dripped with wealth and privilege, and I hated it, hated that my sister was going there, but I knew it was the best place for her.

The second time was when I picked her up from a party. He had a guy pressed against a wall on the side of the house, his tongue deep in his throat, and his hand shoved down the guy's jeans. They weren't even trying to hide what they were doing.

The third time is right now, at this low-rent diner where I'm eating dinner . . . where I'd thought I was safe.

I was wrong.

I don't know what the fuck a rich boy like him is doing in a place like this, but it pisses me off. Can't I have any peace from the loaded motherfuckers who go to that uptight school? The only reason I moved here was to be closer to my sister so I could keep her safe, yet I'm always surrounded by them.

They make me so angry, and Evan? He's the worst.

A bright smile curves his plump lips, showcasing perfect white teeth I bet his mom and dad paid a fortune for. His skin is golden and perfect—no doubt it's been stretched and perfected by the best doctors in the world—and his blond hair, almost the color of ice, is perfectly styled, with two long pieces hanging before his ears, the rest slicked back, falling just above his wide shoulders. He's flawlessly clean in an oversized button-down and slacks, the latest designer bag thrown carelessly over his shoulder.

Basically, he's my opposite.

Fisting my oil-stained hands, I focus on my food and try not to look at him. I tell myself to breathe through the hatred and not taste the woodsy scent that seems to follow him. I need to keep my head down and remember why I'm here—for her. Everything is for her, so I can give her a better life than I ever had.

"Hey, is this seat taken?"

Of fucking course fate couldn't be that kind.

I can actually feel him next to me.

He blocks out the sun, his expensive cologne wrapping around me. "Excuse me?" he repeats, his voice deep and smooth. I hate that I glance at him. I hate that my eyes seek him out even more.

It's all a front.

Rich boys like him aren't nice, not to dirt like me.

"It's taken," I grind out, my voice as deep as thunder.

His eyes flare as he blinks, glancing at the empty seat and then at my large frame perched on the barstool next to it. He arches a brow as if to call me a liar and drops into it anyway.

"I said it's taken."

"Oops." He shrugs, pulling a sticky menu closer with a happy smile.

"Leave now," I order. Usually, that's enough to send anyone running, not to mention the glare I give him. They normally shit themselves or cry.

He ignores me, scanning the menu as my nostrils flare.

"You don't belong here."

"Says who?" he asks, tilting his head to meet my dark gaze. His hands clench the menu, though, giving him away, his biceps straining the material of the shirt. He's built like a rich boy and not with the type of muscles you get from showing off, but from actually working out.

It's probably all for the look of it, not actually useful.

"Me," I respond.

"Ah, too bad, I kind of like it here. It has a nice view." His eyes rove across me, and I slam my mug down on the counter, ignoring the liquid that splashes out. He grins, his eyes cutting back to mine. "What can I say? I like it dirty."

"Get out now," I warn, grinding my jaw. I'm so fucking angry. How dare he look at me like that and mess with me? Does this stupid prick have no sense of self- preservation?

"What the fuck is your problem?" he asks, his eyes flashing as he glares at me. I bet he's never been in a fight in his life, not to mention ever stood up to someone like me.

"You're my problem, rich boy," I snap as I stand, draining my cup. I throw extra bills down and smile tightly at Sandra, the middle-aged waitress working a double with twins at home.

"See you next time, Alek," she calls.

I storm out of the diner, but I hear his soft, expensive shoes tap on the sidewalk behind me and I whirl.

"Alek," he calls. "That's your name?"

"What the fuck do you want, rich boy?" I seethe, stepping closer and towering over him. He might have muscle and be tall for his rich boy school, but I'm much bigger, and we both know it.

"You dropped this." He hands over my worn wallet held together by tape, his eyes scanning me contemptuously before he turns and walks back inside.

He judged and dismissed me like they all do.

I fucking hate rich pricks.

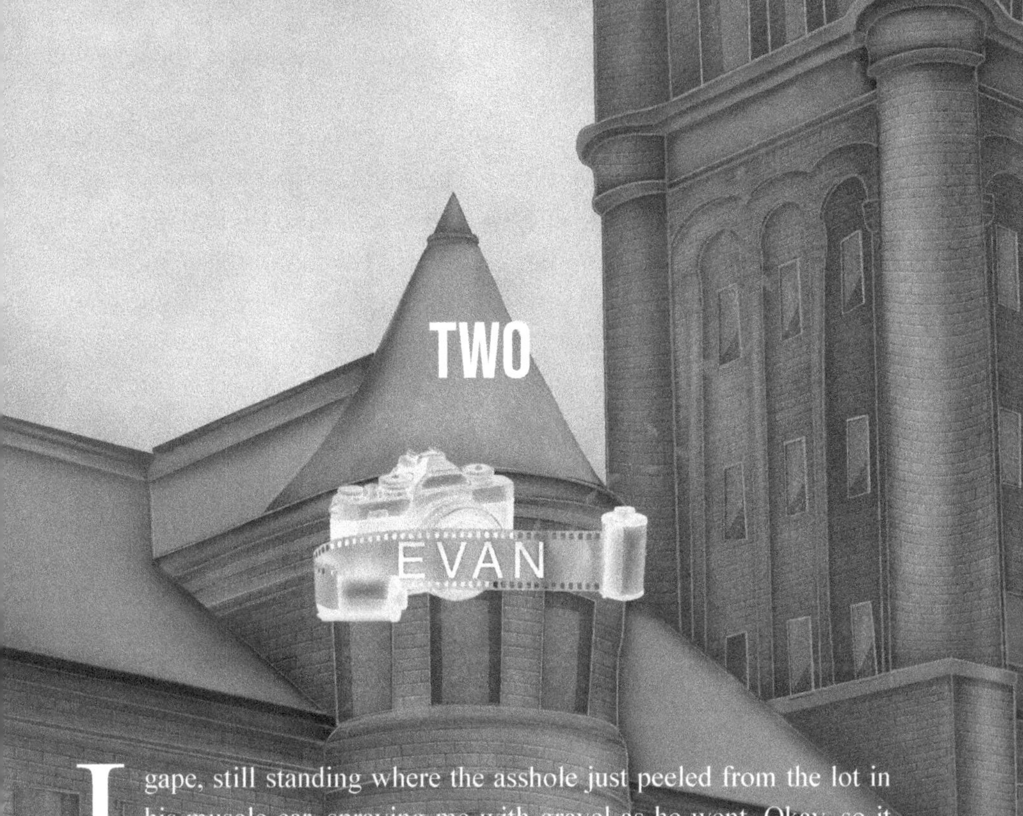

I gape, still standing where the asshole just peeled from the lot in his muscle car, spraying me with gravel as he went. Okay, so it was a nice one, not that I know much about cars, but even I could tell it was a sleek, restored number with a huge exhaust. The leather inside looked hand-stitched, and the bodywork was clearly custom, but still.

Fuck Alek, if that's even his name.

I mean, he was hot, but that doesn't give him the right to be an asshole. Even if he has a scruffy jawline sharp enough to cut you, eyes dark enough to drown in, and black curls on his head. Shit, yeah, they would be good to pull. His hair was shaved on the sides, which I don't usually like, but it worked on him. He was taller than me by a good few inches and so muscular I didn't even know where to look. He also had more tattoos than I could count. His nails were covered in dirt, as if they were stained from a job, not to mention the grease stain he had on his cheek—a cheek pretty enough to kiss. The man was hot as hell, but he clearly has an attitude problem and didn't like me checking him out or being here, but fuck him.

They make the best sandwiches here. I always stop by when I can on the way to my classes. Shaking my head, I head back inside, smiling brightly at the waitress as I place my order and wait. When she slides it over, she leans into me, her eyes twinkling like we're sharing a secret. "He's only an ass to certain people. He doesn't even speak to most people at all." She winks and turns away, leaving me staring after her with an arched eyebrow.

What does that even mean?

"Thanks," I call. Leaving a hefty tip, I tuck the food into my work bag and head out, my hands shoved into my pockets as I walk. I ache to put my headphones on, but I'm trying this new thing where I don't block out the world, even if they feel like a safety blanket.

The walk only takes about twenty minutes, but I soak up the summer rays and do some people watching until I get there. I picked this school since it was so far from home, far enough away from my small, judgmental hometown and family. Plus, it's one of the best, and if I want to become a photographer, then I need to learn from the best.

The best teach at Pine Valley College.

Most people think it's filled with rich folks, and yeah, there are a lot of well-off kids here since they can afford the high tuition, but there are scholarship kids, those who got in on talent, not because of their parents. I'm one of them. I didn't use my parents' money or their name to get in—not that they would have let me unless I picked a major of their choosing, like medicine or accounting . . . Oh, and stopped dating guys.

Yeah, they didn't like that at all.

I cried when I found out I got a scholarship for photography, and that very same day, I had my suitcase packed and I left. They have nothing over me, no way to control me. This is my life, and I'll live it how I want to. That didn't sit well with them, and they haven't spoken to me since. It hurts, even though we were never really that close, but they are still my parents. When I watched others moving their kids in and saying goodbye, I felt lonely.

Luckily, I managed to make some fast and loyal friends, like the pink-haired maniac skipping my way right now. Her bright eyes are enhanced by her thick-rimmed glasses, her wolf cut hair is styled to perfection, and her makeup makes me jealous. Wearing a short dress,

fishnets, and boots, Laila, or Lally to her friends, is effortlessly cool—
so cool I wanted to be friends with her when I saw her, and when she
sat next to me in Introduction to Modern Art, I nearly cried. She looked
at me and smiled and said we would be good friends, and I guess she
was right.

We are joined at the hip, just two orphan kids who found one
another.

"Evvie," she calls happily, stopping before me with a bright smile.
"Are you ready to rock profile taking?"

"Not even close," I reply as I sling my arm around her, kissing the
side of her head as we walk across the open campus to the art building.
The grass is filled with people studying, eating, or playing. The trees
on either side of the path blow in the breeze as we reach the giant,
gothic-inspired building. It never fails to awe me with its beauty, and
the fact I get to study here still makes me feel joy.

"Sorry." I hear a soft squeak, and I stumble as a blur of dark hair
shoots past me and into the building.

"Anders again," Lally says. "She's always late, but she's nice."

I nod as we head up the stairs.

"Yo, Evan, you coming to the party tonight?"

There's a party every night.

"Sure thing, man." I high-five the jock named Liam as I pass. He's
in my history class, and despite the way he looks, he's a big marsh-
mallow inside, and when I randomly told him I was bi, he simply
nodded.

"I get it. Chicks are hot, but there are some hot guys too."

We've been friends ever since, and even though I'm not affiliated
with sports, I seem to be invited to all the football parties, which Lally
and my other friends love since I bring them along so we can openly
ogle all the muscle and hot chicks who hang all over the football
players.

"He's so pretty," Lally murmurs as we pass.

"Eh." I shrug.

"Not your type." She smirks. "You like them brooding and
damaged."

"Do not," I mutter as we navigate through the busy halls.

"There was the starving artist Michelangelo. Oh, and then the nerd with daddy issues named Cynthia—"

"Okay." I cover her lips as she grins, licking my palm until I shoot her a look and let her go. "At least I don't exclusively date closeted girls, or not exclusively since you don't date."

She winks. "They are fun to play with."

Another thing Lally and I bonded over was that our parents didn't approve of our sexual orientations. Unlike mine, Lally's folks actually had her sent to a camp to try and "fix her," as if it were an addiction or a habit she could kick and not how she was born.

Fucking idiots.

"I don't know. I think it's a shame you two don't have the same type. You could share them." Tommy, another of our friends, pops up before us with a bright grin, paint smudged across his face.

"Ew." Lally smacks him. "Bad male. Down, dog."

He chuckles as he steps back. Wearing oversized overalls and a small beanie and carrying his ever-present notebook, he's an art major cliché, but he's also a good guy. "Just kidding, maybe, but Evvie, man, stop collecting all the art dick."

I raise my eyebrows. "I've barely dated since I've been here."

He points in my face. "That doesn't matter. They are all too busy drooling over your model-looking ass to notice. It's hella annoying," he grumbles. "I swear, if you weren't so pretty, we wouldn't be friends."

"But then who would you draw and play COD with?" I taunt as I wrap my arm around him and steer him toward our class.

"Still, not fair," he grouches. "It's always, 'Oh, Tommy, you're roommates with Evan Shaw, right? Can you introduce us?' Boy, girl, teacher, it doesn't matter."

Lally and I stop, our heads swinging his way. "Teacher?" I blurt.

His eyes narrow again. "Not yet, but you never know, and digital arts hottie is mine."

"Mr. Ford?" I exclaim. "Dude, he's a total asshole, and that's coming from me."

"But he's so pretty." Tommy sighs wistfully. "Right, better go or Mr. Ford will have my ass, and not in a fun way. Tonight?"

"Tonight." I nod as we watch him grab his board and run out the door, hitting it as soon as he's outside and running straight into Mr. Ford, whose coffee goes all over them both. "That boy is hopeless."

"So are you, now that you mention it." Lally takes my hand, tugging me inside the auditorium. "Seriously, Ev, what's up with you? You haven't been on a date in ages."

I shrug as I sit, pulling out my notebook, but I can feel her impenetrable gaze on the side of my face, so I sigh as the rows start to fill up. "I'm just bored, you know? None of them excite me. I don't want to be worshiped. I want to be loved, flawed and dirty."

"See, you like walking red flags. That, my man, is a problem." She sighs.

"Then we are problem children together." I chuckle, nudging her side as she slings her leg over her chair.

"Together." Lally winks as she turns to face the front. "At least you might get some dick tonight."

"Doubtful." For some reason, my thoughts turn to the dark-haired asshole from the diner.

He was totally my type.

Shame.

I drag my ass out of the art building when the stars are shining. I'm going home to change before we head out, but fuck, I'm exhausted, not to mention the meeting I have tomorrow.

Another thing about this university is the number of clubs—so many fucking clubs.

I'm just wiping my face when I squint into the darkness, making out the figure huddled in the path. Dark-haired and short, she's familiar.

"Anders?" I call, noticing two burly bastards blocking her path. My eyes narrow, and I stop at her side. "Problem?" I ask her.

She turns her big, haunted brown eyes up to me, eyes I swear I have seen before.

"No, get going," one of the guys responds.

"I wasn't asking you," I snap at him, and then I glance at her, softening my voice at the scared doe expression on her pale face. "Are you okay?"

"They won't let me pass," she admits softly in a smoky voice, as if she doesn't speak much.

I lift my head. They are big bastards with arrogant smirks. It's obvious they are trouble, but that's never bothered me. I step in front of her, crossing my arms. "Move and let the lady pass."

"Lady?" the one on the left scoffs. "We aren't finished with the lady yet."

I am too tired for this shit. "Yes, you are, and if I see you messing with her again—"

"You'll what?" the one on the right growls, stepping closer. He towers over me, trying to intimidate me with his size. If only he knew I climbed men like him for fun, he wouldn't be so sure of himself. This one, however, doesn't want to play. He wants to fight. It's in his eyes. His anger isn't necessarily directed at me, but at anyone.

The campus is empty at this time of night, and despite what it may look like, I'm no stranger to a fight. You don't grow up bisexual in a small town without learning how to take a hit or two and throw a few punches. I don't like to start shit, not after training for years in martial arts, since my hits could do some serious damage. I have to think carefully, so instead, I warn them.

"Make sure you can't," I finish, too tired to verbally spar for once. "Now go."

"Look at this idiot. Fine, we'll play with you first." I see his fist coming and sigh as I sidestep it. Instincts kick in, and I kick out, knocking him backwards as I turn to his friend and duck under his attack before capturing his fist midair, slamming it into his face. He stumbles, shaking his head, so I do it again, and he goes down hard.

"Anders, get back—" I turn to her just as I'm hit from behind. I land on the pavement hard, scratching my arm and face, but I quickly roll us, bringing his arm up behind his back.

"Keep moving and it will break," I warn, my voice cold, but I hear a scream, and I jerk my head up to see the other guy grabbing Anders.

Releasing the one I have, I get to my feet and advance on the second guy. He tosses Anders away and comes at me as I redirect their attention. I stumble under a punch and have to hold myself back. I'm just about to retaliate when a whistle cuts through the air, and then I stumble back as a blur of muscle hits the guys attacking me and Anders. I stare, slack-jawed, as the tattooed wall of muscle beats the shit out of the two guys.

It's brutal as the guy snarls, relishing the blood he spills as he pounds both of the idiots into the ground. He doesn't even stop when they are unconscious.

When he stands, his chest heaving in his leather jacket and his hands dripping with blood, something in my heart kicks. My jeans swell with the pressure, with the beauty this guy just displayed. It was stunning, horrible, and vicious but beauty nonetheless.

Standing, he brushes his curls back and looks at me, his eyes narrowed, and that's when I realize who he is. It's none other than the asshole himself. "You," he hisses.

"You," I respond with a groan. Seriously, could my night get any worse?

Alek, wasn't it? That's where I've seen those eyes—on him.

We glare at each other before he tugs Anders to his side. "Are you okay?" he asks her gruffly. "Is he messing with you?"

"No, he was helping me." She elbows him, seemingly more confident now that he's here. "Thank you, Evan. I mean it."

"No problem." I stick my split knuckles into my pockets with a wince and glare at Alek, my eyes flitting between the two. Curiosity gets the best of me, even though I should just walk away. "Is this your boyfriend?"

"Ew, no. He's my older brother who really needs to stop assaulting people unless he wants to be arrested again," she snaps at him.

Alek stares at her and then me. "You helped her?"

I nod, and he grinds his jaw. "Thank you." It's clear he hates saying that.

I shrug and look at Anders. "Get home safely, okay? If you ever need someone to walk you home from a late class, grab one of us from the photography room. We are always there."

"Thanks, Evan." She smiles brightly, unlike her brother who is glaring daggers at me and pulling her closer like I might snatch her away despite what I just did to protect her.

"You don't need to do that. Just stay away from my sister," Alek warns.

I roll my eyes as I step closer. "Why? Worried this rich prick will defile her?" I taunt him because his disdain for me is clear.

His nostrils flare as I keep moving until I'm pressed against him. Something about him really makes me want to push back.

"Or maybe you're just a backwards homophobe?" I feel his heart racing in anger against my chest, and I know his sister is looking from me to him. "Don't worry, asshole. I won't corrupt your sister, but you on the other hand? Well, you are just too much fun."

I step back as he reaches for me, no doubt to beat the shit out of me for daring to flirt with him because that's exactly what I was doing without realizing it.

I nod at him and grab my bag, getting out of there before he pummels me into the ground.

I might be fast and trained, but Alek? Shit, I've never seen anyone move like him.

He was pure fury, and Lally was right.

I do like red flags.

SHAW DRIVE
NO PARKING
ACTIVE
DRIVEWAY
THE MOMENT
ANDERS AVE
ONE WAY
STOP
TOO
CAR REPAIR
NO PARKING
SALE
SILENT ROSE
Pine Valley
EVER

THREE

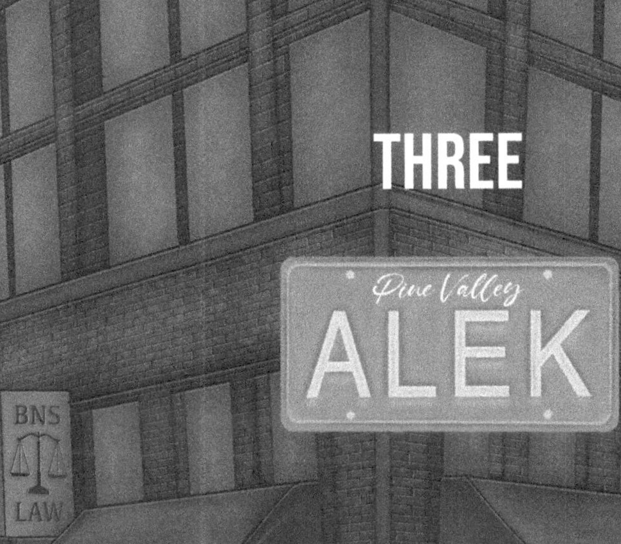

I watch the rich boy, Evan, go in surprise. I thought he was a weak pushover, but I'd been in my car, watching for my sister, when I noticed him. He moved with purpose and intention, both fast and lethal, taking down the two guys almost double his size without even breaking a sweat. I was going to leave him to it until I saw my little sister huddling behind him. I didn't know he had been defending her, but that only makes me narrow my gaze on his retreating back. No guy beats the shit out of someone without a reason.

Does he want my little sister?

He won't get her. She deserves better than him, and anyone who can effortlessly kick ass like that has some serious training or anger issues like me and shouldn't be around her.

"Stop it," Alice scolds, elbowing me.

Yes, Alek Anders and Alice Anders. My mom thought it was funny, go figure.

"What?" I mutter, staring down at her while I ruffle her hair. She smacks my hand away as I smile, watching her fix it.

"He's a nice guy, plus he just helped me," she points out with a narrow-eyed look aimed at me. I glance at him once more before looking back at her. Sometimes, I don't know how we grew up in the same house. She is so innocent, everything I'm not. That's why it's my job to protect her from everyone, especially rich boys like him.

"No guy helps a girl for free," I warn her. "I don't like it."

"Trust me, I'm not Evan Shaw's type." She smiles knowingly, her eyes twinkling as she adds the next part when I just look confused. "You likely would be."

I raise an eyebrow, but she simply rolls her eyes at my denial.

"Trust me, I'm just not. Now let's go before you're late for work again."

I let her take my arm as we head to my car, but my eyes return to Evan's retreating form, wondering what his type is and why I care.

I drop Alice off at home and park my car in my garage. Leaving my everyday car behind, I strip out of my tee and jacket, put on a clean new one, and toss the one I had on today in the laundry so oil doesn't get all over my pristine place. My garage is my baby. I saved up forever to rent the place and gut it out.

The white walls are covered in graffiti and art from some friends, and my everyday car is parked to the left, with my race car to the right. My workbench is behind me with a TV and radio, along with all my paint tools. The LED lights I installed flash from red to blue in each corner as I head over to the bathroom and wash up, brush my curls back, and peer at myself in the mirror. I stare into the eyes I see in my little sister every day, and guilt assaults me for a moment. If Alice knew what type of work I was doing tonight, she would never forgive me.

She's begged me time and time again to be careful, not to do anything stupid, but I do what I have to for her. My sister deserves the world, she deserves a better chance than I ever got, and I'll give it to her no matter what it takes.

Shaking off the emotions I can't afford to have, I turn off the sink, quickly drying off, and head back into the main room.

I grab a drink from the fridge and down it before eyeing my car for tonight. It's a Nissan Skyline. I traded it for a car I spent years rebuilding. When I got it, it was nearly fucked, but I managed to bring it back to life, and now it's my pride and joy. Wrapped in metallic black that shines blue and purple in the light, with hand-painted flames down the side, it's my baby in every sense of the word. It's also how I can afford to send my sister to such a nice school. It took me a few years after dropping out of school to earn it, but I'm here, and now, so is she. That doesn't mean I can afford to stop though. I want to own my own shop one day. It might not happen, but until then, I need to keep working and racing.

Sliding on my black-and-white striped leather jacket, I grab my key and sink into the leather seat in my Skyline. The engine purrs to life, and I hit the button for the garage door and pull out onto the quiet street. It's empty around here, just some other businesses dotted around, but they are usually gone by nightfall, which works well for me. I hit the button again, and the garage door lowers and locks as my lights shine across the dark street, catching on the fluorescent lines.

Hitting the radio, I crank up the rock and lean back in my seat, ready for a long night.

It's busy tonight. The deserted stretch of road is filled with cars pulled to the side, their hoods up to show off their engines and speaker systems. Music pumps from each one as I roll down the middle and pull into an empty space, reversing without even looking. My eyes scan the crowd. It's a mix of guys and girls, racers and viewers, but I find what I'm looking for. Sanjay is in the middle, taking bets and talking to drivers.

Bingo.

He's a few heads taller than the others around him since he's such a lanky fucker. His hair is braided back tonight, and he's in a loose boiler suit and some brand-new kicks. Sliding from my car, I ignore the crowd as they recognize me, instead heading his way as he grins at me.

"There he is, the man of the hour, your god, Alek!" he calls, and the crowd turns to me. I ignore them and the looks I get. I'm used to it, used to the attention and the girls wanting to fuck me. I clasp his hand, sliding money between our palms.

He nods with a grin. Sanjay might be a vain fucker, but he's also smart as hell. "How many tonight?"

"How many do you have?" I ask, looking around. I know some of the drivers here, and they groan when they see me since I'm undefeated, but there are a few newbies as well, all cocky enough to think they can claim my title.

"Five races so far," he replies with a shy smile. It's always a good night for him when I turn up, which is why we get along so well.

"Count me in for all. High stakes, I need the cash," I tell him. Alice's tuition will come around again soon, and I want to make sure I'm prepared, not to mention the new laptop she wants and her rent for the new place she's eyeing.

"You always do. Are you sure you don't run some sort of chop shop?" He smirks. "Or is it for that sweet little sister you are always bragging about? When are you going to introduce me, brother?"

"Never, you're a pig." I smirk as he laughs, and I head back to my car, ignoring the looks and calls. Never give them an inch or they will take a mile.

I'm untouchable to them, the ice-cold asshole who owns these roads, and that's how I like it.

I don't have time for softness or friendship, not in this industry, because it will get you killed.

FOUR

EVAN

The party is like all the others, with drinks, music, and straight guys getting looser with me as the night goes on. Usually, I'm all for it, the life of the party, but I'm not in the mood tonight, too annoyed about what happened earlier.

He's such an asshole. I helped his sister, and he threatened me.

Who the fuck does he think he is? He can't get away with being a dick to everyone he meets just because he's tall, dark, and handsome. Other people might let him get away with it, but I won't. I don't care how good-looking he is or how amazing he smells. He's a fucking bully through and through.

I have no idea how Alice is related to him. They are nothing alike.

"Come on, have another drink," Matty, a football player, slurs, pushing the Solo cup into my hand, his eyes twinkling with intention. He wants to get me drunk so he doesn't feel as bad when we hook up, and he can pretend it never happened tomorrow or that it was the alcohol.

Hell, he could even say I made him.

I've fallen for it before, thinking they genuinely wanted me, but I don't anymore. I learned quickly that some people will never change, and Matty is one of them. He cried once after we hooked up, telling me how he wished he would like girls the way he liked boys, and while I feel genuinely sorry for him since he's struggling with his sexuality, I can't let him use me to work it out.

I have too much self-respect for that.

I didn't used to, but I do now.

I deserve to be with someone who knows exactly what they want and isn't afraid of it. I don't deserve to be someone's dirty secret.

Pushing the cup away, I get to my feet, ignoring my friends looking at me with questioning eyes. "I need some air," is all I tell them, annoyance still running through me at that asshole for ruining my night with his bad mood.

Maybe he needs to get laid. It might cheer him the fuck up.

Heading outside, I lean back against the side of the house, my hands in my pockets. My eyes close as I tip my head back, letting the cool breeze wash away the stench of sweaty bodies and too much alcohol. Maybe tonight just isn't for me. I'm clearly in one of my moods, as Lally calls it, something I can't help. I've been like this for as long as I can remember. Once I spiral, there isn't a way for me to stop. I don't know why, but I can't seem to control the emotions roaring through me.

I only realize my mistake once something hits me. I'm alone on the dark side of the house, the music is loud, and my eyes are closed.

I know better.

I fight back, but there are too many hands, and when my eyes open in confusion, something dark and heavy lands over my head, tightening around my neck. I kick and struggle, giving it all I have, which is a lot, but it's no use, and my hands and feet are bound before I'm lifted into the air and carried away.

My eyes strain against the dark material, trying to make anything out as I shout and twist. Someone grunts as my foot connects with them, but it's useless, and when I hit something hard and roll after being thrown, I freeze. An engine sounds a moment later, and then we are moving.

I can't believe I have been kidnapped. Seriously, what the fuck?

Who the fuck gets kidnapped nowadays? It's kind of embarrassing, not to mention it's pissing me off even more. We drive for what feels like forever, and although I try to memorize the turns, it's useless. I was never good with that type of thing.

I'm hauled out and then dropped to my knees a while later. My eyes strain through the material. All I can see are lights and distorted shapes. Even my hearing is muffled through the thick fabric.

My heart races, and my hands sweat as anticipation and adrenaline pump through me. As soon as this bag comes off, I'm fighting with all I have. I don't know who did this or why, but they have another thing coming if they think I'll make it easy on them.

I burst to my feet, stumbling over the ropes, when the hood is ripped off. I blink, trying to bring everything into focus even as I slam my wrists down onto my leg, breaking the zip ties. My hands are free, but then I freeze as I take in the scene before me.

"Oh, fuck no. I'm not being sacrificed to some weird cult tonight. You got the wrong guy," I tell them, pointing my finger at the hooded figures standing in a semicircle around me.

There are six of them in total. Their heights vary, but they wear the same black robes with hoods covering their faces. Each robe has a symbol on the right breast, and I squint at it before I realize I don't care. The room smells dusty and old, like there isn't enough air, and old bricks line each wall of what I can almost describe as a crypt. The arched brick ceiling makes it dark and creepy, as do the candles flickering with flames throughout.

Definitely a cult.

"I wouldn't. I'm as far from a virgin as you can get," I blurt out, and a chuckle sounds.

"Oh, we know that." A hood is pushed back, and I'm left blinking in shock at Liam.

"Dude, what the hell? Is this some senior prank?" I demand, my arms crossed. "The kidnapping was a bit much."

"It's tradition." He shrugs, and someone next to him pushes their hood back. I get a look at a beautiful black-haired girl who grins at me.

The others push theirs back. They aren't familiar apart from the tattooed asshole at the end. What is it with tattooed assholes right now? Luckily, this one isn't Alek Anders. It's the guy they call Bones from law class. I've heard about him, and yeah, I might have checked him out once or twice. Right now, he's watching me with a dark expression.

Great.

"It's not a swingers club, is it?" I ask slowly. "Because I have to admit, I've done the sharing thing before, but it just doesn't do it for me."

The black-haired girl snorts. "You wish."

"Autumn." Liam sighs before smiling at me.

"Not a cult, not a swingers club, but we should totally discuss the sharing thing." He smiles. "No, Evan, welcome to the Society of the Silent Rose, named after the founder of this school, Albert Rose." He grins at me, and I glance around, unsure.

The words hang in the air, filled with importance and honor, as if I should be shocked and on my knees in gratitude.

"Sorry, never heard of you." The others look at me in horror. "Was I supposed to?"

"Our society is the oldest on campus, the most exclusive. We live through whispers passed down through generations. Usually, you must be blood to be invited. It's an honor."

"Right, uh, so why am I here?" I ask, completely confused. I'm not of ancient blood or whatever, and I certainly don't fit their criteria.

"We have a space to fill, and everyone was allowed to submit a candidate. You were one of them, but we can't tell you who submitted you."

"Liam," I say knowingly, and Autumn sighs. "Oops."

"We investigate the person thoroughly to see if they are the right fit. Tonight, you fought for someone other than yourself. So, Evan Shaw, we would like to invite you to be a member of the Silent Rose."

"What does it entail?" I ask carefully. "Do we have matching outfits? I prefer something with a bit more color than those robes."

Liam chuckles as he grins at me. "Yes, you'll get a robe. It just means you are one of us. A brotherhood, if you will, to lean on throughout your life. When things are hard, we are here. We share opportunities and life lessons, and being a member opens doors you never would have thought possible. We have previous members as far up as the White House. It's a very prestigious honor."

"What's expected in return?" I ask, knowing something like this isn't free.

"You uphold the rules. Our society is to never be revealed or spoken about to another. What happens within these walls, stays within these walls, and when a member calls, you come. That's all. We protect one another and this legacy, and in return, you will be one of us."

I hesitate, looking them over. They are all rich kids with privileged backgrounds apart from Bones. They'll have connections, ones I could use in my future. Besides, I do like being a team player, and a secret society seems like fun.

"Where do I sign up?" I smirk.

Liam booms out a laugh and claps my shoulder as he reaches down and undoes my bindings. "You just did. Come on, let's swear you in."

Autumn holds an ancient-looking book before me. "I, Autumn, scholar of the Society of the Silent Rose, hereby swear in Evan Shaw. His blood will become ours, his life given to our cause, brothers until the end."

Her eyebrow arches, and I lay my hand on top of hers on the book. "I vow it?" The words seem right, and she smiles at me proudly as she presses the book higher and something pricks my hand.

Hissing, I pull it back to see a spiked throne on the top of the book now dripping with my blood. She opens the cover and lets it fall onto the pages inside as I suck the wound and watch.

She snaps it shut. "You're one of us now, Evan. Whatever you need, we are here."

I nod, dropping my hand as I look around, wondering if this is the start of a really bad horror movie or an epic coming of age story. Either way, I'm in it now. No turning back.

Regrets are for pussies.

"Welcome to Silent Rose," Bones says with a jutted chin, and then they part, showing me an arched door at the end of the cavern we are in. As I pass, he leans in. "Don't let the thorns cut you."

Ignoring his warning, I push through the door, my mouth dropping open at what I find.

It looks like the inside of a manor house library, with a roaring fire at the back and couches before it. The wooden walls are covered in expensive works of art, and to the left is a wall covered with books. To the right is a seating area, a game room, and a staircase that leads upstairs.

"You can be anything you want here," Autumn says as she steps past me and then grabs a chalice from the wooden side table. "Now, let's get drunk and celebrate our new member!"

I can get behind that. Grabbing the chalice, I down it as they chant, wiping my mouth as I grin at them.

Secret society, huh? Maybe college won't be so bad after all.

SHAW DRIVE
ANDERS AVE
ONE WAY
NO PARKING
ACTIVE DRIVEWAY
FOR THE MOMENT
STOP
TOO
CAR REPAIR
NO PARKING
SALE
SILENT ROSE
Pine Valley
EVER

FIVE

I have a couple of hours before I need to be at the garage for my shift. Usually, I'd crash and get some much-needed sleep, but for some reason I shower and dress in my overalls, leaning into Alice's door. She has a room here she can use whenever she needs to stay, and after last night, I didn't want her far from me. Her dorm is always empty since she prefers it here.

She looks up from where she's packing her bag with a frown. "You should be asleep. I heard you come in only an hour ago. Busy night at work?"

"Something like that." The wad of cash burns a hole in my pocket, reminding me I need to use it later to pay for her new laptop. "Grab your shit. I'm driving you to school."

"I can take the bus. You need to sleep," she protests, but I just raise my eyebrow and she sighs, knowing better than to argue with me. "You've never driven me to school before. Why now?" she mutters as I grab my keys and lock up after us.

The house isn't bad for what we pay, and it has an underground garage connected to all the houses on the street, which I like. She stares at me the entire way down, and when I start the car, she turns to me. "You're freaking me out. Why are you driving me?"

"I have to be at the garage early, and this is on the way. Seat belt," I tell her.

Her eyes narrow, but she obediently fastens it, and I pull out, heading into early morning traffic. The truth is, I don't know why either. Maybe it's my lingering fear due to what could have happened to her last night after class. She has the pepper spray I bought her, but she didn't use it. I'll need to have another talk with her. Maybe I can ask Bones to help her with some self-defense classes. He's the best at that kind of thing. It might ease my mind a little since I know if I overpower her with my protective instincts, she'll just rebel.

"Don't touch the music," I mutter as she reaches for the dial. She sits back with a sigh, knowing better. Hell, I don't usually let anyone in my car. She's the exception since she's my sister, but she knows better than to fuck with my baby.

It doesn't take us long to get to her fancy as fuck campus, and I park near the art building, idling at the curb as she grabs her bag and looks at me. The sun shines on her dark hair, hair we got from our mom. For a moment, she looks so much like her it hurts, and I lean in, dropping a kiss to her forehead. "Be good today. Call me if you need anything, and don't leave class alone tonight. Get someone to walk you."

"I'll ask Evan," she teases as she leans back, eyes twinkling.

I glare at her. "Anyone but that idiot."

Laughing, she climbs from my car, leaning down to look at me. "I don't know. He's kind of cute. Maybe I will." She slams the door and skips to the sidewalk, heading to class. I fist the wheel as I glare after her.

Evan? Cute?

She's fucking blind.

As if us speaking of the devil made him appear, he skates past me on a board. His straight, icy hair flows in the wind like we are in some fucking commercial. His eyes are bloodshot and red, but there's a smile curving his pierced lip. Wearing baggy jeans, with paint splattered across them, and an oversized shirt, he's the total opposite of me in my all-black attire. For a moment, I debate running him over for making my sister look at him, and my lips curl into a smile at the idea, even as my heart races with the thought. Stupid organ. When he's out of sight, it finally seems to calm down, and so does my anger, so they must be linked.

Shaking my head, I lay my arm across the other seat and reverse, leaving my sister and that idiot to their education.

I skipped out of work early, something I never do, but I'm exhausted and my boss could see that. Luckily, I'm a hard worker, so he let it slide, but I can't make this a regular thing. Rubbing my face, I lean back in my car as I wait. My overalls are tied at my waist, and my black shirt is stretched across my aching muscles. Today was long and hard, and I regret not getting any sleep, but I couldn't just go home. I'd be too worried about Alice, so I'm waiting for her class to end so we can eat and go together. The campus is quiet at this time of night, since her classes run late, and I relax in the peace and quiet until a shrill voice startles me.

"Oh my gosh, I love your car!"

Frowning, I blink at the short, pink-haired girl bouncing on her toes, standing way too close to me. She has a designer bag clutched in her hand, and her perfectly glossed lips curve into a smile. She's cute, I guess, with curves most guys would die to touch, but only annoyance flares through me as her shrill voice comes again, making my aching head hurt worse. "Can I touch it?"

"No," I warn with a deep frown.

"Oh." She wilts for a moment before perking up despite my angry rejection. "Are you here to pick up your girlfriend?"

"No." I shove my hands into my pockets, glaring at her so she gets the picture and steps away, but she just moves closer until her overwhelming perfume nearly makes me sneeze, fluttering her fake lashes like she's trying to take off.

"Well, in that case, how about we go for a drive? I really like your car."

"No," I snap harshly.

"I wouldn't," comes a familiar, husky voice, and I jerk my head around to see Evan leaning on his board, grinning at me. "He's an asshole."

"Oh." The girl looks between us and then smiles at Evan. "I don't mind."

Fuck, can this girl find any self-respect? She's practically throwing herself at me despite the warnings to fuck off.

I sit taller, eyeing Evan despite the girl trying her hardest to get my attention. He looks tired, but he's smiling. Why is he always smiling? I notice dimples in his cheeks as he directs his grin at the girl, and I don't like that.

"Fuck off, rich boy," I snap, drawing his gaze back to me, and his smile turns into a frown, which is better. He shouldn't smile at people all the time, especially her.

"You're much too cute for him," he comments to her, winking. "Trust me, he isn't worth the effort."

"You don't know a thing about me, rich boy," I retort.

"No? You have a younger sister you love, you fight like a beast, and you like cars, especially yours. You think you're better than everyone and hate anyone who comes from money. How am I doing?" He tilts his head, both of us glaring at each other.

"I only hate you, rich boy," I say.

"Really? I feel so fucking special," he sneers, stepping closer, and I push from my car, refusing to back down. He runs his eyes over me.

"Stop it," I warn. "Stop fucking looking at me like that."

"Like what?" he teases, his fucking dimpled smile back in place as a strand of his icy hair blows across his face. I have the insane urge to fist it and drag him closer.

"Like you want me," I hiss. "It's disgusting."

"Trust me, asshole, if I wanted you, you would know it." He grins. "I was just thinking black brings out the color of the asshole in your eyes and makes you look good."

I blink, looking down. My shirt got stained at work, and I borrowed this. It's too tight, and I never wear color. I instantly regret it. "Fuck off. Stop fucking with me."

His tongue plays with his lip ring. "Can I touch your car?" he asks sweetly, fluttering his eyes as he glances up at me, and something about that look has my muscles tightening and my heart skipping a beat.

"You are the last person I would ever let touch my baby," I growl.

"Your baby, huh?" He steps back, eyeing the car. "I can see the resemblance. Both are all souped up with no real drive."

"The fuck did you just say?" I snap. "I'll have you know this engine—"

"Blah, blah, blah, I stroke my dick to car magazines." I gape as he laughs. "What a shame your friend left. I'm sure she would have listened to you ramble on."

It's only then that I notice the girl left during our argument.

"Where did she go?" I frown. When did she go? I'm grateful, but I don't like being unaware of anything.

"Why? Want a taste of rich kids now?" he taunts.

"Fuck off, it's not safe to walk around campus alone at night."

He eyes me, working that fucking lip ring again, and I want to rip it from his mouth. "She left with her friends." He nods after a pink car squealing away. "Guess you were too busy to notice."

My hands ball into fists as I glare at him. "That's because you piss me off, rich boy."

"Name's Evan," he drawls, "but you remember that."

"Trust me, I'll forget everything about you in a minute."

"Really? You keep calling me rich boy and remembering me, so what does that tell you?"

Gripping his oversized shirt, I haul him closer, getting right in his face. "Listen here, rich boy—"

"What, asshole?" He smirks. "Are you going to hit me or kiss me?"

"You fucking—"

"Am I interrupting something?" My sister's voice causes me to whip my head around. Both of her eyebrows are raised as she looks between us. I push him away, and he laughs as he straightens his shirt, gripping his board as he blows her a kiss.

"Nah, just saying hi to your brother and stopping him from scaring off all the girls with his glare," he teases.

I point at him. "Stop fucking talking to my sister."

She clears her throat, marching up to me. "No, you stop being an asshole. I can talk to whomever I want," she snaps, the anger that runs in our family rearing its head. "Thank you for sitting with me at lunch, Evan. I really appreciate it. See you tomorrow."

"Why will you see him tomorrow?" I ask, crossing my arms as I stare her down.

She glares at me. "He's our model for sculpture class."

I blink, turning my head to him to see him grinning. "Nude model." He sweeps his tongue over his lips. "Maybe you should come, asshole. You seem interested."

"Listen here, rich boy—" I start.

"Alek," Alice snaps. "Stop being such a fucking bully just because you're tired. Let's go home and get you some sleep. I'm sick of your attitude."

"Tired, huh? Long night thinking of me?" Evan teases as he drops his board and grins at me. "Try not to dream of me tonight, asshole." He leaves, skating away, and I'm left gaping after him.

"Can you fucking believe that prick?" I seethe as I storm around my car.

Alice laughs. "He gets under your skin," she comments as she climbs in, and I start my engine.

I tighten my hands on my wheel and glare at her. "No, he doesn't."

"Oh yes he does, big brother. Sculpture class is at eleven if you want to come." She winks.

"You shut up as well," I mutter as I pull out, my eyes going back to the rich asshole riding his board without a care, that smile still on his lips.

SIX

I t's Saturday, which means no classes, so I find myself walking in the park. I hold my camera, ready to capture any good shots. I need to build my portfolio, and I prefer to take pictures of people, but good models are hard to find. Either they are awkward in front of the camera or full of themselves. I prefer taking natural shots, capturing the essence of people. I smile as I take a photo of a man kneeling before his wife, tying her shoe as she blushes, and then there's the one of a kid feeding a duck. I can't stop snapping as the sun shines down, trying to capture the beauty in this world when there is so much darkness.

I lift my viewfinder, turning around to find a new subject, when a tattooed hand covers it. Dropping my camera, I stumble back when I see Alek Anders towering before me. "What the fuck?" I sigh. "Are you stalking me now?"

"Taking pictures of people without consent is illegal, you know."

"As is stalking," I retort.

"I wasn't stalking you, rich boy. I was walking to work and saw you being a weirdo." He crosses his arms, and I almost drool at the muscles bunching in his biceps. His eyes narrow when he sees me staring.

"You're working on a Saturday?" I ask.

"Not everyone gets to play all weekend," he snaps. "Some of us have bills to pay that our parents don't cover."

"Who said my parents cover my bills?" I ask, feeling annoyed. "You know nothing about me, Anders, so just head to work where I'm sure you terrify every single customer."

"I'm nice to everyone else." He smirks his lips tilting tauntingly, and I hate myself for wanting to taste them.

It really isn't fair how attractive this man is without even trying. "Lucky me," I mutter, and I walk away, lifting my camera to take pictures.

"I mean it, get consent," he calls, always having to have the last word.

Lifting the viewfinder with a mischievous smirk, I take his picture as he walks away. He stills as a dog runs up to him, and despite his intimidating exterior and constant frown, he bends down to the fluffy ball of happiness, a rare smile on his lips as he pets it. I snap a picture. Like he feels it, he swings his gaze to me, and I quickly turn away.

I try to forget all about Alek Anders as I take pictures, but hours later, I give up and head to work. Despite what he thinks, I also have a job. My scholarship covers a lot, but I still need money to live on.

I haven't been there long, and I don't want to make a bad impression, so I arrive at the café early and change. I immediately loved this place. Deadly Sweet is totally my vibe, with art covering every wall. There is an internet side to the left where people game and compete, and to the right is a more traditional café, but it's very modern, and pretty much every waiter here is an artist of some kind—oh, and male since it's a hot waiter café. I straighten the frills on my shirt and tuck the back into my pants. Checking my hair, I smudge my eyeliner and head out to get started.

The customers are mostly college girls, which suits me just fine. I get paid to flirt for hours, and the tips are great.

Hours later, I'm bent over a table, clearing, when I feel someone behind me.

"Be right there," I call since I'm also working the counter, but when I straighten and turn, I almost groan.

"Are you fucking kidding me? You are everywhere I turn," snaps an angry voice.

Alek Anders.

"I work here, asshole. What about you? Didn't know you were into hot waiters," I snark.

"Wait, what?" He swings his gaze to his sister, who giggles at his side. "You said you knew a nice place."

"I do, this one." She grins at me. "Looking good, Evan. The frills really suit you."

"So I'm told." I smirk as I clear the table and step past him, looking him over. He looks so out of place and uncomfortable. "Find an empty table or leave like we both know you want to. Your fragile masculinity can't handle it."

I head to the back, cleaning the plates, and when I come out, I'm surprised to see him sitting stiffly at a table, his sister talking away. Leaning into the bar, I cover my smile with my hand as I watch him look around uncomfortably.

I don't imagine this is his sort of place, not enough grease or cars or masked chicks and men talking shit, but he sure as fuck looks good in the lighting here. It caresses his curls, highlighting his tattoos and muscles, and I'm not the only one who notices.

"Damn, who's that hottie?" Sang leans into my side, ogling Alek. His black hair is pushed back, and his pale skin glistens with the glitter he put on to get more tips. He's bigger than me and muscular. He's also hot as fuck, and if we weren't such good friends, I would have hit that for sure.

"Alek Anders, not your type." I laugh as I nudge him, turning to face him. "We both know you like them dainty and small so you can throw them around."

"Very true." He leans in. "Want to find out?" I laugh as I push him. Our flirting is just that—flirting. It's something fun to pass the time, but when I turn and head over to the Anders's table, I see Alek glaring at Sang, so I step in his path.

"Don't like men flirting?" I taunt. "Then you should leave."

"Is that your boyfriend?" he comments, sneering the word.

"Why, going to be a homophobe?" I retort, crossing my arms. "You can leave. We don't have your type here, asshole."

"Problem, Evvie?" Sang calls, heading my way since he runs this place. He frowns at Alek. "Are you harassing my staff?"

"Me?" Alek looks him over. "Seems like you were doing that all on your own. Aren't there rules against the boss flirting with their employees?"

Sang's eyebrows rise as he looks at me, and I sigh. "He's an asshole all the time."

"Jesus, Alek, stop it," Alice hisses. "You're so embarrassing. Evan, I'm so sorry. He's just moody because he's hungry."

Sang's eyes narrow as he leans into the table and Alek, not the least bit intimidated despite the glare Alek gives him. "That better be it. If I hear you are being rude to my staff, we will have a problem. Enjoy your meal." He straightens and nods at me. "Let me know if he harasses you."

"I can handle it." I smile in thanks, and he squeezes my shoulder as he heads back to work. Alek glares at his back, and I wait. "Well?" I prompt.

"What?" he snaps.

"Your order," I reply. "Or would you rather I just stand here so you can keep checking me out."

He snorts, looking me over. "You look like a tablecloth my nana owned."

"Really? Well, she must have good taste," I retort.

"Honestly, would you two just fuck or fight already?" Alice comments dryly, and we both turn to her, but she's too busy scanning the menu to notice our incredulous looks.

"You know what? Call me when you're ready," I snap, putting my pad away and moving past their table to the one farther down. I force a smile at the college girls who giggle as I come their way.

"All done?" I comment, nodding at the check.

"Yes, thank you," one gushes, handing it back, and I pocket the cash as she leans in. "My number is on the back, too, just in case." They hightail it out of there.

Chuckling, I shake my head. The number of times we get hit on is insane, but it's just a job, nothing more. I never call or text.

They don't interest me.

My eyes go back to Alek, who's watching me, and I find myself wishing he would leave his number.

He'd probably call just to threaten me.

ALEK

Honestly, what man wears frills?

Okay, so he doesn't look terrible, but seriously? The black, long-sleeved shirt has frills at the collar and sleeves, and yes, they might compliment his hair and work for him, but it's ridiculous, and those pants? They are so tight I can see everything. No wonder every single customer is looking, never mind flirting. He eats it up, winking and teasing. I notice the other waiters do as well, but it doesn't piss me off as much as it does with Evan. He's doing it just to upset me. I know it.

"You're staring again." I turn around to see my sister playing with her plate as she grins. "Want me to leave him your number like that table did?"

"Shut up and eat your food," I mutter. She surprised me at work, wanting to go to dinner, and I can't say I'm unhappy. Now that she is at school and I'm working so much, I barely get to see her, and we have always been close.

"Seriously, Alek, what's your issue with him? I know it's not because he's bi. I know you too well for that. What is it?" she demands. "He's nice."

"He's another rich idiot who thinks the world owes him some-thing," I snap. Does everyone else think I'm an asshole to him because he likes both men and women? I don't like that. I don't give a fuck who anyone likes as long as it doesn't affect me.

"He's right. You don't know him," Alice drawls. "He's a scholar-ship kid." I blink at her, and she nods. "I heard rumors that his parents kicked him out when they found out he liked men, so he made his own way here, earning a scholarship for his talent. He's working just like you. Maybe you misjudged him." I look back at him and wonder if she's right.

I didn't expect that.

"They kicked him out?" I mutter. She knows where to hit. We have our own family trauma and shit, and ours is no less fucked up. I don't want to like Evan Shaw, but finding out his life isn't perfect softens me a little.

"Yup. Apparently, he doesn't even speak to them. He puts up a good front, but I saw him staring at a picture he took of a happy family the other day, and he looked so sad. Remind you of anyone?" She nudges me. "I'm just saying, you don't know him, not really. Maybe you should stop lashing out because of your insecurities and prejudice."

"Need a refill?" His voice startles me, and I wonder if he overheard us as he pours Alice another iced coffee. He must feel my gaze because his eyes cut to me. "What?" he barks.

"Nothing," I admit.

His eyebrows rise, and I look away, hating that Alice got into my head.

"I heard you are looking for models," Alice comments. She has always been good at connecting with people. Conversations are easy for her, and everyone likes her. I'm the total opposite, and as much as I hate to admit it, I'm more like our father.

I certainly have his temper. Do I have his prejudice as well?

"Yeah, it's for my end of semester project, so I still have time," he replies. "Is your food okay?"

"It's amazing. Maybe Alek could help," Alice says.

"What?" we both snap at the same time, glaring at her as she grins.

"What?" She blinks. "It's a paid position for models. You said the other day you might take another side gig, and I hate to see you working so much just to pay for my school."

I feel Evan's eyes burning into the side of my head, but I ignore it, fisting my hands under the table. "It's fine. Eat," I tell her, my voice rough. I hate that he knows that about me. I don't want to appear weak in front of this man at all.

"There are a lot of students searching for models," he finally comments. "It's good pay. I can give you their information."

"No thanks," I mutter, glaring at them. "We're fine."

"Alek," Alice begins. "When are you going to start working on your own dreams and stop helping me chase mine?"

"Enough," I warn. "Eat, I need to get back to work."

Her expression becomes sad, and she hangs her head, playing with her food. I want to take it back. I know she's worried, and I love her for it, so I take her hand. "It's not your job to worry about me, Alley," I mumble. "It's my job to look after you, okay? Don't worry so much."

"You're tired all the time, and you used to talk about the garage you wanted. You don't anymore, and I feel like it's my fault," she whispers.

"No, baby sis. I'm just so happy you are doing what you love. That's enough for me, I promise."

It is only then I realize Evan is still here, and I shoot him a narrow-eyed look. He simply observes me with something in his eyes I don't want to analyze. He hurries away, and I watch him go.

When it's time to pay, Evan is nowhere in sight, so I grab another waiter. "Oh, it's okay. Your check was taken care of." He grins.

"What? By whom?" I ask. I have a bad feeling.

"Uh, he told me not to tell you." He winces when I glare. "Evan."

That fucking asshole. "Where is he?"

"On break." The guy points to the back corridor as I stand, pissed as hell. "Go home, Alice," I snap, heading straight for the corridor that leads to the back despite the guy shouting that I can't go back there.

There are only a few doors, so I find the workers' area quickly. I slam the door closed behind me, and Evan jumps, turning with a wide-eyed look.

"Anders?" He frowns as I stomp over.

"I don't need your fucking pity," I growl, throwing cash at him.

"It wasn't pity," he starts, but I back him up against the wall.

"I don't need your fucking charity either. I can pay for my own fucking meals, rich boy," I snarl, slamming my fist into the wall next to his head. He doesn't even flinch, just stares me down.

"It wasn't charity," he retorts. "Jesus, I was just trying to be nice and mend bridges. Why are you such an asshole?"

"I don't need anyone to understand me. Least of all you." I push him into the wall, my chest heaving in anger as his scent wraps around me. His eyes drop to my lips, and I hate the way my body reacts.

I hate that I want him to look.

"Fuck you," he snaps, equally as angry. "I won't be nice next time."

"Nice, rich boy?" I hiss. "You're nothing—"

My head snaps to the side from his slap. Licking my stinging lip, I slowly turn my head back to look at him. His eyes are wide. No doubt he's shocked at his own actions, but I'm not. If he wants to fight, then fine. I slam my fist into his face in retaliation, making him recoil with a cry. "What the fuck, Anders?"

Grabbing his head before he can say more, I crush my lips to his. He freezes before fisting my shirt, pulling me closer, his teeth digging into my lower lip so hard I taste my own blood. It only urges me on, and I swallow his groan as I press every hard inch of him against the wall, pinning him as I lick his teeth and dominate his mouth. He gasps as I kiss him, deepening it until it hurts.

Desire and anger fuel me, wrapping around me until I'm lost in him.

I'm not in my right mind, and when I hear a voice outside, I realize what I'm doing.

I pull back, my eyes wide in horror, my lip bleeding from his teeth.

I kissed him.

He watches me, his eyes wide and confused, and before he can say a word, I turn and race out of there.

I can still taste him in my mouth, no matter how much I wipe it away.

SEVEN

A lek Anders kissed me.

He also hit me, which isn't okay, but some dark part of me liked the pain because that meant I pushed him so much he snapped. That's probably fucked up, but I don't care.

I spend the rest of my shift thinking about it. I have never been kissed like that, with nothing but pure, raw desire. No, I've never been kissed like that before, and I hate that it was with that asshole. I don't even know if he likes guys, although it's obvious he doesn't want to. He ran away so fast, I was surprised there wasn't an Alek shaped hole in the wall. I remind myself I need to forget about it as I sprawl across my twin-sized bed in my shared dorm.

He kissed me. So what? He regrets it, and I don't want to be some-one's regret.

There are plenty of people who want me, so then why do I crave attention from someone who doesn't?

It doesn't help that I saw a different side of him today. He's working to put Alice through school. Shit, maybe he isn't such an asshole, which doesn't help.

My phone vibrates, and I grab it, expecting it to be Lally, but I'm surprised when I see the unknown number.

Unknown: If you tell anyone what happened today, I will kill you.

My eyebrows rise. Only one person would text me that, and I hate that I want to squeal when I realize he must have asked around for my number. I really am fucked in the head.

Evan: Who is this?

I wait, watching him type, my heart racing as I sit up, staring my phone intently.

Unknown: You go around kissing a lot of people?

Unknown: Forget I said that and forget what happened today. It was nothing.

Evan: Jealous that I do? How did you get my number?

Unknown: Alice had it, said you gave it to her in case she got scared. Now stop texting me.

Chuckling, I thumb out a response.

Evan: You texted me first.

I click the information and quickly add his number, changing his name and picture to the one I took the other day—the one of him smiling.

Asshole: Fine. Now delete my number.

Evan: Why would I do that? You're so much fun to wind up ;)

He doesn't reply, and I frown, wondering what he's doing. Is he thinking of me? Thinking of our kiss?

I need to know, and there's only one way to get Alek Anders to react to me, and that's pissing him off.

> Evan: What are you wearing?

> Asshole: None of your fucking business, rich boy. Seriously, delete my number.

> Evan: I think you wanted me to have it. Why else would you ask for it then text me when you could have just confronted me when you saw me again?

> Asshole: I don't plan to see you again.

> Evan: Liar. I'm betting you sleep naked, right?

He doesn't reply, and I lean back, snapping a quick picture before sending it.

> Asshole: Are those ducks on your pajama shirt?

> Asshole: Forget I asked.

I can't contain my smile, and I bite my lip, ignoring my thumping heart.

> Evan: Yes. Prefer it off?

I pull my shirt down and unbutton it a little, snapping a picture and sending it.

There's a pause, and I wonder if I went too far.

> Asshole: Stop sending me pictures. You're making me feel sick. I'm blocking your number.

Shit, he would too, and for some reason, I don't want him to.

> Evan: What if something is wrong with Alice and I need to get a hold of you?

It's a low, dirty move, but I don't care.

> Asshole: Fine, but only use this in case of emergencies.

> Evan: What consists of an emergency? What if I need someone to hit me and then kiss me? Or what if I need a getaway driver?

> Asshole: I'm blocking you.

I can't help but laugh as I bury my head in my duvet before I lift my head and try to act cool.

> Evan: Fine, I'll stop.

It is quiet then, and I can't resist.

> Evan: Night, Anders, dream of me and my ducks.

ALEK

I reread the text over and over, leaning back in my bed, my comforter pooled at my waist. Frowning, I go to block the number and then hesitate. If I do and something goes wrong with Alice, I would never forgive myself.

Instead, I reread his texts before opening the second picture. His head is tilted so his hair falls over one eye, and his shirt is half unbuttoned, displaying the stacked muscles on his chest. I find myself staring. I go to hit delete, but for some fucking reason, I save it.

Blackmail, I tell myself.

Groaning, I throw my phone away and cover my face. What the fuck is wrong with me?

Why did I kiss that asshole?

I blame my emotions. I am never good at controlling them when I get carried away. That has to be it. I wanted to shut him up. Yes, that's it. No other reason.

It won't happen again, that's for sure.

Rich boy doesn't get to come in here and fuck with my life. It's perfect the way it is.

I don't need the complication he would provide, and that's exactly what he is—a complication.

I don't even like men, I like women, and I'll prove that to him and everyone who says differently.

Rolling to my side, I scrunch my duvet and bury my head in it.

Why do my dreams center around ducks and frills?

SHAW DRIVE
ANDERS AVE
ONE WAY
STOP
ACTIVE DRIVEWAY
NO PARKING
THE MOMENT
TOO
CAR REPAIR
NO PARKING
SALE
SILENT ROSE
Pine Valley
EVER

EIGHT

I'm only taking her to school so she doesn't have to walk. That's the only reason.

It's definitely not to catch a glimpse of the icy-haired menace who keeps texting me no matter how much I ignore him.

"I need to work tonight," I tell her. I have a big race. It's worth a lot of money, and if I win, I will finally be able to put a down payment on a garage. I don't want to get her hopes up though. "I'll be home late, so get someone to walk with you. Not Evan."

"You didn't call him rich boy. Okay, bye!" she calls as she slams her door and runs off.

Brat.

I hesitate. Evan is like clockwork, always on time for class, but I don't see him anywhere. Good, that's good, I didn't want to see him. I pull out my phone to check the time. I have no notifications, and his last text was yesterday at dinner—a picture of him eating a burger with it smeared all over his face like a fucking idiot.

Frowning, I notice his red eyes and pale skin that I didn't before.

I hesitate before I turn my engine off and get out. I only need to confront him and tell him to leave me alone. I grab a blue-haired guy as he moves past. "You know Evan Shaw?" I ask.

He looks me over before nodding. "He isn't here though."

"Why?" I demand.

"He's sick. He missed his first lecture too." He takes off, and I stare after him.

Fine, it's none of my business. Besides, at least he might leave me alone. He's sick . . . It isn't because I hit him, is it? He had a bruise, but he didn't seem to care. No, he is sick, and it has nothing to do with me.

Nothing at all.

I managed to work all day without thinking of Evan Shaw or that fucking kiss, but when I finish and pack up to go to the race, I check my phone. Still nothing from him.

Is he really sick?

Alice said he had no family anymore, no one to look after him, but his friends will check on him, right?

For fuck's sake, Alice will be pissed if I let him die. She'll blame me.

That's the only reason I do what I do next. He needs to get better so I can kick his ass and warn him away.

There's a store next door. I don't know what's wrong with him, so I just clear the shelves of anything he could need. On the way out, I spot a bistro across the way, and despite the looks I get for going in there, I get a soup to go and then climb into my car, freezing. I don't know where he lives.

Pulling my phone out, I search for him on Instagram, easily finding him since he has tons of followers and posts. I skim his photos, idly noting they are good before I find one where he's in front of a door. I memorize the number before heading there. Later, I'll tell him what a moron he is for posting that for anyone to find. At the building's entrance, I grab a skinny kid. "Which room is Evan Shaw's?"

He looks at me over, confused. "Eighteen C."

I nod and stomp upstairs. Once at the wooden door that looks like every other one here, I grind my jaw. I debate leaving it on his doorstep, but what if he's dead? Slamming my knuckles into the door, I wait impatiently.

There's no answer, so I knock again. There is a groan and a crash, so I rip the door open, noting it's not locked, and storm in.

Evan is struggling in his duvet on a twin bed. His hair is sticking up all over, which is my first clue he's sick, not to mention his nose is red and dripping, his skin is pale and clammy, his eyes are bloodshot, and he's shivering even though it's boiling in here.

"Anders?" he questions as he sits up, frowning. "Shit, am I seeing stuff now?"

The other bed is empty, and I scan the room. The left side is decorated in all dark colors and posters. Evan's, the right side, is bright with color and photos. Setting the bags down on the table, I head over without saying a word. I slide my hands under him and lift him upright, throwing his duvet back at him. He frowns, wrapping it around his body.

"Wait, you're really here. Why?" His face is puffy and adorable.

No, ugly.

"Alice made me," I mutter. "She was worried." I grab the bag and throw it his way. "Here, medicine."

"Oh, thanks." He searches inside, his eyes widening. "Did you buy the whole store?"

"I didn't know what was wrong," I grumble, my eyes lingering on the bruise on his cheek. Guilt spears me for a moment.

He nods and sits back, shivering.

"Have you eaten?" I ask.

"I'm not hungry." He sighs, closing his eyes. He must be sick because he isn't even fighting me.

I frown, not liking this defeated side of him. He isn't fun if he isn't sassy. Pulling out the soup container and spoon, I grab water and sit on the edge of his bed, ignoring its creak as I hand it over. "You need to eat."

He watches me. "Why are you here?"

"Alice," I remind him as I thrust the food at him. "Eat or don't, I don't care."

I stand then, ready to leave, when his hand catches my wrist. I look down. His hand barely spans my tattooed wrist, and something about that has a spark of desire flaming through me. "Thank you, Alek. I mean it, even if Alice made you."

"Whatever, rich boy." I jerk my hand away, ignoring the burn lingering on my skin. "Eat and take your medicine."

When I'm at the door, his voice stops me again. "If I didn't know better, I would say you're worried."

"You wish, rich boy." I slam the door and then hesitate as I hear him laugh, but it turns into a cough and then a groan.

Grinding my teeth, I glance at the hallway, knowing I need to leave or I'll miss the race—one that I was lucky enough to get my name in for since so many want in.

Smashing my head into the door, I rip it open again, angry at myself. I stomp over and pat his back as he coughs, probably harder than I need to, and then I sit. "Eat," I demand.

He eyes me worriedly but eats every last bite, and I throw him the water. He sips it before I clean up. "Now sleep."

He snuggles down, still coughing, wrapped up like a burrito. "You can leave."

"I am. Just making sure you don't die or Alice won't forgive me."

"Sure, keep telling yourself that," he mutters, but he's asleep before I can respond.

I should leave now, but I clean up his mess and then sit on the office chair, watching him.

He's getting worse. He has a fever now and won't stop moaning in his sleep. I run a towel under the faucet and keep putting it on his forehead, which seems to help. Water runs over my hands as I head back to reapply the new one.

He's on his back, only wearing some shorts now since he insisted on stripping. I force my eyes to his face, not his body, and reach for his head, but he jerks away, still half asleep.

"Stop being a fucking brat," I snap, pressing him back to the bed.

He groans, his eyes barely fluttering open in his feverish state. "Anders?" he slurs.

I search his face. "Yeah, baby, it's me."

"It's hot," he whines.

"I know, baby," I murmur, dripping the water over his face. "Your fever will break soon, just sleep."

"I hate being sick." He whimpers, the sound piercing straight to my heart.

I nod. "Everyone does."

"I want my mom." He sighs, and I swallow, looking at him.

"You want me to call her?" I reach for his phone.

"Don't bother, she won't answer." He laughs bitterly before it ends in a cough that has him curling up on his side. "No one would."

My heart breaks a little.

He sighs and snuggles up around my arm, nodding off like a kitten while I'm left staring at him. Unlike when he's awake, I let myself drink him in.

He really is beautiful, like a work of art. He's all sharp edges and plush lips. The combination of his features shouldn't work, but it does. My fingers drift across his face, feeling his soft skin before pressing against his parted lips. They are obscenely soft and so full they should be on a woman.

I remove my hand before I do something stupid again.

Brushing his hair back, I rub the silken strands between my fingers, knowing if he ever caught me, I'd kill him, but I can't seem to resist.

"What are you doing to me, rich boy?" I murmur.

He doesn't answer, and that's for the best.

His fever breaks a few hours later, and once I'm sure he's over the worst of it, I lay out his medicine and leave, making sure to write a message for him to lock his door. It's the early hours of the morning, and I know I missed the race, not to mention put everything in jeopardy, just to look after a rich boy I hate—one I can't seem to stay away from, even when I know I should.

Once I get home, I climb into bed, my fingers tracing my own lips as I remember the way his felt pressed against them. It was better than anything I've ever experienced.

Hating myself, I slide my hand down my chest and circle my hard length, recalling the way he tasted. I imagine the way his mouth would part for me then wrap around my cock.

My eyes close of their own accord, and I remember the way his stacked chest looked in his low-slung shorts. I visualize the way my hand would look tracing those muscles, his own soft ones reaching for me. His eyes are wide and bright, his lips parting for me as I press my cock into his mouth.

I have to bite back a moan as I tighten my fist, wishing it were him. Instead, I imagine him sucking me down. He'd fight me, tease me, and I jerk in my palm at the thought.

"Alek." He moans around my length, my name on his lips. I lift my hips in my bed as I jerk my cock quicker, harder, and rougher. "Let me taste you. Let me feel you come."

Jesus fucking Christ.

I come with a muted bellow, spilling over my hand. My chest heaves as I squeeze my eyes shut, angry in the wake of the ebbing pleasure.

Disgust and hatred fill me as I lie in my bed, my own cum on my stomach.

I need to stay away from Evan Shaw. That much is clear.

NINE

It's been two days since I've been at school, and my phone has been blowing up with texts from my friends and emails with assignments I need to catch up on. It keeps me busy but not busy enough that I don't remember what happened the other night.

Was Alek Anders really here?

If it wasn't for the medicine and food he left, I might have thought it was a fever-induced fantasy, but no, he was here, and he stayed all night, looking after me. Why? Because Alice asked him to? Part of me wishes it was because he was worried, but I know that's stupid. Men like Anders don't worry, especially about people like me. The sad part is, despite him being forced, he is the only person who has ever looked after me. Usually when I was sick, I had to stick it out alone, so having someone there was nice.

Fuck, I'm pathetic. Talk about mommy issues.

I'm so distracted by my spiraling thoughts I nearly throw my board when a familiar beep sounds. My head jerks up, and I see a grinning Alice climbing from Alek's muscle car. She waves happily as the brooding asshole pulls his shades down, peering at me from the driver's seat. His eyes are red and puffy, and he looks exhausted, but I wave. He ignores me, pushing his shades up and peeling away without another glance.

He's still an asshole. Was he really the one who looked after me the other night, or does he have a doppelganger? One who's nice and holds my hand through a fever.

Alice's hand slides through my arm as she smiles up at me. "We've missed you the last few days."

"Course you have, cupcake. I'm a delight," I tease, kissing her head as we maneuver down the path toward the building our classes are in. At the door, I glance back at where Alek's car was.

Why was he so tired?

Why am I worried?

He's not mine. He made that very clear.

Classes were exhausting in a good way. I had a lot to catch up on, but I'm a fast learner. By dinner, however, my energy is waning. I'm still not a hundred percent after being sick, so I grab copious amounts of coffee and fill my tray before slumping into a seat at the table.

Lally and Tommy are out filming today, so I'm mostly alone, which sucks, but the quiet is nice. At least I don't have to join in and smile and laugh. I can just be tired in peace. Sipping my coffee, I look out of the window for a moment when I hear a loud exhaust. It's just a car shooting past, though, and not the one I seem to look for everywhere.

"Hey." The happy voice brings me from my thoughts, and I smile as I turn around to see Alice flopping into a seat opposite me.

I have no idea how two siblings could be more different, but they are. Alice is pure sunshine while Alek is like midnight. "How were your classes?" I ask, sitting up straighter as she starts to cut her food.

"Good. I think I made the right choice." She nods, smiling up at me. "You?"

"Tiring, but good. That reminds me, thank you for sending Alek with the medicine. It really helped," I tell her. When I went to bed, I hadn't even thought about going out to get medicine—okay, I had, but I didn't have the energy. I was being selfish and just wanted to feel sorry for myself.

Alice blinks at me, her fork halfway to her mouth. "Alek? Medicine?" She blinks as she stares. "What are you talking about?"

"Oh, uh, the other night . . . Just, thank you," I say, blushing slightly.

"Evan, are you sure you're feeling alright? Maybe you came back too quickly. I didn't send Alek with any medicine."

I just stare, and she stares right back.

Alice didn't ask her brother to check on me? Then why did he, and how did he know to bring me medicine and food?

Did Alek Anders come to look after me and lie about it?

If he did, he'll only get pissed off if Alice knows, so I force out a laugh. "Shit, sorry, I haven't been sleeping well. Must just be brain fog."

She nods slowly, chewing her mouthful as she peers at me. "Are you sure you're okay?"

"Yeah, just tired." I toast her with my coffee. "Nothing some caffeine can't fix." Swallowing, I lean in with my signature grin. "So, are there any boys or girls you like so far?" I wiggle my eyebrows, and when she blushes with a small laugh, I know the distraction worked.

I spend the rest of dinner doing that, hoping she forgets my random question. If she brings it up with him, he'll kill me, yet part of me wants to know why and how this will turn out. You don't look after somebody you hate, which begs the question—does Alek Anders really hate me, or does he just wish he did?

I guess it's time for me to find out. I never was one to back down, not if there's something I want, and I want tall, dark, and broody. It seems I might actually get him after all.

Game on, Anders.

SHAW DRIVE
ANDERS AVE
ONE WAY
THE MOMENT
STOP
NO PARKING
ACTIVE DRIVEWAY
NO PARKING
SALE
SILENT ROSE
Pine Valley
EVER

TEN

My eyes burn, I'm that tired, and I drop the wrench for the second time in five minutes. I worked all last night, and I wasn't supposed to be here this morning, but I picked up the shift so I could take Alice to school, which means no sleep. I did it so she wouldn't have to walk, to make sure she was safe—definitely not to see if Evan Shaw was back at school and feeling better.

I totally haven't done this for the past two days just to catch a glimpse of him to make sure he was okay after I left. It isn't like I could text him because he might get the wrong idea, and he never texted me, not even a thank you, so I refuse to be the one to bend first.

Not that I care if he's okay or not.

Annoyed at my own thoughts, I slam the wrench down harder than I need to, wiping my stained hands on my cloth and stomping away. "I'm taking a break."

"Come back in a better mood!" Whistler yells, the only bastard in here who dares to say anything to me. At six-six, with a beard whiter than snow and hair to match, the tattooed ex-gangster is a terrifying bastard to most. We know he's really a teddy bear, but that doesn't stop the fucker from mouthing off at me every chance he gets. Hell, nearly all the guys are scared of him, but not me, so I flip him the bird as I head to the back of the shop and the break room there.

"Eat shit, old man."

His rough laughter follows me in, even making my own lips twitch.

My mood doesn't improve throughout the day at all, especially when I check my phone after work and see Evan's text.

> Evan: Too busy dreaming of me to sleep last night? You looked rough this morning.

Ignoring it, I pocket my phone and take off to race despite my exhaustion. I need the cash, and honestly, I need to work off some of these emotions. I don't want to take them home to Alice, something I always promised I wouldn't do as soon as I realized I had my father's temper. No, she deserves better, so despite the fact that I'm driving when it could be dangerous, I head to the one place where I can truly be me and leave it all behind.

I barely speak to anyone when I pull up, ignoring the booze and the music. I put in my buy-in and head straight back to my car for the first race. My dark, bleak expression scares everyone away, thank fuck, and I close my eyes and lean back in my seat while I wait for the others. As soon as I do, though, I see Evan's grinning face, so I open them again and fiddle with the radio, refusing to let my mind betray me.

He's not important. I don't give a shit about him.

The only person I care about is my sister, the one I silently proceed to give a better life to. That also means improving my own, getting my garage, and supporting her. I have no room for distractions, even ones with pouty lips and a wicked smile.

Shaking my head, I crank the music up, the bass flowing through the car and into my blood. Adrenaline courses through my veins when I get the nod and start my engine, heading to the line.

There are five cars for the first race. I recognize only two of the drivers. Some are like me and come often, trying their luck, while others are trying to make a name for themselves. It's clear that's the case with a young guy in a souped-up Dodge SRT Demon next to me. He smirks at me as he revs his engine.

Rolling my eyes, I focus on my own race, knowing none of them can beat me.

I'm the best.

When the flag drops, he and I shoot off at the same time, but by the first corner, I'm in the lead. His headlights shine on my rear as he tries to keep up, but I effortlessly drift around the corners of the empty streets. Fans are spread around, screaming for us, and I let the adrenaline consume me.

On the fourth corner, something goes wrong. The Dodge tries to pass me, almost hitting me, and I have no choice but to jerk away to avoid being thrown over the barrier. The maneuver lets him slip past, so I gun it after him, knowing my car can beat his on this stretch of road. He's pushing it, though, so hard he doesn't see the fan running across the road to get a better look until the last minute.

Time seems to slow as my eyes widen, and I know he's going to hit her, but at the last second, he sees her and jerks his wheel to avoid her, except he's going too fast and doesn't have control.

I know it's going to happen before it does, and all I can do is watch.

He avoided hitting the fan, but he can't avoid this.

Horror fills me as I watch the car flip and roll in front of me, coming so close that I have a split second to react. Instinct kicks in, and I yank the wheel, pulling the brake so I drift around the flipping wreckage, but metal flies through my open window, slicing my arm. The slight pain fades due to my adrenaline. I start to fishtail, so I release the break, spin the wheel, and turn the other way so I'm moving in an S, and when I straighten out, I realize I crossed the line first. I won, but none of that matters. I leap from my car and run toward the wreck. The frame is crushed, and battered metal is spread across the road. The hissing and popping of the engine reaches me as it lies on its side, blocking the road.

I can hear the engines of the incoming racers, and I know I don't have much time. I grip the undercarriage, ignoring it as it cuts into my palms, my blood making my hands slippery, and haul myself up and over. The driver is leaning against the steering wheel, but his head is at an odd angle, and I worry for a moment he's dead until he groans.

I don't know him at all, but I reach down and demand, "Give me your hand." I know he shouldn't be moved, but the roar is getting closer, and we are sitting ducks. If he stays here, then he's dead. He blinks his big blue eyes at me. There's blood running in rivulets down his face, and his shirt is ripped and covered in blood too. "Now!" I yell, and it seems to snap him from his shock.

He offers me his hand, but I realize his seat belt is still on. Turning, I slam my foot into a twisted part of the door, snapping a bit off with my boot and gripping it, ignoring the sharp pain as it digs into my cuts, then I saw at the belt until it snaps free. Grabbing his hand again, I try to lift him, but he's heavy, and my hands are coated in my blood, so he slips back into his seat.

My head jerks up, the roar so loud that I have no choice, and I see cars barreling toward us. I reach back down to the guy who is panicking now, breathing so loudly I can hear it over the engines.

"I am not dying here. Give me your hand now!" I shout, and this time his palm slaps into mine. I grip it as tightly as I can, and using all my strength, I pull him free of the wreckage, the momentum carrying us off the side. I hit the pavement with a groan, his weight crushing me, but I turn and drag him to my car, throwing him inside and gunning it just as the others try to avoid his wrecked vehicle.

I drive only a few feet to give them room to stop, and then I turn to the dazed man. "Are you okay?" I ask as the crowd converges on us.

"You saved my life," he whispers, staring at me in shock.

"Don't mention it. Go get checked out. You don't know what injuries the shock is hiding."

He nods, his hands shaking as he tries to open my door.

"Hey, kid." He turns to look at me, still in shock. "It's not worth winning if your life is on the line. Remember that. There's always another race; there isn't another life. Drive smarter, not harder."

He nods slowly and climbs out of my car and into the waiting crowd, where his friends gather around him, helping him away and, hopefully, to the hospital. His injuries could have been a lot worse, but I bet he has some broken bones.

He's lucky to be alive and he knows it.

You don't walk away from an accident like that as the same kind of person who went into it.

Leaving my car running, since it won't be long until the cops are here, I head over to Sanjay who is watching, slack-jawed and sad. It isn't the first accident in the races, and it won't be the last. There is a reason this is illegal, but there's also a reason we all keep coming back.

"Good save, man," he calls as he slaps my back. "That kid owes you his life."

I shrug it off, wilting a little under the praise. I just did what anyone else would do.

"Your winnings." He slaps them into my hand. I look at the cash I desperately need and hand it back over.

"Give it to the kid who's on his way to the hospital. He would have won if he didn't crash," I mutter.

"Uh-uh, he crashed because he was being an idiot," Sanjay snaps. "It was reckless."

"But it's what's fair." I slap his arm. "I have to go sleep. See you later."

Without a backwards glance, I climb into my car and drive away before the cops show up and start asking questions. I can't afford another arrest.

I can't go home with these injuries. Alice will worry, and I don't want that for her, so on the way back, I stop at a pharmacy that's still open. Luckily, I can sling my jacket on to hide the worst of the bloodstains so I won't get strange looks. I clean up my hands with a bottle of water and wrap them in some tape I have for sparring and head inside. I've had worse, and I can clean the wounds myself. I already checked. They don't need stitches, but they are going to hurt like a son if a bitch for a while, especially now that the adrenaline has left me. Once I'm inside the brightly lit shop, I grab some sugar and chocolate to help combat that and head to the aisle I want.

I fill the basket with anything I might need. When you hurt yourself often enough, you learn the essentials of taking care of injuries. We never had the money to be seen when we were kids, and our parents didn't really care, so it was always up to me.

Hauling my basket onto the counter, I wait for it all to be scanned, and then I hand over the cash. I'm going to need extra shifts to cover everything. Hell, my money is on a goddamn spreadsheet. I don't spend anything without looking first, but these are essentials. I remind myself that unexpected issues arise. I won't go broke from it, but I hate that I'm eating into Alice's school funds. She needs a new laptop, so I have to save for that.

I'm just grabbing the bag when a familiar voice stops me.

The hair on the back of my neck rises.

"Anders?"

ELEVEN

lek Anders turns to face me, his expression like thunder. His nostrils flare as he looks over me where I stand behind him in line, as if I stalked him here or it's my fault I needed meds. Without a word, he thanks the cashier and stomps out of the store.

Fuck him, but then I realize I still need to thank him, and my mom didn't raise a bitch. Well, she didn't really raise me, but you get my drift.

Quickly slapping my money on the counter for my meds, I hurry after Alek as he marches through the deserted lot to his car at the back. I didn't even see it at first since it's parked away from everything.

He's already opening the door, sitting in his seat and rooting through his bag. Rolling my eyes, I stop next to him, but he studiously ignores me like that might make me disappear.

Nice try, asshole. People have tried that my whole life. It didn't work then, and it won't work now.

"You can go back to ignoring me in a minute," I mutter, leaning into his open doorway, my arm on the top of his car. "I just wanted to thank you for looking after me."

"Alice made me," he grits out. At least he's talking to me now.

"Liar," I retort, and his head snaps up, his dark eyes narrowing on me. For a moment, I debate if this is really the hill I want to die on, but I have a feeling Alek Anders is worth the effort. I raise an eyebrow as his eyes narrow further.

I watch his muscles bunch before he strikes out at me.

Catching his fist, I tell him, "Nice try. I let you get one in, but no more." I tighten my hand around his, and he hisses, yanking it back, or trying to, and I frown, turning his hand despite his protests and prying his fist open.

There's a wicked gash on his palm, and it's still bleeding.

That's when I notice the bag on the pavement between his legs, filled with cleaning supplies and bandages, the handle coated in blood.

"Shit, what the fuck happened?" I ask, worried. Those are some nasty gashes. Are they knife marks?

"Nothing." He yanks his hand away, avoiding my eyes.

"Fine, but is the other guy alive?" I joke.

He glances up at me, and for a moment, we just stare. I crouch, ignoring the wet pavement dirtying the thousand dollar jeans—some of the last I have from my past—and grab the bag. I pretend like I don't see him staring at me like he's debating how best to murder me and get away with it.

Rifling through the bag, I lay out what I need as he watches me with a withering expression. I ignore the death glare and gently grab his arm. He tries to pull it back, and I lose my patience.

"Stop it," I snap, and he stills at my angry tone. "You can't bandage these yourself, and since you're a stubborn fuck determined not to see a doctor, I'll do it. I dressed enough wounds during Mauy Thai, not to mention after fights." I jerk his arm back, and for once, he doesn't fight me.

"Get in a lot of fights, do you, rich boy?" he asks, needing to have the last word, but I talk to distract him from what I'm about to do because it will sting like a bitch.

"As a bisexual man from a tiny town? Yes," I answer.

He's quiet for a moment, and I glance up to see him watching me with a considerate expression. "Now don't go feeling sorry for me, Anders. It isn't your style."

"You fucking wish. I'm just thinking they didn't hit you hard enough to dent that pretty face," he snaps. I can't help but laugh, even as a slight blush stains my cheeks.

"You think I'm pretty, huh?" I wink.

"You fucking wish—" I dab the antiseptic into the wound, and he yells, pulling away.

Rolling my eyes, I grab his arm and lay it across his knee. "Stop being a big baby," I chastise and blow over the wet wound to dry it.

A shudder runs through him that makes me really happy, but I don't comment on it. He might try to hit me again, and it will only make his wound worse. I quickly bandage his hand, making sure to wrap it well because I have a feeling he's the type to pull off bandages so he can work better.

I hold my hand out for the next arm. He grinds his jaw but hands it over, and I clean that one, making sure to blow on it again. "Why did you do it?" I ask as I roll out the bandages.

"Do what?" he asks, but he sounds distracted.

"Bring me food and meds and look after me. I know Alice didn't ask you to," I reply carefully, not meeting his eyes as I wrap his hand. He's quiet, and I don't think he'll answer, or he'll try to hit me again, so it surprises me when he speaks.

"If you die, then who am I going to torture?" he mutters, and when I meet his gaze, there's a small smile on his lips. "Besides, only I get to end you, rich boy, not some illness."

I can't help but grin, and when I release his hand, I narrow my gaze on him. There's blood on his shirt, and he's holding his arm weird. Just how hurt is Alek? Hell, he'll probably deny it just to piss me off, but while we have a soft sort of truce happening, I decide to push it a little. He'll never accept help otherwise. He's too proud for that.

"Any more?" I murmur while peering up at him from between his legs. I watch his Adam's apple bob as he swallows then mutely jerks his head in a nod. He reluctantly strips his jacket off to show me his arm, knowing better than to argue. The cut's shallow, but it runs the length of his forearm. I turn it over to see it better, trying to ignore the veins bulging in his muscular arm.

After carefully cleaning the wound, I grab the bandages.

"You didn't do the thing," he mutters as I blink up at him. He looks embarrassed for a moment and then angry. "The blowing thing. Don't you need to?"

I purse my lips to swallow my smile, then I lean in and blow on the wound. Both of us know I don't need to. Alek Anders likes my touch, even if he doesn't want to admit it. I push it one step further just because I can't resist and I eat up Ander's reaction. He acts like my existence is a sin, but when it's just us, I can see hunger in his eyes and the way his body leans into mine. Pressing my lips next to the wound, I lay a gentle kiss on his skin as I meet his dark eyes, watching as he swallows nervously.

I lean back and dress the wound, knowing better than to push it any further. I would definitely get hit again, but I'm starting to think it might be worth it.

"There." I lean back on my knees, smiling sweetly up at him like I didn't just lay a claim on him, one he doesn't understand yet. "Now we're even," I say as I stand and try to dust off my knees, but they are wet and filthy, so I leave it.

His eyes drop to them, and his mouth purses.

"You fucked up your designer pants, though I bet you have a million." It's sly but not mean.

"Nah, only this pair. I could only bring what I could carry." I shrug. "It's fine. I never liked them that much anyway."

"I didn't ask," he snaps.

"Sure." Gripping my bag, I toss it over my shoulders. "Later, Alek, try not to scare too many people tonight."

I take two steps before his voice stops me. "Rich boy."

I swallow my smirk as I turn to face him.

Oh yes, Alek Anders will be mine. He just doesn't know it yet.

SHAW DRIVE
ANDERS AVE
ONE WAY
STOP
NO PARKING
ACTIVE DRIVEWAY
THE MOMENT
TOO
NO PARKING
SALE
SILENT ROSE
Pine Valley
EVER

TWELVE

ALEK

He turns to face me, one perfectly shaped eyebrow raised. His piercings flash in the light, and his hair is wavy tonight, which is a first. Maybe he didn't style it? It hangs around his face, one side pushed behind his ear, and I realize he looks younger. His face is . . . different. Does he wear makeup? His eyes are usually darker, but tonight, they pop. When I just stare, hesitating, he tilts his head.

"Alek?" he retorts, not backing down.

Hell, he even stopped me from hitting him and then casually dropped to his knees and took care of my wounds, ruining his expensive pants in the meantime, all without asking for a thank you. He said I could call us even. Is that the only reason why?

Nobody has ever bandaged my wounds for me before, not even Alice.

I get hurt so often that I'm used to it, but something about this fiery, silver-haired man blowing on my wound made me weak. I shouldn't have hit him. Why did I? Why did I want more after he pressed his lips to my skin?

Shaking my head, I remind myself that offering him a ride is just what a nice guy would do. It's what I should do for my sister's friend

—nothing more, nothing less. It's late, and he's still recovering from being sick. He could get hurt.

I'm just being nice.

That little voice inside chuckles. Since when am I nice to anyone?

"Get in," I demand gruffly, and then I let him choose. I won't make him. Sliding into my car, I throw the bag in the back and start the engine, but he just stands there.

"Get in," I call again.

He treads closer, leaning into my window. "I didn't hear that."

"Where are you going?" I ask instead.

What if he's going to his boyfriend's or out? It is late, after all.

Shit, I shouldn't have said anything. My hand grips the wheel harder.

"Home," he says, and my grip relaxes.

"Fine, get in," I mutter, cranking up the heat.

"No, I'll walk. It's fine," he starts, and I turn my head, meeting his bright eyes.

"Evan, get in the fucking car." For a moment, he just stares at me before he sighs and heads around the front, getting in the passenger seat and dropping his bag between his feet. His arms are covered in goose bumps, so I crank up the heat all the way before I pull out of the lot.

The silence stretches on, and when I glance over at him, he's watching me. "What?" I ask quietly.

"Did Alice ask you to?" he teases.

I yank the wheel and pull over, ignoring the honking traffic. "Get out."

Laughing, he settles deeper into the seat. "Get out," I snap.

"No. Now, are you going to drive, or are we going to stare at each other all night?" He leans over the stick, his eyes dropping to my lips. "Unless you want to do something else."

Snarling, I swerve back into traffic, ignoring his chuckle as it throws him back into the seat. "Belt," I demand.

He ignores me, and at the next stoplight, I lean over, grab it, and click it into place. When I look up, I find him inches away. He wears a serious expression on his face, glancing from my lips to my eyes.

I swallow hard, my gaze dropping to his when a horn blares behind us, breaking the moment, and I move away, gunning it.

It doesn't take me too long to pull up at Evan's dorm, idling in the parking lot. I frown at my own hands as an unfamiliar feeling grips me. I'm almost reluctant to let him leave, feeling sad about how quickly we got here.

Idiot.

When I glance over, he's watching me, seemingly with no intention of getting out, and I relax, ignoring my internal battle. "What?" I finally ask, my voice softer in the dark, empty night.

It's just us, and we are so close I could reach out and touch him.

I won't, but the thought is there.

"What happened to your arm and hands?" he asks, taking me by surprise.

I glance down at them. I'd forgotten about them despite the pain. I shrug, and he sighs, grabbing his bag and preparing to open the door. Something about that makes me feel uneasy, so I reach over and slam the door shut, sitting back as his wide eyes turn to me. "I was racing tonight, and there was an accident. I helped someone after they crashed but got cut up."

"Racing?" He frowns, looking around my car. "As in car racing?"

I nod. "Street racing, to be exact."

He blinks, sitting back in his seat, and my tight chest seems to ease. "I didn't know you raced. Makes sense though. Are they okay?"

"I hope so. Their friends took them to the hospital," I reply, although I didn't check further than that.

"But their friends didn't help them and you did?" he asks, and I shrug, looking out the front window. "Does the great Alek Anders have a soft side?"

"Don't go thinking stupid shit like that. I just didn't want to be one of those dicks sitting on the sideline, watching while someone got hurt," I mutter.

"Uh-huh, sure, whatever you tell yourself. So you race this car? Isn't it illegal?" he asks, getting more comfortable as he turns to me.

I sit back in my seat and turn to him. I should make him leave, tell him to stop asking questions. Maybe it's the night making this feel like a dream, or maybe it's how close I came to dying, but I answer.

"Not this car. I have a Skyline I race. I built it from scratch. It's illegal, so don't tell anyone, rich boy," I warn.

"Your secret's safe with me." He gives me a wide smile that drives me fucking insane, and it does something weird to my chest. "So you build cars? Alice mentioned you work at a garage."

For a moment, I stiffen. "What, not good enough for you rich bastards?"

He blinks, taken aback. "What do you mean? I was just curious if you enjoy it."

I think about his words as I look at him. There's no judgment in his tone or eyes, just confusion, so I relax. "I do in some ways, but also, it's all I'm good at. I needed money for Alice, so it made sense."

"I doubt it's all you're good at. I have a feeling you are actually good at many things but don't let yourself be."

"What do you mean?" I ask.

"Maybe you're scared to want anything more." He shrugs. "Or maybe you have just spent so long taking care of your sister, you stopped looking at your own life."

"You don't know anything," I snap as I look away.

"No? You drive her to school nearly every day so she doesn't have to walk and she's safe. You work at a garage and race to earn money for her school. You love her so deeply, it's evident. You do everything for her, but what do you do for yourself?" he asks, and I glance over. My chest tightens at how deeply he understands me with just a few meetings.

The truth is, I don't know.

"If you want to be a mechanic and nothing else, good, then do it. Do what makes you happy, but don't do it just because you're scared or because you are living for your sister. I don't think she would like that. She loves you, and she wants you to be happy."

"And what do you know about being happy, rich boy?" I counter defensively, lashing out in fear.

His smile disappears, and I hate that. His expression becomes sad. "Not a lot, but I'm trying."

"How?" I ask, and unlike most people, he doesn't look away. He contemplates his words, and when he speaks, he holds my gaze, not a hint of shame in those bright orbs.

"I cut out the toxic people who made me sad. I walked away from my family and their expectations, and even though it hurt, it was for the best. I knew they would never accept me, never love me how I am, and I was so tired of trying to be someone they would love to the point where I wasn't even myself anymore. I cut them out. I chose my own path, my own future, and I'm fighting every day to follow my dreams. I might not know a lot about being happy, but I want to. I want to find out what it means to have a life I'm proud of, even if it's never grand or epic. I just want to be able to look at myself in the mirror and tell myself I love who I am and that I am proud of the path I've made. I think that's the true meaning of being happy. It isn't about the big, exciting stuff, but the small moments that make up your life, the memorable ones." He trails off. "But what do I know? I'm still young and trying to figure it all out."

"I think you know more than most. I'm older, and I still haven't figured out the key to being happy," I admit softly, moved by his words. Evan Shaw isn't what I thought he was at all. It's clear he's been through a lot. Maybe he isn't just a spoiled rich boy. In fact, at the moment, I'm almost jealous of his openness with himself, with his ability to call out his own flaws and try to fix them. "I want to own my own garage one day. It isn't a big dream, nothing crazy, but I want to own it and hire people like me—people who have no opportunities. I want to give them a chance. I also want to build and restore cars. I think that would make me happy."

"So do it," he says. "Who gets to say that dream isn't big enough?"

"I'm trying but . . . Alice always comes first." I meet his gaze once more. "I have to give her a better life than I had. I can't fail her like everyone failed me."

"And what about you? Who looks after you? Who puts you first?" he argues. "This is your life, Alek. I know you love Alice, and she's so lucky to have a brother like you, but if you don't put yourself first, nobody ever will, and one day, you'll look back and wonder what if."

I stare at Evan, and he stares right back. "When did you get so smart, rich boy?"

"I always have been. You were just too busy hating me to notice." He winks, making me chuckle, but it ends in a yawn, exhaustion setting into my bones even as I fight it. I want to keep talking to him. He notices me when no one else ever has. He looks past the scars, the ink, and the oil to the man underneath. He isn't scared of me despite everything I have thrown at him.

"You look exhausted. I'm betting you don't even sleep in case she needs you." He snorts. "I'll let you get home. Thank you for driving me back. Text me when you get there so I know you didn't wreck or something." He opens his door and slips out, and I don't stop him, but I do call out.

"Why, would you miss me?" I tease.

"No." He grins as he leans back in, his bright smile making my chest tight once more. "Just need a heads-up so I can choose my outfit for your funeral."

I can't help but smile, imagining what horrendous outfit this fashion diva would wear at my funeral, and he points at me, grinning widely. "I got you to smile. Night, Anders." He leaves, and I watch him cross the lot toward his building. When he reaches the door, he looks back at me, his grin firmly in place, and then he lifts his hand to wave before disappearing inside.

I wave back, even though he's already gone, and it's only then I admit to myself that I would have stayed here all night talking to him despite my exhaustion.

I guess I do some things for myself, and they all seem to revolve around him.

Shaking my head at my own feelings, I wait until I see his light come on, and then I head home. He's right. I need to sleep.

Once I'm home, I check on Alice and find her passed out on her desk, her books spread out around her. Turning off her light, I drape a blanket over her and head to my room. I take off my shirt and pull my wallet and phone out of my jeans, ready to crash, but I hesitate, looking at my phone.

I tell myself I won't, but I open it and click on the message thread.

Alek: I'm home.

I pause before thumbing out another message.

Alek: So put away the lace and veil.

A minute later, a picture comes through. He's in the shower, his chest bare. I can't see any more, but it stops me in my tracks before I notice his pout and the soap making his hair stick up, and I laugh.

Rich Boy: Shame, I have the perfect pearl necklace I could clutch while I scream your name dramatically so everyone would stare.

Pushing my jeans down, I text back as I crash into my bed.

Alek: There wouldn't be many there to stare.

Rich Boy: Damn, all that performance wasted for nothing? Good thing you're alive then. Now get some sleep, Anders.

Alek: Are you ordering me, rich boy?

Rich Boy: You know it. You can hit me for it next time.

My lips twitch even as I thumb out another message.

Alek: Stop texting me while you're naked. It's weird.

Rich Boy: Then this will shock you—I'm
pretty much always naked when I text you.
Now sleep.

Idiot.

Alek: Night.

Rich Boy: Night, Anders, don't dream about
me too much.

Putting my phone down, I bury my face in my pillow to hide my stupid grin, but I know I'll dream of the boy with the icy hair and the sunshine smile.

SHAW DRIVE
ANDERS AVE
ONE WAY
ACTIVE DRIVEWAY
THE MOMENT
STOP
TOO
SALE
NO PARKING
SILENT ROSE
Pine Valley
EVER

THIRTEEN

ALEK

Last night, I might have realized that Evan lives far from campus, but that has nothing to do with what I'm doing.

Nothing at all.

I woke up early, packed Alice some breakfast, and dragged her out earlier than we usually leave. I use the excuse that I need to be at work, which she falls for. She doesn't notice the different route we are taking either. It's purely to see the scenic view, nothing else.

We pass the park, and then I slow down, looking for him since he has to take this road to school. What if he went a different way?

"Hey, that's Evan! Pull over. Let's give him a ride," Alice demands, smacking my side.

"No," I mutter, my gaze tracking him.

"Alek," she warns.

Grumbling to myself, I pull over right next to him. He's oblivious, looking down at his camera, so I roll down my window to call out, but Alice beats me to it. "Evan, hey!"

His head jerks up, and he blinks into the early morning sun. When he sees us, a bright smile curves his lips. "Anders duo." He nods. "What are you doing here?"

"Going to school. Get in, we'll give you a ride," Alice calls as she grabs her bag and climbs into the back, leaving the passenger seat open for Evan.

He spares me a look, and I roll my eyes. "You heard her." I sigh, pushing my shades down to peer at him. "Get in, rich boy, before I run you over."

He grins, dropping his camera to the strap and lifting his bag higher, then he steps off the curb, looking both ways before opening the door and sliding in.

He looks good in my passenger seat, which only pisses me off. Despite the fact I came this way, I'm annoyed and glare at him as he straps in.

"Isn't your house the other way?" he asks, confused. "That's the way you headed last night."

Shit.

"Last night?" Alice asks, appearing between the seats with a grin.

Double shit.

"Sit back. Seat belts or I'll leave you both," I snarl.

"He's not a morning person," Alice warns.

"Or an afternoon person," Evan teases, making her laugh as she sits back. It's nice seeing her joke with him. She can be super quiet sometimes, but she seems to open up around him.

"Don't expect me to pick you up again," I snap as I pull out into early morning traffic and purposely ignore him. It's childish, but true.

"I didn't today," he replies, and when I glance over, he's frowning at me.

He's right, he didn't. I came this way to see him, so why am I so angry?

It's because I went out of my way to look after him, and I don't understand why.

I'm quiet the whole way there, and I know the atmosphere in the car is tense, so it doesn't surprise me when they both climb out quickly when we pull up at campus. Evan waves tersely and waits for Alice, who leans into my window.

"Stop being an ass. You like the boy, so flirt, don't be a mean idiot." She huffs before heading his way, their arms linked as they chatter and walk toward their building. I could never be like that with him.

I could never touch him like that in public or handle the stares we would get. It pisses me off and only puts me in a worse mood, knowing he's more suited to my sister.

I gun it to work despite being early and shove my headphones in, ignoring everyone else. Not long after I get there, my phone buzzes, and I pull it out.

Rich Boy: How is your wound? Are you in pain? I can bring you some Tylenol.

I stare at the message, this morning flashing through my mind. We can never be together. We can never be anything. Besides, I don't even like him like that, so I should just stop leading him on. It's not fair to him, at least that's what I tell myself anyway as I block his number and toss my phone into my toolbox, focusing on the car before me.

While I work, Evan's words from last night float into my mind. I deserve to dream and be happy.

What would make me happy?

Truthfully, I don't even know anymore, but something about his sunshine smile, even for a moment, made me believe I had the right to be.

Reality has set back in, though, and it's better this way.

I should have known better. My past is a stark reminder of why I can't have Evan Shaw—a truth that Alice doesn't even know, nor will she ever.

It's another reason I moved here—one I will never share.

FOURTEEN

I stare at my phone for the hundredth time in the last hour. He hasn't responded to any of my messages. I told myself at dinner I wouldn't text again. He obviously doesn't want to talk to me, but I still type out a message as I lean back in my chair, waiting for the lecture to start, Lally talking happily at my side.

> Evan: Ah, so we are back to ignoring me now, huh?

This time, the message doesn't send, and I gape. "Lally," I interrupt.

"Huh?" She leans over as I thrust my phone at her.

"What does that mean?"

She scans the messages and winces. "Uh, doesn't that mean they blocked your number?"

"Seriously?" I mutter, staring at my phone. "What an asshole." Dropping it to my desk, I glare at the front of the room. I feel Lally watching me, but I ignore her, suddenly in a terrible mood. When she glances away, I snatch up my phone, and despite the fact I know they won't go through, I text him.

> Evan: Seriously, you blocked me?

> Evan: What the hell is your problem?

> Evan: I know you're an asshole, but seriously?

> Evan: I didn't ask you to drive me home last night or to pick me up this morning.

> Evan: You could have just texted me and told me to leave you alone, said no. It's called communication, you fucking dick.

> Evan: But no, you blocked me because you have the emotional intelligence of a sausage.

> Evan: You want me to leave you alone? Fine, I will.

I quickly change his name to "Asshole—do not answer."

My mood sours with each undelivered notification, so I turn my phone off and shove it in my bag. I'm sick of this hot-and-cold treatment. He hit me, kissed me. He spent last night talking to me, letting me in, then he flirted with me all night and blocked me.

I don't understand him one fucking bit.

Have you ever met anyone you just know will break your heart, yet you can't seem to stop yourself from giving it to them, even knowing the outcome?

Alek Anders is that person. I know loving him would be foolish and only end in pain, but I can't seem to stop myself, and I hate that more.

It's like watching a car crash, which only makes me worry about his injuries and in turn pisses me off more.

For fuck's sake.

Club 37 is a mix between a dive bar and a neon club. It shouldn't work, but it does. Lots of art students come here, and the owner is an alumnus, which is great since he lets us in for free. A ton of others from the area come through, mostly older people since it's the hottest place in town, so it's crammed.

It doesn't take me long to get sweaty, the club music pounding through me, unwinding my tight muscles as we make our way through the crowd to the booth our friends grabbed. It's overflowing with people, and they cheer when they see us, thrusting drinks our way. I grab the shot and down it, then another as they continue cheering. Their faces blur. Usually, I'm the life of the party, but tonight, I just want to forget, so I let them ply me with liquor until I'm buzzed. I laugh and joke with them, surrounded by people who care about me and would never block me just because of their own issues.

"Let's dance!" I shout and grab Lally's and Tommy's hands. I tug them onto the dance floor filled with writhing bodies, the strobe lights turning it all into a flashing kaleidoscope. Lally spins before me, and Tommy pulls me against him as we dance and grind together. I forget about everything else and just move to the music. The liquor heats my blood, making me feel free, happy, and horny.

Lally is right. It has been too long since I've been laid. That's why I fell for Anders so quickly. It's just need, but I can take care of that tonight, and I know that when Lally looks at a hot blonde and dances over to her that I won't be the only one. I wink at Tommy as he goes for a drink, leaving me alone.

I feel eyes on me, and within minutes of my friends' disappearance, a guy appears before me. He's really fucking cute. He doesn't have that rough edge like Anders has, but he's muscular, taller than me, and has styled blond hair. He doesn't have any tattoos, but he does wear a silver chain around his neck and a matching bracelet on his wrist. He looks good, and he's the exact opposite of Anders.

Perfect.

"Can I dance with you?" he calls loudly, having to lean in, his mouth practically pressed against my ear.

"Sure," I respond, though I don't think he can hear me, so instead I let him pull me closer. His hands grip my hips as I grin at him. He grins back as we move together to the music. His hand slowly slides down and around until he grips my ass and grinds into me. I see hunger in his eyes as they drop to my lips before he leans in.

"Are you here alone?" he asks.

"Just with some friends, you?" I reply, moving closer until I'm pressed against him so he can hear me.

"Just my friends," he says, kissing my pulse point. "How about after this dance, I buy you a drink?"

I purposely brush my lips over his ear, feeling him shiver. "Sounds great."

A hot guy flirting with me? Yeah, it's exactly what I need, and one dance turns into two until we are both hot and heavy, our lustful eyes locked on one another. I signal Lally so she knows I'm safe, and she nods, then we head to the bar. I plop into a little table tucked into the corner as he goes to order, and when he comes back, I can't help but grin.

He really is hot.

He hands it over and sits right next to me, his leg pressed to mine. His hand drops to my thigh and squeezes as he leans in. "So what's your name?"

"Evan. Yours?" I reply, sipping the fruity drink.

"Tait," he answers. "Are you single, Evan?"

"Very." I nod as I lean closer, getting a good whiff of expensive cologne. "But you really don't want to ask that and make small talk, do you?" I flirt, my fingers trailing up and down his chest as he glances from my eyes to my lips. "Why don't you ask what you really want to ask?"

"Do you want to get out of here?" he blurts.

Smirking, I lean back and down my drink before I stand and offer him my hand.

Fuck Anders. Tonight, I won't think about him at all.

NO PARKING
ACTIVE
DRIVEWAY
SHAW DRIVE
THE MOMENT
ANDERS AVE
ONE WAY
STOP
TOO
SILENT ROSE
DADDY SWEET
CAR REPAIR
NO PARKING
SALE
Pine Valley
EVER

FIFTEEN

ALEK

I won two races tonight. I needed the high, the risk of danger. Despite my injured hands and jacked arm, I still won, and then I decided I needed a drink. It didn't take much to convince Skylar, another of the racers I'm pretty close to, to join me for one. I even let him pick the place, and it had been going well. Sky is a good guy. He's fun to be around, and we are friends despite not knowing much about each other outside of racing, but then Evan turned up with a gaggle of friends.

He looks so fucking good, I hate him on sight. He hasn't even seen me, completely focused on the people fawning all over him. His smile is so wide it hurts to see. Doesn't he care that we aren't talking?

Isn't he upset?

He doesn't look like it as he jokes and flirts and then dances with his friends. He's acting like I'm nothing to him, as if us talking the other night didn't mean anything. Hell, to him, it probably didn't. I'm probably another person waiting in a long line for him.

I know that's not fair, since I'm the one who blocked him, but of all the fucking places, why did he have to show up here looking so fucking good when I'm trying my best to stay away from him?

"Who's the blond hottie you're staring so hard at?" Sky's deep, mocking voice has my head whipping around, and I meet his shrewd gaze. With eyes darker than mine, Sky is a mean-looking bastard. He's big and muscular, with most of his hair pulled back into a bun tonight. Some might even call him handsome, but my tastes seem to be stuck on the ball of sunshine dancing like he doesn't have a care in the world.

"No one, my sister's friend," I reply, sipping my drink.

"He's hot. Is he single?" Sky asks, leaning back with a wicked grin.

"No, he's fucking not. Don't go near him," I warn, and Sky laughs, leaning back farther to escape my anger, holding his hands up.

"Shit, man, sorry. Didn't realize he was yours."

"He's not mine, don't be an idiot," I mutter, looking away from his knowing eyes. I reach for the glass bottle on the table, pouring myself another drink and shooting it before pouring another.

"Uh-huh, since when do you care about anyone else? If he isn't yours, I could just go over there—"

My head jerks up, my glare only making him laugh before it fades and he winces. "Shit, looks like someone beat me to it. Are you going to go over there to defend your territory?"

My head swings around, my heart missing a beat when I see the blond idiot dancing against Evan, who doesn't seem to care. No, he seems into it. I watch the guy's hands grip Evan's ass, pulling him closer, as jealousy and anger fill me.

"How the fuck can they be so open about that shit?" I ask, gripping my glass tighter to stop myself from racing over there and beating the shit out of the bastard for touching what's mine.

"Alek Anders, don't tell me you're homophobic." I look over at Sky, who wears a serious expression as he leans into me. "Because let me tell you, we'll have some problems. Love is love, man."

My eyebrows rise as I read the very dark look in his eyes, which is so out of place on the jovial race head. "I'm not. It's just—"

"He's yours, and you're acting irrationally, but you sound like an asshole, and as your very gay friend, be careful. You might get away with that shit elsewhere, but not with me. If he's not yours, then he's allowed to dance with and fuck whoever he wants," Sky says, toasting me.

I mean, I didn't know Sky was gay. Not that it matters but—

"He can't fuck whoever he wants," I mutter.

"So he's not yours, but he isn't allowed to be anyone else's." Sky snorts. "That's stupid. Make up your mind, man, before you lose him. If you want him, then take him. If not, I'm betting there are plenty out there who do want him, but you need to decide. Don't play with his feelings. That's not cool."

I stare at Sky, shocked by his words. We don't usually talk about anything deeper than cars. Where is this shit coming from, and why do I suddenly want to talk about it with him? "You're not upset that I want him?"

Sky watches me sadly before leaning closer. "I don't care who you love or fuck, Alek. Love is love. Gender doesn't matter. I don't know what kind of backwards people you've been around to make you believe you loving or wanting who you want is wrong, but that's their problem, not yours. Do you want him?"

I stare before slightly inclining my head, admitting to him what I don't even want to admit to myself.

"Then what's the problem? You are allowed to want who you want and be attracted to who you want. Fuck what anyone else thinks. If they have a problem, then that says more about who they are than you. I'm not saying it will be easy—trust me on this—but it's worth it. Being honest with yourself lifts a weight off you." Sky nods, pouring me another drink. "I mean it, Anders. Be who you are and fuck everyone else." He downs his drink, and I drain mine.

"You're a pretty good guy, Sky," I mutter.

"Glad you finally noticed. It's only taken me a year of friendship," he scoffs. "Even now, we wouldn't be here if you weren't stressing over that man."

I wince because he's right. I've never tried to deepen our friendship. I use Sky.

He laughs. "Don't worry about it, man. I know that's how you are, but you need to decide what you want quickly."

My head snaps around again to see Evan and the blond sitting at a table, way too close and smiling at each other with a look that makes my blood boil.

I can't believe him. My hands tighten around my drink in anger, and when he stands, grinning down at the guy, I feel the glass break, cutting into my already mangled palm, but I don't care.

"Shit, Alek, what the fuck?" Sky snarls, jumping back from the spilling liquid.

I watch Evan leave with the guy, waving to his friends who just let him go with a fucking stranger.

Shoving to my feet, I throw some bills down without even sparing Sky another glance. "I'm out."

"About fucking time!" he calls. "Get your man!"

By the time I make it through the club, Evan has disappeared with the idiot. I push through the crowd, knocking people out of my way with a snarl that gets the others moving. I don't feel like myself. The anger and jealousy coursing through my veins is insane, and I'm not thinking clearly, but despite all that and what Sky said, I can't let Evan leave with him.

I burst out into the cold air, searching for them. Panic consumes me, but then I catch sight of a familiar icy head ducking into an alley a few feet away. I stomp after them, stilling at the end of the alley when I see Evan pinned to the wall, the blond all over him, their teeth and tongues clashing as they kiss. Evan's hands are in his hair, and he's kissing him back.

Evan is kissing him.

Something stabs into my heart, but it doesn't stop me from closing the distance and ripping the blond away from him without even a glance. He flies backwards, and I glare at Evan, who blinks owlishly at me before his cheeks redden in anger as he straightens.

"Anders, what the fuck? Are you okay?" He goes to move past me to the blond, who's struggling to his feet, but I hold up my arm and block him, turning to the blond myself.

"Leave," I order, unable to grit out more words when I see his bruised lips.

He glares at me, dusting off his ass and looking from me to Evan despite the threat I present. I am practically vibrating with anger, ready to strike. "Evan, are you okay?"

"I'm fine, it's okay, you can leave. I'll deal with this guy." I glance over to see Evan blushing and rubbing his head nervously, messing up his pretty hair.

"Don't apologize to him. Leave," I tell the blond again. It's the last chance he will get, and I watch him give Evan another look before he hurries from the alley, then I turn to Evan as I try to hold back my fury. "You should be apologizing to me."

"To you?" His eyes widen incredulously. "Why the fuck would I say sorry to you?"

The anger snaps inside me, and I turn, slamming my fist into the wall. I feel my knuckles split and the cuts on my palm reopen, but even that sharp pain doesn't push back these feelings inside me.

"What the fuck, Anders? What is your fucking problem?" A hand hits my back, sending me stumbling forward, and I turn to see him spitting fire. Evan is angrier than I've ever seen him. "You don't get to do this shit. You don't get to block me then show up here—"

Rather than hitting the wall, I grab him and slam him into it. My mouth crashes onto his. He fights me at first, hitting me, and although it hurts, I don't relent. I don't let go. I pour all of my jealousy, confusion, and anger into that kiss until he groans, softening against me and kissing me back.

His fists turn into clenching hands, pulling me closer as our bodies rub together, all hard muscles and warmth. "You're mine, pretty boy," I tell him, kissing him again until he whimpers. The sound snaps me out of it, and I stumble back. Desire burns so hotly in my veins, I'm surprised I haven't exploded. My fists clench as I stare at him, his lips parted and raw as he gapes at me before he laughs bitterly.

"At least you didn't hit me this time," he mutters, wiping his mouth with the back of his hand. "I guess that's something."

Shit, I really am an asshole.

Even if I want him, I don't deserve Evan.

I could live a million lives and never deserve a man like Evan Shaw, and he knows it.

Grinding my jaw, I spin on my heel and race away.

"So you're back to ignoring me again?" he calls, and I still. "Fine. I'm fucking done, Anders. I'm so fucking done with whatever this is." When he barges past me, he hits me, knocking me to the left, and when I meet his gaze, his eyes are cold.

"Don't call, don't text, don't show up outside of my house with excuses, don't come after me, and don't stop me from hooking up with people. I'm not yours and never will be. You made that very clear, and I'm done. I'm done chasing you. I'm done being used and tossed aside by you when it suits you. I'm not your fucking plaything to figure out your feelings and use to dispel them. I'm done." He turns and walks away, and it's my turn to stare after him.

I feel like I just lost something very fucking important to me, like I just lost my boyfriend, but how can it end when it never even started?

SHAW DRIVE
ANDERS AVE
ONE WAY
STOP
ACTIVE DRIVEWAY
THE MOMENT
NO PARKING
SALE
SILENT ROSE
EVER

SIXTEEN

ALEK

I should leave him alone.

I hurt him, I made him angry, but I can't seem to stop myself.

I know I'm stalking him, but I need to make sure he gets home okay after drinking and walking alone. I quiet my steps and hang back as he stomps toward his dorm. Luckily, Club 37 is on the other side of the campus, closer to his dorm, but it's still a walk, and he had a lot to drink. He's so annoyed, grumbling to himself, that he doesn't even sense me behind him, which pisses me off.

I want to shake some sense into him, but I don't want to fight again.

I'm tired of him being angry at me.

When he disappears into his dorm, I linger outside for a little while, watching his light come on, his silhouette framed in the window. Part of me aches, knowing I lost something that could have been amazing, but I know it's for the best.

I could never belong to someone, especially Evan. I'm too damaged for that, and he deserves better. He deserves someone who can proudly stand at his side and show him off. He deserves someone who knows what he wants and isn't as confused as me.

I mean, fuck, I don't even like guys . . . Do I?

I need to deal with my confusion, so I head to the gym. I let it morph into anger—anger at myself, anger that the one person I'm attracted to is a guy after everything that happened.

I strip down. Luckily, the gym is empty at this time. It's a small one, mainly for bodybuilders and calisthenics, but it has a separate kickboxing area, and that's where I take up shop. I need to beat something up. I need to get all these emotions out.

I want to feel pain as my feet and fists hit the bag, splitting open my wounds. That sharp pain only spurs me on more.

I lose myself in the burning of my muscles, pushing myself harder and faster, the bag swinging so wildly that I eventually have to stop. I lean on my knees, breathing heavily, sweat dripping down my body, and I smile bitterly when I realize it didn't work.

My thoughts instantly go back to him.

Is he okay? Is he still mad?

Fuck! I slam my leg into the bag before collapsing on the floor, my arm across my face, trying to block everything out, but all that does is throw me into darkness, and in that darkness, bright sunshine appears before the image contorts to his furious face. My cock hardens uncomfortably in my pants, even as my heart aches.

What am I doing?

I am so fucking confused. I wouldn't let anyone else talk to me like that, but then again, I wouldn't go out of my way to insert myself into someone's life like I'm doing with Evan. Dropping my hand, I press my fingers to my lips, remembering the way he felt when I kissed him.

It was soft but hard, and his body wasn't like a girl's when it was pressed against mine. He was all hard muscle, but I didn't hate it or the way his dick rubbed against mine as we came together. Shit, no, I didn't hate it. I might have even liked it.

Why does this keep happening?

Why can't I stay away from Evan Shaw? He's no good, not for me at least. He's everything I hate and everything I don't need. I have to focus on my future and taking care of Alice, not beating the shit out of things, refusing to sleep or eat since he's all I can think about.

Why can't I just stop?

Why does that smiling bastard have such a hold on me?

Why can't I just be normal?

I don't want to think about Evan. I don't want to want him. I don't want to wonder what his skin would feel like against mine or imagine his eyes flashing as I pin him. I don't want to want a boy.

I just wish my body would listen, my heart too. Can't it remember what happened before?

Why is it doing this to me, and why now?

I know I'm messed up inside, a total headcase, but I'm spiraling. My past mixes with my current issues, leaving me raw and angry. I wouldn't mind liking Evan if he was a girl, and that's fucking me up. The worst part is I know it's fucking him up to. I don't want that. Despite all my anger toward him at first, Evan is a good guy. He also knows what he likes and wants. He shouldn't be made to feel like it's wrong just because I can't wrap my head around it.

I should let him go, but I can't.

I reach for my phone, staring at it for a moment before I make a decision. I swipe through the options before I hit unblock.

A string of messages from the last few days comes through, and I grin as I read them, but the last one makes me sit up.

It's from tonight, before we saw each other.

> Rich Boy: Fine, Alek. I get the message. I'm done. Tonight, I'm going to forget all about you, so don't worry anymore. I'll leave you alone.

Something inside me squeezes, and despite knowing I shouldn't, my instincts take over, and I type a quick message, hitting send before I can stop myself.

> Alek: Don't.

SEVENTEEN

One word, that's all I get. No apology, nothing. Just "Don't."

I can't help but reread the text for the millionth time. What does he mean? Don't give up? Don't stop chasing him? Fuck, he couldn't have explained? No.

I have to admit that when my phone went off last night as I was lying in bed and the delivered notification popped up, followed by the read receipts showing he'd read all my messages, I felt a sick sense of satisfaction.

He unblocked me and reached out first.

Whether Alek Anders knows it or not, he doesn't want to let me go, which only makes me more confused and pissed off.

Dropping my phone to the library desk without replying, I bury my head in my hands. I've been distracted all day, which doesn't bode well for me. I have assignments due that are worth a good percentage of my grade. I need to focus on my work, on my friends, on the things that bring me happiness . . .

All I can think about is Alek Anders and the flurry of emotions he causes inside me. It's eight at night, and I've been staring at the same essay question for four hours. Giving up for the night, I start to pack up when my phone buzzes again.

I'm ashamed of how fast I snatch it up, hope blooming in my chest, only to deflate when I realize it isn't him.

> Unknown: Tonight, 9PM. Meet behind the library.

Huh? I look up and around before peering back at my phone just as another message comes through.

> Unknown: You didn't forget about us, did you, newbie? You're one of us. It's time for your first meeting.

It has to be Silent Rose.

Oh, well, I mean I kind of did forget about the whole secret society thing, especially since I haven't heard or seen anything after I was kidnapped and inducted. I figured it was like a one-time thing. Apparently not. It's just what I need though, a distraction, something not tainted by Alek Anders.

This is all mine and has nothing to do with him.

It's normal. It's college—well, maybe not normal, but it's college and what I should be doing.

> Evan: See you then.

Finishing packing my bag, I head out to wait since there is no point in hanging around. The library is huge, so it takes me a little while to get through the old building. Once I stand outside the well-lit front, I shove my hands into my pockets and look around. There are students milling about, and I watch them for a moment before walking off the path, onto the grass, and around the building. There's a gate at the side, but it is unlocked despite the sign saying "No trespassing." The creak of the hinges is loud away from the hustle and bustle here, and I shut it behind me, almost jumping when a lock falls into place.

Okay, not creepy at all.

Shrugging it off, I carry on, my sneakers sinking into the slightly wet grass as I round the building to the back, where the campus lights don't reach. It's dim back here, almost too dark to see until my eyes adjust.

The bushes and flowers continue against the building, and I follow them until I reach the back of it. I scan the area. There isn't much, just some trees and grass stretching across to the other buildings on the other side. There's also a garbage center to the right against a metal fence, but the rest is too dark to see, so with nothing else to do, I wait.

I bounce on my toes nervously as I check the time on my phone. It's almost nine, and I start to worry. Looking around once, I search for signs of anyone, a creepy feeling building within me. What if this isn't them? What if it's a setup or something?

Biting my lower lip, I tell myself if no one is here in another ten minutes, I'll leave and pretend I never came.

Five minutes pass, and I pick my bag up, ready to leave. "I knew it was a setup," I mutter.

"Why would we be setting you up?" a voice calls, and my head jerks up as Liam materializes seemingly out of nowhere. "Evan?" he asks with a frown.

I shrug halfheartedly, deflating. I guess you can take the boy out of the small town, but not the small town out of the boy. How many times did I agree to go out with someone only for it to be a trap? I have to remind myself that this isn't the same place, and they aren't those small-minded assholes.

I'm one of them. I'm part of something.

All the cloak and dagger stuff is kind of fun when you're not worried about being killed. "So it's just us?" I finally respond.

Chuckling, he slings his arm across my shoulders and steers me over the grass. "Nah, everyone else is already here. Sorry I'm late. I was at practice and the coach made us run laps."

"No worries." I let him lead me farther still. "Um, where are we going?"

"You'll see," is all he says as he grins down at me, far too happy that we are venturing off into the dark, but oh well. If I die tonight, at least it will be a good story.

I mean, "you'll see" is definitely what a weirdo serial killer says right before they throw you in their dungeon with lotion to make a skin coat out of you. I do have very nice skin, but still, I would be a very bad prisoner. I'm too needy, but I bet I could get some good naps in. Plus, I do like red flags, and a guy going to that much effort to get your attention?

I'm about to tell him all this when we circle some trees and stop, leaving me blinking in shock.

There is a small marble structure here, statues of pine trees framing a wooden door with a huge lock across it. It's hidden well, so well that if you didn't know where it was, you would probably never find it. There's a fence to the right almost blocking it off, and the trees cover it entirely from the campus's view. It feels like a different world. The gray marble building looks like something from the past, and the plaque above the door is in a foreign language.

Intra ea cum secretis ut.

"What does it mean?" I ask softly, nodding at the plaque.

"Not a fucking clue. They told me, but I'm shitty at Latin. Ask the others, they'll remember. I don't know why they couldn't just write it in English, the dramatic fuckers." He chuckles as he heads over and pulls a key from his pocket. It's an antique brass one, and it slides into the lock. The chain drops, and he pushes the door open before turning to smile at me, then he holds the key out to me.

I gape as I turn my head from the secret doorway to a grinning Liam. "You didn't think we would leave you in the dark, did you? You're one of us now, and that means knowing the secret and getting the key to the door. This is more than a club or a hobby, Evan. This is a partnership. It's a family. A place to go when you have no one else, and it's yours now." He pushes me into the open doorway, and I stumble inside.

It's just a small room, which is disappointing, and there are busts placed around the walls on small shelves. The floor is uneven concrete, and there is a wooden table cut into the back of the marble room with candles scattered across it. Liam heads past me, the door shutting behind us with a bang, making me jump. He isn't bothered, though, and at the table, he reaches sideways, pressing on one of the busts that turns, and then there's a cranking noise.

The table lifts, revealing a dark passage. He whistles as he grabs a candle, lights it, and leans in, hitting something. Light blares within as he blows the candle out and puts it back, and I can see stone stairs leading down.

"After you, newbie." He grins, waiting.

Okay, I know what I said about being a bad skin suit and all, and really I didn't think I'd be one of those dumb blonds in a horror movie, but I'm just too fucking curious. Besides, my hair is dyed, it's not natural, so it doesn't count, right?

Heading his way, I stop at the top of the stairs. "If you decide to skin me and use it for a skin suit, please, for the love of God, at least do it in a fashionable way," I tell him as I step inside, his laughter chasing me as I descend the steep stone steps. At the bottom, I find an oval tunnel leading off into the distance, with buzzing, old-style lights hanging from ropes all the way down. Nothing else.

I hear the door slam shut above us, and then he's at my side again. It's just wide enough for us to walk that way without brushing against each other, but not much else.

"These tunnels were built when the school was founded. They were forgotten for a while before our society began, and ever since, we have used them to meet and get around. No one else knows they are here, not even the staff. People just assume it's locked and they can't get in," he offers when I stay silent. "It's useful for us. We can get to our hideout without being questioned or seen. You'll get this key tonight, and you can come here whenever you want, not just when we are meeting. What is ours is yours now—our knowledge, our houses, our families, our names, and our power."

"How often do we meet?" I ask, although it's probably something I should have asked before. "And do I need to do anything?"

He shakes his head. "We meet every month, more if we want or if there is a problem. At the end of the year, we have a big blowout as well. No, you don't need to do anything really. Just keep the secret and be one of us. If a member asks for help, you help no matter what, and that's it."

"What if it's to move a body? I'll be honest, I wouldn't do well in prison. I'm too pretty." That makes him laugh again as the tunnel curves.

"Don't worry, we've only moved a few bodies throughout the years, and we never got caught." He winks, but I have no idea if he's joking or not, but then we reach another door.

This one is metal, and there's a sliding window at the top. No lock, no handle.

Liam raps his fist against the metal in a series of knocks—great, a secret code. I'm going to need to write all of this down. The sound echoes, and when he's done, the door cranks open. It's so dramatic, but I love it.

"After you, newbie."

I step inside to find myself back where I was last time. The lights are on now, though, and there's no kidnapping. The members are spread around, drinking and chatting, so it's just like a party.

"Ah, you're finally here," Bones says from his spot on a sofa.

I nod and head over, sitting in one of the chairs while Liam grabs two beers, handing me one as he reclines on another settee.

"Okay, okay, meeting time." Autumn claps. "Let's discuss the matters we need to, then we can get drunk and fuck around."

"What matters? Oh god, it isn't to vote to change the color of the crest again, is it?" Liam mutters in annoyance.

"No, we settled on gold." She huffs as she looks around. "We were considering taking another member next month. We think it would be good to get our numbers up, but we need to vote. Hands up if you agree." Some stick their hands up, and I just sip my beer as she turns to me. "Evan?"

"Oh, um, I didn't know I was allowed to vote." I slowly stick my hand up.

"You're one of us," she reminds me with a grin. "Okay, so it's agreed we will add someone. Start scouting, and report hopeful names to me whenever you have them. We can look into those we think could fit. Next matter." Someone groans, and her eyes narrow. "Tee"—she glances at him—"is looking for an internship this semester and needs our help. What do we have?"

"My father owns a law firm," Bones says. "I can swing that if you need experience there."

He sighs. "I need it more in big businesses."

"My uncle is the CEO of some big trading company. I'll call in a favor and get you one," Ollie replies.

"Awesome, so that's taken care of. Anything else?" she calls. "Anyone have any worries or need help with anything?" Her gaze lands on me. "Evan, we heard you've had issues with some guy . . . Anders, was it?"

My eyes widen at that. Shit, how do they know? Just how closely do they pay attention to our lives? "Uh, nothing I can't handle."

"Are you sure? We could take care of it for you. I didn't look into him, but we could take his job."

"Get him kicked out of his apartment," someone suggests.

"Get him expelled if he's a student," another adds.

"Oh, um, no, no, it's fine. We are . . . friends. Just been in a fight," I offer protectively. I don't want them to touch Alek. The fact that they are so easily talking about destroying his life pisses me off. I know it's to help me, but he worked so hard to get where he is, yet they are talking about ruining it all.

"Okay, let us know if you need any help. That's what we are here for."

I nod, sinking into my seat. They are just trying to be nice. It isn't their fault they don't know about him and me—whatever the hell there is to know. I'll just need to be careful and make sure they don't go after him.

"Alright, now that shit is out of the way, let's get drunk and play some games!" Music blares as they jump up. Some head to the pool table, and others hurry over to the drinks, laughing and joking as I sit there.

What the hell have I gotten myself into?

Honestly, it's kind of fun. No one treats me strangely, and they all accept me. We drink and play games, and I start to relax. It feels more like a club than a society, but then I remember their earlier offer. They could easily manipulate people's lives to get what they want. They are dangerous, that's for sure, but it seems like once you are in, you are in. I'm one of them just like that.

Collapsing into the sofa, I sip my drink as I watch them dance and laugh loudly. It isn't even a bad thing. It's kind of nice to have a place to go and a family who accepts me. Isn't that what I've always wanted?

Bones collapses next to me, his face flushed and grin wide for once. "So are you enjoying being one of us elite bastards?"

My eyebrows rise at that. I never quite know how to take him. They say he's a brutal bastard, but he seems nice enough to those he likes. "It's different. Not what I was expecting."

"You were thinking we wore cloaks and wanted to take over the world?" He smirks, taking a sip. "That's every other month."

I can't help but laugh, and he leans in. "You can relax, Shaw. We know everything about you. There's nothing that would turn us off." My eyes widen, and he nods. "It's my job to find out every dark, dirty secret for those we might add—yours included. We know it all."

"That seems unfair," I snap out of anger and concern.

"True, but we keep folders, and you are welcome to read ours as well. Fair is fair. I just thought you should know. You're one of us. They keep saying it, but it's true. We accept you for everything you are and have been, so stop worrying. You don't need to pretend."

I didn't even know I was, but somehow, this guy knew.

"Oh, and with that Anders guy . . . we mean it. We can help, but don't worry. We won't if you don't want us to." He grins slyly. "I'd love to take him down a peg."

"I can handle him."

He smirks and presses his beer to mine. "To handling assholes."

I toast him and take a drink. "Is that why you want to be a lawyer?" I ask.

"Partly." He shrugs. "I like the control and power, plus it means I know how to get away with things and can protect the people I love." He stands. "You can leave whenever. You look tired. We've added you to the group chat, so just drop us a message if you need anything." He wanders away, and I look around to see some people have already left.

I want to stay, but he's right. I'm tired. I down my beer and wave goodbye, heading out alone. The brass key burns in my pocket, and his words ring in my head.

What did he mean, get away with things?

Once outside the marble building, I wander back over the grass, trying to remember my way. Eventually, I reach the lit part of campus. It's late or early, depending on how you look at it, but there are still some people around. I could get a taxi, but I decide to walk home. The fresh air is nice, and the alcohol is still buzzing in my veins, but about halfway back, I feel eyes on me.

I speed up my steps, feeling like I'm being stalked or chased.

It's uncomfortable, and when I'm back in my room, I lock the door with a frown.

Maybe it was just my imagination?

Fuck, I hope so.

SHAW DRIVE
ANDERS AVE
ONE WAY
NO PARKING
ACTIVE DRIVEWAY
THE MOMENT
STOP
TATTOO
NO PARKING
SALE
SILENT ROSE
Pine Valley
EVER

EIGHTEEN

Evan is ignoring me.

He didn't text me back. I know he read it though, and I have checked if he blocked me often. He hasn't, which is somehow worse. It's a taste of my own medicine, and I fucking hate it.

Despite my need for money, I spent last night waiting for him. It was late when he emerged from campus and came home. It pissed me off. Where had he been and with whom? I wanted to demand answers, but I don't deserve them. Instead, I stalked him home like a creeper to make sure he got there safely, and then I went home and silently fumed all night, stalking his socials to make sure no one tagged him in anything and to see if he posted.

He didn't.

I have no idea where he was or what he was doing. I tell myself he was near the library. He could have been studying, but I don't know for sure, and I hate that. He doesn't owe me anything, he isn't mine, but the idea of someone else touching him?

Yeah, it makes me pissed as hell.

He said he gave up, but did he really mean it?

It was all I wanted, but now, it hurts and annoys me.

That's why I wait after dropping Alice off. He's late today, but he eventually hurries by, fixing his hair as he runs, his unbuttoned shirt exposing tan abs, and my hands curl into fists at the show he's giving everyone. He doesn't even seem to notice people watching him with lustful eyes—like me, the girls sitting on the grass giggling, or the guy skating past.

No, he's completely oblivious, and I hate it. I nearly marched out there to button every single button so no one else could see him, but he'd probably hit me. I'd deserve it. His bag falls from his shoulder, and I hear him curse as he stops to pick it up. He throws it over his shoulder, blowing out his cheeks which are red from running, and then his head jerks around like he feels me. His eyes meet mine, and for a moment, he stares at me before he turns away and hurries to his building, dismissing me.

I'll admit I sit here for far too long, telling myself I can't march into his school and drag him out and demand he speak to me. Instead, I head to work. It's the only thing I seem to do besides stalk Evan Shaw.

He has ignored me every morning this week.

It's been five fucking days of him purposely not looking at me no matter what I do, like talking loudly to Alice, cranking my music up, and revving my engine. He doesn't look at me once. He ignores me like I'm not there, and it's pissing me off.

I am there every morning regardless, just to get a glimpse of him under the guise of dropping Alice off. I'm pathetic, and that's only confirmed when Alice turns up at dinnertime at the garage.

Her arms are crossed, and her eyes are narrowed.

Worry slides through me as I dry my hands on a rag, heading her way and pulling her out of earshot. "Are you okay?" I ask. She would only come here if something was wrong.

"Yes, you." She pokes me in the chest. "Whatever you did, apologize now."

"What?" I frown.

"You did something to Evan, apologize."

"He said something? Is he okay? Is he upset—"

"No, he doesn't need to say anything. He doesn't look at you anymore, and you've been stalking him all week like a creep." I blink. "Yeah, I noticed, so apologize for whatever you did."

"Why do you assume I did something?" I grumble instead of denying it.

"Alek, you're my brother, and I love you, but you're an ass." She sighs. "And dumb. You did something, now fix it because staring holes through his head every morning isn't working, and I hate seeing you stomp around, sulking every night."

"I don't sulk," I protest, and her eyebrow arches. "I . . . brood. It's different."

"How?" She tilts her head.

"It's . . . manly."

"Well, you and your manly sulking—I'm sorry, I mean brooding, need to fuck off and fix this or I'm going to kill you." She pats my chest. "Good talk, by the way. He's at work right now." She starts to walk away.

"I don't need to know that. I don't even like Evan—"

She waves at me, interrupting my denial. "Fix it, now!"

Fuck.

I glance back at the garage then at her retreating form. He's at work? I suppose he can't avoid me there. We can sort this out once and for all because Alice is right. If this carries on, I'm going to end up killing someone or being arrested for stalking.

I need to eat dinner, or that's what I tell myself.

It doesn't matter if his work is in the other direction or a thirty-minute walk or that I don't have the time to go there. I'm just hungry. That's all.

I just so happen to sit in his section as well. It's purely coincidental.

When he heads my way, scribbling in a notebook, not even seeing me, my heart pounds. He's wearing those stupid fucking frills that he looks ridiculously good in, his hair is partially clipped back, and there is glitter across his cheeks and eyelids. He looks hot, and I hate that, hate that I'm covered in grease with bags under my eyes from over-thinking everything while he looks this fucking good.

His head comes up as he starts to speak when he reaches my table, a practiced speech spilling out. "Hello, welcome to—" He stops, a deep sigh filling him as his expression turns from friendly to angry. "Fuck, I seriously can't get rid of you, can I?"

That means he missed me, right?

"I need dinner." I shrug. "That's all."

"Uh-huh, and the forty or fifty restaurants and take-out places near your work aren't enough? You had to come to the one place I work at? The one place you complained about not wanting to ever come to?" He calls me out on my shit, and I actually feel my cheeks heat. "Why the fuck are you here, Anders?"

I pick up the menu and randomly point. "For that, it sounds good."

His eyebrow arches as he looks at it. "The princess dessert?"

Motherfucker.

Either I admit I came to see him or say I want the dessert. He waits as I debate which is the lesser evil, his smirk growing as time ticks on, and I know I can't back down. "Yes, the princess dessert. Is that a problem?"

"No problem at all." He grins mischievously. "Coming right up, princess."

He wanders away, and I know I fucked up. I just don't know how. Ten minutes later, I realize why.

He comes out with a plate that requires two hands and puts it down before me with a flourish, and I just gawk. There are flowers every-where, pink glitter on everything, and a tiara on the side of the plate.

Picking up the silver and pink tiara, he happily plops it on my head. "Such a pretty princess," he coos. "Do you want your picture like everyone else?" Before I can stop him, he pulls his phone out and snaps one of me. Pink dessert, tiara, and flaming cheeks.

Thrusting back from the table, I stand, clenching my fists. He doesn't step back. "Problem, princess?"

Grinding my teeth, I tug off the tiara and drop it to the table, deciding I can't get any more embarrassed, so what the hell? "Why are you ignoring me?"

His cheeks heat as he looks around. "I'm at work."

"I noticed, but you won't talk to me any other way. Why are you ignoring me?" I grumble.

"Why do you care?" he retorts.

"I just do," I admit. "You didn't reply."

"To your one-word answer? Or the fact that you kissed me again and then tried to ignore me?" My cheeks are so hot they are burning. "Honestly, Anders, what is there to say? We are better off staying away from one another. We are like a volcano and a tornado. We don't go together. You wanted me to leave you alone, so I am." He goes to walk away, but I grab his arm, stopping him.

"I don't want that." I force the words out, knowing if I don't, I'll lose him forever, and if there is one thing I have realized this week, even if I don't want to, it's that I want Evan Shaw in my life.

"You don't know what you want," he says, looking at me, "and I don't have time to wait for you to figure it out, not when it comes with the brunt of your anger. I can't do that, Anders."

Releasing his arm, I sit back and think. I don't know how to fix this. I'm not good at words, and it's clear something is broken between us. It's my fault.

My eyes drop to the dessert. "I'm sorry," I say.

He's quiet, and when I look at him, he appears shocked.

I nod. "I am."

He stares before nodding slowly, and my eyes drop to the dessert again.

"I'll take it away," he mutters, grabbing for it, but I pick up a fork.

"I'll eat it. It looks good." Without caring about the giggles or looks, I devour every single overly sweet, flowery pink bite of the dessert just to see him smile.

It's worth it.

Things might not be fixed between us, but that smile tells me we aren't broken beyond repair.

I can live with that, even if I will never be able to look at the color pink again.

NINETEEN

I still can't get over Alek Anders apologizing to me.

I didn't think he knew how to, but there he was, apologizing in a tiara. It doesn't change everything that happened—it's just too messy between us. I need to focus on my studies, but I'll admit it softened me to him. I stopped purposely, not looking his way this morning, and the little grin he wore was almost one of vivacity. I tell myself it doesn't mean anything.

All thoughts of him disappear soon, though, because today is a big day.

It's shoot day, and I've been working toward this all week. All my planning, location reconnaissance, and information gathering has led to this. It's a big part of my grade, and the professor finally signed off on my proposal at the beginning of the week. I didn't want to waste any time on starting it.

I head to the equipment building, picking up everything I need. Luckily, Lally and Tommy are assisting me today, and they are already waiting to help me haul everything to the location I chose—the park.

It's one of the first places I found when I explored Pine Valley, and it's beautiful right now. The weatherman forecasted sun today, but I had my fingers crossed all week just in case. Fortunately, they were right. The sun shines brightly, warming us as we set up near the water with blossoms in the background. People mill about, looking on curiously.

Once I'm content, I step back. "Okay, my model should be here soon. Lally, you're on makeup. I want sleek and minimal. Think *Vogue*. Tommy, you are helping me with lighting, right?"

"Yes, you've told us a million times. It's going to be great, Evvie." He slaps my shoulder. "Oh, hey, look, there's your model."

I turn to see Terrie heading my way, grinning. I wave, so happy she agreed to be part of this. I know a lot of media students wanted her. She's beautiful, like drop-dead stunning, and so kind, and she agreed to help me if I would assist with her figure studies class. She said she liked the way my body looked, so it's a good deal.

"Hey, Terrie." I hug her. "Thank you. I won't take too much time. I know you have the film later as well."

"Never too busy for you, Evvie." She grins. "Let's do this."

"Let's."

Despite my nerves, I give it my all.

This is what I want, this is my future, and I'm never happier than I am when taking photographs. Today is no different.

We spent two hours shooting, and Terrie hurried off after, but I think I got everything I needed. The photos are going to be amazing, I just know it. She was a natural, letting me direct her how I wanted without complaint, and the camera loved her.

After turning my equipment back in, I thank Lally and Tommy by buying them a meal before heading back to campus. Technically, I have a month to get the pictures turned in, but I'm eager to see and edit them, so I walk to the photo lab. There are a few other students using the computers in here, all with headphones on, so I pick one at the back and plug in my hard drive.

When they load, I could cry. They are so pretty and exactly how I imagined them. Sometimes, it's hard to translate my ideas into reality, but these are exactly how I wanted them to be, and I feel so proud as I prepare them for editing. I can do this. This is what I'm here for—to become a photographer. Forget everything else.

I spend the next hour picking out photos I think are the best and ready to edit. I'm so lost in my task, I don't even hear someone next to me until they tap on the desk, making me jump. My head snaps up.

"Evan." The professor smiles when he sees me sitting in the photo lab, peering at the unedited pictures on the screen. "You did your shoot today. How did it go?" He sits on a rolling chair, and I lean back, my eyes aching.

"Good. They haven't been edited yet, but I think they are what I wanted."

"Can I see?" He raises his eyebrow, and I nod. The professor rolls closer and clicks through the unedited, raw files, and my heart races at his silence. Nervousness fills me as well as excitement.

The minutes drag on, and I worry when he finally sits back, watching me for a moment.

"The compositions are beautiful. The coloring, the lighting, even the model . . . Everything is perfect." He smiles, and I sag in relief, but the smile disappears. "But it's missing heart, purpose, a story. It's missing emotion. We capture images to convey something. All these show me is perfection. It has no passion. Do you understand? I don't just want to see your technical skills. I want to see you and who you are. Find out what you want to take pictures of. Remember what inspired you to get into photography. Was it something you saw and couldn't resist capturing? Find out what you're passionate about, Evan. These pictures are good, but they aren't going to get you where you need to go, and I know you can do better." It's said nicely, and the criticism is meant to help me, but I crumble.

I keep it in, though, and nod as he stands, squeezing my shoulder. "Don't take it too hard. You still have plenty of time. I can teach skills, but I can't teach heart, so find yours."

Fuck.

I slump back, defeated, and stare at the photos. Is he right?

I was so worried about them being beautiful that I forgot the first rule—why I'm taking them.

I picked Terrie because she was gorgeous, and I picked the park because it was perfect. He's right. I'm not saying anything with them. Not only did I waste his time, but I also wasted this whole day. Packing up in defeat, I wander around campus, feeling dejected.

I don't know what I'm going to shoot now. I was so sure. What if I'm not meant to do this? What if I'm not good enough to be a photographer? What if I have no original ideas or passion for it? What if all this time, I was chasing this dream, but I'm not good enough for it?

That thought bums me out more. There are plenty of talented photographers out there, but it takes more than being proficient with a camera to be successful. It's understanding what you're taking and the audience viewing it. It's what I've wanted to be for so long, and I can't imagine doing anything else.

I know I'm overthinking, but how could I not?

I think over everything my teacher said as I walk. Is he right? Do I have nothing to say?

What am I passionate about?

Taking photos, that's all I know. I've never really considered my object/model to be my passion. They're just an instrument I need to use. I've never felt connected to or emotional about them, and maybe that's the problem. Maybe I need to find something that ignites my emotions.

Only one thing pops into my head right away—Alek Anders. Good or bad, I feel when I'm with him. I feel stronger than I have ever felt, like he taught me what true emotions are.

Rage, desire, happiness, guilt, and want are all magnified with him.

As if my thoughts conjured the asshole, I see him before me.

I don't know how or why I ended up at the park once more, only that my feet brought me here. Hell, I can still see where we were shooting earlier. It's later now, but there he sits, alone on a bench, with a sandwich in one hand and a book in the other. His eyes are locked on it, his brow furrowed slightly. My heart kick-starts. It's like I come to life when I see him.

Every argument, fight, kiss, and stolen moment fuels me.

Before I realize what I've done, I lift my camera and take a picture. It's black and white because the settings are fucked, but as I look down at it, I realize it might as well be the first real photo I have ever taken. It's raw and gritty, but it has emotion.

There is longing, want, hatred, and desire.

It captures what it's like looking in from the outside, never quite fitting in or getting what I want.

This is the passion my teacher was talking about. I could turn in those other images, but they would pale in comparison to this quickly shot photo. They are empty. Pretty, but empty.

He told me to find my passion, and I did, it just so happens to be Alek Anders, and that's both a good and bad thing. My life seems so entwined with his, like the threads of fate keep bringing us back together.

What we have together is just that—passion. It's fucked up, but it's something worth exploring, even if it hurts in the long run. It might not be everyone's version, but it's mine, and maybe by exploring what makes me feel, I'll start to understand and become a better photographer.

I decide to take one more chance with him.

I tell myself this is the last time. I won't come back after this if he kicks me away again. No more hot and cold. This is it.

Taking a deep breath, I sit silently next to him. I know the moment he notices me, his inhale loud, but I just stare down at my camera.

"Evan?"

Not rich boy, not an insult.

Just my name with a lilt of hope in it.

I know no matter where this goes, it'll be worth it.

It's worth all the pain it can cause.

NO PARKING
ACTIVE
DRIVEWAY
SHAW DRIVE
THE
MOMENT
ANDERS AVE
ONE WAY
STOP
TOO
NO
PARKING
SALE
SILENT ROSE
Pine Valley
EVER

TWENTY

ALEK

His head lifts, and his eyes clash with mine, his usual vibrancy gone. He appears lost, and I hate the dejected look on his beautiful face. I hate the way he just stares, as if he's unsure if he should be here.

I keep reminding myself of all the reasons why I should avoid Evan Shaw, but one look at his face right now and I know all the reasons I should stay.

He needs me, and I'm a bastard because I stay. I let him need me. I let it bind us together even though I shouldn't. This won't end well, but then again, every ending is a messy one no matter what people tell themselves. There is no such thing as a good ending. It's just an end—messy, hurtful, and isolating—but it doesn't mean it isn't worth taking the chance.

"Evan?" I repeat, and he blinks. When his bright eyes meet mine once more, they burn, and that allows me to breathe easier. "Are you okay?" I ask as the wind whistles through the trees.

His brows furrow slightly, making this adorable little crease between them. "I will be," is all he says, his voice soft and almost sorrowful.

He's here, though, next to me despite everything.

I glance down at my half-eaten sandwich, and without a word, since I tend to fuck things up between us when I speak, I hand over the other half. He takes it with a blink, glancing from it to me before taking a bite. I look back at my book and continue eating, a comfortable, companionable silence stretching between us.

When I finish eating and finish my chapter, I close my book and lean back against the bench. He's fiddling with his camera, and I watch his long fingers as they move expertly over it. "How are your courses going?"

He jerks from the suddenness of my voice, swinging his head around to look at me. Embarrassment heats my cheeks. I really am rusty at this shit, but he doesn't seem to mind as a small smile tilts up his pink lips.

"It's going well. I really like my teachers and classes. Some of them are hard, but the good kind of hard, you know? They push you to think and do better. Then again, I was confident about this project, and my teacher just told me to rethink my entire photo shoot. I was so confident about it." His smile fades as he gazes at the water. "Have you ever felt like that? Like you were so right, so sure of your actions, but then they turn out to be completely wrong, and it just leaves you feeling—"

"Lost," I finish.

He nods, glancing back at me. "So, yeah, he says I need to find my passion, something else to photograph, so that's why I'm here, searching for it."

"Did you find it?" I ask. If anyone can, it's Evan. No matter what I think of him, it's clear he doesn't give up. Hell, him chasing me tells me that.

"I think so." The secretive smile makes my head tilt, and he just keeps watching me, wearing that same look that drove me mad ages ago but now makes me uncomfortably hot.

I need to fill the silence. I need him to understand. "I'm sorry for, well, everything," I offer gruffly. "I know it was fucked up." I push the words out before I can chicken out and swallow them. "Evan, I don't know what you want from me. I don't even know what to offer you. I don't even know myself. I can't figure it out. I'm a fucking mess inside." He chuckles, making my own lips quirk. I take a deep breath and stare into his bright eyes, telling myself to have at least half the courage he does. "But I . . . like being with you." I gesture between us. "Like this. Hell, even when we're fighting, I like it. I know that's not enough, but it's all I have for now. That's all I can give you." I snap my mouth shut as he stares at me.

His hand comes out, and I jerk, expecting a slap, but it just covers mine on my thigh.

"Then that's enough for now."

EVAN

"What?" he stutters, still staring at my hand on his. "How can that be enough?"

"I get to decide what's enough or not." I shrug, and his head lifts, his dark eyes meeting mine. I have no doubt we look like polar opposites right now. He's all darkness, and I'm all sunshine, yet here on this bench, we can be anything we want, and I want to be his. "Because I like this too, and I don't feel this way about anyone else," I tell him truthfully. "You asked if I found my passion, and I did. It's you. I've never felt this deeply before. So how about we just have this truce between us?" I remove my hand and sit back, waiting.

Alek is always so hard to read, and now is no different as he stares at his hand on his thigh, thinking through my words. For all his bravery and strength, Alek is scared to feel.

He reaches over before stilling. "Can I touch you?"

My heart stops beating for a moment before it begins to pound in my chest because I know for Alek Anders to reach for me, to touch me, it means he's trying. He's saying this is enough too—at least for now. I nod my head, afraid if I speak, I'll scare him off.

He's skittish like that.

His big hand slowly covers mine and then lifts, and our palms meet, my fingertips barely reaching halfway up his. Mine are tan, and his are pale. His are scarred, while mine are soft, yet they seem to fit perfectly together for a moment. His dark eyes meet mine, and then slowly, so slowly I swear I don't even breathe, he leans in. His lips press against the back of my hand. It's just a soft, chaste kiss, but I swear I feel it all the way to my soul.

It's like he just laid claim to my heart.

Biting my lower lip, I watch his lips tilt in a smile, and then he reaches over, pressing his thumb to my mouth, where my teeth hold my lip prisoner. "Don't do that, it just makes me want to bite it myself."

My eyes widen in shock as he grins and sits back like he didn't just flirt with me.

Alek Anders just flirted with me, and I swear my heart goes into a frenzy.

I glance back at the water, still wide-eyed and confused as he twines our hands together and lets them hit the bench, his on the bottom as if to protect mine from the wood. We just sit here, holding hands and enjoying the silence.

Something new blooms between us like spring.

Voices eventually make us break apart, but I don't mind when he takes his hand back because I know he gave himself part of me, and one day, he'll be ready to show the world—or at least I hope because hope is all we have. This is complicated and hard, and it might hurt in the long run, but something tells me it's worth it, that he is worth it. If Alek Anders isn't ready for the world to know about his sexuality, then that's okay. I can be his secret until he's ready.

I'm not going anywhere.

Our eyes meet, and I know I'd let this beautiful man wreck me just to call him mine.

TWENTY-ONE

The whole next day is like a fairy tale. I am in such a good mood despite my professor's response to my project. I feel like I'm floating. Hell, when I got in the night before, I was kicking and squealing like a fucking schoolboy again, which prompted Tommy to chuck a pillow at my head.

We texted nearly all night, and despite my exhaustion, it was worth it.

As if my thoughts make it happen, my phone buzzes.

> Alek: What time do you finish today?

> Evan: In about half an hour.

I glance at the board and type out some notes, all while holding my phone with my other hand, waiting for his response.

> Alek: I'll meet you out front. Let's go for a drive.

> Evan: What about work or Alice?

Alek: Do you want to go to the river or not,
rich boy?

I can't help but smile, and I press my lips together to hide it as I type back.

Evan: Fine, princess, see you then.

Alek: Keep it up, rich boy.

Evan: Or what? *Winky face*

My heart beats fast, and my smile is so wide I can't contain it.

Alek: Or you'll regret calling me princess.

Evan: We both know I'd like it. Now stop
distracting me, princess.

I send a picture of my lecture for meaning.

Alek: *Image*

A photo comes through, and he's reclining in his car seat with his eyebrow arched. I can see the parking lot behind him, and it sends butterflies soaring through me. He's already here, waiting for me. Does that mean he was already on campus and texted me, hoping to see me?

Fuck. Now I really can't focus. In fact, I don't hear a word that's said for the next thirty minutes, and when it's over, I hurry to my feet.

"Evvie, want to hang—" Tommy starts.

"Can't, busy. Sorry. Love you. Bye." I stuff my shit in my bag, and I'm out of the door after waving in under a minute.

I get outside so fast, I'm panting, and I see his car idling. He's leaning against it, completely ignoring the girls watching him, and for a moment, I'm awestruck by how hot he is before his eyebrow arches impatiently. I cover the distance quickly, and he opens the door for me. I slide in, noticing his hand above my head so I don't hit it, and those damn butterflies start again as he shuts it and rounds the hood, getting in and revving the engine.

"Alice?" I ask as he lays his arm across the back of my seat, his fingers tracing over my neck. He watches me before looking back and reversing, but even once we are out on the road, he keeps his hand there, and slowly, his long fingers curl around the nape of my neck, holding it possessively. The warm claim makes me swallow hard. "Alek?" My voice is rough.

"She's staying late. She has an assignment that's due, so it's just you and me. Is that a problem, rich boy?"

"Not at all," I reply, leaning into his touch. He glances at me for a moment, and his grip tightens before he focuses on the road. "Where are we going?"

"I want to show you something," is all he says. I relax in my seat and stare out of the window, letting him drive me wherever he wants.

About thirty minutes later, we roll through a downtown area. The shops are just shutting down, the lights turning off for the night. Alek seems to know where he's going, and once we turn down a side road, he pulls up to a double-shutter door of a black, one-story, brick building.

"Huh?" I question, but he hits a button, and the garage door rolls up. He waits until it's open all the way and slowly drives in before turning the engine off and looking at me. As we are plunged into darkness, I hear the crank of the shutter going down behind us, sealing us in. "What, are you planning to fuck or kill me here?"

"You wish." He smirks, but it drops quickly, and his eyes lower to my lips. He leans closer, but bright lights suddenly turn on, and we both jump apart.

Laughing, I climb from the car and look around, blinking in surprise.

"What is this place?" I ask as he leans against his car, watching me. It's big enough for two cars, his usual and a shiny, low one next to us. There's a seating area in the back with a TV, radio, leather sofas, and fridge. A wooden staircase leads up to a small loft, which I can't see into from here, and there's a sliding door at the back that's partially open to show me a bathroom.

"This is my workshop. When I'm not working at the garage, I'm here, working on my cars," he admits. "Come on." He turns to keep me in view as I wander. "I've never brought anyone here before, not even Alice."

I whirl around to see him, my gaze moving from the graffiti on the walls to him. "And why's that, princess? Why did you bring me here?"

Something about calling this big, tattooed bastard a princess and getting away with it is addictive. It's like a shared secret, and despite his protests, I can tell he secretly likes it. I even set the picture of him eating the dessert as my screensaver. He hates it, but it's so fucking cute.

He watches me for a moment. "I wanted to share it with you," is all he says, but it's enough.

Alek is trying to let me in, and showing me this, his safe space, is a big step. It's clear it's his passion, something I was searching for. Is that why he brought me here?

I could let it go, but something tells me now is the time to push, so I don't stop until I stand before him. I tilt my head back to meet his unsure gaze. "Why did you bring me here, Alek?"

"Because it's important and so are you," he whispers. "Because I want you to know me the way nobody else does. I want you to see that I'm more than just an angry thug."

My heart aches for him. Reaching out, I take his hand. "Then show me that side nobody else gets to see. Let me see you, Alek Anders, because I have a feeling you are a lot more than an angry thug. I have a feeling that you're as beautiful inside as you are on the outside."

I watch Alek work. At first, he was nervous, and he kept glancing at me, but he's relaxed now, and it's enjoyable watching him tune up his car. He told me his Skyline is his race car, and he even let me sit in it. I just observe him quietly until he gets annoyed—or more like embarrassed.

"Stop watching me, rich boy. Do homework or something," he mutters, but his cheeks are hot.

"But this view is so much better," I flirt, pulling out my laptop and stretching my legs out on the sofa. I pull up the image of him. I can still see him over my laptop, and both views only make me that much hotter. I can't stop smiling, but I do as I'm told. I edit the photo, knowing it's rough, but there's something about it that captivates me. It's imperfectly perfect, just like him. It's dark shades of gray but so mesmerizing it nearly hurts.

Time passes comfortably like this, both of us working, just happy to be together. When I shut my laptop, he glances over and shuts the hood. He wipes his hand on a rag and heads my way, sitting on the coffee table and leaning into me. "What are you going to take photos of now? Have you decided?" he asks, no doubt remembering my confession yesterday.

I have a feeling there isn't much that Alek Anders forgets.

"I have decided," I admit as I glance at him. He might hate it and turn me down, but I can't stop myself from speaking. "I want to take pictures of you."

He recoils, blinking. "Me?" He looks down at himself. "I'm not really model material, rich boy."

Laughing, I lean back into the leather. "The professor told me to take pictures of something I'm passionate about." I tilt my head, running my eyes over him. "That's you," I state without an ounce of shame.

His eyes widen, and he stares, frozen. Grinning, I sit up and slide to the floor on my knees between his parted legs. I place my hands on his thighs as I sit up so my face is level with his. "May I, Alek? May I take pictures of you?"

He swallows, glancing at my lips. "Evan," he warns.

"Be my muse," I murmur as I lean in, nearly pressing my lips to his. "Please." I feel his resolve weakening, and even though I know it's cheap, I kiss him softly. I want to convince him and, well, kiss him. I have since the moment I saw him leaning against his car, so I take my shot. He doesn't push me away, but he doesn't touch me either. He just lets me kiss him, and when I pull back slightly, his eyes are closed.

"Say yes, princess," I demand as I lean in once more like I'm going to kiss him again, "and I'll show my gratitude any way you want."

I feel him wavering, and his head moves ever so slightly, but it's enough so his lips brush mine. I pull back, and he chases me. "Say yes and you can kiss me all you want."

"Evan," he snaps, and his hand cups the back of my head, yanking me closer until my lips crush against his. I relax into his grip, my eyes fluttering closed. It's demanding and rough until it softens, and then his lips just brush against mine, leaving lingering kisses as if he can't resist. I know the feeling.

My hands curl into his chest, pulling him closer. I push up from my knees and straddle his lap. His hands drop to my hips, holding me, and then I kiss him back, sliding my tongue between his parted lips. He gasps, pressing my hard body against his. I can feel his length hardening against mine as I groan, sliding my hands up to grip his shoulders as I rub against him until I have to pull back to breathe.

"Yes," he whispers roughly as I blink, bringing his dark eyes into view. Everything else is forgotten.

"Huh?" I respond, my eyes on his lips, wanting them on me again.

He chuckles darkly. "Yes, rich boy, you can take my picture."

"I can?" I stutter over the words, trying to remember why that's important, but it's not nearly as important as getting his lips back on mine.

One of his hands slides up my back, gripping the nape of my neck as he tugs me closer again and crushes his lips to mine in a hard, swift kiss. "Yes, rich boy, you can take my picture." He stands, lifting me effortlessly. He only has one arm around me, yet he carries me like I'm weightless. "Get your camera before I change my mind." His eyes darken as they drop to my lips. "Or I decide I need more convincing, and I let you do what I see in your eyes." He lowers me down his body until my feet hit the floor.

"Now, Evan," he orders when I just stare.
Camera. Right.
Pictures.
Fuck.
Who really convinced whom then?

NO PARKING
ACTIVE
DRIVEWAY
SHAW DRIVE
THE
MOMENT
ANDERS AVE
ONE WAY
STOP
NO
PARKING
SALE
SILENT ROSE
Pine Valley
EVER

He stares at me for a moment, his lips bruised from my rough kiss, his hair mussed from my touch. He looks way too fucking handsome for his own good. Turning away before I follow through on my threat, I curl my hands into fists to stop myself from reaching for him. I don't know what's gotten into me, but I want him pressed against me. Instead, I force myself away, lingering near my car as I breathe deeply, trying to push down the desire plaguing me. If he's taking my picture, then I can't be hard. That would be fucking weird, but when I turn back to see him fiddling with his camera, his bottom lip caught between his teeth in concentration, my cock jerks, and I have to turn away again.

I chant random shit in my head, trying to fight my need to fuck Evan Shaw, which is stronger than I've ever felt since I was a fucking teenager and couldn't control myself.

"Are you sure about this?" he asks. "Others will have to see them."

"It's fine," I respond gruffly, glancing over my shoulder to see him wandering around, playing with my lighting. He doesn't have all his equipment, but he seems to make it work, and I watch him as he snaps pictures, testing areas before smiling at me. "Okay then, let's do this."

"Where do you want me?" I glance around. Despite my bravado in agreeing, I'm not very photogenic, and he'll soon realize that.

He heads my way, and I let him lead me around until he's happy with me before my Skyline. "Okay, can you lean against it?" I lean back, my arms crossed, and he smiles. "Not so stiff. Don't look so angry." I relax my arms, and he snaps a picture, looking at me before frowning and heading my way.

His warm hand cups my chin, tilting it down. "Relax, princess. It's just me. Focus on me, not the lens. Just me. Use your eyes to tell me everything you want to tell me in lieu of words. Just focus on my face and nothing else, okay?"

I watch him step back and smile softly at me as he lifts the camera again. He lines up the shot and then moves his face away so I meet his eyes. "You look so fucking hot, Anders," he says, and my lips tilt up without me meaning to, and I hear the click.

"Bastard," I mutter as he chuckles, peering at the photo he took.

"You look good, but something is missing." He drops his camera and sweeps his eyes over me before he snaps his fingers, and then he grins. "Do you trust me?"

"Not even a little with that look in your eye," I reply, but I straighten anyway. "What is it?"

"Can you put on those coveralls but, like, tie them at your waist and have your chest bare? We can rub some oil across you and have you posing around the garage. I want grunge. I want it to be you, not some perfect pose. Just you." Honestly, I was worried when he said naked torso. I know I have nice muscles, but this is different. The fact that he wants this to be authentic to me helps me make up my mind. Plus, there is a twinkle in his eye that makes it very hard for me to say no.

"Give me a second." Grabbing my coveralls that are still stained, I slip into the bathroom and change, tying them at my waist as I check myself over. They hang low, showing off my abs and Adonis belt, and I worry it's too much, but when I come out, the appreciation in Evan's gaze makes it worthwhile. He actually gulps, his eyes on my chest like he can't look away. The raw hunger in his gaze makes me bite back my smile. Evan Shaw is just as affected by me as I am by him.

"Are you sure this wasn't for you?" I tease as his cheeks heat, turning an adorable shade of red that I want to see all the time.

"Maybe a little." He grins. "Okay, oil up, baby."

Rolling my eyes, I head over to the rag I was using and rub it over my chest, letting it stain my muscles like he wants. He nods but heads over, taking the rag and rubbing some over my cheek and forehead before stepping back, eyeing me.

"Photos," I remind him when he just continues to stare. He blinks and turns away, blushing, but I can't help smiling at him so obviously checking me out. Rattling Evan is fun, since he doesn't usually bat an eyelash at anything I do. He goes toe to toe with me, but seeing him almost shy is ridiculously cute.

Heading back his way, I pose like he showed me and focus on his eyes, not on the camera that makes me stiff and nervous. I just look at him, losing myself in his bright irises. His gaze runs over me obsessively, like I'm the only thing that exists to him. It's addictive. When I look at myself through Evan's eyes, I feel important. I feel like someone worthy of love, of being wanted the way he wants me. I've never felt good enough, but to him, I'm more than sufficient.

I don't even notice him snapping pictures, only him moving until he grins widely at me and kisses my cheek. The warmth from his lips lingers on my skin as I lift my hand to capture it. "Amazing. Okay, lean back more and just relax, then move around your garage. Be as natural as possible, and I'll keep taking pictures. Just imagine—"

"I'm flirting with you," I finish, and his grin widens.

"Yeah." His eyes fall to my lips, and I step back, grinning.

"Then you can't kiss me again until you're done taking your pictures," I murmur, leaning into my Skyline as I eye him hungrily, wishing he were pressed against me again.

He snaps a picture, even as he seems slightly dazed, and I slowly start to relax and have fun. The way his eyes narrow and his desire for me grows with each pose is addictive. I bend over under my hood, then I sit inside the car, my hand on the wheel. I keep going until he drops the camera and closes the distance between us in two steps, kissing me as I laugh.

The sound soon shifts into a moan, and I turn us, backing him into my car, burying my hand in his fucking hair and yanking him closer. His hands slide down my chest hungrily, making my dick jerk as my other hand drops to his hip and slides lower. Grabbing his ass, I haul him against me, making him moan my name, and it only spurs me on.

Pulling away, I open the back door to the Skyline and crawl in, dragging him with me. I want him in my car. I want his scent to fill it so every time I look back here, I'll remember. I forget all the reasons why I shouldn't do this, all my concerns and the past, and for this moment, I just let myself live and take what I want—Evan Shaw.

I pull him onto my lap so he's straddling me, his head above mine. His bright eyes shine, and I swear I can hear his heart pounding, but that could be mine. He looks so fucking pretty above me, with my hands on his perfect skin. Sliding one down his side, I grip the base of his shirt and tug it up. "Off," I order, my voice rougher than I've ever heard it, but I can't stop. I need his skin on mine more than I need my next breath.

I watch his Adam's apple bob as he leans back and grabs the back of his shirt and pulls it up and off, throwing it away so his chest is bare for me.

Sitting back, I greedily trace his muscles with my eyes. He's built —not as thick as me, but he has muscles I know took time to build. I glance up to his eyes as I lift my hand and press it against his chest. I can feel his heart racing through his skin, and as I slide my big palm down between his pecs and over his abs, he sucks in a breath, his teeth catching his lip again. I arch up and bite down until he releases it. "I told you," I mutter, gripping his sides as I pull him closer. "Don't bite this lip, it's mine."

Our kiss turns desperate, our teeth clashing as our hands drag over each other's skin like we can't get enough. My car rocks with the force of our bodies meeting as he rolls his hips above me, moaning my name. It's all greedy hands and desperate touches, and I fucking love it.

I love feeling his hard skin under my hands, the unyielding muscles and soft noises he makes and the pressure of his dick against mine.

It's fucking amazing, and I lose myself in him, forcing Evan closer still, needing more.

My phone buzzes, breaking us apart. We pant as our eyes meet, and we burst into laughter. Scrambling for my ringing phone, I answer without looking as Evan leans into me, curling into my chest. He places a kiss on my throat, and my smile only grows.

"What?" I bark roughly.

"Dude, you know most people say hi, right?" Alice snaps. "Bring home burritos."

"No," I retort.

"Yes." She hangs up.

Groaning, I throw my phone away and wrap my arms around him. "My sister is a cockblocker."

His chuckle makes goose bumps rise across my skin. "I could go for a burrito."

My smile only grows, and I kiss his shoulder, holding him tighter to me. I want this moment to last forever. Here, in the darkness, nothing else matters, nothing but him in my arms.

"Burritos it is then, baby," I tell him. "Just give me five more minutes."

His happy sigh makes me kiss the top of his head as his hands stroke my sides, and my eyes close as my head hits the back of my seat. My cock is hard, but my heart is happy.

How could something that makes me feel this alive ever be wrong?

STARFIRE
RACING

TWENTY-THREE

I'm floating. There is no other way to describe it.

I have never felt this happy. I might not be telling people about us right now, but us keeping this a secret only makes it more exciting. Every stolen moment, lingering touch, or look leaves me breathless, and when we kiss?

Yeah, it's never been this good, like we are meant to be together. It seems Alek agrees. He's still angry and an asshole, but he can also be flirty, funny, and kind of sweet—not that I would tell him that to his face because he would probably hit me. Even thinking about it makes me grin.

> Alek: I keep finding blond hair in my car. You are worse than a girl.

A picture comes through of his grumpy face holding up a blond strand.

> Evan: That could be anyone's.

> Alek: You are the only blond who's been in my car.

Evan: So you let brunettes inside it? The betrayal.

Alek: The only other person allowed in my car is my sister, you rich idiot.

Evan: Maybe I need to put my name on it so everyone knows it's my seat then.

Alek: Don't you even dare, pretty boy.

I want to squeal, but I swallow it down. I can't hold back my smile though. It's quiet in the library, so I have to duck my head and bite my lip to stop it, especially with Lally and Tommy working on their footage for their project just across from me. I know they know something is going on, but they are good enough friends to let me tell them when I'm ready.

Evan: So mean.

Alek: You love it. I have to work late tonight, so I won't have time to see you.

Evan: That's okay. I need to edit tonight anyway. I think Lally and I are going to pull an all-nighter in the photo lab.

Alek: Okay, don't work too hard, and make sure you eat.

I bite back a bigger smile, glancing around in case anyone is watching when my phone vibrates again.

Alek: Now show me that pretty face since I won't get to see you.

Keeping the phone low and on silent, I pout as I snap a picture and send it. I look at Lally to see her watching me with a knowing grin on her lips. I quickly look away when my phone buzzes under the table.

Alek: Such a pretty boy, I hate it.

Alek: I want to see more of you.

Evan: I'm in the library, you perv.

Alek: Go to the bathroom, rich boy, now, and send me a picture, or I'll turn up there and see for myself.

I almost want to dare him to, but we both need to work, so I mutter an excuse to my friends and hurry to the bathroom on this floor. After ensuring it's empty, I step into a stall and lock the door. I stare at my phone, biting my lip. I'm not normally shy, but something about Alek makes me shaky. He went from hitting me when kissing me to being obsessed with seeing me, and it's addictive.

Taking a deep breath, I gather my courage and snap a picture of me with a smirk from a high angle, my shirt lifted to show a sliver of skin.

Alek: Fuck.

Alek: I want my hands on you. Lift your shirt higher and give me something good to get through work.

Desire makes my cheeks burn hot as I lift my shirt to flash my abs and send it, waiting with bated breath for him to reply.

Alek: Look at you, pretty boy, so goddamn sexy. I wonder what those muscles taste like. You have no idea what you do to me or how crazy you fucking make me.

His praise does something to me. It makes me hot and needy. I want it all. I want to hear those words whispered in my ear.

A picture comes through, and my eyes widen. I slam my phone to my chest and look around like someone could be here before realizing how ridiculous that is and peeking back at it. It's of Alek in the bathroom at work, and it's focused on the mirror, slightly blurred. His coveralls are shoved down, and he has his hand down them, leaving no doubt about what he's doing.

Desire pounds through me so fiercely, I can't resist. I slide my hands down my abs and shove it into my cargos, wrapping my hand around my dick. I stroke myself as I look at him, but my phone suddenly vibrates, making me jump.

Alek: Are you touching yourself, rich boy?

My heart stops. How did he know?

Alek: Show me. I want to see.

I snap a picture of my hands in my cargos, and my phone rings. I lift it with a shaky hand and answer.

"Hello?" I whisper, my voice rough.

"Don't speak. Let me hear you touch yourself, rich boy. Let me hear you come."

"I—"

"Now," he demands, his voice sharp and hard. He sounds so angry, but it's so fucking hot.

My hand tightens around my cock as I stroke myself, wishing it were him, and the thought of his hand touching me like this has me softly moaning his name.

"Shit, rich boy," he murmurs. "My name sounds so fucking good on your lips. Do it again." I hear rustling, and his breathing picks up. The idea of him touching himself where someone could find him, so hot for me he can't stop, turns me on.

My eyes close as I widen my legs, stroking harder, moaning his name again.

"That's it, pretty boy," he growls. "How hard are you right now?" When I just pant, his voice comes stronger. "Tell me."

"Hard, so hard," I whine, uncaring who hears. I need to come too badly. I've needed to since the first time we kissed, and our make out session in his car the other day didn't help. I'm on edge, and I've barely touched myself. "I need to come."

"Me too, pretty boy." He groans into my ear. "Fuck, getting you like this is all I think about. Every time I close my eyes, I see those pretty lips and wish they were wrapped around my cock like my fist is right now."

A groan slips free as my back hits the stall, my balls drawing up in pleasure.

"That's it, pretty boy. I can tell you're close. It's in your breathing. You're doing so well. Keep quiet and make yourself come for me. Imagine it's my hand touching you, my lips kissing down your abs and bruising those pretty lips. Be a good boy and come for me."

"Alek," I beg.

"I'm here, pretty boy. Come for me," he demands, his voice hoarse, and I can't stop myself. My cock jerks in my fist, and I bite down until I taste blood as a whimper chokes from my throat. Desire courses through me until I explode. Cum spills over my fist and into my pants, making a mess as I pant and writhe. It doesn't stop as pleasure rolls through me, and when I hear him groan my name quietly into the phone, it only makes it harder.

When I can finally stop, my legs shake, my fist is sticky, and my lips ache. "Good boy," he praises. "Show me how you look right now." I send a picture, and he groans. "Now clean yourself up—no one else gets to see you like that—and get back to work. The quicker you're done, the quicker I get to see you." He hangs up.

I pant, still confused and aroused.

Honestly, it was so hard to clean up the mess, but I did it, and I ignored Lally and Tommy who teased me all afternoon before we went for a meal and then set up camp in the photo lab. It isn't late, so it's still busy, but we manage to secure a corner together, which is rare. We all have our headphones on, but being together offers support. Besides, I trust their vision and ideas, and when I show them a photo I'm editing, they both point out it's better in black and white. I wasn't sure, but I trust in them, so I start to edit them all that way, seeing the vision.

I'm so engrossed in them that I jump when someone taps my shoulder. When I see my professor behind me, a bag over his shoulder, I get hit by a sense of déjà vu. I minimize my work and pull off my headphones, smiling.

"You found something to shoot?" he asks. "I was worried I was too harsh—"

"No, you were exactly right. I needed that push, the honest truth," I reply.

"Can I see?" he asks excitedly.

Biting my lower lip, I look back at my computer, hesitating. "It's raw and unedited. I don't know . . ." I look back, but he seems crestfallen, so I blow out a breath. "Okay." Besides, it's better to know now, right?

I pull up the images and click through them. He looks over my shoulder the entire time, and I wait with bated breath. When it's on the last one, I turn to look at him. His eyes are wide, and I don't know if that's a good or bad thing.

"Damn, Evan." He nods. "You're very talented. This is exactly what I was looking for. I can feel your passion for the subject, and I love the gritty nature of the images. You definitely have talent for portraits and expressing the person in them. I can actually feel him. They are incredible, Evan, truly."

"Really?" I murmur, holding my breath.

"So worth starting over. I'll leave you to it, and trust in yourself, Evan, because you are very talented." He smiles and waves as he heads out.

Lally and Tommy wait for him to leave before jumping on me. "He loves it! He's never reacted like that before, you star!"

"Evan, you are going to be so fucking famous, rich, and get all that dick," Tommy adds, making me laugh as I glance back at the computer, which is open on Alek's image, because he's the only dick I care about.

"We should celebrate!" Lally grins.

"Totally," Tommy agrees.

"Uh, deadlines," I remind them.

"Shit," they both say at the same time. "Later."

Grinning, I look back at the screen. It's all because of Alek. "Damn, who is that? Your boyfriend?" I glance over my shoulder to see George leaning into my chair. He's a year above me and majoring in photography too, so it's no surprise he's here.

I glance back at my screen, which shows Alek leaning into his car, and hesitate before forcing a smile. "No, just a friend who agreed to be my model." It isn't a lie. I don't know what Alek and I are. We haven't agreed on dating or anything, even if he feels like he's mine. Besides, he isn't ready for anyone to know.

"They are really good." George claps my shoulder, and I nod in thanks, watching him wander off.

"Friend my ass," Lally mutters, making my lips quirk.

She doesn't know the half of it. Friends don't kiss the way we do, that's for sure.

Alek: Are you done?

I blink at the text. It's early morning. We have been working all night and just called it a day with none of us being able to focus anymore. I'm heading back to get some sleep before my classes start.

Evan: Just finished. Packing up now, why?

Alek: I'm outside. I'll give you a ride home.
We both need to crash.

I blink stupidly but smile anyway and wish Lally and Tommy a good night before heading through the building. Alek is waiting outside, leaning into a rail and looking every inch a movie star. For a moment, I just stare.

"It's rude to stare, rich boy," he calls without looking.

Smirking, I head his way, and he takes my bag, slinging it over his shoulder, and falls in step at my side as we head to his car. He opens the door, carefully putting my bag in the back when I pat my pockets. "Shit, I left my card with Lally. One sec."

"Hurry up, rich boy. I'm tired."

I stand on my toes and kiss his cheek as I dash off. Luckily, Lally is still here, and I take it from her with a mumbled, "Thanks," and head back out, only to stop on the sidewalk. George is talking to Alek.

"You're Evan Shaw's boyfriend?" he asks, and I stiffen.

Alek laughs quickly. "Nah, he's my sister's friend. I'm just here to give him a ride."

My heart sinks at his declaration, and he glances at me as he straightens. I swallow down that feeling and force a smile. I knew he wouldn't tell people, so why did it hurt so much to hear it out loud?

"There you are. Hurry up, I'm exhausted," he snaps.

Nodding, I head his way, smiling at George. "See you in class, Evan."

"Nice to meet you, man. Like I said, if you ever want to model again, let me know."

I watch him go, a jealous feeling in my stomach which doesn't disappear as I look at Alek, who doesn't seem the least bit bothered about the fact that he just lied to someone about me.

He opens the door for me, and I slip inside, quietly putting on my belt and looking out the window.

I was so happy, but it all tastes bitter now.

Will I ever be more than his sister's friend to anyone in public?

SHAW DRIVE
ANDERS AVE
ONE WAY
STOP
NO PARKING
ACTIVE
DRIVEWAY
THE
MOMENT
TOO
CAR REPAIR
NO
PARKING
SALE
SILENT ROSE
Pine Valley
EVER

TWENTY-FOUR

Evan is quiet, too quiet. I know why, and I feel like shit, but I don't know how to change it. Words aren't my strong suit. Instead, I turn the wheel.

"Where are we going?" he mumbles. He looks tired and has bags under his eyes, but it's his frown I hate most.

"I'm guessing you haven't eaten, so I'm going to take you on a breakfast date," I admit gruffly. It's all I can do to look after him.

"Oh," is all he says, and I hate that most. Evan is many things, but quiet isn't one of them, not unless something is bothering him.

Everything had been going so well. We were having fun and growing closer, and last night over the phone . . . yeah, I was hoping to explore that further, but right now, I need his frown to turn into a smile. I need my sunshine back.

I park on Main Street and get out, opening his door for him. I block his head as he exits, so he doesn't hit it, and once we're on the sidewalk, I put my hand in my pocket to stop myself from reaching for him. There aren't many people around at this time, but I'm worried he'll reject me, and I don't think I could handle that.

The diner we met at for the first time is open, and I push inside, holding the door for him. I wave at a tired waitress and head to a booth, letting him slide in first, then I slide in opposite, locking my feet around his under the table. It's a small touch, but I need it to know he doesn't hate me.

He doesn't pull away, which is a good sign, but he's quiet, and I'm unsure how to fill the silence. Usually, he handles the conversations and I listen, but today is different. Luckily, I'm saved by the waitress. "Orange juice and omelet please, cheese and spinach." I look at Evan. "Rich boy?"

He jerks, blinks, and smiles softly at the waitress. I watch her smile back automatically. She can't help it, and I hate it. Jealousy fills me, even though she's easily his mom's age. "Could I get an apple juice and pancakes please?"

"Sure thing, sweetie. Anything else? Maybe some fruit?" she offers kindly, not even sparing me a glance.

"Fruit would be great, thank you so much." His smile brightens, and I watch her cheeks tint as she hurries away to put in his order.

His smile drops after, and he glances out of the window. "Evan." I wait for his eyes to drift to me, and I reach for his hand but then stop when the door opens, admitting four college girls. They glance our way and giggle before heading to another booth. Swallowing, I pull my hand back, and he watches me, a knowing sort of bitterness in his gaze. I hate that I put it there.

I'm not even surprised when the waitress comes back and places a huge bowl of fruit in front of him with the yogurt next to it. "On the house, cutie." She winks and dashes away.

He picks at his fruit as I watch him. "Eat," I command. Rolling his eyes, he stabs a strawberry harder than necessary and shoves it into his mouth, chewing dramatically.

"You're such a brat," I mutter, and he flinches, dropping his eyes to the table. "Shit, rich boy, I'm sorry." I rub my face. "About everything, okay? That guy took me by surprise and I panicked. I really am sorry."

He nods, picking at his fruit, but he still seems sad. I'd carve out my heart right now and hand it over if it would get rid of that look. Evan's face is made for smiling, not frowning.

"How about you come with me to a race tonight?" I lean over and take his hand, uncaring who is watching. "I've never taken anyone before, but I want you there."

His head lifts, his eyes brightening. "Really?"

"Really." I nod. "So . . . you want to come?"

The smile he bestows upon me makes me feel like a fucking king. If that little gesture can make him happy, I truly am an asshole. He doesn't ask for anything, and I hate that I keep hurting him. I'll try to make him happy from now on so he never has to look so sad again. "I'd love to."

"Good." I steal a strawberry and then grab another, feeding it to him. "It's a date."

Today was long, but I'm excited to see Evan. He was happier during our breakfast date, and I hated leaving him at his dorm, but we both needed sleep. He texted me throughout the day, though, and he seems fine now, which is a relief. I'm excited to show him a different side of me tonight.

I wait for him after his classes, and he hurries over, sliding into my passenger seat. "Is my outfit okay?" he asks, almost bouncing in his seat. "I've never been street racing."

I look him over, desire spiraling through me. My boy always looks good, but tonight he looks extra fine. He's wearing black cargo pants with white graffiti print over them, a white tank, and a loose shirt over the top. "You look hot," I murmur, "but you might be cold." I grab my leather jacket from the back seat, the one Alice bought me and I've worn ever since, and hand it over. "Here, wear that too."

He blinks, his grin growing as he slips it on, and I watch as he buries his nose in the leather.

"You smelling me, rich boy?" I tease.

His eyes twinkle as they look at me. "Hmm." He nods. "You smell delicious."

Coughing, I focus on pulling away without crashing as he chuckles.

I take us to my garage, and once there, I get out. When he rounds the car, I swear I stumble. My jacket looks so fucking good on him. The sleeves are slightly too long, and it's baggy, but it works, and seeing it has feelings of possessiveness and satisfaction rolling through me. I can't stop myself from backing him into my car, gripping his chin, and kissing him swiftly.

"What was that for?" he asks, grinning.

"Just because," I reply. "Come on." Taking his hand, I lead him over to my Skyline and open the door. "You're the first one to ever sit in my passenger seat."

His cocky smile is worth it as he leans into me. "Good." He kisses me as he slips inside, and I shut the door before getting in the driver's seat and reaching over. I fasten his seat belt.

"Stick with me tonight, okay?"

"I'm yours." He shrugs, and fuck if that doesn't make me hard.

"That's right, you're mine, rich boy, so stay in that seat and don't look at anyone else," I order before kissing him again. "And watch your man win every fucking race."

I see desire in his eyes and can't help but grin.

It doesn't take us long to get to the races, and I watch his wide-eyed fascination as I cruise through the streets slower than I normally would, but I want my boy to see everything and for everyone to see him.

When I reverse into an open space, he turns to me, grinning widely. "There are so many cars. Do you know everyone here? Can I go look?"

"No. I hate everyone, all people," I point out, and his eyebrow rises. "Except you. Stay, and let me go sign up."

Getting out, I glare tightly at some of the girls heading Evan's way, and they quickly turn around and head to a different car. Once I'm sure no one will move in once I'm gone, I search the crowd for Sanjay. It's less crowded tonight, which is good. It shouldn't be too much for him, and it gives me an excuse to get out of here early and spend some time with Evan.

Sanjay waves when he spots me, and I stomp over, my hand in my jacket as I barge through the crowd. Someone starts to protest before realizing who I am, and then they swiftly step away, leaving me alone with Sanjay and his usual adoring fans.

"I've never seen you bring someone, never mind let them in your precious car." Sanjay grins. "You going to introduce me?"

Rolling my eyes, I hand over my money. "Not a fucking chance. Just two tonight."

"Two? You usually race all of them." His eyebrow rises higher.

Glancing over my shoulder, I smile. "Yeah, well, I have something better to do later." Clapping Sanjay on the shoulder, I head back to my car where Evan is waiting dutifully.

"So what now?" he asks as I climb back in.

"Now, we race." Leaning over, I cup the back of his neck, uncaring who is watching. "So hang on, rich boy, and let's see if you can handle me."

His eyes drop to my lips before meeting mine again. "I can handle you, Anders. The question is, can you keep up?"

Chuckling, I sit back. "I guess we'll find out, rich boy." Starting my engine, I pull up to the cars that are already lining up. I spot a familiar one at the back and one at the front. The others are newbies, so not much competition unless there is a wild card. We do pass Skylar's car on the side though, so I guess he's racing tonight. "How do you know if you win?" Evan asks, sitting up taller in his seat as I idle at the line.

"You just know, baby." I smirk as I crank the radio down and look him over. "You look good in my passenger seat."

"And if you win, I'll look good in your back seat."

"Is that my prize?" I ask, eyebrow arching.

"Win and find out," he retorts, his eyes blazing.

Desire pounds through me as I lean in, almost kissing him. "Then I will never lose again." Sitting back, I rev my engine and wait for the flag to fall. When it does, I shoot out like lightning. I don't lose because I need the money, but tonight I'll win because I want him in my back seat again. I want the prize he'll give me.

I weave through the cars with deft movements, instinct kicking in as adrenaline pumps through me. Evan lets out a cheer, his head spinning to see the cars we are passing, and yeah, I might show off a little as I pull the handbrake, spinning us in a circle until we face them before jerking us back around and speeding away from the chasing cars.

"Shit! That was sexy," he says.

Smirking, I focus on the road, the familiar paths prompting me to drive faster and more dangerously, but I've never driven so safely before. I would never risk the most precious thing in my life sitting in my passenger seat.

The first race is far too easy, and I spin donuts after the finish line, my eyes on Evan. When I slide to a stop, he reaches over and kisses me on the mouth as the smoke clouds around us from my exhaust. "Good fucking job, baby!" he praises.

"One more, then you're mine," I warn him as I pull to the side and wait for the next race. I keep my eyes on him the entire time, just like his are on me. Anticipation builds in his gaze, and heat fills his cheeks as he watches me.

I can't look away, both of us knowing exactly what's going to happen if I win tonight. Evan Shaw will be all mine. Maybe that should scare me, since it isn't something I've done before, but with the way he's watching me and the desire pooling inside me, I know I don't care. We'll figure it out together, but I need him.

I need him spread across my back seat while I claim my winnings.

I need the paradise I tasted on his lips.

I need him, and I'm tired of being scared of that.

I know what crossing that line means. This isn't fun. This is me deciding that he's mine and I like boys—no, one boy, him.

He must see it written in my gaze because he leans closer, gripping my chin and pulling me down. "Not getting scared, are you, Anders? I thought you never lost."

"I don't," I snap, knowing he's winding me up.

"All talk." His eyes drop to my body. "I guess I could go find someone else who could act—" He turns and grabs the handle, but before he can leave, I pull his door shut as my lips meet his ear.

"You'll be begging for forgiveness for this shit later, you brat," I warn, loving it when he shivers against me. "Try to leave again and see what happens."

His eyes meet mine over his shoulder. I see a dare in them, but I simply arch an eyebrow. For once, he backs down, but his hand lands on my thigh, sliding higher and higher. "Then win, Anders, or I'll find someone who can."

It's a challenge, and we both know I won't back down.

He has given me the excuse I need to win, not just to fuck him.

He's fucking incredible.

I want to tell him that, to thank him, but I hear the horn that indicates the next race is lining up.

"Well, Anders?" he prompts.

Grinding my jaw and biting down on my retort, I drive us to the line once more. This time, the lineup is filled with racers I know, good ones, including Sky, and I sit up taller, knowing it's going to be one hell of a ride. That will only make my win that much sweeter as I claim the bratty, pretty boy's ass.

This time, I don't fuck around. As soon as the flag is down, I'm off. I don't show off, just maintain pure concentration as I wind through the crowd, drifting around a corner. I meet Sky's eyes through his passenger window as we level out, and he smirks as he guns it, shooting past me. I ride his bumper until the next corner and then feint left. When he goes to block me, I jerk right and shoot past him, flipping him off as I go.

Not one to give up, he rides my tail for the next three corners, taking every chance to try and slip past me. The field narrows down to him and me as we level out on the home stretch. It's one of the tightest races of my career, and he knows it as he winks at me, edging forward. He makes me work for it, my engine overheating as I force us to go faster. We might not be able to stop in time, but I'm not losing this race. When Sky brakes so he doesn't crash at the end, I speed up, sliding over the line and slamming on the brakes as I jerk the wheel. I control the movement so we spin until we stop just inches away from the screaming crowd.

My heart is pounding, but my eyes lock on Evan. He's staring at me, his eyes wide with wonder.

"Are you okay?" I ask.

He nods silently, so I reach over.

"Rich boy, are you okay?"

"Yeah, I'm fine," he croaks before coughing. "I guess you won." The lusty smile he gives me makes me laugh, and I climb out of the car to check my engine as he gets out after me. Sanjay waves at me, handing over a stack of cash as he goes to calm the crowd. The other cars stop behind us. Once I'm sure my engine isn't going to explode, I point at the car and leave Evan there as I head over to Sky, who's climbing from his.

"Shit, man," he says. "You nearly went too far that time."

"Nah, I had it under control." I accept his arm as a greeting, and he shakes his head as we pull back.

"Fucker, you were determined to win," he mutters.

"I had something important on the line." He follows my gaze to Evan, who is watching us, a crowd moving closer to him and my car.

"Uh-huh, I bet. Come on then, let's go meet your boy." Before I can stop him, he heads Evan's way. I quickly catch up.

"Don't even think about it," I mutter.

"You scared I'll steal him?" Sky grins, running his eyes over Evan. Stepping before him, I cross my arms, blocking his view.

I smirk. "No, because you would be dead before you touched him."

Sky laughs, slinging an arm around my shoulders and steering us to a grinning Evan. "He's not my type anyway. I like them moody and a little crazy," he whispers in my ear. I watch Evan's eyes narrow us so I duck away, not wanting him to be pissed at me after we just made up. Instead, I head his way and lean next to him against my car, making sure our thighs touch.

"Only two for you?" Sky asks.

"Yeah. Thought I'd leave some winnings for you for a change." My eyes drift to Evan though. I want my winnings. The entire time I talk to Sky, all I can think about is bending Evan over in my back seat and finding out if he feels as good as he tastes.

His eyes find mine as he looks up at me through his lashes, driving me insane, and when Sky chuckles, I realize we have just been staring at each other.

"Jesus, just get out of here, will you? You two are practically undressing each other in front of me. I feel like I need popcorn or some shit."

Without sparing him a look, I open the passenger seat and wait for Evan to climb in. Sliding across the trunk, I get into the driver's seat and pull away before his belt is even in place. I leave the racers and Sky far behind as the darkness of the empty roads closes in on us, only ratcheting up my desire. I can smell him all over me, in my car, and on my skin. I want more of it. I grip the wheel to stop myself from touching him because I know as soon as I do, it will be over.

I haven't been able to sleep or think about anything else apart from us getting hot and heavy in my car. It's been driving me crazy, and tonight, I'm giving in.

"I like your friend." Evan grins as I speed away.

"Don't," I grunt, unable to form a sentence around my desire, and the little, rich prick doesn't help when he leans over and brushes his mouth up my throat to my ear. His hand lands on my hard cock.

"Can you drive if I'm playing with you?" he teases.

"Rich boy," I warn, but his tongue darts out and tastes my pulse.

"Eyes on the road, Anders," he says when I glance at him. "I'm trusting you not to crash while I play."

I force my eyes to the road in front of us. My heart races, and desire spirals through me, making it difficult to breathe as his hand massages my dick through my jeans. His mouth glides down my neck and back up before he bites down hard enough to mark me, and the slight pain makes me hiss, the wheel jerking in my grip as he chuckles.

Luckily, no one is on the road or we would have crashed, especially when he opens my jeans and unzips me, sliding his hand inside and gripping my length. I lift my hips as I struggle to breathe.

He hums, licking my ear and biting the lobe. "You're so big, Anders. I can't wait to feel you stretching my ass."

Holy fuck.

Those words send images through my head, ones that have me speeding up. I need to get us somewhere safe before I lose it. I'm not an idiot. As soon as I started realizing I was interested in Evan, I did some research, not wanting to look like a fumbling moron. I didn't expect to like what I saw so much, and the idea of Evan like that . . .

"You like that? I can feel you. Do you want to be buried in my ass, Alek? Do you want to fill me with your cum?"

"Rich boy," I growl, my eyes narrowing on the road. It's so hard to concentrate, it's not even funny.

Leaning down, he places a kiss on my cock, and I'm lost.

Jerking the wheel to the side, I stop us in the darkness of a dead-end road. My lights are still on, but I don't care. I rip off my seat belt and reach for him. He gasps as my lips press to his, and then I shove him into the back seat, crawling after him as he chuckles.

"I want my winnings, rich boy."

TWENTY-FIVE

I crash backward in the seat as he pins me, his lips finding mine. Our teeth clack together, and I taste my own blood from my lips. His hands tear at my clothes and delve under, tracing over my skin and branding me with his claim. I gasp into his mouth, arching up and begging for more.

He sits back abruptly, his eyes so dark they are black. He watches me, and I smirk.

"You won me, now what are you going to do with me?" I taunt, and it gets him moving. His hands frame my face and drag me up so I'm on my knees.

"Just looking at what's mine, rich boy," he murmurs, his gaze sweeping over my face. I was wrong. His eyes aren't black. Up close, they are on fire, flaming with desire.

"Clothes off, pretty boy—everything but my jacket. I want you wearing that while I fuck you."

I shiver, loving this possessive streak in him. I'm not ashamed to admit it makes me harder than I've ever been.

He reaches for my shirt when I'm too slow, and he helps me struggle from it before he slides his jacket back onto my shoulders. I reach for my pants and undo them before shoving them down, then I lie back and slide them off, kicking them away until I'm naked on his back seat.

His eyes devour me, his lips parting when they land on my hard dick. I reach down and palm myself, squeezing as I stroke, and he watches me, his chest heaving. Suddenly, he smacks my hand away. "You don't get to touch yourself, rich boy, not when you're with me."

Groaning, I lean up and search for his mouth again, needing that brutal edge. He gives it to me, kissing me hard as his hands slide up my thighs and grip me. Desire courses through me as I groan into his mouth, lifting my hips as I thrust my cock into his hands.

"Please, Anders," I beg, not above it when I need him this badly.

I've wanted him all this time, and it's been driving me crazy. I want more. I want it all. He looks nervous, though, as he sits back, releasing me. This isn't my first time, but it's his, and I need to remember that. I shouldn't push him no matter how much I want him.

"Alek." I cup his cheeks as I lean up, our faces inches apart so he can focus on my words. "We don't have to do this if you aren't ready."

"You think I'm scared? No, rich boy, I'm fucking frozen with how goddamn beautiful you look spread over my back seat. I've never wanted anyone as much in my entire fucking life, so yeah, maybe I'm scared I'm going to fuck this up or that I'm going to hurt you with how much I want you." He says it so confidently, so proudly, that I nearly come on the spot.

My eyelashes flutter as a coy smile curves my lips at his declaration. "Not possible, Anders. I'll like it however I can get it. Hard, painful, soft—I want it all. You don't think I want a man like you without wanting the pain that comes with it? Baby, you hit me when you kissed me, and I went home and jacked off. Your actions and words are always laced with venom, and I love it. Sink it into me, fucking fill me with it, and fill my body with agony. I'll beg you to keep going. Whatever you dish out, Anders, I can take it," I promise as I run my lips down his throat. "Now take your clothes off. I want to see you. I want your muscles on display for me while you fuck me."

He opens the door with a groan and slides out as I sit up, watching as he removes his shirt and throws it into the front before shoving his jeans and boxers down, letting me look at his large, hard cock. It's leaking for me and so thick and long, I have to grip my shaft to stop myself from coming at the sight. He's going to feel so fucking good inside me.

I can't look away as he crawls inside and over my body as I fall back.

My eyes feast on him as he leans above me, his arms bunching with the movements, and his abs rub across my cock. He's so fucking beautiful, and I tell him so as I kiss him. "You can have me, baby, any way you want. You want me on my front—"

"Uh-uh, on your back, rich boy. I want to see your pretty face when I take what's mine," he says, and shit if my heart doesn't fucking clench at that not so innocent warning.

Lying back for him, I slide my hand up his thick, muscular thigh, liking the way the hair tickles my palm before I grip his long length and guide him between my legs.

His eyes widen, and he reaches down, scrambling across the floorboards for something without looking away, and when he lifts a bottle, I smirk. He blushes hard. "I have been researching. I thought we might need this."

"And you kept it here?" I grin, tightening my hand on his dick until he groans, bowing over me.

"Enough talking," he snaps and uncaps the bottle, drizzling the cold lube across his fingers. He reluctantly pulls his cock away from me as his wet fingers slide over my dick, then my balls and lower, pressing against my hole. He glances down, watching his movements, and I spread my legs wider, lifting them so they are on his shoulders.

He groans, slipping his digits inside me, and I close my eyes, my back arching as he innocently prods my prostate. My cock throbs in pleasure as he slides his fingers in and out, working in a third, all while watching me with obsession and hunger in his gaze.

"No more," I beg. "I can't take any more. I need you inside me. I need your cock, not your fingers."

Snarling, he yanks his fingers out of my ass and squirts the lube on his cock, and we guide him to my ass together. Our eyes meet once more as he hesitates. "I can take you, baby. Trust me . . . Fill me . . ."

"I'll try to be gentle," he stutters as he pushes into me, both of us groaning at the feeling. The sharp discomfort only lasts a second as he slides deeper before pulling out and rocking his hips forward.

"I don't want gentle, baby. I want you, brutal and hard. Fuck me," I order, placing my hands on his shoulders and digging my nails into his skin. He hisses in pain, his hips snapping forward in retribution, filling me to the brim with his huge cock, and I cry out.

"Shit, sorry, pretty boy—"

"Don't stop!" I implore, lifting my hips to take him deeper, and he groans in response. My eyes open, locking on his brutal face, and his eyes are focused on his cock as he pulls from my ass and slides back in, making me feel so fucking full I can barely breathe. Each time he fills me, he hits my prostate, and I dig my nails in deeper.

"Look at you." His voice is filled with awe as he thrusts harder, filling me until the car is rocking with the force. "Fuck, pretty boy, you are goddamn perfection. You were made to be under me, taking my dick."

"Do I feel good?" I ask, my heart hammering in my chest as I slide my hands greedily across his exposed muscles, pinching his nipples and watching him snarl above me.

"Hot, so fucking hot and tight." One hand hits the ceiling of his car as he thrusts before he groans and drops lower, covering my body.

His mouth slants over mine once more in a blazing, possessive kiss. I kiss him back, eating at his mouth as our bodies move. Pleasure spirals through me, my cock rubbing against his abs, leaking all over them as I rock my hips. Whining into his mouth, I push him up, needing to breathe. I turn my head, and he bites my neck brutally before sucking.

"You feel so good, pretty boy." His voice is a wicked rasp, filling the interior of the rocking car. "You're never getting away from me now. You're mine. You're wearing my fucking mark, and I'm going to stain this ass so no one else can have it," he says as he lifts his torso again, blocking more of the light as he fucks me. His thrusts become brutal and hard, hurting even as they feel so good, I bite my lip until I taste blood.

I watch his biceps flex with the movements, his fingers digging into my muscles as he snarls my name.

My hand slides up his shoulder and around the back of his neck, feeling the solid muscle there as I tug him down for another fierce kiss.

I buck my hips, needing more.

Sensations assault me—the feeling of his huge dick pounding into me, his hands trailing over my body, his eyes pinning me beneath him as we break apart. It's too much.

"Alek," I beg, closing my eyes as I grip my cock and stroke it. I can feel him watching, and he swells inside my ass to the point of pain. His thrusts turn vicious, uncoordinated as he rams into me, forcing himself deeper.

It hurts so fucking much.

I love it.

My balls draw up with pleasure, and I can't hold back anymore. "Alek!" It's a hoarse cry, a warning.

"Come for me, pretty boy, let me see it," he demands above me like my avenging angel.

My hips buck, and my shout fills the car as my cock jerks, throbbing in time with my heart as I come, shooting hot ropes of my release all over my chest and his.

His palm smears it across my heaving chest before he lifts his hand and licks it clean, then he drops it to the seat and fills me twice more.

"Alek." I part my legs wider. "Come inside me. Let me feel it."

It's all the encouragement he needs, and he cries out in the next second, his cock jerking inside me. It pulses with his release as he fills me until I feel it dripping down us.

His hips rock, pushing him deeper, and then he collapses above me, his weight almost too much. Smiling happily, I wrap my legs and arms around him, uncaring about the mess, and kiss his head and face as I stroke his back.

"That was—" He lifts his head slightly as he searches my gaze.

"Incredible," I offer breathlessly, and our lips come together in the dark, our hands sliding over each other's bodies leisurely as we explore. When we break apart to breathe, we are both smiling.

He cups my face and brushes back some of my sweaty hair. "I adore you, pretty boy."

Rolling my lips inwards, I search his eyes, letting some of my truth leak out in the darkness of his car. "I adore you too."

Alek's car is still steamed up inside by the time we pull up to a cute two-story house. He gives me a knowing look, his eyes dropping down my body and heating again. "Uh-uh, let's get inside before you throw me in your back seat again." I grin. I'm so happy. I got everything I wanted tonight.

I expected him to take me home, but he gruffly declared I was staying at his house. I'm not going to complain about that since my dorm is cramped and I don't want Tommy's questions all night. Besides, spending the night in Alek Anders's bed? Fuck yes, sign me up, even if it's just to sleep next to him.

"Come on, rich boy." He gets out, and I follow him up the three concrete steps to the door. There are plants and flowers in boxes outside of the porch with a welcome mat that reads "Fuck off."

I laugh, and he grins as he unlocks the door. When I follow him in, he lifts his fingers to his lips in a shush gesture. "Alice is here. She'll be asleep, and she gets cranky if you wake her."

I nod and stay silent as he locks up, grabbing us some water as I linger in the entryway. To the left is a small, cozy living room with a huge TV and leather couches. There's also a coffee table with flowers on it and pictures on shelves with books. The hallway in front of me leads to a kitchen I can see from here, done in soft greens. The walls are paneled with wood, with more pictures hanging on them. I squint into the dark, seeing Alek and Alice in them from different ages. It's totally not what I was expecting, and as he takes my hand and leads me upstairs, I smile.

It's fucking cute. The second floor is decorated in pastels and has three doors—one closed, one open to show a bathroom, and the other partially open at the end of the hall. He pushes inside the last, hitting a switch with his elbow and holding the water so he doesn't have to let go of my hand.

It's his bedroom, with a king-sized bed pushed against the back wall under the window, perfectly made sheets spread over the top. There's a bench at the end with boots underneath, a TV on the opposite wall, and a desk to the left covered in mechanic books and car diagrams. Posters of different cars hang on the walls, and there is a dresser to the right of the door. There's even a soft blue rug on the floor, and as he kicks the door shut behind me, I look around. He hands me a water, and I take a sip as he heads over to his dresser, taking off his shirt and shoving his jeans down. Wearing nothing but his boxers, he roots around in a drawer before pulling out a black shirt.

"Here." He throws me the shirt. "You can sleep in mine."

I slip mine off and hang up his jacket before sliding his shirt on. It's massive on me but comfy as hell, and when he comes toward me, his eyes darkening, I can't help but blush. "You look good in my shirt, rich boy," he murmurs, grabbing my hips before he smacks my ass. "Get into bed, you have school tomorrow."

"Yes, Daddy," I tease as I climb in, but he smacks me until I scoot over so I'm under the window. "Is that your side?" I tease.

"Nah, I sleep in the middle," he replies as he plugs both of our phones in and goes to turn off the light. "But this way, I can protect you," he says. He doesn't even realize what he said, but my heart takes flight as I slip under the covers and lay my head on his pillow as he plunges us into darkness.

I feel the bed dip as he gets in, turning to face me. Our hands are inches away on the pillow, so I close the distance, linking them. His fingers twine with mine as he watches me. His face is in shadows, but I can still see his beauty.

He watches me for a moment before the dark seems to make him brave and vulnerable—or maybe it's what we shared tonight. I don't know, but it's a different side of him.

"When did you realize you . . ." He trails off, looking unsure.

"Liked boys?" I question with an arched brow, and his chin dips in a nod as I smile.

"I was young, maybe eleven or twelve," I murmur. "Some guy kissed me on a dare, and I realized I didn't hate it. I guess I always looked at both girls and guys growing up. I understood the attraction to both. It was hard to figure out by myself, since I thought it was shameful to want something I shouldn't, but I couldn't help it. My parents didn't like it," I scoff.

"You mentioned your parents before. You don't speak?"

"Not anymore. They couldn't accept me. They even tried to bribe me to be 'normal,' as if liking boys wasn't." I laugh bitterly. "They are old-money rich, and they thought I was disgraceful. They tried everything to change me, and I did everything not to lose myself until I could get out of there. They love me in their own way, the person they want me to be, not the person I am. Sometimes I hate them, and sometimes I can't bring myself to. I guess I miss having parents, but having ones who don't love and accept you for who you are isn't better than having none."

He squeezes my hand. "They are stupid not to love you, Evan." I smile. "What was it like growing up open like that?"

"Hard," I admit, "especially in the small town I was from. There weren't many who understood or accepted me. Even the guys I dated mostly hid what they were in fear of the repercussions. I didn't like that, and I didn't see the point in hiding. It made me an outcast. I was bullied a lot, so I started taking lessons to learn how to protect myself. My dad once told me I couldn't be gay and weak. It was a barb, but I took it seriously. Still, I wouldn't change growing up like that. It shaped me into who I am, and now I can face anything. I can be anything as long as I am true to myself. It didn't mean it didn't hurt, but it was a good kind of hurt, you know?"

He watches me before reaching out and caressing my cheeks softly. "I wish I had half the strength you do, Evan," he says, speaking so softly I barely catch it. "I never had the chance to figure out who I was, nor the strength. My parents aren't around. They died when Alice was young, and she was suddenly just mine. I was her entire family. She lost her parents, and I had to be her rock, her safe place, so I put everything about me on the back burner, and I became what she needed. I didn't even realize that I had been drifting until I met you, just existing for her and not myself. I wasn't happy or sad, just here." He swallows, moving closer. "I need you to know, Evan, there's a reason I am the way I am . . . with this. With us." I frown, confused, and he groans. "I'm not ready to talk about it, but it's not you, okay? I wish I were as strong as you are, and I wish I could own it, but I can't. I hope I can one day."

"Shh." I kiss him. "I don't need you to tell me if you aren't ready, but when you are, I'll be here, and I'm glad you're finding out who you are and what makes you happy, Alek. You deserve it. You took on so much looking after Alice so young, providing for her, but you don't have to do it alone now."

"I've always been alone," he whispers.

"Not anymore," I reply, kissing his hand as I settle in. The smile he gives me is soft and sleepy, and we lapse into silence, lost in our own thoughts. I'm unable to look away from him, wondering what happened to make him so closed off from his own needs and wants. It's obvious Alek has been through a lot—losing his parents and becoming Alice's only family and parental figure so young—but the way he spoke, it's obvious there's something else to it. I hope someday he'll feel like he can share it with me. I hope I can be his safe space like he is for his sister. I have a feeling he needs that, and maybe I do too.

I want to be needed and wanted, when my whole childhood, I wasn't.

"Night, pretty boy," he mumbles, settling into the bed and tightening his grip on my hand as if he's afraid I'll disappear.

"Night, princess," I respond equally as softly, not wanting to disturb him.

As his eyes close, I can't look away. I'm obsessed with the peaceful look that transforms his face as he falls asleep. I didn't even realize how much tension he held in his face until now, as if the weight of the world is on his shoulders. He admitted he feels like he does everything alone, and as I stare at his younger looking face, my heart breaks for the boy who had to grow up too fast. No wonder he's such an asshole.

I place a gentle kiss on his forehead, lingering for as long as I dare. "Sleep, princess. You aren't alone now. I'm here."

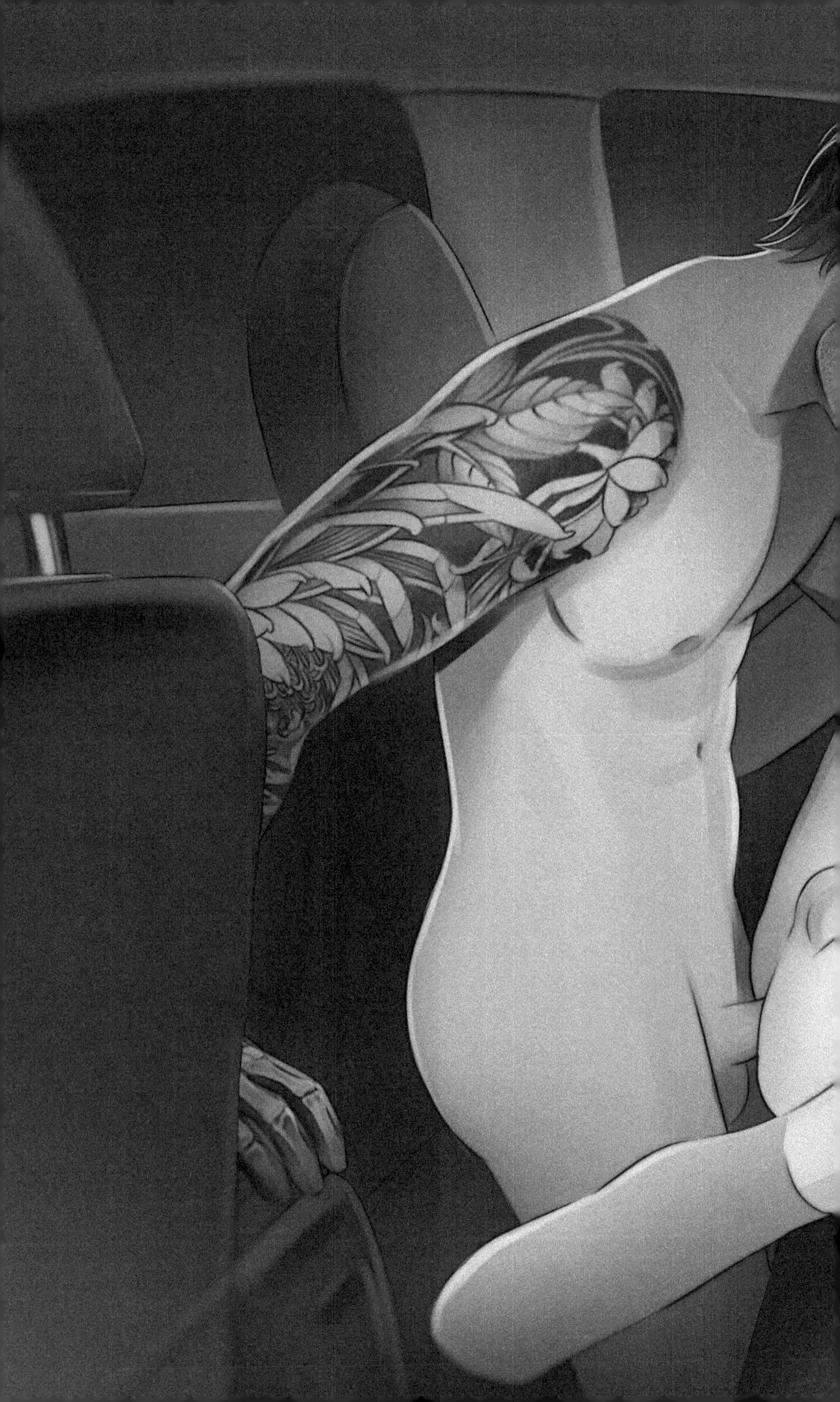

FREE PARKING
ACTIVE
DRIVEWAY
SHAW DRIVE
THE MOMENT
ONE WAY
TOO
STOP
ANDERS AVE
SILENT ROSE
NO PARKING
SALE
Pine Valley
EVER

TWENTY-SIX

ALEK

I jerk awake, blinking in confusion as the early morning sun shines right into my eyes. There's a soft, sleepy sigh, and my eyes drop, widening when I find Evan pressed against me. He's wrapped tightly in my arms, both of us in the middle of the bed and as close together as we can possibly get. His head rests on my chest, and his hands are curled on my torso.

For a moment, I just stare, my heart thudding painfully in my chest. He's so fucking pretty. His bratty mouth is quiet for once, and his long lashes fan across his sharp cheekbones. He looks good in my arms. It feels right having him in my bed.

I should get up and get Alice ready for school.

I should move, but I don't. I tighten my hold on him, pressing my nose to his hair and inhaling. I allow myself this weakness that I would never allow in public. Here, I let myself cling to him, closing my eyes once more.

I wish we could be like this all the time. I wish I weren't so scared of my past because loving Evan Shaw could just about heal anybody.

I want our whispered nights in the dark, I want laughter,and I want pain. I want it all with him.

I just don't know if I'm strong enough to take it because I might ruin it like everything else.

Chased out of my peaceful moment by my thoughts, I place a tender kiss on his head and gently roll him over before slipping my arms from him. He sighs, and I freeze, but he just snuggles deeper into my bed, snoring once more.

Sneaking out of my bed so I don't wake the angel sleeping there, I pull on jeans and a shirt and slip out of my room, heading downstairs to make Alice's breakfast. I start the coffee and begin making sausage and bacon, then eggs and toast. The scent of food fills the house, and right on cue, I hear Alice banging around in her room, the familiar sound going straight to my aching heart and easing something within me.

No matter what, I'll always have her and this—our routine, the familiar.

Even when I had nothing else, I had us. One day, I know she'll have her own house and family, and I'll miss the sound of her clumsily falling out of bed to come for breakfast. The house will be quiet, and I'll be alone because no matter what I want, I know nobody could love me forever.

She comes down moments later, her eyes closed as she shuffles inside, sniffing the air like a bloodhound. I watch her, memorizing the moment. Her hair is pushed up onto her head, and there is a crease on her cheek from her pillow. She grew up so fast, but some things never change. I wish they could stay like this forever, but they won't.

Proof of that is the groan coming from the stairs as another person heads our way.

I chuckle as Evan shuffles into the kitchen, his eyes half open and his hair sticking up from sleep. "Food," he declares.

I glance between Alice and Evan as he sinks into a seat, both of them half asleep but sniffing the air, and I can't help but smile. For one more day, this house is filled with love and laughter, with people and memories. I'll cherish them so when I'm alone once more, I can look back and remember the better days when I was happy.

Laying the food on the table, I pour Alice coffee with the sugar she likes and put it between her hands before she sips it like a zombie. I pour Evan one as well, trying to figure out if he likes cream or sugar. I take a wild guess and set it before him before making my own and sitting down. I sip mine, watching them both nurse their coffees until more life comes back into their eyes. Once they are more awake, I dish up food, making Evan a plate and then Alice. She takes a bite woodenly as Evan shoots me a small, sleepy smile.

"Morning, princess," he mumbles.

"Good morning, pretty boy," I reply, kissing his cheek since I can't help myself.

Alice suddenly gasps, making me jerk back, her eyebrow arched as she turns to Evan and points. "You! You're here!"

"Uh-huh, he's been here this whole time," I point out as I relax back, confused about how comfortable I am with him around my sister. I don't let anyone close to her, since she's the only good thing in my life, but I know Evan would never hurt her. Hell, he would help me protect her.

"It's too early for your sass, brother," she snipes, turning to Evan. "I don't function before caffeine, but you're here."

"Close your mouth," I warn as I grab another slice of toast, butter it, and put it on Evan's plate. She looks between us, grinning, before wiggling her brows at me.

"So, Evan, did you spend the night? I had my headphones on, just for future reference."

He blushes but grins.

"Enough, Alice," I tell her, but I can't hide my smile.

Why does Evan Shaw fit so perfectly into our little kitchen and our tiny, broken family as if he were always meant to be here?

A boy without his parents' love and one craving it.

"I did." He nods, shooting me a look as if he's unsure how much to say. "It was late, so better here than heading back and waking my roomie."

"Uh-huh, does this mean I have a new daddy?" she jokes as Evan chokes on his toast. "Can I call you Papa?"

"Dear God, I thought you were the sane sibling." He coughs as I hand him some juice and pat his back.

"Nah, I hide it better. Plus, he makes me look sane." She points her thumb at me as I sigh. "So you like my brother, huh? Why? He's an ass."

"A pretty one." Evan grins.

"Ew, too much." She gets to her feet. "I better get dressed." She walks my way, kissing my head as she passes. "I'm glad he's here. I'll make sure to put in my noise canceling headphones from now on." She laughs as she hurries away.

"Get ready, you scoundrel!" I call.

"Make me!" she shouts back as I sigh. When I glance at Evan, he's smiling.

"What?" I grumble.

"I like your house. Mine was always empty and quiet. I like the craziness. It's nice." He shrugs as he takes a bite, and my heart breaks for him. I can't imagine growing up in a cold, empty house without love. Our little family might be broken and slightly insane, but it's filled with love and laughter.

My heart breaks for Evan right there and then, so I kiss him swiftly. "Then come here every day. It can be yours too. I'm not saying you won't get sick of the bickering but . . ." I laugh. "It's yours."

"I wish," he offers softly, and I lean back, watching him, but he seems to shake it off and then smiles brightly at me.

"I better get changed. I'm stealing a shirt." He heads upstairs and I watch him go.

What did he mean?

Does he not plan to stay?

"Alice! Fuck, why isn't the door locked?" I hear a moment later, and all my negative thoughts morph into laughter.

He wanted crazy after all.

I drive them both to school, Evan riding in my passenger seat where he belongs. I pull into the familiar parking lot, under one of the oak trees. Students mill about on the grass in the sun, while others rush onto campus for their classes.

"Thanks for the ride," Alice mutters from the back.

"Yes, thanks for the ride, Anders." Evan winks. "I really enjoyed it."

Sweet fuck. I swallow hard as I reach behind my seat and grab what I was looking for before I change my mind.

"Here." I hand over a lunch box.

He blinks, looking from it to me. "What is this?"

"Your lunch. I didn't know if you ate here or not but—" I scrub my neck in embarrassment. "Just take it." I shove it at him as a slow smile curls up his lips.

"You softie. Thank you, princess."

"Wait, where the fuck is my lunch?" Alice asks from the back.

"You're old enough to get your own," I snap.

"So is he!" she protests.

"He's pretty," I retort, reaching back and pushing her toward the door as he watches us.

"I'm pretty too. This is favoritism, and I will not stand for it!" she argues as she gets out.

Rolling my eyes, I grin at him. "I'll text you later."

"Sure, have fun at work." He leans in to kiss me before my eyes shoot to the people watching, and then he leans back, his smile wilting slightly. "See you later, princess." He's gone before I can speak again, and I wish I let him kiss me if only just to see his smile, but also to get me through my day without seeing him.

My eyes linger on him, even though I should leave, but I'm glad I didn't when I see a buff guy pushing away from a bench and heading his way, smiling and stepping way too close to Evan. He's flirting, I realize, even from here.

Jealousy courses through me, and even though I have no right, I get out of my car before I can question what I'm doing. As soon as I reach them, I tug Evan away from him and to my side, eyeing the guy with an angry expression.

"Alek?" Evan asks, confused.

"You forgot this." I hand him his camera that he left in my passenger seat. Luckily, I have that excuse, but it doesn't stop my jealousy, my eyes on the guy. "See you after class, baby."

"Um, see you later." He looks from me to the guy before ducking and hurrying away.

I arch my brow at the guy who backs away, holding his hands up with a knowing grin before he leaves.

Shit, did I just claim Evan Shaw in front of everyone?

TWENTY-SEVEN

I still can't get over Alek's possessive display this morning. Fortunately, there weren't many people around to question it, but I know he's probably worried. He doesn't run away, however, and he texts me all day, checking in and being sweet. It's different, and I like it. It seems like something has really shifted between us after yesterday, and I couldn't be happier.

> Alek: Can I see you tonight?

> Evan: I promised I'd go for a meal with my friends.

I'm not the type to ditch them just because I'm seeing a guy, a superhot guy but still. My friends have to be prioritized as well.

> Alek: :(

> Alek: Okay, let me know if you have time after.

> Evan: Will do, princess.

I focus on my class after that, and the day passes quickly.

I slump into my seat at the restaurant Lally chose. It's a fusion restaurant, new and hot, and I'm surprised we managed to get a table, but she always achieves it somehow. She brings us to the strangest places, and we have the best time. It's one of her strengths.

"I'm starving," Tommy complains as he leans back in his seat.

"Me too," I add, sipping my water as I glance at them with a grin. It feels like it's been forever since I got to hang out with them, but in actuality, it was just last week, and we see each other every day. I know it's important to set aside a time for all of us to get together. They've been with me through everything and are amazing friends, so I keep my phone in my bag, no matter how many times I hear it vibrate, and instead I keep my attention on them.

"It will be worth it, I promise," Lally says, since we let her order for us, trusting her taste. "But there are more important matters to deal with." She wiggles her eyebrows at me. "Did I see Alek Anders dropping you off this morning, you slut?"

Tommy whoops, leaning over with his hand up. "Nice one, getting that closet dick, bro. He didn't come home last night."

"I am not high-fiving that," I mutter, but I can't help smiling even as I shake my head. "It isn't like that."

"Uh-huh, so what's it like?" Lally asks, leaning in. Tommy looks at her and then mimics her movement. Both of them rest their chins on their fists as they watch me with matching grins.

"Well—"

"Evan." I turn at the familiar voice, smiling when I see Autumn with some friends.

"Hi." Getting up, I give her a quick hug. "You eating?"

"Just finished. It's amazing." She grins at Lally and Tommy, and they nod, confused. "Just thought I'd say hi. Have a good night, guys. See you later, Evan."

I nod and wave as she leaves, and when I sit back down, Lally and Tommy both turn to me. "Who was that?"

"I'm allowed to have other friends," I point out.

Lally gasps dramatically. "You are cheating on us?"

"The horror!" Tommy yells.

"Okay, okay." I laugh, holding my hands up. "We met in a class, that's all." I know I can't tell them about Silent Rose, so I lie, which I hate doing to my friends, but luckily, they accept it.

"Fine, we'll let this slide . . . if you tell us about Alek," Lally replies.

Groaning, I rub my head, but they just wait. Scooting closer, I drop my voice. "We are . . . seeing each other."

They squeal, slapping their hands together as I watch before leaning in, uncaring about the eyes on us since they are so loud.

"How's it going?"

"Tell us everything."

They speak at the same time, and I can't help but smile, their excitement for me contagious. I don't know why I was so worried. I know they are my friends and will always be there for me, support and love me no matter who I date, but they are important to me, so their opinions matter. I realize I want them to like Alek and care about him because I do.

"It's never been like this," I admit softly. "I've dated—"

"Lots."

I glare at Tommy, who laughs. "But it's never been this . . . exciting. It's like everything is new. Everything is a first for me. I've never felt so intensely for someone before. I can't stand to be apart from him, and I'm obsessed with everything he does. I can't stop thinking about him. I've never been this attracted to someone. Even kissing feels different. There's just—"

"Fireworks." Lally nods. "You lucky bastard."

"Right, fireworks. It's amazing . . ." I trail off, and her eyes narrow. "He's just shy about it being public. He isn't ready, and that's fine. I can wait, and I understand how hard this is, but it makes me feel like I'm doing something wrong, you know? I reached for his hand yesterday without realizing it and then instantly felt guilty when he panicked."

Lally and Tommy share a frown as they lean back, and I hold my hands up. "He isn't mean or anything. I was the one who was willing to wait for him to be ready. He didn't want me to. I just, yeah, I don't know. I guess I didn't expect it to be so hard. I just want to shout about who I'm dating. He's so amazing, but I guess it will just take time."

I don't like the looks they are giving me, but Lally finally sighs, sitting forward. "I'm glad you're happy, Evan, and if you say he's a good guy, we will believe you. I just hope he can accept your relationship and give you what you want, that's all," she offers. "We worry because we care."

"I know," I say as Tommy covers my hand.

"Give him time and let him get used to it. I'm guessing it's all new for him too, but he wouldn't be fighting for this if he didn't care."

"Also true," Lally adds.

"Oh, I know! There's a party tonight. How about you invite him? We can meet him, and he can hang with all your friends—no pressure, no prying eyes, just fun. It might help loosen him up," Tommy suggests.

"That's a great idea!" Lally agrees. "It's a good place for him to see that no one cares and to get to know you and this side of your life if you want him to be a part of it."

"I don't know . . . Do you think so?" I ask worriedly, biting my bottom lip.

"It's your choice, Evan, but I think it would be good for both of you," Lally replies.

I glance at my bag where my phone is and back at them. "Okay, let me ask him." Grabbing it, I head outside and call him.

"Baby?" he answers. "How's your meal?"

"It's good. Lally and Tommy want me to invite you to a party tonight."

He's silent, and I panic as I lean back against the wall of the restaurant.

"No pressure, it will be busy and probably not your scene, but you can meet my friends. Only Lally and Tommy sort of know about us, but you really don't have to—"

His chuckle cuts me off. "You're cute when you're nervous." I feel my cheeks heat as he carries on. "You want me to come?"

"You really don't have to. It's probably silly—"

"Evan, do you want me to come?" he asks, cutting off my mumbling.

"Yes," I answer.

"Then I'll be there. I'll drive. Want me to pick all three of you up?"

My heart melts as I smile widely. "I'd love that. I'll text you the address."

"Sounds good, rich boy, see you then." It goes quiet, and I think he hung up, so I'm putting my phone away when his voice comes again. "I'm glad you called and asked me." He hangs up, leaving me grinning.

When I head back inside, Lally and Tommy are watching me, their hands out and fingers crossed. "He's coming."

The cheer they let out has every head turning in our direction as I laugh.

NO PARKING
ACTIVE
DRIVEWAY
SHAW DRIVE
THE MOMENT
ANDERS AVE
ONE WAY
STOP
TOO
CAR REPAIR
NO PARKING
SALE
SILENT ROSE
EVER

TWENTY-EIGHT

Evan looks good tonight. I can't take my eyes off him as I pull up to the address he gave me to pick him and his friends up. He has on a long-sleeved top, his thumbs through cutouts on the sleeves. It's a deep gunmetal gray with white grooves down the arms. The neckline is slightly torn, and it ends mid-waist, so when he turns or moves, it exposes his abs. The sight shouldn't make me hard or feel possessive, but it does. All his skin on display, his tight waist . . .

Shit.

The pants don't help. They might be loose cargos, but they hang low, showing off his boxers, and the chains looping around them have some very bad ideas entering my head.

Nothing else matters, though, except his wide smile and his wave when he spots me.

I won't admit that I was in the car, counting down the minutes until it was time to meet, or that I spent an hour picking out an outfit. I even asked Alice for help, wanting to look good for him and his friends. I know this is important, and I want to make a good impression, but one look at my sunshine and all that anxiety flees. A smile curves my lips as I pull up alongside them and hop out, ignoring the honking traffic since I shouldn't stop here. Usually, I wouldn't care about helping others into the car, but again, I know these are important people to my boy.

"Hey, princess," he greets, winking at me as his eyes drop to my outfit. I feel severely underdressed in my black shirt and jeans. My boots have yellow laces, and I styled my hair, but I suddenly feel very . . . out of it. "Looking good." Instantly, those feelings disappear too.

"Perv," I mutter, glancing at his friends. "You must be rich b— Evan's friends."

"I'm Lally, and this is Tommy." A pink-haired girl grins. Covered in piercings and tattoos, she looks more like someone I would hang out with, but the e-girl outfit she has on has my eyebrows rising. Nodding, I open the door, and she clambers into the back. Tommy salutes me as he follows her. He's wearing loose overalls without a shirt underneath and a beanie. Shutting the door, I head around to the passenger side and open the door before Evan can.

His eyebrows rise, and I smile as I slide my hand across the base of his spine, feeling his soft skin as I lean in. He shivers as his eyes land on my lips. "You look good enough to eat, pretty boy."

"Later, if you're good," he promises, both of us lost in each other's eyes until a honk makes him jump.

I flip the driver off as I guide Evan inside, my hand automatically going above his head as he slides in, and I shut the door behind him. Hurrying around, I reach over and fasten his belt—a habit.

"Aww, you two are so cute." Lally grins, popping her head between the seats. "It's nice to finally meet you. Should we call you asshole or Alek?"

"Alek is fine," I mutter, embarrassed as I glance back. "Belts."

"He's all bark and no bite. Well, some bite," Evan teases as he reaches for the radio and flips through the music. I let him as I pull out into traffic.

My cheeks heat as I focus on the road, but his friends just laugh. "Nice ride," Tommy says. "You build it?"

I nod, unsure what to say. I've never been good with the social side of things or small talk, and I worry I'm doing it wrong.

"Nice, love the artwork. You should do some dope paintings on other cars. People would pay for it." He nods, and I glance at him in the rearview mirror.

"I do it for some friends. I've thought about it," I tell him. The subject is something I'm interested in, so I find myself relaxing. "I can always show you one day."

"Hell yes, I'm down for that." Tommy grins and nudges Lally. "I like him."

Lally smiles, but she watches me closely, and I know she won't be won over so easily. Evan told me a lot about her, and I'm glad he has her. She's very protective, which I like.

I focus on the road. I mapped the drive earlier when Evan texted me the party address, so I leave him singing along to the radio as we drive, Lally and Tommy chatting away in the back.

It's . . . nice.

My hand drifts from the stick to his thigh before I remember we aren't alone and I snatch it back. Grinning at me, he grabs my hand and laces our fingers together, uncaring about his friends. It shouldn't make me float, but it does. I like that they know about us, plus they seem nice. There was no judgment, no teasing, just acceptance, as if Evan liking me was enough.

Lifting his hand, I kissed the back of it at the next light. "I missed you tonight," I admit quietly.

"Did you?" He kisses my cheek, his voice coming before he leans away. "Then we can spend the night making up for it."

Grinding my jaw at the hungry look in his eyes, I jerk my gaze back to the road before I do something super inappropriate. Laughing, he tightens his hold on my hand as I pull onto the street the party is being held at. I'm not usually one for a frat party, but Evan invited me so I'll go.

If it's filled with idiots, though, I might just have to kidnap him. There is only so much sports talk I can handle. It surprises me when we pull up outside and see jocks there. "I didn't know you were a jock kid."

"Evan is friends with everyone," Lally supplies happily. "He's all about breaking stereotypes. Equal rights and all that."

My eyebrows rise, and he shrugs as he gets out. I meet him around the front of the car, itching to reach for his hand, but I shove mine in my pockets. The grass is filled with students, some waving at Evan. There's no flying under the radar here. I don't know why I thought Evan was an outcast, but it seems he knows everyone.

I must look overwhelmed because Lally loops her arm through mine and leans in as she drags me after him and Tommy to the huge house where music is currently playing. "Don't worry, it gets easier, and I found the perfect response to the drunk jocks. No matter what they say, just say 'no way,' and drinking makes it easier to enjoy. School experience and all." She grins at me, letting me in on the secret.

"I don't drink and drive, especially with Evan in the car," I mutter, "but I'll try the no way thing."

"Evan! You came!" a big burly bastard calls out. He's currently helping an upside-down guy drink from a keg.

"Hey, Liam." Evan waves. "Nice party."

"You know it. Have a good night, man." He turns back to the bros surrounding him as I stare.

This is for Evan, I remind myself.

When we get inside, Evan steers us away from the packed dining room that has become a dance floor and to the back porch, where there are some couches surrounding a fire pit. The music still blasts out here with people drinking and partying, but it's chiller than inside. Lally pushes me down and grabs Evan, shoving him down next to me. "We'll get drinks!" she yells and then drags a confused Tommy away.

Evan is pressed against my side, so I move away slightly, not wanting him to worry. He arches his brow but turns to face me. "First college party?"

"First and last probably," I admit.

"Not your scene, asshole?" He smirks, leaning in to hear me better.

"I much prefer the quietness of my garage, especially when you're bent over my car," I flirt, and he throws his head back as he laughs. When he looks at me again, his eyes are sparkling.

"Let me let you in on a secret, princess. I prefer that too. I also like that you're a grumpy, antisocial bastard but still came just because I asked." His lips brush my ear. "I'll make it up to you later."

"You better," I grouch, especially when a stream of shirtless guys run outside, chanting. Dear fucking god, what have I gotten myself into?

His laughter at my reaction is contagious, however, and I find myself relaxing.

For him, I remind myself again.

If I didn't know frat parties were for me, I would now.

Lally's "no way" only works so much. It seems like every time I go to the bathroom or to get Evan a drink, they home in on me. They must think my big build means I'm an athlete, and it's tiresome. The bass pounds in my head, and I'm sweaty from winding through the crowd, but Evan is having a good time, and that's all that matters.

He's a little drunk and getting super touchy, which I wouldn't normally mind, but the crowd that formed around him, as if drawn to him like a magnet, is starting to notice and giving me knowing looks. I'm not ready for questions, not yet, so I keep my distance as much as I can without being obvious. Besides, I'm sober and getting grumpier by the minute, and I don't want to ruin his night. It's not his fault this isn't my thing, and I'm really trying for him, but I just don't get it.

He's flourishing as the center of attention. Hell, even with me, his laughter is contagious, and the stories he tells has everyone on the edges of their seats. He's good, but I can tell he's getting tired of keeping it up, of trying to be the life and soul of the party. If I didn't know Evan as well as I do, I might not have noticed.

When I hand him his drink, his hand lingers on mine before I step back. "So, Alek, right?" one of his many adoring fans says.

I nod, meeting their eyes as they lean in. "You're Evan's friend?"

I rub my neck as I nod again, and he waits for me to say something.

"It seems he has a lot of friends." I shrug, and I feel Evan's disappointment, but he soon perks up.

"Alek is amazing with cars, aren't you?" He turns his hopeful gaze to me, and I can't say no.

"I'm okay." It's clear they are waiting for more, so I rack my brain. "Um, I rebuilt a Skyline from scratch."

"Like from *Fast and Furious*?" one of the girls asks. "That's so hot. Are you single?"

My eyes widen, but Lally slides in. "You're such a car whore, Heather. Aren't the eight cars your daddy bought you enough?"

The girl laughs, flipping her hair over her shoulder as she replies to Lally. "Why? Want to try one out?"

"You wish." Lally grins and winks at me.

"Can you hold this for a sec?" Evan asks, passing me his drink.

"Sure, bro." I hold it as he stands, and he blinks at the word "bro."

"Um, okay, bro?" he responds, shaking his head. "I'm heading to the bathroom."

I go to follow him, but he points at me and the chair. "Sit, bro, I'll be right back. Friends don't need an escort."

Shit, I'm going to pay for that one later. I watch him storm off as I groan.

Lally flops down next to me, leaning in so our conversation is quiet and not overheard.

"So are you looking after my Evvie well?" she asks, sipping her drink as she watches me with hard eyes. Lally is a force of nature. Hell, I've seen guys less intimidating than her, and they are ex-criminals.

"Uh-uh, your Evvie has a bad temper and likes to square up to me. I don't think he needs protection from me, maybe the other way around," I point out.

"Very true." She laughs. "Just don't hurt him, okay?" she says protectively. "We get it. We've all been where you are, and you're figuring shit out. That's fine, but don't hurt him in the process. He's been hurt enough, and it's obvious he really likes you."

"Baby," the girl from earlier whines, trying to get Lally's attention.

"Wait your turn, sweetheart," Lally replies before turning back to me, and I can't help but laugh. Oh yeah, she's trouble. It seems all of Evan's friends are wild cards. I process her words as I watch her.

"How do you know?" I ask, not reacting to her anger or barb. She's protective of him. I get it.

"You wouldn't be here if he didn't," she points out. "Just be good to him, okay?"

"I'm glad he has you," I tell her. "It's obvious you care about him a lot. The last thing I want to do is hurt him."

She seems taken aback, blinking as she sips her drink. "Well, okay then." She smiles as if we have come to some sort of agreement, although I have no idea what.

"You should go after him," she suggests.

"Thank you." I leap to my feet and hurry inside, searching the party for Evan as she laughs and returns to the girl smiling seductively at her. I think Lally has her own ride home tonight.

I ask around and then head upstairs where they tell me to go. It's a maze of rooms up here, but as I duck around another almost empty corridor, I see him. A grin curls my lips before I stop dead in my tracks as the other person with him comes into view.

Anger fills me, as does a dark, cloying jealousy as I watch the man step closer. He presses his hand against Evan's chest as he leans into the wall. Evan doesn't remove it, and from the way Evan's looking at him, it's clear they know each other well.

His ex?

It's definitely someone he fucked, if the way the other guy is hungrily eyeing him is anything to go by.

He's taller than Evan and built, with blond hair and a wicked grin. He's a pretty boy and the total opposite of me. My hands fist at my sides, and fury races through me, mixing with my jealousy. I want to punch that smug look off his face.

Why isn't Evan pushing him away?

"I said no." Evan's voice reaches me as he straightens, stepping away from him.

How many times has he said no? My jealousy shifts to pure anger, and before I know it, I'm storming toward them. Evan sees me, his eyes widening. I grab his neck, yank him behind me, and turn to the guy.

"Hey, I was talking—" I don't let the guy finish. I slam my fist into his face, sending him staggering into the wall. Before I can let another punch fly, Evan's hand touches the base of my spine, stopping me. Grinding my jaw, I turn and grab his arm harshly, yanking him into the closest room, slamming the door closed, and engaging the lock.

At the moment, I don't care who sees us, and I don't care what they say.

My chest heaves as I stare at Evan while he backs into the sink. We are in a bathroom. I notice, but I can't focus on anything but him. I'm being an asshole, but I don't care. Covering the distance between us before I go back out there and break the man's hand for touching what's mine, I grab Evan's chin and press my lips to his. He kisses me back for a minute before pulling away. He tries to move away from me, but I pin his body between mine and the sink, not willing to let him go.

"Seriously, Alek, you're such an asshole," he hisses, his nostrils flaring. Fuck, he's so hot when he's angry. "You bro me, you won't even touch me all night, so worried they would figure out you're fucking me, then you come storming up here and do that? You won't even let people know we're dating. Hell, I don't even know if we're dating, yet you're mad another guy tried to talk to me—"

I cover his mouth, watching his eyes widen as I lean down. "Let me get one thing very clear, Evan. You are mine. We are dating. I have spent the entire evening smiling and small talking with your friends, and it wasn't because I like them. It was because I like you. I want you and want you to be happy. This is the last place I would ever want to be, but I came for you." His lips move against my palm. Sliding my hand down, I circle his throat. "So yes, I don't like him touching what's mine or the fact that you let him. Either I come in here and kiss the ever-loving shit out of you until I forget or I go out there and beat the shit out of him. It's your choice, baby."

I wait, watching his eyes look between mine before his mouth parts, and then he kisses me. "Good boy," I croon into his lips, dragging him closer.

He whimpers into my mouth, the sound going right to my cock, which has practically been hard since I saw him waiting for me on the sidewalk. My other hand slides under his cropped shirt, stroking his abs as I bite and suck his mouth. "I hate this fucking shirt just as much as I love it. I hate that they can all see you, but I love that I can touch you," I tell him as I tilt his head and run my lips along his neck. He rolls his hips into me, letting me feel his hardness beneath his cargos.

"Alek, please," he begs.

"I love the way you say my name when you want my dick, rich boy," I growl as I drop to my knees. Pushing his shirt up, I slide my lips along his abs, kissing him until he's panting, and then I suck on his nipples, watching as he swallows hard.

I fucking love how he reacts to me.

"Yes, baby?" I murmur as I lick down his abs and stop at the waistband of his pants, teasing him.

"Please," he implores, his hands grabbing my shoulders, urging me up. Chuckling darkly, I get back to my feet, wrapping my hand around his throat once more as I tilt his head back and kiss him.

Turning him to face the mirror, I keep one hand on his throat so he knows he belongs to me, while the other slides into his pants, circling his cock. "Moan for me, pretty boy, and let them all hear. Let that asshole hear who you are going home with tonight."

His head falls back against my shoulder as he watches me touch him through the mirror. The stark difference between us has me grinding into his ass. He's all golden and bright, and I look like the fucking devil behind him, all dark hair and eyes. It's a fucking sight, and I wish I could film it.

Later, I remind myself.

"Look at you," I murmur into his ear as I slide my lips down his neck. He reaches down, pushing his pants out of the way so I can see my hand palming his huge, hard dick. "Look how pretty you are. Whom do you belong to, rich boy?"

He just pants, his eyes locked on my hand, so I stop moving.

"Evan," I growl.

"You. I belong to you, now fucking touch me."

Chuckling, I bite his ear in warning. "So needy, pretty boy. You want me to let you come?"

"Yes." He groans, thrusting his cock into my hand.

"Then use me," I tell him, circling his cock. "Make yourself come while I watch."

His eyes clash with mine in the mirror as he thrusts into my hand, using it like he would his own.

Fuck, he's so pretty. Licking his neck, I keep my eyes on him, unable to look away as he writhes. I feel him jerking in my hand, and I know he's close.

He pulls his shirt up, exposing his rolling abs as he fucks himself into my grip, his cheeks red with desire. God, he's fucking perfection. I almost blow my load just from watching him, but I hold back. When I do come, it will be inside his ass.

Licking up his neck, I release my breath over his ear. "Come for me, pretty boy."

He lets out a whimper, biting down on his bottom lip as he thrusts into my hand and stills, coming all over me as he bites back his cry. Sliding my hand from his neck, I pull his lip from his teeth. "Let them hear, pretty boy," I order as his hips roll. He cries out louder, spilling in my hand until he finally slumps back into me.

Turning him to me, I pull up his pants and button them for him before I kiss him. "I was just going to play with you, but made me all needy, rich boy. It's your fault, so you need to deal with it. I refuse to take your perfect ass here though." I rub my thumb across his lips as he blinks. "But we have other ways. Put that pretty mouth to good use." I push him down, gripping his icy hair. "Show your boyfriend how grateful you are for him."

His eyes simmer at the word, his lips parting as he eagerly unbuckles my jeans and shoves them down. "Like that, do you? Me calling myself your boyfriend?"

He nods, his tongue darting out to wet his lips as his eyes land on my cock.

"Show me how much you like it," I demand.

He wraps his lips around the tip of my cock, sucking hard. The pressure makes my back bow as desire storms through me. He watches me, his eyes dancing with amusement and lust, as he opens his jaw wider and slides me into his wet, hot mouth. The sight causes me to thrust forward, forcing myself down his throat. He lets me as he breathes heavily through his nose. I hit the back of his throat and slide deeper still.

One of his hands circles the base of my cock, squeezing, while the other grips my thigh, tugging me closer as he licks and sucks my length. "Pretty boy." I slide my hand into his hair, messing it up as I pull out and thrust into his waiting mouth. "Jesus, fuck, I love the way you take me. You look goddamn beautiful while doing it. This mouth was made for me, wasn't it? Made for me to touch, taste, and fuck, just like that hot, little body. Every inch was made for me."

He nods, sucking me deeper and working me with his hand when he can't take me any farther.

"Fuck, look at you, baby," I murmur. "You are a goddamn work of art. I can't get enough of you. I need you all the fucking time. What have you done to me, rich boy?" I ramble as I fuck his mouth, unable to hold back, watching him worship me. It has things unlocking inside me, and when he hums around my cock, I explode with a shout, coming down his throat. I pull him up and rub his neck. "Swallow all of it," I demand, watching his Adam's apple bob as he swallows my cum.

I lean us into the sink as he wraps his arms around me and kisses me softly. "I'm yours, Alek," he promises, his voice slightly hoarse. His lips are raw and swollen and so fucking pretty I can't help kissing him again.

"Don't forget it," I murmur, leaning my head into his shoulder as I try to recover. When I can breathe normally, I fasten my pants and wash my hands as he watches me, a grin dancing over his lips.

"Stop looking at me like that, Evan," I warn.

"Or what?" he asks, leaning into the door.

"Or I'll take your ass right here and now rather than when we get home." I peer up at him as I dry my hands, our eyes meeting in the mirror. "Where I plan to spend all night buried inside you, pumping you so full of my cum, you'll be dripping for days."

He swallows, his eyes widening as I chuckle and head his way.

"That's what I thought. Let's go back to your friends before they send out a search party." Smirking, I rub his bruised, raw lips. They leave nothing to the imagination.

As soon as Evan goes out there, they will all know he's been fucking around, and I love that mark of possession on him.

We stay at the party for a few hours after our bathroom break. Everyone knew what happened, even if they didn't say anything, which I'm thankful for. I don't know how Alek would have reacted.

We stumble from the house, wrangling a very drunk Lally and Tommy into the car, and head back to campus. We idle outside of the dorms as Tommy watches Lally fall to the ground for the second time. "She was so pretty. Such a pussy tease."

"Uh-huh, so you said. You're a mess, come on." Tommy waves at us, hoisting her over his shoulder. "See you later, guys. Have a good night." He winks as he heads toward our dorm, where he'll let Lally crash. Lally has always been a messy drunk, especially if she doesn't get her way, which she didn't tonight.

"I'm sorry she nearly vomited in your car." I wince.

"It's fine, baby," he replies, kissing my knuckles as he smiles. "Are you ready for bed?"

I swallow with a nod, knowing exactly what he means from the glint in his eyes and the wicked grin tugging at his lips. He promised to fuck me all night.

We barely park before he's out of the car, yanking me out of my seat and throwing me over his shoulder. He storms through the front door, slamming it and tossing me onto the sofa. "Alice is at her apartment tonight," he says, his eyes wild as he removes his shirt and shoves his jeans down. "And I can't wait. Bend over the couch, pretty boy."

My eyes slide down his body, and I note every hard inch of muscle leading to his huge, hard dick, his thick thighs begging to be grabbed as he stalks toward me.

"Evan," he warns, the streetlights shining behind him. The lights are on in here, casting a low light over the room, and there's a dangerous glint in his eyes, the one that makes me harder than hell.

"You want me, princess? Come and get me," I taunt as I back away.

"Evan," he snaps.

Laughing, I turn and race toward the kitchen. He catches me in the hall, throwing his weight into me so we hit the wall, denting it, but he doesn't care. He rips off my top before I escape, sliding away and darting into the kitchen. He follows, stalking me, and lifts my shirt to his nose, inhaling.

"When I catch you, pretty boy, I'm going to make you regret running."

"Oh, big bad Alek," I tease. "Too slow to catch weak rich boy."

He dives over the table I'm hiding behind. I skid around it and run back into the hall. This time, I make it to the stairs before I'm slammed into the steps. It takes my breath away, and the pictures on the wall rattle with the force. My boots are yanked off, then my pants before I turn and kick him away. He falls back a few steps, and I manage to get to my feet and turn, intending to race up the stairs, but his arm bands around me and flings me through the air.

I hit the couch none too gently, and I'm pushed down on it. My ass is yanked into the air, and I gasp when he spits, his saliva hitting my ass and dribbling between my cheeks.

"I warned you. I was going to be nice, but now I don't think I will. I think I'll make it hurt."

"Alek!" I gasp as he pushes my head down. I can barely breathe against the leather as he kicks my legs wider, and I feel his cock press against my ass. "Don't you dare—" My warning ends in a cry as he starts to push inside me.

He stretches me to the point of pain, making it hurt like he promised.

I should have known better than to taunt the devil.

I whimper as he pushes deeper into me, his thick cock invading me to the point of agony. "Shh," he murmurs, rubbing my back, and then he spits again and pulls out, wetting his cock and pushing back in. "Good boy, take all of me." His grip is bruising on my hips as he yanks me back, sliding those final few inches home.

The burn is too much, and I try to pull away, but he pulls me back, holding me prisoner, and then he fucks me with hard, brutal thrusts as tears fall from my eyes.

Softly, so different than the way he's fucking me, he brushes them away. "God, you feel so good, baby, so fucking good. Shh, I've got you."

I cry out as he tilts my hips up, finding that spot inside me that has my eyes crossing and agony mixing with such intense pleasure, I nearly black out.

"That's it, pretty boy, cry for me. Fuck, I love the way you look under me, stretched out like this. I love how tight your pretty ass is wrapped around my cock. You feel so fucking good." His hand slides down my back and cups my balls, squeezing before wrapping around my cock and stroking me as he pummels into my ass. "I want this all fucking day and night—you under me, over me, on me, riding me, taking me . . . letting me claim what's mine."

Fuck, I created a monster, but I can't seem to care as I push back, needing that sharp edge of pain only he seems to give me.

"Alek, princess, please," I beg, thrusting into his hand as he fucks my ass.

"Please, what? Tell me, Evan."

"Please fuck me harder," I implore, pushing backward. "I want it to hurt."

He bends over my back, letting me feel every hard inch of his skin as he powers into me, his hand tightening on my cock. "Like this, pretty boy? You want to feel me with every step you take? Want me to ruin you?"

"Yes, yes, yes," I chant, my voice tight as pleasure spirals through me so strongly, I struggle not to fall.

My cock jerks in his grip as I bite down on the couch, muffling my cries as he hammers into me. His teeth find my neck and sink in, marking me. The sharp edge of pain blends with pleasure until I can't take it anymore. My balls draw up, and my cock swells in his grip.

"That's it, baby, come for me," he orders against my neck.

With a gasp, I fall over the edge. Ropes of cum splatter my chest, his hand, and the leather as I shake and jerk from the ecstasy racing through me. He continues to fuck my tightening ass, his crooning voice in my ear. He drags his hands over every inch of me as I whimper.

"Alek."

"Shh, you can take it. I want you to come again." He turns my head, kissing me deeply and swallowing my moans as his thrusts become slow and rolling. Slowly, my cock starts to harden again. My need for him is great, and I push back to meet him, nipping his lips in the dark.

"There you are, pretty boy," he praises as he leans back, wrapping his hand around my throat and dragging me up to my knees as he pummels my ass. His other hand slides down my abs to grip my dick again, working it hard and fast with my own cum. His massive cock swells inside me, and I know he's close, his breathing heavy in my ear.

"Come for me," he orders, slamming into me so deeply it hurts, hitting that spot that has me bellowing in ecstasy. As he wanted, I come again as he groans my name, pushing deeper still, and I feel his hot cum fill me as his hand tightens on my throat, pressing me against him so neither of us have an inch of space.

He turns my head with his hand and drops a kiss onto my lips. "Good boy, now let's clean you up and get you in my bed so I can start all over again."

The wicked promise sends a shiver of need through me, one I know he controls.

Alek is sleeping soundly on his back, with one arm behind his head, and the other gripping me tightly, his leg thrown over mine. The sheets are pooled low, showing off his abs and muscles, and I get distracted for a moment by his beauty before I focus on his face.

I can't sleep, unease making my mind turn.

He struggled tonight. He didn't want anyone to know we were together, yet he got jealous. That's a good sign, right? It leaves me feeling . . . vulnerable. Will he ever be able to admit what we are? I thought so, but I'm scared he won't. I'm scared I'll always be a secret in the dark he reaches for. The brutal truth is, though, that I don't think I could ever get over Alek Anders. He showed up in my life like a whirlwind, and I might have acted like it, but I never hated him. I wanted him, and I think I always will. There's something in this broken, brutal man that calls to me and makes me want to fix him, to love him.

I'm starting to love him. Maybe that's why I'm sitting here with fear pounding in my chest—because I'm falling in love with Alek, but I don't know if he could ever love me or accept that he loves me.

Where does that leave me?

I'm so scared to fall alone, afraid he won't be there to catch me and will turn away from me like everyone else. I'm terrified I still won't be enough to be loved. Maybe I'm more fucked up from my past than I realized, but as I stroke his peaceful face, I can't help the terror that races through my blood.

"Please love me," I whisper. "Please don't be like everyone else. I don't think I could stand it."

Everyone I love leaves and hurts me.

Will he be different?

Laying my head on his chest, I close my eyes and fight back tears as he sighs and wraps his arms around me, holding me tight without even realizing it, and for the first time in my life, I feel hope.

Hope that we can face this together.

That hope is crushed early the next morning—no, not crushed, shattered, stomped on, and left behind like a glittering pool of glass, the shards so sharp they cut into me, making me bleed as I stare at the man I care for.

Sitting at Alek's table, I scroll through my school emails when it pops up.

I quickly scan the text and sit up straighter, my hand almost shaking as I reread it to make sure what I'm seeing is correct.

"You okay, rich boy?" Alek murmurs, his foot locked around mine under the table as he eats. He pauses, looking me over. "You look like an excited, yappy dog about to pee."

"Lovely," I mutter, sliding my phone over, excitement racing through me along with trepidation, although I don't know why.

He reads it swiftly before pushing it back across to me without saying a word.

"Well?"

"No."

"No?" I repeat, blinking. "No what?"

"You need my permission. That's why you showed me, right?" he asks, shoving toast into his mouth. "No."

"Alek, my professor wants to put my images in the end of term showcase. That's a really big deal. Industry professionals will be there—"

"Even more of a reason for me to say no," he snaps, his fork clattering to his plate as I stare into his angry eyes.

"You're angry about this," I murmur.

"I'm not." He sighs. "I'm just—no, okay?"

Now I know why I was worried, because I knew how he would react. I knew he wouldn't want this. If I were a girl, would he have the same response?

"This is important, Alek," I whisper, clutching my phone as he stands and throws his plate in the sink. His back is to me, his hands braced on the counter. "This is a really big deal. They never choose first years for this. It could be what makes my career, and it makes me even happier that it's with pictures of you . . . someone I care about."

"I don't want that many people to see me like that," he mutters, shame lacing his tone.

"Like what?" I ask as I stand.

"Jesus, Evan, just fucking no!" he yells as he turns, his fists clenched at his sides. "You know what they'll think, what they'll all say." His eyes are wide now, panicked.

Rounding the table slowly, I cover his hands. "Hey, it's okay. They won't think anything at all. They'll be awed by you, just like I am. It's going to be okay. Can you just think—"

"I said no," he snaps, pulling his hands from me and pushing me back in the process. I hit the table hard, rattling the pots as he stares at me. "Can't you respect what I want? I did it for you, not for everyone else. Doesn't the fact that I don't want people to see me like that matter to you?"

"If I were a girl showing those photos, would you care?" I retort, and he freezes but doesn't reply. "So it isn't because of what they are, but who took them. Is that right? You think they'll see my name attached and assume you're my boyfriend. So fucking what if they do? Can't I show you off?"

"Just fucking stop." He pinches his nose. "I'm going to be late for work. Catch the bus or take a taxi today." He stomps upstairs, and I watch him go.

My hope shatters around me since I just got my answer.

Alek Anders will never want the world to know about us, too scared of what it means.

So where does that leave us?

It leaves me a devastated mess in his kitchen, realizing I fell in love with a man who will never love me the way I do him.

SHAW DRIVE
ANDERS AVE
ONE WAY
NO PARKING
ACTIVE DRIVEWAY
THE MOMENT
STOP
ZOO
NO PARKING
SALE
SILENT ROSE
Pine Valley
EVER

THIRTY

I should be at work, but I find myself at the racetrack, watching Sky cut corners and push his car to the limit. He might be an illegal racer, but he's trying his hardest to become legit and part of a team here in Pine Valley. When he pulls up and gets out, tugging off his helmet, I nod at him.

His eyebrow rises as he waves at someone watching and heads my way, hopping the short wall between us. I lean back into my car as he pushes his sweaty black hair from his face.

"I've never seen you here before. You okay, man?" I stay silent, staring at my feet, and he sighs. "Alek, what's wrong?"

"What do you mean?" I mutter.

"I've known you for years, and you've never sought me out, so something is wrong and you want advice or a friendly ear. You don't have any other friends, hence you being here, so spill it. What's up?"

"Smart-ass," I mutter.

"No one else could put up with you," he scoffs, "and since I'm guessing it's about Evan . . ." I meet his eyes, and he nods. "So I'm right. What did you do?"

"Why do you assume I did something?"

His eyebrow arches again. "Alek, you're an idiot, grumpy and rude—"

"Thanks."

"You can't speak without putting your foot in your mouth, and you don't know how to express yourself normally, so I'm assuming you fucked up, and now you're wondering how to fix it. Am I right?" Sky asks, nudging my shoulder.

"I shouldn't have come here. You're an ass." I push off my car, but he grabs my arm and tugs me back.

"Come on, tell me. That's what friends are for. I know you don't like to need or rely on anybody, but you can trust me, Alek. I might tease you, but we're friends, and I want you to be happy, so talk."

"Don't you need to practice?" I ask, my eyes landing on the track.

"The track will still be there. My friend is more important," he replies without an ounce of hesitation.

Kicking the rocks with my boots, I debate how to start, but it just blurts out of me. "I said some stupid shit, and then I stormed upstairs. When I came down, he was gone. Shit, I should have stayed, but I was scared and angry, and I just needed a minute so I didn't say something that would hurt him out of fear, but I saw that sad puppy-dog look in his eyes, saw the hurt, and I just left. Now he's gone and not replying to my texts, and I don't even blame him."

"Okay, okay, start at the beginning. What did you fight over?" he asks. I hear no judgment in his voice. He's just trying to work through it, and I realize Sky is right. I need someone to listen and help. I need someone who doesn't love me the way Evan does to tell me the truth.

I explain what happened, and he listens. "Okay, so you actually didn't want those pictures to be shown because Evan took them or—"

"No, of course not. Shit, I'm so proud of him. He was worried, and for his photos to be recognized? I know it's a big deal. I'm just worried how people will react," I admit. "That they'll know."

"Know that you two are together?" he asks, and when I nod, he meets my eyes, considering his response for a moment. "Would that be such a bad thing, Alek? The world isn't the same as it was before, and there is nothing wrong with loving Evan, with loving a man. Why are you so scared?"

"I'm not scared," I snap, but I slump back into the car, my eyes on the track. "You don't understand. You're so proud of who you are—"

"I wasn't always. I'm not saying I had it easy, Alek, because I didn't. You aren't the only one who struggled to accept who he is, but would it really be such a bad thing to be loved like that? Evan is so proud of you, he wants to show you off and talk about you. He's letting you into his life, he's reaching for you over and over, and you're pushing him away. I wonder if it's because you are really scared of everyone finding out or if you think you don't deserve his love." He straightens. "If you can't accept it publicity, at least accept it privately."

"What do you mean?" I whisper.

"That you are falling in love with a man . . . that you are gay, Alek. You have to accept that and love yourself for it or no one will ever be able to, and if you aren't careful, you'll lose a man who is willing to wait and hold you through it, and you'll regret it forever. Trust me on that and just talk to him. Tell him why you're scared and let him understand because right now, he thinks you're ashamed of him. He thinks he should be a secret, and I'm guessing he thinks it means he isn't good enough to be loved."

"What?" I snap. "Nothing could be further from the truth. He's so fucking amazing. He's smart, talented, kind, and strong, and he has this laugh that just makes everything better. The world is brighter when he's around! How could he ever think he isn't good enough to be loved?"

"Words are cheap, Alek. Actions speak more. Evan strikes me as the type of person who takes everything to heart. If he's been hurt in the past, then that scar is still there. It's your job to help heal it, not create more. Figure out what you want and fast because"—his hand lands on my shoulder—"rather you want to admit it or not, you already love that boy."

"I can't lose him," I admit, "but I don't know if I'm ready."

"You can't have both." He smiles sadly. "Be someone he's proud of. Be someone you're proud of. You are strong, Alek, the strongest person I know, so if anyone can stand up and shout about who they are, it's you. Fuck what anyone else thinks or says. It doesn't matter. All that matters is the people you care for and what they think, and we are here, right behind you, supporting you."

"You're right," I murmur.

"Say that again." He smirks, making me laugh.

"Don't get cocky." I push him back. "Thank you for being my friend, Sky, even when I'm stubborn—"

"Or rude or mean or an asshole." He laughs as I smack him again. My phone vibrates, and I pull it out, hoping it's Evan, but my heart sinks and drops at the text I see displayed on my screen.

Alice: There's been an accident on campus.

My heart freezes, and my body becomes cold as the world buzzes around me. My eyes catch on the word—accident.

Alice.

Evan.

I get into my car without a word and race toward the only people in this world I care about. All the while, my heart pounds with fear that either of them could be hurt and that I could lose them.

No, I can't.

My foot hits the pedal as I race through red lights to get to them.

THIRTY-ONE

I did as Alek suggested. I left, taking the bus to campus, needing that time to think. I wear my headphones, blasting my music as the world passes, and I ignore people I know as I walk the path toward the art building. I'm early, earlier than even the teachers, but I need time to think.

My phone buzzes, and I stop walking, pulling it out.

> Alek: I'm sorry. Can we talk?

> Alek: Did you get to school safely?

> Alek: I'm sorry I ruined a good night.

> Alek: No, a great fucking night. Just text me back, pretty boy.

I debate responding, my fingers hovering over the keys before I sigh and put my phone away just as something hits me hard. I fly to the side, hitting the ground, my headphones falling off. The music turns into screams as I stare into Tommy's worried, terrified eyes.

"Evan!" he snaps. "We were shouting at you."

"What? Why?" I look past him as he crouches before me. My entire body turns cold as I freeze, the screams making sense now.

The tree I stopped under blows in the breeze, and hanging from its lowest branches, swaying like leaves in the wind, are two bodies hanging from their necks, right above where I was standing.

There's a crack, the branch beginning to break, and Tommy shakes me. "Are you okay?"

I nod, climbing to my feet as we both turn to stare.

Nausea crawls up my throat, and I swallow bile. I've never seen a dead body before, and these—oh god. Their necks are bent at strange angles, their bones sticking through where dark brown rope is wrapped around them multiple times. It's hard to make out their faces from here, and I'm grateful for that. Their skin is a weird color, and the birds and insects on them make me turn my head and gag.

My horror only grows as what I'm seeing sinks in.

Two people are hanging.

Dead.

"What's going on? Oh my god!" Alice screams. I quickly grab her and turn her around, my hand over her eyes.

"Don't look," I tell her. "Has anyone called the police?"

"One of them did." Tommy points at the crowd. I spy some people taking pictures, and my stomach rolls. Even in death, they can't find peace from this world.

"Come on." Holding Alice, I grab Tommy and lead them to the building to avoid the crowd and bodies. Alice is pale and shaking, so I grab us some coffee, my hands wrapped around the warm mug, but I can barely feel it.

Is this shock?

Alice's hand shakes as she types out a message. I keep my arm around her as we sit in the cafeteria.

"They were dead," Tommy whispers.

I nod, unsure what to say.

"Did they kill themselves?" he asks. "Why here? Why like that?"

"I don't know," I admit. "Let's wait for the police, okay? Alice, are you okay?"

Her head jerks up, her face pale, and she nods too rapidly. "I texted Alek."

"That's good." I take her hand, and we all stare out of the window as sirens split the air and police descend upon the campus, alongside news crews.

We sit and watch it all, quiet and horrified.

Did they kill themselves?

It repeats in my head.

Everyone is being interviewed. There are so many cops, they make quick work of it, but they let Alice, Tommy, and me stick together.

"So that's all you saw?" the older officer asks. He has to be in his mid-forties, with salt-and-pepper hair and kind eyes that have seen too much. His name tag reads "Winchester." His partner, on the other hand, is younger, with short black hair and cold eyes. He writes everything down carefully.

"Yes, I pulled them inside after. I didn't want Alice to see anymore," I admit. "Are they . . . Did they kill themselves?"

"We will have to wait for the investigation," Winchester replies. "We are asking everyone here if they knew them."

"We didn't see their faces," I tell him. "I didn't want to."

He nods and pulls out his phone and slides it across to show two pictures side by side. They are up close photographs of the bodies, showing only their faces. "We have positive identification of them, Kenny Rogers and Dodge Kennedy. They attended this university, and their roommates reported them missing weeks ago."

Ice flows through my veins as I stare at the images.

"I don't know them. Sorry, it's a big school," Tommy admits.

"And you, Mr. Shaw?" the younger one asks.

My head snaps up as I meet his eyes. "I know them," I say, and they both focus on me. "They were hassling Alice on her way home one night."

"When was this?" he asks.

"Um, a few weeks ago?" I reply.

"Tuesday the fourteenth," Alice says. "I remember because I had a meeting with a teacher just before."

"That was the night they disappeared." They share a look and then look back at me. "And what happened?"

"They tried to assault her, and I stepped in to stop it." I leave Alek out, not liking how they are looking at me as it is. They would take one look at him and wouldn't hear anything he said.

"Did you hurt them?" the younger one asks.

"No, I just stopped them. They disappeared after?"

"Evan Shaw, we need you to come with us."

I stand, looking between them. "Why?"

"Because you might be the last person who saw them alive, and then you found the bodies. It's suspicious," he snaps.

"We just need to ask you some questions." Winchester frowns at his partner and then smiles at me kindly. "Can you come with us?"

I know it's a question, but if I protest, they won't leave me alone. Nodding, I grab my bag and give Alice a meaningful look, telling her not to bring up Alek, and then I meet Tommy's wide, shocked eyes. "Stay with her until her brother arrives, okay?"

"Of course, man. Are you going to be okay? Should I call someone?" he asks as the officers stop at my side to guide me out of the room.

"No need for that. It's just an informal chat." Winchester smiles. "You should head back to class or home. Please come to us if you hear anything." They grab my arms.

Informal my ass.

I'm basically being arrested.

They think I had something to do with their deaths, which tells me this wasn't suicide. This was murder.

I do throw up this time.

NO PARKING
ACTIVE
DRIVEWAY
SHAW DRIVE
THE
MOMENT
ONE WAY
STOP
ANDERS AVE
TOO
SILENT ROSE
NO
PARKING
SALE
Pine Valley
EVER

THIRTY-TWO

When I see all the police and the news crews, the panic I feel can't be contained. I grab someone at random as they hurry past. "Have you seen Alice Anders and Evan Shaw?"

The girl nods. "They went inside." She points, and I sprint up the stairs, taking them two at a time, only to run into Alice at Tommy's side just inside the door.

Tommy nods. "Alek."

"Alice, are you okay?" I grab her, looking her over. "Talk to me."

"I'm okay, I'm okay," she replies, covering my hands. "Shh, I'm okay, I promise."

Relief makes me slump, but then I look around. "Where's Evan?"

They share a look, one I don't like, and my heart skips a beat. "Alice, where the fuck is my boyfriend?"

"He was taken away by the cops," she whispers.

"What?" I snap, peering into her eyes. "Why?"

"There were two bodies, Alek, hanging here. They were the guys who bothered me. They knew Evan assaulted them, and they took him away. I'm worried. He isn't going to be blamed for saving me, is he?" Tears flow down her cheeks, and I pull her closer, kissing her head. I try to contain my anger and panic as I comfort her, but my entire focus is on my boy.

"No, it's okay. It's probably just routine," I say, but I look at Tommy, who appears concerned.

"Tommy, I need you to take Alice home, okay? Or to your dorm, or call Lally." I kiss her head and brush her tears away like I did when she was a kid. "Are you sure you're okay?"

She nods, wrapping her arms around herself. "Where are you going?"

"I need to help Evan," I reply, torn between my duty to my sister and the man I . . . well, him.

"How?" she asks.

"I don't know, but I have to try." I point at Tommy again. "Straight home, and call me if anything happens." Turning, I yank my phone out as I race to my car.

Evan. Arrested. Bodies. The words repeat in my head.

God, pretty boy, please be okay.

"Where the hell have you been?" I snap, pushing away from the police station wall as Bones heads my way, dressed head to toe in a fancy as fuck suit that cost more than my entire house. He's the only person I could think of. I'd consider him a friend, or at least a sparring partner. He teaches a lot of self-defense classes, but I know he is training to be a lawyer and his dad is one.

"Is he inside?" he asks calmly, appearing smooth and cold as usual.

I nod, clenching my fists. "They won't let me in or tell me anything, just that it's an informal chat."

"Good, that's good. They can't charge him or haven't yet." He straightens his tie. "Don't worry, Alek, I've got this."

"Shouldn't we call your dad or something?" I ask. I mean, he hasn't passed his exams yet.

"No need, I can handle this. Besides, Evan is one of ours." I frown at that, and he smiles. "Don't worry, just wait here."

I can't do anything but watch him head inside the station, and then I wait again. Minutes turn into an hour, and then two. I'm about to storm in and drag them out when the door opens. A pale-faced, exhausted Evan comes out after Bones, who looks pissed.

"What the hell took so long?" I demand as I stop before them.

Evan's eyes widen when he sees me. "Alek?" He frowns. "What are you doing here?"

"He called me." Bones shrugs. "Just remember what I said, Evan. Ignore them, you told them everything you know. They have nothing on you. Come to me if they bother you again." He pats Evan's shoulder before nodding at me and heading back to his car, leaving Evan and me staring at each other.

I cover the distance, but he steps back, and I drop my hands. "Are you okay?"

"Yeah, just tired, and my head hurts," he admits as he walks past me. I follow him to the sidewalk where he turns to face me. The distance between us is killing me.

"What happened?" I ask, my hands in my pockets to stop myself from reaching for him, assuring myself he's okay.

"Those two guys that we beat up . . ." He lowers his voice. "They are dead. I admitted to what happened that night, but I left you out."

"You didn't have to—"

"I wanted to protect you," he protests. "They questioned me, but they have nothing, so they had to let me go, which they weren't happy about, and Bones was pissed." He looks up at me. "I also didn't mention your name because I was worried."

"Worried?" I repeat, confusion lacing my tone.

"I have to ask," he murmurs. "Did you do it? Did you kill them?"

"Me?" I snort. "I'm flattered you think I'm capable of murder, though I am sad you think I wouldn't hide it better, but no, I didn't kill them, Evan. I would have if they touched my sister, so don't think I'm a good guy."

He relaxes, scrubbing at his face. "I had to ask."

"Pretty boy . . ." I step closer, and his hand drops.

"I'm really tired, Alek. Can we do this later?"

My heart aches, but I nod. "Okay, let me take you home, and we can talk tomorrow—"

"Can we not?" My heart stops as he looks away. "Can we just not talk tomorrow?"

"What do you mean?" I whisper, panic filling me as my stomach plummets. Staring at his pale face, I have a sinking feeling I've lost him. "Are you breaking up with me?"

"We would have to be dating for me to break up with you," he retorts, his voice filled with venom as he looks at me before he sighs again, his shoulders dropping. "I just need some time to process, and I think we both need some space."

"This morning—" I start. "I was wrong." I don't know what else to say, and when I don't explain further, he laughs bitterly.

"You want to know why I wanted to show those photos? Not because of what you are doing in them, but because it's you and I'm so proud to be yours, even if it's in secret, but you don't feel the same. You're not proud, you're ashamed, and that fucking hurts, so give me space."

I take one step back, letting him track the movement. "You want space? There, that's all the space you'll get from me."

"Alek," he snaps, annoyance flaring in his eyes. "You don't get to control this or order me around. You don't get to stop me from being hurt or upset. You made the choice to deny us this morning. Now, I'm allowed to make my choice to figure out how I feel about all this." He waves his hand between us, his voice deadly serious and laced with pain.

He's right, and I hate it. I step back again, my heart aching something fierce. "Sure, okay," I respond coolly, calmly, even though my insides are anything but. If I push this now, I'll lose him and he'll leave. He's hanging on by a thread.

"Let me take you home," I offer, hoping for one more moment in his presence.

· · ·

He shakes his head. "I'll walk." He hesitates, grinding his jaw before he meets my gaze. "Thank you for calling Bones. Bye, Anders."

He called me Anders, not Alek, princess, or asshole. Anders.

He's putting space between us, and I hate it. I hate that I ruined the only good thing I had. He turns without another word and wanders away, looking far too lonely and tired.

As I watch him go, I wonder how everything went so wrong.

How could we go from being so happy to being so broken?

THIRTY-THREE

"Two college students' bodies were found today—" I skip to the next channel numbly. "The deceased are students at Pine Valley." Hitting the off button, I stare at the black screen. It feels weird to be in my dorm since I've been spending so many nights at Alek's, but I need my own space to think.

While I was being asked the same thing over and over, and then left alone, it was all I could think about—us and how to put it into perspective. Life's too short to be unhappy, and I don't want to be unhappy. I like Alek a lot, but I don't want to hurt him nor myself by loving him. We both need to figure out what we want, and to do that, I can't see him because when I do, all I think about is him, and nothing else matters but our own little world.

Lally sighs, her head resting on one shoulder. Tommy's on the other as we sit on my single bed, our legs hanging over the side. "I can't believe they hung themselves. I mean, they were assholes from what you said, but still . . ."

I don't say anything about what I uncovered while being questioned. I don't want to worry my friends any more than I already have.

"Are you okay, Evan? You're quiet," Tommy asks.

"Mm." I can feel them looking at me. They were here when I got back. Tommy escorted Alice home, and then he called Lally. They grilled me as soon as I walked in, but I told them how tired I was, and luckily, they let it drop, but they refuse to leave me, knowing something is wrong.

"I can't believe they took you to the station. What assholes!" Lally snaps. "If I could, I'd march down there and grill their asses."

That makes my lips curve. "I'm surprised you weren't rallying outside."

"I stopped her." Tommy snorts. "Alek seemed to have it under control, and I didn't want her to get thrown in jail alongside you."

"Cellmates," Lally whispers as I nod, but the sound of Alek's name makes my heart clench.

"Where is Alek?" Tommy asks.

"Home." I shrug, and they must hear something in my tone.

"Uh-oh, trouble in paradise?" Lally asks.

Sighing dramatically, I place my head on her lap, and she strokes my hair as I continue to stare at the black TV screen.

"Tell your besties," Tommy urges, rubbing my legs. "We might not help you commit murder—" He groans as a pillow hits him. "What?"

It does the trick, and I smile, turning to look up at my ceiling. I'm unable to look at them as I speak, telling them about the email and our fight. They are quiet for a moment until Lally's serious voice comes.

"Do you love Alek, Evan?"

I turn to meet her hard gaze. "I think I'm starting to," I admit fearfully. "Maybe I should just do as he says and not show the photos and just accept us as we are. Maybe it's enough and I'm just pushing for too much. I knew when we started this that he wasn't ready. It isn't fair for me to punish him now."

"That's bullshit," Tommy snaps. "He said time, and that means evolution. If it's staying the same, then how is that changing anything? I get not wanting to be open yet and feeling confused, but there is a difference between that and forcing the person you love to deny their future over your own fear."

"Maybe he just cares more than he lets on?" I suggest as I sit up.

"Evan Shaw, you fucking listen to me right this second," Lally snaps, and my eyes widen at her angry tone as she points right in my face.

"Do you really feel that fucking low about yourself that you would put up with someone treating you like shit? Treating you so fucking badly just because you're desperate to be loved and accepted, even if that means he never makes you a priority, shows you off, or claims you publicly? Tell me you have more respect for yourself than that, Evan. You deserve to be loved loudly and in public. You deserve to be happy, not sad and worried because you made the mistake of kissing him in public or taking his hand or showing some pictures. Don't fucking settle, Evan. I mean it. I know you think Alek Anders is your soulmate, but what if you're just a passing fling to him? Have you ever thought about that? You're just an experiment, something to try. To you, he's your forever, but to him, you're just for now. I love you, Evan, but I don't like who you are becoming. My best friend would never accept this. The man who fought every single person, including his family, to be openly bi would never accept a love that meant he had to hide who he was. We want you to be happy, and I thought Alek was it too, but if he isn't, then cut him loose. You don't bend for him or change who you are for someone you love. You grow with them. So tell me, Evan, is Alek worth it? Is he worth it all?"

Is that what it comes down to?

I spent so long fighting to be proud of who I am, so can I go back to being ashamed of it just to keep him? Can I change who I am just to keep the person I love?

"I love him," I whisper, admitting it for the first time. "I love him, and it hurts."

"I know." They both take my hands. "Love shouldn't hurt like that, Evan. Love should make you stronger, not weaker. It shouldn't put you in knots. I love you, Evan, we both do, and we are worried for you. We've never seen you like this for anyone—like you have become a mirror, reflecting what Alek wants to see, not who you really are. We want you to be happy."

"I know." I feel tears dripping down my face, and I dash them away. "What if I can't walk away? What if I'm not strong enough to?"

"Then you aren't the Evan we know and love," Tommy murmurs. "You aren't the Evan who stands up for those weaker than himself, and you're not the Evan who stepped in front of me when we got jumped when my old friends found out I was bi. You're not the guy who fights for everyone. Remember who you are, Evan, because you are fucking amazing, and if you need to walk away, then do it. Don't settle just because you think it's all you deserve."

He wraps his arms around me, and Lally does as well so they are both holding me. I cry in their embrace. "I thought he was the one."

"I know." Lally kisses my cheek, holding me tighter. "He still might be, but you need to fight for yourself, Evan, for your heart. Don't hand it to someone who doesn't deserve you. If it gets broken, we'll be right here with ice cream and bad movies, ready to cry with you. We are your family."

That only makes me sob harder, and I cry for everything I've lost.

For the boy who just wanted his parents' love and approval.

For the boy who only wanted his first love to end happily.

For the boy who can't help but fall for the one who wishes he were everything he's not.

For the man who would do anything for the man he's fallen in love with, while he would only do the bare minimum.

For the heart I healed and gave away again, only to be broken once more.

This time, I'll keep it. I'll give it to myself.

Alek Anders might be the love of my life, but I'm not his, and that's what it boils down to.

I thought he was my forever, but for him, I'm just his present, and it hurts.

Lally and Tommy are snoring. She's on the floor, between our beds, our hands still linked as I stare at the ceiling. I should be worried about the police and the bodies, but all I can think about is my aching heart.

It's breaking, and I hate it. I know they are right.

I either have to love him fully or let him go. There can't be any in-between. I need answers, but I'm scared to get them because I know it will mean the end of us.

My phone buzzes, and I turn my head, checking it.

Alek: I'm sorry, Evan.

I snort and look away. He's sorry. He's *always* sorry. It's Alek's move. He breaks it and then tries to fix it. He's so focused on protecting his family and his life, he doesn't even seem to care about his own heart and fixing that.

I know Alek is hesitant for a reason, and I know a little about his past. I thought I could wait and maybe fix him, but you can't fix people who don't want to be fixed.

Some people want to remain broken because it's easier.

I know I'm young, but even at my age, I know there will never be another Alek Anders. He was born to be mine and be loved by me. We were born to be together, but this world is cruel and it tears apart happiness, and sometimes love isn't enough.

It can't change everything.

I loved my parents, even through their prejudice and hatred, and they still rejected me.

I loved my friends through their confusion, and they still walked away.

I loved a man through his hesitancy, and it did nothing but pull us apart.

I loved myself even when others said I shouldn't, and I'm still here, hurt and wondering why I'm not good enough.

I'm just so lost.

How the hell am I supposed to have this all figured out like everyone expects? I'm supposed to have a dream and follow it, but also work hard, have fun, and enjoy life without making mistakes. I am supposed to love but not too much or too openly. This whole life is a contradiction, and it's so fucking exhausting sometimes just to be alive.

I'm trying to figure things out and find my way, but it just feels like I'm failing all the time and doing everything wrong. I'm standing still where I am, while everyone else is moving on.

I just want Alek to hold me and tell me it's going to be okay, but I can't even have that.

I can't even have the man I love. Isn't that some bullshit?

NO PARKING
ACTIVE
DRIVEWAY
SHAW DRIVE
THE
MOMENT
ANDERS AVE
ONE WAY
TOO
STOP
SILENT ROSE
NO
PARKING
SALE
EVER

THIRTY-FOUR

ALEK

"**I** can't believe they are partying after everything."

I lift my head from the kitchen table, where I had been aimlessly staring at my phone, hoping Evan would call or text. I haven't heard from him since yesterday when he said he needed space.

Well, he's had some, and I fucking hate it. I don't want space. I want him.

"Who is?" I murmur. I forced Alice to move back here. I don't know what the fuck is happening on her campus, but two people are dead, two people who harassed her, and I want to keep her as safe as possible. She's the only thing in this world I care about—well, her and Evan, who is currently ignoring me.

"People at our school. I mean, seriously, what kind of—oh shit, is that Evan?" I'm up and over the sofa in an instant, grabbing her phone. She yelps and tries to take it back. It's an Instagram story panning around a party, and my eyes narrow.

"Where?" I ask.

"Maybe it wasn't . . ." She trails off when we see Evan. He's laughing and surrounded by his friends. Some guy has his arm around his shoulders and is leaning into him, and I see red.

Leaping up, I point in her face. "Text me the address and do not leave this fucking house. Lock up after me." Snatching my keys, I rush out the door and climb in my car a moment later. Jealousy and anger fuel me as I pull into traffic, almost backing into a car.

I check my phone and put in the address. It's on the other side of campus, and I fume the entire drive.

How can he ignore me and then go out and flirt and hang on some other guy? He said he needed space, and he's doing this? Yeah, it pisses me off, but it also makes me so jealous I can barely see straight. I don't even park when I pull up. I just abandon my car and storm inside. People move out of my way, no doubt seeing the look in my eyes and not wanting to fuck with me.

"Hey, Alek," Lally calls with a frown as I search the crowd.

"Where is he?" I demand.

Her eyes widen, and she steps into my path. "Nope, not happening, big guy. You need to calm down before you find him. I'm not having you raining all that down on him."

Breathing heavily, I fist my hands at my sides and try to calm down. "I'm not going to hurt him."

"You already have," she says softly. It lands, and I flinch. "Alek, why don't you go, and he'll talk to you when he's ready?"

"I can't," I tell her, and his laughter reaches me. The sound is more familiar than my own heartbeat, and so bright and beautiful it makes my soul ache. I fight the smile that wants to curl my lips because he didn't laugh for me.

Moving past Lally, I follow the sound and find him sitting in the middle of the living room. He's telling some story, and everyone hangs onto his every word. A girl has her hand on his thigh. She leans into his side, her eyes bright with alcohol and desire, and he doesn't seem to care.

I feel like an intruder, and I hate it.

I hate that she's touching him when I can't.

I hate that he's happy while I'm falling apart without him.

"Evan," I call.

He turns, and the chatter dies down, every eye turning to us. I see people nudging their friends and whispering, but I don't care. All I care about is how his smile dies when he sees me and he stands.

"Alek, what are you doing here?" he asks, sounding confused, a cup dangling from his hands.

"I'm here for you," I answer without shame. He runs his eyes over me like he always does, but this time, when they clash with mine, there's a coolness there I don't like.

"How did you know I was here?" he asks, and it's silent except for our conversation. I hesitate, and he frowns, heading my way as I move closer.

He meets me in the middle of the room. "I don't like that she's all over you," I say slowly.

"You have no right to be jealous or pissed," he retorts, crossing his arms.

"No? How about the fact that you're out here partying when two people just died, and you're drinking."

He flinches. "To forget you," he admits.

"You wanted space." I step toward him. "This is as far as you get now."

He stares at me, so sad that it breaks my heart. "Please stop, Alek."

"I can't," I reply. "I tried, but I can't. You did this, rich boy. You came after me, made me care, and made me need you," I hiss. "It's your fault."

"My fault?" His laugh is so bitter, it kills me. "You're right about that. It's my fault for falling in love with you."

My heart stops and then races. "You love me?"

"I do, and I'm an idiot." He looks me over once more like I'm a stranger. "Because the truth is, Alek, you are never going to want to admit to being with me. You are never going to love me enough to get over that I'm not a girl. I know you're hurting and fucked up from your past, but I can't keep doing this."

"Pretty boy, please," I beg, reaching for him. "Let's just go somewhere and talk privately."

"Always private." He looks away for a moment. "No, I'm done with privacy." I swallow as he meets my eyes again. "If you want me, then kiss me right here, in front of all of these people. Otherwise, I'm walking away for good. I can't do this. I can't keep hurting myself just to keep you. I can't love you if it means hating myself. Kiss me, Alek, right here, right now, or lose me."

"I can't," I croak. "Please, please don't ask me to. Please, baby."

He nods, pursing his lips in a pained smile. "Then we're done." He turns, but I grab his arm. He looks back at me, tears swimming in his bright gaze. I hate that I put them there. I hate myself so much right now.

"Last chance, Alek," he warns. "Claim me in front of everyone or let me go."

"Please don't do this, Evan," I plead. I can't lose him, but I can't do this. Doesn't he see my panic? The whole party fades, the edges blackening until I feel like I'll pass out.

I'm back there, at that other party, even though I'm here, holding on to Evan, then he takes his arm away, my lifeline holding me to the present.

"Then it's over." He leaves, and I fall backwards into my memories.

I don't even know how I make it out of the party, but when I'm back in my car, Lally is leaning against my side, the door open. "Should I call your sister?" she murmurs kindly.

I turn my head away, not wanting her to see me cry.

Why does it just feel like I lost my entire world?

"Okay, do you need me to drive with you? You shouldn't be alone right now."

"No," I croak. "Just be with him. Thanks." I shut the door before she can protest, and despite my words, I barely remember the drive home or collapsing into my bed and rolling over to bury my nose in my comforter.

The tears come then, and I bite down on my tongue so hard to stop Alice from overhearing that I taste blood.

I cry silently for what we could have been if I was strong enough, but I'm not. I'm weak, just like they said—weak and wrong.

THIRTY-FIVE

It was stupid to go to that party, but I needed an escape. I needed to numb myself and not feel for a moment. I never expected to see him there nor to assault him like that. I practically forced him to out himself. That's fucked up, but I think I needed to so I could end this before I got hurt even more.

Maybe I'm scared, or maybe I'm just done with loving someone who can never love me back. Either way, it's over, and I'm back to being alone again.

My friends are around me, they haven't left my side since the party on Saturday, but I feel alone. He's all I think about. I find myself reaching for my phone to call him so I can tell him about something minor that happened. I sleep in his shirt and look for him in every crowd, but he's just gone, like he was never part of my life to begin with.

I should feel relieved, but as I stare at the empty spot his car usually fills near my campus building, I only feel tired and sad.

It isn't fair. Why does everyone else get to be happy?

Why does everyone else get to be with the person they love?

Does everyone have to fight this hard not to go back to the person who broke their heart?

The campus is tense and quiet. Some students have skipped school this week, while other classes have been canceled, and there's an increase in security and police presence. The tree is still cordoned off with tape, a stark reminder of what happened, and as I stare at it, I can't help but feel like we are all waiting for something else to happen, which wouldn't surprise me since they were murdered.

The murderer is still out here, free and among us.

I don't remember what happened in my classes. I do have a meeting with my photography advisor to discuss the images, but I know I can't use them. I can't do that to Alek when he doesn't want them in the showcase. I might be a bastard who tried to force him to accept us, but I'm not that much of a bastard. Maybe that's why I've been antsy all day. I'm angry at myself for doing that.

When the message comes, I'm almost relieved.

I head straight there after class, unlocking the mausoleum with my key and taking the tunnel like Liam showed me. It doesn't take long, and when I head into the manor house, no one is there. I must be the first. I slump into one of the sofas, letting my head hit the back as I close my eyes.

"There's my jailbird," comes a voice sometime later. I crack an eye open and smile as Bones walks my way.

"Thanks for that, by the way. I know Alek called you—"

"Eh." He drops into the chair next to me. "I was already on my way when he called. One of us saw it go down and alerted us. Like we said, Evan, you're one of ours, and we have your back."

"You were going to come and defend me not knowing if I did it?" I snort.

"You're not a killer, Evan." He looks at me meaningfully. "But yes."

"Good, you're here," Autumn calls, hustling in with the others in tow. Everyone quickly spreads out as the meeting starts. "Okay, Evan, give us a rundown. What happened?"

"I was one of many who found the bodies. I went inside to protect a friend when the police came to speak to me." I tell them what they probably already know, and then glance at Bones.

Unlike what I told everyone else, I lean forward and tell them everything I heard. I don't know why, but it seems important that they know. Besides, I'm worried, and if anyone understands, it will be them.

"The cops also said they think they had drugs in their systems to keep them compliant and knocked out or they wouldn't have been able to move them. They also had injuries consistent with them being held against their will. They didn't outright say it, but they don't think this is suicide. They think this is murder and that the bodies were placed there for a reason. They were trying to dig." I glance around at the shocked faces. "Those two boys were murdered and hung there for a reason."

Autumn looks pale, and she rubs her face. "It's happening again." It's so soft that I barely hear it, but I frown.

"What did you say?" I ask.

Lifting her head, she swallows hard. "That it's happening again." She glances around. "None of you were here. It was five years ago, so before our time, but my older brother was head of Silent Rose then, and he told me all about it. There were some suspicious deaths on campus. They were suspected murders, and they were covered up. It was a big fucking deal."

"How? Why?" I ask.

"The guy they arrested for it at first was a member, but he was proven innocent, and they had to drop the cases, but yeah."

"And they died like that?" I murmur.

"The hanging is new, but the drugs and restraints? Yeah, they died like that and were left on campus as a warning—of what, nobody knew."

"You need to talk to your brother again or any members from back then," Bones murmurs. "We need to know who did it, then we can catch them before anyone else gets hurt. Evan almost took the fall, and the police are still looking at him, not for the actual killer. We need to clear his name."

I peer at Bones in shock, and he catches my gaze and nods. "You're one of us, Evan. We'll protect you, and we'll fix this. Until then, lie low, and don't do anything stupid or give them any reason to come after you, okay? We all know you didn't do this, so let us prove it."

Swallowing the lump in my throat, I nod stiffly.

So this is what it feels like to have a family.

As I glance around at the other members, I have the insane urge to cry. This might have started as some fun, but knowing they are willing to protect me makes me feel like I've finally found a home.

SHAW DRIVE
NO PARKING
ACTIVE DRIVEWAY
THE MOMENT
ANDERS AVE
ONE WAY
TOO
STOP
CAR REPAIR
NO PARKING
SALE
SILENT ROSE
Pine Valley
EVER

THIRTY-SIX

ALEK

"Why, for the love of all that is holy, are we here?" Alice gapes, turning her face up to meet my wide, innocent eyes. Her hair is up in a bun, and she's wearing some leggings and an oversized shirt since I caught her during her movie marathon. "You like to work out, not me, so find yourself a buddy to do it with, not your sister. I am not made for exercise. I am made for comfort, naps, and snacks," she warns.

"I know all too well." I smirk, draping my arm over her shoulders and steering her across the parking lot to the gym. It's late, so it's empty, which is good since I know she'd be embarrassed if it wasn't. "I tried to get you to work out with me for years, and I kept finding you hiding behind machines, watching K-dramas on your phone."

"It's called exercising my mind and imagination." She huffs, trying to escape my hold, but she finally gives up and slumps reluctantly.

"Or watching, as you call them, daddy hotties." I smirk as I push through the door.

"Hey, I'm all about equal opportunities. The women are hot too. I'm no better than a man." That makes me raise my eyebrows, but she doesn't seem to realize what she said so I let it slide. Alice will talk to me when she's ready. If you push her, she fights back. My sister is as stubborn as I am, maybe even more so—she just hides it behind a polite smile.

Bones is already warming up inside, dancing across the gym mats while he waits. I texted him to make sure he was wearing a shirt because I'm not scarring my sister. Luckily, he agreed to do me this favor, which lets me know he's probably worried about what's happening on campus too. Besides, he always makes time to train anyone in self-defense—it's like his passion or hobby.

"Why am I here?" Alice asks, looking over at Bones.

"He's going to teach you some self-defense until I'm sure you can handle yourself in an emergency."

"Alek," she whines, pouting up at me.

"Not going to work, kid." I shrug. "I'm serious about this. Please, for me. I hate that something like that happened here. For fuck's sake, it's supposed to be the safest school in the country, not to mention the richest. I need to keep you safe."

Her eyes narrow on me, and it's times like these I'm scared of my sister. I swear she can read my mind.

"You're just upset and worried about Evan and using me as scapegoat to avoid being alone and overthinking everything," Alice mutters.

"Ouch." I press my hand to my chest. "Hitting me where it hurts. Please. Alley cat, do this for me? You're the only family I have left."

"Using the dead family card, you bastard, but you know it's true." She sighs as she turns to look at Bones. "But I'll do it for you, and when you stop worrying about me, you can start worrying about fixing your love life."

"I'll never stop worrying about you," I admit as I ruffle her hair. "That's what big brothers are for."

"And sisters are here to be a pain in the ass." She elbows me away. "Call Evan. Fix it."

As she rolls her shoulders back, walking toward Bones who is waiting for her, I can't help but let my own droop. "I can't. It's broken," I whisper, not wanting her to worry about me. It's my job to worry about her, not the other way around, and yes, maybe I'm using her as a reason to keep going, but I also want to keep her safe.

I wonder if Evan would train with Bones. I know he's skilled and can protect himself, but I don't like that he's on campus where this happened. He might hate me, might not want to see me again, but he'll understand that, right?

Pulling out my phone, I bring up our messages, hesitating over the keys. Will he ignore me? Probably. My stacked messages from the last week are still on read. Thumbing back, I swallow the pain in my heart as I read the flirtatious ones from before. I open the last picture he sent and rub my thumb across his smiling lips, wishing more than anything that I could fix this and be the man he deserves.

Clicking off it before I cry like a fucking loser, I hit call instead, hoping he'll answer. I walk outside, standing by the glass so I can keep my eye on Bones and Alice as I wait anxiously for him to pick up. It rings and rings, and I'm about to give up when the line clicks on.

My breathing is almost a pant, excitement and fear warring within me, and I'm left fighting in silence, unsure what to say.

"What, Alek?" He sighs.

"You answered," I blurt like a moron, my cheeks heating, but luckily he can't see.

"You're stubborn, so I knew you would just keep calling until I did. What's wrong?" He sounds tired, and I hate that it's probably my fault.

"I just want to make sure you're okay with everything that happened and—" I ramble.

"I'm fine." The word kills my hope. It's cold and calm, leaving no room for argument or for me to start a conversation. He's drawing a line, and I hate it, even if I know it's for the best.

I don't deserve Evan Shaw. I don't deserve to be happy or loved. This is just a reminder, but it doesn't stop me from trying. He's the only shred of light in the darkness of my life—the only shred of decency and happiness I've ever felt.

"Pretty boy . . ." I swallow, knowing I have no right to call him that now. "Evvie, please, I'm sorry. If I could just—"

"You keep saying sorry," he murmurs. "I didn't even think you knew how to apologize, but here we are. A relationship shouldn't be you constantly hurting me and then apologizing. It should be filled with you finding ways not to hurt me again after apologizing. Just stop calling, Alek, okay? You're making this harder." His voice is soft, pained, and I hate it.

I hate all of this. I just want him here in my arms where he belongs. "If it's this hard, it isn't right," I admit.

He's quiet for a moment. "I realized something tonight." There's shuffling in the background—is he in bed? Was he thinking of me like I am of him? Does he miss me like I miss him? "I didn't mind waiting for you when I had hope. I could have waited forever, but you will never love me enough to overcome whatever it is that's stopping you from being you because you like your life. You like being miserable. You like being unhappy because it means you never have to lose anything again, and you will never want me more than that. Maybe it was wrong of me to try and force you to out yourself at the party, and I'm sorry for that, but I had to know what you would choose. It wasn't about you kissing or claiming me. It was about looking into your eyes while you thought about it. Do you know what I saw, Alek? You're scared. You're scared to be happy. You're scared to love someone, and because of that, you close yourself off and stop yourself from wanting anything so you don't get hurt. Maybe I'm foolish for trying with you when I knew how it would end, but at least I tried. I'm honest with myself and with my life. You? You're not really living. You exist. You work. You look after Alice. You never want anything for yourself—"

"I want you," I interrupt, my voice tight. "I want you. You're the only thing I have ever wanted or taken for myself."

"And you didn't want me enough to fight for it, not when things got hard. I love you, Alek, but right now, I really don't like you. Sometimes I wish I'd never met you." Tears fill my eyes, and they fall unchecked. "But then I remember the happiness we had, even briefly, and I can't regret that. I just hope one day you meet someone you care more about than protecting yourself. I hope you find someone to love, because it isn't me."

He hangs up, and I'm left crying against a silent phone. "I already did—you," I admit.

I know he's right. He saw right through me even when I didn't want him to. I'm a coward. I'm so scared of getting hurt that I thought I could protect myself and love him, but that's not possible. You can't protect your heart and give only what you wish to someone. You have to be vulnerable, weak, and trust them not to hurt you even when you know they could. I didn't do that. I was halfway out the door the entire time, so when it shut after me, it didn't hurt.

But it does. It fucking hurts, so all that stupid bullshit didn't work because I'm still fucking hurting despite it.

Turning, I press my forehead to the glass, seeing Alice beyond, but my eyes blur with tears, and all I can think about is the past and the reason I am this way.

"Come on, Alek, they'll never know," Matty promises, the party music still pounding. He's lying under me, his hands gripping my biceps. I fell after he yanked me through the door.

"Matty, stop," I demand as his hand pulls my shirt up, sliding across my chest, but I can't bite back my groan or the way I react. I never can, and I hate that I react to him. I've tried to kiss girls, to fuck them like all my friends, but I just can't. Nothing works. I can get hard alone, but with a girl? No. One touch of Matty's hand, though, and I'm as hard as a rock. He smirks like he knows, his hand drifting down to press against my cock, and I moan, jerking in his hand. "Please," I beg. "Don't."

"Why? You like it." He leans up, licking my lips. "We both know you do. You want me, Alek, right?"

I try to back away and stop this, but then his lips are on mine, and he's kissing me. His hand stroking me through my jeans and his soft lips feel so good, I give in to this want inside me, the one that scares me. I let go, trusting him as I kiss him back, pressing him to the bed. The hard press of his muscles against mine almost makes me spill in my jeans.

Breaking the kiss with a gasp, I stare into his wide eyes as he strokes me. "You want me?"

He nods, his lips red from my kiss.

"Have you ever—" I start, unsure what to say, my cheeks flaming.

"Been with a guy? No, we can figure it out," he replies. "Don't you want to?"

"I do," I admit. "More than anything, I want to know what you feel like. I can't stop imagining you under me."

Leaning down, I trust in him as I kiss down his face to his neck. He turns to give me better access, sighing slightly, and I blame it on that. I blame being so lost in him and this new desire that I don't hear it at first.

"What the fuck?" The shout jerks me upright, my eyes widening as I glance at the door to see most of the football team watching me kiss their quarterback.

I look back at Matty, and he meets my gaze. I see fear and confusion there when his eyes were clear moments ago. His expression turns mean, which isn't something I've seen before.

Matty's eyes widen as he glances at the door and the crowd. "You see this shit? He forced himself on me. He was saying all kinds of messed up stuff." He pushes me off him, scrambling away as he glares at me. "He's so fucking gay. You were right. That's why he kept looking at me. Can you believe it?"

"What?" I sit up, confused as I stare at them. "Matty—"

"Don't say my name, you faggot," he spits as he straightens his designer shirt. "You disgust me. I can't believe you thought we were friends. We just had to be sure. I guess you're so desperate for anyone to like you that you thought we actually wanted you here tonight."

"You tried to force Matty?" Terrance, the linebacker, cracks his knuckles as he heads into the room, the rest of the team following, kicking the door shut behind them. "Let's beat the gay out of you, Anders."

I leap from the bed, but they surround me. There are so many of them, I don't stand a chance. I'm on the floor before I know it, curling up to protect my head, but the pain is constant as they slam their boots into me. I feel my cheek split, my lip burst open, and my head ring with the hits. Something inside feels wrong, broken, and I want to scream as the beating continues.

Is this how I'll die?

It feels like it. The pain is so intense, I can barely see, but they suddenly stop. "Shit, are those cops?" one of them calls.

Groaning, I try to sit up, but my arm slips in my blood and I hit the floor hard, the sharp pain making me cry out.

"Maybe, but I don't care, I'm going to kill the gay boy first," Terrance snaps. He will kill me simply for being this.

Banging downstairs distracts him for a moment, and I force myself upright despite the agony around my body, the cracked or broken ribs making it hard to breathe, then I turn to the second story window and throw myself out of it. If I stay, I'm dead. I hit the ground hard, almost crying from the pain, but I swallow it back as other partygoers rush across the lawn and to their cars to escape the cops.

I run because I have no other option. The cops won't care, nobody will. When I glance back, I see Matty in the window with tears in his eyes. "I'm sorry," he calls.

Ignoring him, I run as hard as I can, trying to outpace what happened tonight.

By the time I make it home, I'm limping and in agony. I know my face is a mess, and there's blood all over my shirt. I just hope everyone is asleep, but as I slip in the back door, I know I'm unlucky. My father is on the sofa, beer in hand, watching some game reruns.

He hears the door open and glances over, blinking as he leaps to his feet and rushes over. Concern and anger gleam in his eyes—probably because he wasn't the one who put the bruises there.

"What the hell happened to you?" my father rages, turning my face to see the bruises and blood. "Jesus, Alek, you let yourself get beat up like this? Why didn't you kick their ass?"

"There were too many of them," I snap, yanking my face from his grip, but I freeze when he slams me back against the wall, his arm across my throat.

"Did you just talk back to me, boy?"

"No, sir," I force out, biting back the tears that want to fall. I've had a shitty night. Can't he just let it go for once?

"You better not have." He steps away, grabbing his beer as he

looks at the TV once more. "Wash up and avoid your mom and sister for a few days. They don't need to see you like that."

He stands at the back of the couch, dismissing me. Usually, I would hurry away, glad that's the end of it, but tonight, I push from the wall and try my luck. Something inside me needs to have his eyes on me and for him to know the truth, even though I know it's a bad idea.

I am just so tired of hiding and figuring this out alone.

Maybe he can help.

As I force the words out, it's my hope that I won't have to go through this alone. That, despite his anger, he'll support me as his son, love me, and give me guidance when I feel like I'm a boat without an anchor.

"I'm gay. They beat me because I'm gay," I snap, but he doesn't even look at me, and my heart sinks, but I don't back down now. I'm so very fucking tired and alone. "Dad, did you hear me?"

"You're wrong." He finally looks at me, and my whole world shrinks when I see his expression. "No son of mine is gay. You're just young and stupid. You'll find a nice girl and settle down."

"And if I don't?" I spit.

"Then I'll help them beat the gay right out of you, boy. No son of mine is a sissy, so don't you ever say that shit again." My head hits the wall from the force of the bottle hitting my face. I feel glass and blood sprinkling down my head from the impact as I stare in shock. "If you ever say it again, I'll kill you, understand? If I ever see you with a boy, I'll kill you myself. Now get out of my sight."

As I gape at my father, hatred builds inside me—one for myself for being born this way.

I will never be the kid he could love, nor will I be the kid others would be friends with and invite to parties.

I hate myself, and I hate them all.

Opening my eyes, I blink to clear away my tears. I hate how it's all coming back now. I tried so hard to be normal, to be the kid he could love, and to be accepted into this society that punishes you for being different. I tried and failed.

I know I can't blame my past for my actions now. Yes, I was young, and what happened was fucked up, but I'm older now. I know what Matty and the others did was wrong. I know my father was wrong and that being gay isn't a problem. It's who I am, but it doesn't stop old insecurities and fears from forcing my hand. It doesn't stop me from thinking that everyone I trust or let close will hurt or betray me simply for what I want.

I dropped out of school and got a job, and when my parents died, I grieved them. I moved on and grew up, so why can't I let go of that scared teenager?

I used to hate Matty, but as I think back on it now, I just feel sorry for him. He was obviously scared and worried, and he used me as a scapegoat, but aren't I doing the same thing now to Evan?

Look how that made me feel.

Evan is right, I'm scared, but I really wish I weren't.

I wish I were brave enough to accept who I am and love without worry.

As I watch my sister learning to protect herself, I know I have a choice to make—to stay stuck in the past, never accepting myself and being happy, or to be brave like her. I could show her it's okay to be who she is and to love whoever she wants. She looks up to me, so it's my duty to lead the way—not just for her, but for me as well—and to be the change I needed back then.

Can I break the cycle?

THIRTY-SEVEN

Staring at my phone, I debate if I'm wrong. Am I? Or am I just missing him?

It's stupid to get this attached to someone so quickly, but you can't help who you love, and I love Alek Anders. I hate it. I hate that it's hard to breathe. I hate that I'm just going through the motions, looking for him everywhere. He hurt me, and we are over, yet I'm here, staring at pictures on my phone of when we were together.

I was happier than I have ever been before, and the wide smile on my face as he poses behind me in this image is proof of that. My phone is filled with stolen moments and snapshots, and I can't force myself to get rid of them.

His phone call last night didn't help. It didn't make me feel better to take it out on him when I know he's struggling. That's the thing—when you love someone, you make excuses for them. You don't want to hurt them even when they hurt you. Even now, I hope he's okay and he isn't overworking and not sleeping.

Love is a foolish, fickle bitch, and I want it gone.

I don't want to be in pain anymore. Rubbing my chest, I place my phone face down just as the chair opposite me in the dining hall is scraped back. I jerk my head up and see Alice. She slumps into it, groaning as she rubs her arms. I stare, and she tilts her head.

"What? We are friends, aren't we? He didn't get me in the divorce," she jokes. I've noticed the more comfortable she feels around someone, the more she speaks, and she's right. We are friends. I like Alice, but she reminds me of her brother. I can't look into her eyes without seeing him.

I simply nod, and she sighs, reaching over as she flips my phone, seeing the picture there. I snatch it back from her and sit deeper into the chair, embarrassed she caught me.

"Evan."

"Don't, okay? I don't need you to defend him or anything."

"I'm not going to. I'm your friend, remember? Are you okay?" She reaches over, holding my hand. It's soft and warm, but I wish it were bigger, tattooed, and his. Still, I let her comfort me.

"Not even a little," I admit with a bitter laugh, meeting her eyes once more, the eyes of someone I love in a different face. They are so alike sometimes, it's scary.

"Is he okay?" I ask.

"You want the truth?" she counters, and I love her for that. She might be his sister, but she's also my friend, and it's clear when Alice cares, she cares deeply. She's like her brother in that regard. I nod, and she smiles.

"No." Her smile is sad. "He isn't. I've never seen him like this. It's like the energy is gone from him. He's barely eating or sleeping—hell, he even missed work."

I hate that concern winds through me.

"I know you don't want to hear it, Evan, but no matter what happened or what you think, my brother cares about you a lot. Losing you has wrecked him," she admits.

"But he didn't care enough," I mutter like a petulant child.

"Evan, my brother didn't even know he had a heart until he met you. All he has done for the last few years is look after me, never wanting anything for himself. He's slow to admit when he feels some-thing. He's dumb about it, but he's trying."

"Alice." I stop her, and she waits. "All my life, I've been told what I am is wrong, sick, and perverted. I don't want my relationship to be like that. I want my love to be my safe space, my happy place, where I can be unapologetically me."

"And you couldn't with him?" she asks honestly.

"How can I when he can't even be honest with himself?" I shrug.

"Forget everyone else and what they want, Evan. What do you want? Does it matter to you if Alek loves you silently or loudly? Or do you just think it should matter?" She squeezes my hand. "He might be slow, but he shows you in a million ways. His actions are his promise to you, Evan, even if he doesn't realize it. Think of everything he does for you. That passenger seat? It's yours. He doesn't even let me sit in it, and nobody else can ever sit in his car. He made you food every morning, no matter how late he worked, because he was worried you weren't eating enough. He picked you up almost every day just so you didn't have to walk home. He helped you with your shoot because it made you happy. I'm sure there are a million other little things, but that's what I saw—my brother, a man who looks after people he loves, was looking after you.

"He only takes care of people he cares about, Evan, and that has only ever been me. He let you into our lives, our house, and his heart. He does it silently without complaining, not because he doesn't want people to know, but because it's who he is. He might never be the type to scream that you are his, but he will show this world through his actions if you let him. I'm not saying he isn't a fool, but he has spent years fighting who he is." She leans closer. "Our father hated him, convinced him it was wrong to be gay. There is a reason he's the way he is, Evan. I'm not saying it's right, but he's trying. Despite it all, he's trying. I'm not trying to ruin this or stop you from being happy, but if you're not happy moving on from him, then why are you doing it? Life's too short to hold yourself back, Evan. You deserve to be loved, to feel safe and happy, but there will never be another who will love you the way he does."

"Alice."

"No," she snaps. "My brother has looked out for me my entire life.

I owe him everything, and I want him to be happy, and you make him happy, Evan. You make him so fucking happy. You made him dream again, dream about a future he thought was gone. Maybe I shouldn't be saying this, but I see two people I care about hurting themselves for the other, and I can't stand it. You either need to love him or completely let him go, Evan, but if you let him go, you'll never have him again. He'll close up and never trust another person, so can you try to love him, no matter how dumb he's being? Can you love him enough for both of you, even when he hates himself?"

I peer into her determined eyes. They remind me so much of her brother's, and she's right. I love him, and it hurts to stay away. He does show me, and I know that party was a mistake. Did I overlook his pain, thinking mine was greater? Could the reason lie in his past?

I don't know if we can ever be the way we were or if this can work, but she's right about one thing—I want it to. I've never wanted something so much, and it hurts to be away from him. It hurts so much, I feel like I'm dying.

Alek Anders is stubborn, angry, and foolish, but he's mine.

"You're stubborn, just like him," I mutter.

"Yeah, I am." She grins proudly. "No matter what you choose, Evan, do it for you, no one else, and I'll still be your friend." She rolls her shoulders, groaning. "But for the love of all that is holy, please fuck the shit out of my brother because he kills me with his boredom and heartache."

I burst out laughing.

Is she right?

Can this be salvaged?

Is it worth it?

Is he worth it?

The answer is yes. He might not think so, but I do.

I think he's worth the heartache, the worry and sleepless nights, and if we try again and it breaks once more, at least I'll have no regrets because I know letting Alek Anders go would be the biggest mistake of my life.

I don't know why I came here other than it sort of feels like our place. I never expected to see him, that's for sure. I skipped my classes to come here and think about what I want before I reached out, but it seems fate has other ideas.

Sitting on a bench before the pond, under the blooming cherry blossom tree, is Alek Anders, his shoulders rounded as if he's carrying the weight of the world. When I step closer, he doesn't even hear me. I can see his profile, and he looks tired. He's wearing some black jeans with white seams and his normal leather jacket, and despite his exhaustion, he looks good. My heart misses a beat, thumping faster simply from seeing him.

I could leave before he notices, but I drift closer and sit down on the other end of the bench, my hand next to his. I feel his head swing my way, but I keep my eyes on the water. "I didn't know you were here. I was coming to think."

"I see," he murmurs, his voice hoarse. I turn my head, meeting his brown eyes. Alice is right. He will never love another, never let another in. That is just who Alek is, and he loves so much it would be a shame to this world.

Being loved by Alek Anders would be something beautiful, I think.

"I was going to call you," I admit, and he blinks in shock, hope blooming in his eyes before it dies.

"I'll keep an eye on Alice at home. You don't have to worry." He shrugs, looking away, so sure that everything is never about him, even now.

"I didn't want to talk about Alice. I wanted to talk about us." I look back at the water, letting the stillness give me strength.

"Is there an us?" he asks. He sounds angry, but I know better now. Alek's pain is masked behind his anger—anger he directs at a world that has never helped him and people who never cared about him.

"I don't know," I answer honestly, not wanting to lie to him, "but I think I want there to be." I meet his gaze. "I need answers, though, Alek. I need to understand."

"Understand?" he parrots.

"You said you couldn't at the party, that you had your reasons. I want to hear them now if you will tell me. I want to know why. I want to understand. I'm ready if you are."

NO PARKING
ACTIVE DRIVEWAY
SHAW DRIVE
THE MOMENT
ANDERS AVE
ONE WAY
TOO
STOP
CAR REPAIR
NO PARKING
SALE
SILENT ROSE
Pine Valley
EVER

THIRTY-EIGHT

ALEK

His words repeat in my head as hope dares to take root in my chest, hope that Evan isn't gone yet.

He mistakes my silence for refusal and turns away. "I'm sorry. I shouldn't have asked—"

"No," I croak, sitting up taller. "I'll tell you anything you want to know. If pulling myself apart will let me keep you, I'll do it time and time again," I say as he looks at me. "I can't live without you, rich boy. I've realized that these last few days. You're the best thing to ever storm into my life, and I don't want to lose you. I was a dumbass, but if you give me another chance, I'll do and be better. I want to try. I want to deserve you. Do you think we can ever fix this?"

"I don't know, but we can try," he murmurs. "What did you mean?"

Looking away, I debate how to start before I turn to him and let it pour from me. I tell him about the party and Matty. "I thought I could trust him, and I almost died that night, Evan, just because they found out I liked a guy, and the guy himself was part of it. It fucked me up, but when I got home, my dad didn't care, and I got so mad. I was so fucking tired of hiding who I was to make everyone happy that I admitted I was gay. He lost it and attacked me. He told me if I ever said it again, he would kill me."

"Alek."

"He wasn't a good dad. He was always filled with anger. Usually, it was directed at me for doing stupid shit. I suppose it forced me to grow up faster—"

"Alek, you shouldn't have had to grow up faster. You should have been allowed to be a kid. You should have been protected and cared for. You didn't need to grow up. You needed to be loved."

I swallow as I stare into his eyes. "I thought it was wrong to be what I was, and I convinced myself I was wrong, that I wasn't gay, to make them happy so it never happened again. I started a new life, and I tried so hard to be what everyone wanted, especially after my parents died. I thought it would free me, but I had to grow up and take care of Alice, and I knew in a world where people like me were not accepted, it would cause her issues. I was scared, Evan, so I buried it deep down, but I didn't even realize it until I met you. I think that's why I hated you so much at first—because I wanted you. I saw you, and you made it all come back. You made me want things I swore were just a bad dream or a teenage rebellion.

"You forced me to face who I was, but then I didn't care because I got you, and I had never been so happy. I was finally open with myself and learning that it was okay, and I'm sorry, Evan, but when you asked me to kiss you at the party, it just all came back. I couldn't breathe, and it felt like the past all over again. I should have told you, but talking was never my strong suit. I always fuck things up; it's who I am. I don't deserve you, Evan, but I fucking want you more than I've ever wanted anything. You are the only thing in this world that makes me happy, that makes me have hope. You are the only person I have ever let in, let love me, even when I didn't think I was allowed to be loved."

He watches me, his eyes glassy as I speak, and I surge forward, letting it pour from me. "I messed this up, and I hurt you, but I never wanted to. You're the last person in this world I wanted to hurt, but I did, and I'm sorry. I'm sorry I'm still letting my past mess with my present. I'm really trying to come to terms with everything. I'm not saying I won't hurt you again or fuck up, but I'll do everything I can to fix it. Evan Shaw, you are my entire world. I wasn't living until you came along. I was existing. You brought sunshine back into my life, you brought back hope and dreams and laughter, and I can't go back to living without it . . . to living without you."

Swallowing my pride, I reach over and lay my hand next to his, letting him choose. "I wish—no, I want to be what you want, what you need. I want to be able to kiss you in a party full of people. I want to take your hand in public and let everyone know you're mine. I want to be everything you need, and I swear I'll try, Evan. Give me one chance, pretty boy, and I'll love you with everything inside me until the day I die."

His fingers slowly cover mine, and I know we are going to be okay. Tears drip from my eyes, and he reaches up, wiping them away. "Okay," he whispers. "We'll do this together and face your past and our future. We don't have to rush this. Let's try again, but no more secrets or hiding. If we are in this, we are in this together."

"Together," I murmur, pressing my forehead to his. "I missed you so much, pretty boy."

"I missed you too," he whispers, and his eyes drop to my lips before he goes to pull away, but I wrap my hand around the back of his head and kiss him softly. How could something this good ever be bad? I don't care who's around me. I don't care about anything but us.

I no longer care who sees or what they think. There is nothing worse they can do to me than what I've done to myself, and there is nothing in this world that holds a candle to losing Evan. I'll take their judgment if I get to keep my sunshine. I'll be his darkness and his barrier from it all.

"I love you," I whisper proudly.

"I love you too," he replies with a grin. "And one day, you'll love yourself the way I love you. I promise, Alek, that I'll erase everything they did to you, and if I ever meet them, I'll kill them for what they put you through." He means it, and for some reason, it makes me cry, knowing this sunshine would risk it all just to hurt those who hurt me.

"I might just let you," I admit weakly.

Laying my head on his shoulder, I let him hold me as I let go of all anger, pain, and resentment.

I just exist in Evan's arms, letting him put me back together.

We sit in comfortable silence, our hands twined on his thigh, our arms around one another as we look at the water. Hope flourishes between us—a second chance.

It's the happiest I've ever been, and I know I'll never let Evan go again. This is it for me. The boy I was never supposed to fall for has become my everything, and no matter what anyone else thinks, we are in this for the long run.

We are a forever kind of thing, and that's so beautiful.

I don't need to shine like him, but I will be his umbrella from the rain.

With the good comes the bad, however, and when my phone vibrates, I sit up and accept the call without glancing at it.

"Alek," the shaky voice says.

"Alice, what's wrong?" I ask, instantly on high alert. Evan is right there with me, his eyes wide and worried. "Alice."

"Can you come home?" she sobs. "Please, just come home."

"I'll be right there. Stay there." I hang up and grab Evan, dragging him toward my car.

"What is it?" he asks. "Is she okay?"

"Something's wrong," I croak, terror making my heart race.

Please, whoever is listening, don't hurt my sister just because I'm happy.

THIRTY-NINE

We arrive at Alek's house in record time—I'm pretty sure he even dusted a cop that was chasing us—and he's out of the car within seconds, racing toward the door. I'm hot on his heels, both of us bursting in to find a trembling Alice sitting on the couch, pointing at some flowers on the coffee table in front of her. My brows furrow, adrenaline pumping through my heart.

"What is it?" Alek asks, covering the distance and gripping her face. His love and worry for his sister pour from him. "Alice, talk to me. What happened?" He practically shakes her, his voice demanding and high-pitched.

"The flowers," she whispers. "They were on the doorstep when I got back."

"Flowers . . . You're okay?" he asks. "Alice."

"I'm okay, just read the note." She seems to gather herself together. "I read it and freaked. I just wanted you home. I didn't feel safe."

Frowning, I stride over and take the note. "There's no delivery address, which means someone dropped them off," I observe as I flip the card open, my eyes widening as I scan the words. "Shit."

"What? What does it say? I swear if some freaky boy has some ideas—" He heads my way, looking over my shoulder, going silent as soon as he reads it.

This isn't some guy wanting to get in her pants.

This is a fucking stalker.

Alice, you looked so pretty today in the white dress. It's my favorite thing you have worn. I don't want others looking though. Don't make me jealous or upset. Look what I had to do to those boys who tried to take you from me.

Yours always.

"Oh, this is some freaking stalker shit," I hiss, and I hand the note to a furious Alek and head her way, wrapping my arms around her. "I'm so sorry, sweetie. We are here, and you're safe. We'll report it to the police right away. Don't let it get to you."

"He's watching me, whoever it is. He knew what I was wearing. And it sounds like he hurt those two boys on campus?" she asks.

I share a worried look with Alek. "It could just be a bluff, someone playing a prank and trying to scare you." I cup her face, wanting to reassure her. "But don't worry, you won't be alone. Whoever this is, Alek will hunt them down and kick their ass. You trust your brother to keep you safe, right?"

She nods, tears glistening in her eyes, so I brush them away and place a gentle kiss on her forehead. I like Alice, she's like a little sister to me, and I hate seeing her upset. "We both will. Don't worry."

I meet Alek's eyes over her head. He's furious, fisting the card, but he mouths, "Thank you."

I wink and hold her closer as he walks away to call the police. Whoever this is, joke or not, we have to report it. If what they said is true, then the person who murdered those two guys has set his sights on Alice.

The police were here for hours. They took the note and flowers away and left Alice with a contact number. I'm glad they are taking it seriously. I don't think they would have if it hadn't mentioned the two dead boys. Luckily, different officers than the ones who arrested me responded to the call, but I have no doubt they will find out and think I'm the one behind it again.

I'm exhausted, but we stay up with Alice since she doesn't want to sleep. She's curled up between us, a film playing on the TV. Alek's arm is behind her on the sofa, mine too, and our hands are linked behind her head, his thumb stroking along mine.

An hour later, she finally falls asleep, and Alek slowly stands, scooping her into his arms like she's a child before he heads upstairs. I follow and pull her comforter back as he lowers her into bed. We both tuck her in carefully, and I tap on her lamp in case she wakes up scared. We share a look over her head, a soft one, and then he offers me his hand.

"Come on, baby, time for bed."

Nodding, I take his hand, and at the door, we both look back. "She'll be okay," I say, leaning up to kiss his cheek. "She has you. Nobody would dare fuck with Alek Anders."

"Nobody but you." He smirks as he shuts her door.

Laughing quietly, I hold his hand as I walk backwards to his room, remembering the last time I was here. His eyes track me. "Very true, but I have a feeling you like it when I fuck with you."

"You have no idea, pretty boy," he growls as I open the door and step into his room. He kicks it shut behind him, his gaze predatory and dark.

Stepping closer, I lean up and nip his chin. "Then show me."

I go to step back, but his hand slides around my waist and presses against my spine, drawing me closer as he tips my head back and his lips slant over mine. "Shirt off, pretty boy. Let me see what's mine." He releases me as I pant.

Eyes narrowing, I step away. "This?" I tease, playing with the edge. "Ask nicely."

His jaw grinds, and he practically vibrates as he resists throwing me down and having his wicked way with me.

"No?" I sigh, dropping it. "I guess I'll go to sleep then—"

"Please, Evan."

"Good boy." I wink as I reach down and pull my shirt off, letting him get his fill of my muscular chest. His eyes narrow and his lips part as I drag my hand down my chest to my jeans and open the button. "These too?"

He nods silently, and I wait, my eyebrow arched. "Yes, please."

"Good boys get rewards," I say as I unzip them and shove them down, kicking them off. I'm in nothing but tight boxers. I fall back onto his bed, propping myself up on my elbows as I watch him.

"What rewards?" he asks gruffly, his Adam's apple bobbing.

"Me," I answer as I slide my hand into my boxers and stroke my length. He finally snaps, and I laugh as he storms across the room, but my laugh turns into a moan as he grips my hand through the material.

He holds my gaze as he leans over me. "Don't touch what's mine, pretty boy," he warns. "Hands up."

I do as I'm told, and he rips off his shirt and quickly ties my hands above my head, stretching me out as he leans back and devours me with his eyes like I'm a feast and he doesn't know where to start. My heart races with desire. Smirking like he knows what I'm thinking, he leans down and brushes his lips across my throat, leaving teasing kisses and licks before biting my Adam's apple as I moan.

Chuckling, he moves across my chest, his lips warm and teasing as they close around my nipple. I'm breathless as his tongue slides across my abs and stops at my waistband. His hand follows the trail his mouth took and then slides into my boxers, gripping my cock.

"There you are, pretty boy." His dark eyes watch me as I arch into his touch, thrusting into his hand. "I've missed this, missed you. Remind me whom you belong to." He squeezes my length to the point of pain, yet I love it. "Whose is this?"

"Mine."

"Wrong answer." He lets go and strips my boxers off, dragging his mouth up my leg until his breath blows over my cock. "Whose is this?"

I swallow hard, willing to say anything if it means I get him. "Yours, yours."

"Now who's a good boy?" he purrs as his mouth seals around the tip of my cock, and he sucks.

My back bows off the bed, eyes rolling back from the pressure. Desire courses through me, and I grip his shirt as I try to hold back.

Chuckling, he releases me and slides up my body, placing a kiss over my racing heart. "I wanted to take my time with you tonight, baby, but you're all wound up and needy, aren't you?" I nod, and he hums. "I guess I'll have to take the edge off first, and then I can play with you all night."

"Please, Alek," I beg, reaching for him, but he slams my hands back down.

"Keep them there. I'll make you feel better, pretty boy. I've got you. You know you only have to ask."

Leaning back, he quickly strips off his jeans, leaving him naked and oh so fucking beautiful. My eyes drag along every inch of exposed skin, but he doesn't give me nearly enough time to look as he climbs up on the bed. I jump when he quickly lubes his fingers and presses them inside me, working them in my ass as his mouth meets mine in a frenzied kiss. He fingers me as I groan into him, pushing into his hand for more, before he pulls them free, and then I feel him roll the condom on. His hands rove over my waist as I feel his cock against my ass.

Leaning back, he groans as he looks at me. "So fucking pretty, baby."

He presses against me, one hand lifting my thigh so it's up by his head as his other holds his cock and presses it against my ass. We are so close, our lips meeting as he leans down and pushes into me.

It's brutal and slow.

We are so close and connected. It's different this time.

This isn't just fucking. This is deeper.

He stretches every inch of me, filling me so deeply it's almost too much, and then he starts to move, slowly rolling his hips. I claw at my bindings, wanting to feel his skin as he presses my leg higher with each deep, hard thrust.

The bed creaks from the force, our breaths mingling. "You're mine, pretty boy," he states. "Alek's boy, you hear me?"

I nod jerkily. "Please."

"If anyone tries to take you away, I'll kill them," he promises against my lips. "You're going to be like this every morning and night—under me, over me, taking me."

Jesus fucking Christ.

He leans back, gripping my hips as he slams into me, forcing me to take him. My dick jerks in need, leaking all over.

"Goddamn, look at you. You're a fucking work of art, Evan Shaw," he praises, his dark eyes dragging along my body as he fucks me, tilting my hips until he rubs across that spot that nearly has me coming, and then he reaches up.

He rips off the bindings and his hands curl into mine above my head as we kiss once more, our rhythm speeding up as our bodies come together. His cock is so deep inside me, I know it will hurt with each step I take tomorrow, but it will be so worth it.

"My Evan," he says against my lips. "Mine, mine, all mine."

"Yours," I whimper, wrapping my legs around him, urging him to do more. His rolling thrusts have me rocking into him, desire shooting through me until I can't breathe.

My toes curl, my entire body locks up, and then with a yell muted against his skin, I come all over us. His cock jerks inside me, and then he hammers into me until his groans follow mine. His cum fills my ass as he presses me down to the bed, breathing heavily.

He opens his eyes, meeting mine, and then leans down, kissing me once more. "Mine, pretty boy."

"Yours," I murmur.

FORTY

I promised Alek I would keep an eye on Alice. He wanted her to stay home, but she's determined not to let this psycho ruin her life, and honestly, I fucking admire her for it. She's so much more like her brother than she knows. He drops us both off, and I walk her to class, promising to meet after.

"Evan, go, I'm fine." She sighs, rolling her eyes before she smiles. "I'm glad you two made up."

"Yeah? Me too," I reply, blushing hard, hoping she didn't hear us this morning. Alek kept his promise—he kept me up all night, and I loved it.

She laughs, no doubt reading my face. "Don't worry, noise canceling headphones, remember?" She squeezes my arm. "Thank you for loving him and making him smile. I know he's a pain in the ass, but he deserves you, Evan. He deserves to be happy. Hell, you two even have me believing in love again."

"You'll find someone, Alice, who will treasure you and know how incredible you are," I promise.

"I know." She smiles and waves me off. "Now go. Don't be late because of me. I'll text you if anything comes up."

I watch her go inside, shoving my hands in my pockets, then I head out of the building, ready to meet for the workshop that's happening near the foundation, but I only take two steps when two familiar police officers step into my path.

"Evan," Winchester greets.

"Here to take me to the station again?" I ask casually.

"No, we heard what happened and wanted to talk." He holds his hands up, and I nod, looking around.

"Follow me." I head over to a free bench, ignoring the looks I'm receiving as they sit opposite me. I know there are rumors, but the important people in my life know the truth, and that's all that matters.

"We heard about the delivery at your friend's house."

"Boyfriend," I correct. Honestly, it doesn't really matter, but it does to me. They hesitate, the younger one taken aback.

"Boyfriend, right." He coughs. "We are aware the person is claiming to be behind the deaths—"

"Murders, you mean?" I ask, tilting my head. "They were murdered."

"That information isn't available. How do you know?" the younger one asks.

"You basically told me. I'm not an idiot." I sigh, sitting back. "I had nothing to do with it. I would never put Alice in danger, nor would I ever kill someone."

"We know it wasn't you." They share a look. Maybe they are starting to figure it out. "But we are worried someone is trying to frame you."

"Frame me? Why would anyone want to do that?" I snap.

"You tell us. Who hates you enough to do that? Evan, this is serious. You could have been charged for two counts of first-degree murder, and now there are these new stalking allegations. Someone is trying to ruin your life and get you out of the way. Why?"

The only reason that comes to mind is Alice. Whoever it is wants her, right? They killed people who hurt her and sent her flowers. The only connection I have is Alice.

But why me, and why now?

I shrug. "I have no idea. I didn't think anyone hated me that much.

There are people who don't like me, but nothing that serious." Standing, I pull my bag on. "Maybe instead of wasting my time and hassling me, you should find out who is behind this. Oh, and put some protection on Alice so she doesn't get hurt in the meantime."

"Evan."

I stop and look back. Winchester seems worried.

"Someone like this will escalate before we stop them. We are doing everything we can, but the truth is, we are in the dark. Be careful. If they are trying to frame you and it fails . . . who knows what they will do."

Comforting thought.

Nodding, I head toward the workshop, but I'm distracted and not in the mood to make small talk. Instead, I find myself hanging out in the library, pulling my phone out and texting Autumn.

This is getting out of hand. We need to know who is behind this. She mentioned her brother. He has to know something, right?

Autumn: I tried, Evan. He won't talk to me at all. All he said was that it was bad and it's buried for a reason. I'm worried.

Evan: Me too.

Autumn: I'll keep digging and let you know if I find anything.

Evan: Thanks.

Gnawing my lip, I dial Alek's number.

"Baby, what's wrong?" he asks. There's a clattering sound and voices before I hear his footsteps. "Are you okay? Is Alice?"

"I'm worried, Alek," I admit. "Alice is fine, and so am I, but the police were here again."

He swears, and I hear rummaging. "I'm on my way—"

"They've left, but the shit they said . . ." I rub my face. "Alek, this is worse than we thought."

"I'm on my way. Meet me at our spot," he snaps, and then his voice softens. "I'm coming, okay? Just hold on."

Nodding, I hang up.

I tell him everything. He's silent the entire time, turned in the driver's seat to see me. Neither of us want to leave Alice, so we are in our spot outside the art building—private but close.

"Shit, Evan," he growls. "Why didn't you tell me?"

"Honestly, I wanted to be wrong, but I'm not, and now with what they said, I think whoever it is wants me out of Alice's life. What if they are right? What if they come after me when they can't frame me? Or worse, after her?"

"Shh." He presses his forehead to mine. "I'll keep you both safe. Nobody is laying a hand on either of you."

"Alek, this person is crazy. They killed two people—"

"And you think I wouldn't to protect my family? You are my family, Evan. You and Alice are all I have. I'll kill them before they hurt either of you."

I search his eyes, realizing he's serious. "And if you're hurt?" I whisper, my heart racing. "I couldn't live with that."

"Shh, it's fine. We will be okay, alright? We'll be extra careful from now on and lie low until the police figure out who this fucker is. We'll stick together."

I nod, letting him kiss me softly. "I'm sorry to call you from work," I mumble, playing with his shirt.

"I'm glad you did. I'm glad you needed me," he admits. "I like when you lean on me, pretty boy. I like being able to help."

"Masochist." I smirk, and he laughs as he leans back.

"Want to see something that will make you happy?" he asks.

"If it's your dick, we might need to go somewhere private," I tease.

Sighing, he climbs from the car and opens my door. "You wish, pretty boy." He winks and points.

I follow his gaze, noticing what I hadn't when I first climbed in. I blink, staring at the words proudly displayed across the footwell of the passenger side of his precious baby.

EVAN'S SEAT

"Holy shit, you defaced your car for me. That's so romantic." I grin, going to kiss him, but I hesitate. He doesn't. He drags me closer, kissing me without hesitation.

"I'm finding, pretty boy, that I would do anything for you. Don't believe me? Pull the visor down."

Frowning, I do as he says, catching the Polaroid that falls out. It's of me. We had been playing around one night at his palace. I'm in his arms, smiling at the camera. "How long has this been here?" I ask softly.

"Since the night we took it," he replies, carefully putting it back and shutting it before he grabs my chin and tugs my face up. "I wanted you close at all times, and there is no one else who belongs in this seat but you. I even make Alice sit in the back. It's yours, just like I am."

Biting my lip to stop my wide grin, I smack his chest. "You soppy asshole."

Laughing, he kisses my forehead. "You love it, pretty boy."

"You two better not be fucking!" Alice calls, and I peek around him to see her heading my way.

"Nah, that's later," Alek retorts, opening the back door. "Come on, let me treat my two favorite people to lunch."

Climbing from the seat, I sling my arm around Alice, kissing her cheek. "He's paying, so let's make the most of it. I'm thinking buffet and cake."

She giggles, and I help her into the back before climbing into the front. Alek sighs but smiles as he shuts our doors and heads around to drive.

Peeking back at her, I wink as she laughs, and I know Alek is right.

I'd do anything to protect her. Alek might be my boyfriend, but Alice is the sister I never had.

I'll keep them both safe no matter what it takes.

SHAW DRIVE
ANDERS AVE
ONE WAY
THE MOMENT
NO PARKING
ACTIVE DRIVEWAY
STOP
TOO
NO PARKING
SALE
SILENT ROSE
Pine Valley
EVER

FORTY-ONE

ALEK

Alice is studying late tonight, and I've snuck into the library with Evan to keep an eye on her. He's also busy, though, and I'm bored. He told me off twice already, and people around us keep looking, but I don't care. Annoying him is my favorite game. He gets this look in his eyes that makes me hard as fuck.

He has his nose buried in a book, looking between that and his laptop. Running my foot up his leg, I press it against his crotch, making him jump with a yelp. Someone glares, and he winces before throwing me a dirty look and knocking my foot away.

Smirking, I sit up straight and place my hand on his leg, working it up under the table. He smacks me away, so I grab one of his books.

Sighing, he slams his book shut, making me jump, and narrows his eyes. "You, follow me," he orders as he stands, ignoring the looks he gets as he stomps away.

Grinning, I follow him, shooting Alice another look before I do. She's surrounded by people, so I happily follow my boyfriend—right into the bathroom. "Get out," he snaps at a guy at the sinks. He gives us both a look but hightails it out of here, and then Evan turns to me.

"You are acting like a needy child—"

I head his way, and he backs up, stumbling into a stall. I follow, shutting the door behind me.

"Seriously, Alek, if you can't sit still—"

"What?" I murmur as I trap him against the door.

His anger quickly changes.

"Is this where you sent me those pictures?"

He nods, his eyes wide.

"Show me what I missed that day."

"Alek—"

"Play with me, baby," I murmur, "and I'll let you study in peace for at least an hour."

"One hour?" he grumbles. "Insatiable."

"You made me this way. Now show me," I order.

Licking his lips, he sighs. "If I play with you, do you promise to behave?"

"For a whole hour." I grin innocently.

Grumbling, he tugs his shirt up, flashing his abs.

"I remember that picture. I stared at it every night," I tell him as my eyes drop to his hand as he slides it into his pants. "I remember the sound of you panting on the phone. I was so fucking hard, everyone knew what I was doing in that tiny bathroom, but I couldn't help it. After seeing you, hearing you, I needed to get off."

He swallows hard, and I step closer, pressing my mouth to his ear. "Pant for me, baby. Let me hear you again."

His breathing picks up, and I slide my hand down his abs and cover his over his dick. "Look how hard you are for me," I murmur, licking his ear as he leans into me. "I love it when you get mouthy. It makes me think of fucking those pouty lips."

"Alek." Hearing my name on his lips makes me snarl, and I grab his pants and shove them down so I have better access.

Turning him, I press his face against the stall wall, sliding my hand down his length as I press against his ass. "You want me to fuck you here, pretty boy, where anyone can hear? Want me to be buried in this sweet ass while I touch you? Is that what you imagined that day?"

"Alek," he groans, putting his palms on the stall as he thrusts into my hand. "Please."

"Please what?" I demand, ignoring my own hard cock.

"Fuck me," he says, meeting my eyes over his shoulder. "Please fuck me."

"Because you asked so nicely, pretty boy," I promise. Pulling my cock out, I rub it across his ass, my other hand gripping and squeezing his cheeks. His eyes close, his cock jerking in my grip.

"Open up wider, baby," I order. His legs open farther, and I lift him slightly, not bothering with a condom. I want my boy raw. I want to feel every inch of him gripping me, and he says nothing as I press against his ass and work myself in, all while stroking him.

When I'm buried fully inside him, we are both panting, our bodies locked together. "Hold on, pretty boy, this is going to be hard and fast."

"I can take it. I can take you." He pants, pushing back to urge me on.

Chuckling, I slam my hand against the wall and pull out, plunging back in. The thrust makes him hit the wall, rattling the whole stall. Each time I fill his ass, I thrust him into my waiting hand, and he cries out, begging for more.

Turning his head, I swallow his moans with my mouth, kissing him while I fuck him. He's so fucking tight around my cock, gripping me like he never wants to let go of me. I pummel into him as he pants my name, taking everything I give him and more as he leaks in my hand.

Finally, neither of us can take any more.

He yells, rolling his hips as I feel his cum spill over my hand, his ass clenching around my cock. I bury myself as deep inside him as I can as my red-hot release slams through my body.

Biting his neck, I muffle my groan against his skin as I come, spilling inside his pretty ass.

I stay there before pulling my teeth free and kissing my mark, then I slowly slide my softening dick from his ass. He whimpers, and I kiss his racing pulse. "You did so well, pretty boy."

As he slumps, I reach down and pull up his jeans. "Don't clean up," I tell him. "I'll only behave if we go out there and I know I'm still deep inside you." Turning him to me, I lick my hand clean of his release as he watches, and then I kiss him. "I'll behave now."

"And I'm the brat?" he mutters, cheeks blazing, but he's grinning.

"My brat," I reply as I open the stall. The bathroom is empty, which is a surprise, but I quickly wash my hands, and then I take his.

Grinning, I hold his hand as we walk out of the bathroom door, only to freeze. Alice is standing there with a knowing look in her eyes and books in her arms. "I just want you to know, if I end up in therapy because I had to play door bouncer so you two could hump like bunnies, you're paying for it. Now come on, I'm done if you are." She arches her eyebrow.

"Your fault." Evan elbows me and smiles at her, grabbing her books before taking her arm. "He's a terrible person, Alice. I'm weak and innocent and he's corrupting me. He wouldn't even let me study in peace."

I watch them wander away with a grin. I grab our stuff quickly, carrying Evan's bag and following after them.

He isn't wrong. I'm weak when it comes to him.

FORTY-TWO

Maybe it's selfish to say things are good, but they are, at least with Alek and me. We can't keep our hands off each other, and he doesn't seem to care too much who is looking. I guess losing me woke him up a little. I still don't push it, but I find him reaching for me more often, and yeah, it might put a goofy grin on my face. However, we are both still worried about Alice, and the police aren't any closer to figuring out who killed those two or sent the flowers.

It has us all on edge, especially Alek. Usually, I let him take it out on me, letting him fuck me until he can relax, but it seems inappropriate with his sister in the car, not to mention my best friend.

"Nice bag, Anders," Lally comments, picking one up from the footwell. "I didn't expect you to carry a man bag."

Lally teases Alek as often as she can. I expected him to snap at her or hate it, but it seems they have some sort of truce, and I'll admit it makes me happy to see my boyfriend getting along so well with my best friend. Hell, Alek and Tommy talk for hours about cars when he comes to my dorm.

Glancing back, I spot a black shoulder bag and look at Alek. "You never carry a bag."

His ears are turning bright red, his eyes locked on the road as he drives us to campus. He just shrugs. I grip his bicep, squeezing until he glances at me.

"Baby?" I know it's his weakness, his eyes practically flaming with desire.

"I started carrying it for you," he admits quietly. "I noticed you were struggling to carry your camera and books all the time, so I figured I'd carry it in case you needed help."

"Oh my god," both girls say in the back, but my eyes are locked on a blushing Alek.

"What?" he asks when I just stare at him.

Leaning closer, I drop my voice. "You are so getting laid tonight," I whisper as I kiss his cheek.

His smile is wide as he winks at me, even as he continues to blush, but luckily he focuses on parking so it calms him down a little.

"You are so whipped, Anders," Lally remarks with a laugh.

"Shut up, pinkie," Alek retorts as he turns off the engine.

"What do you think, cutie?" Lally asks, nudging Alice. "Is your brother whipped?"

Alice blushes so hard, I think she might pass out, and I shoot Lally a warning look, but she only winks at me. Like me, she's a terrible flirt, but when Alice smiles, I let it go. She's been through a lot recently, so if Lally can cheer her up, then so be it.

"So whipped. Last night, Evan mentioned he was craving pastries, and this morning, Alek set an alarm on his phone on silent so it wouldn't wake Evan, and then he went and stood in line at Evan's favorite bakery to get them for him."

My mouth drops open as I gape at Alek. He never told me that. I just figured he had them.

"When you two get married, I want to be best man," Lally says.

"Who else would be?" I wink as Alek's head snaps around to me. I expect him to freak about our joke, but he just watches me seriously.

"You'd marry me?" he asks quietly.

"Baby, seeing you in a tux with a ring while locking you down? Yeah, I'd marry you. Now come on, we need to get the kids to school."

"Hey!" Alice protests as I laugh, climbing from the car, but within seconds, I'm pressed back against it, and Alek's mouth is on mine. I gasp in surprise, gripping his wide shoulders as he pins me, kissing the life out of me.

"Come on, cutie, they could be at it for a while. I'll walk you to class. Bye, Daddy One and Daddy Two, see you at dinner," Lally calls.

I wave, but my hand drops when Alek bites my lip. Pulling away, I pout as he rubs his thumb across the stinging bite, his eyes smoldering for me.

"What was that for?" I mumble.

"The idea of marrying you made me want to kiss the shit out of you," he answers without shame, smiling brightly as he steps back. "Okay, let's get you to class—wait, where did they go?" He frowns at the empty back seat.

"They left." I snicker as I take his hand. "I have a free period before my next class. Want to hang around campus and feel each other up like a horny couple?"

The smirk he gives me makes me cough, and it's my turn to blush. I hold his hand tighter and tug him after me. "Come on."

We did exactly that. We lounged on the grass, touching and teasing each other, and we laughed and talked. It was so nice just spending time with him in the sunshine.

Sighing in contentment, I look down at Alek, who has his head on my lap. He's lying on the rim of the fountain in the middle of campus, one hand covering mine on his chest, the other playing with grass. I can't help but smile as I play with his hair.

"I can feel you staring at me, rich boy," he rumbles, his chest rising with a deep breath.

"Can you blame me?" I tease, kissing his forehead with a grin. "You're so beautiful."

"I'm handsome or arrogant—"

"Nope, beautiful." I laugh as I sit up. Our words trail off, both of us content in comfortable silence.

"I'm worried about Alice," he finally admits. I know he is. He hasn't been sleeping, and it's obvious. I just wish there were more I could do to help.

"I know," I murmur, squeezing his hand in support. "The police are doing their job—"

"Not fast enough." He sits up, eyeing me as he pushes his sunglasses up on top of his head. "What if something happens in the meantime? I can't lose her, Evan. She is all I have. She's my entire family—"

Grabbing him, I tug him into my arms, rubbing his back.

"I know she is. You won't lose her. Alice is a smart girl, and we are all here." Pulling away, I cup his cheeks, looking into his terrified eyes. Sometimes I forget that Alek is only a few years older than me. He acts so confident and strong, but he's still barely an adult. He lost his parents, and now he's facing losing his sister, and he looks lost. He needs a purpose. Alek isn't the type of guy to sit on the sidelines.

"How about we snoop around?" I offer. "Look into it as much as we can? I'm not saying we will find anything, since the police are already investigating, but it might help you feel better."

His brows draw together as he watches me. "What could we find out?"

Running my eyes over his face, I debate how much to say. I don't want to break the rules of Silent Rose, but this is the love of my life and it is life or death, so surely they will understand. "There were murders like this before," I admit. "My friend told me her brother was here when it happened. Apparently, it was covered up as suicides, but everyone knows it wasn't. They never found who did it. Maybe if we can look into that, we might find some clues."

"It can't be the same person, though, if that was years ago, right?" Alek muses.

"They don't have to go to school to be here, Alek." I point at him. "They could work at the college or even close by. Maybe they aren't connected, but maybe they are, and it's obvious the police won't be looking into that link since they closed those cases years ago."

"Good point. Where would we even start?" He sighs. "Also, what friend?" His eyes narrow. "Is it a guy?"

"Not every guy I'm friends with is trying to fuck me, Anders," I scoff.

His eyebrow arches. "Most would have said that about me, but you have this way about you, pretty boy."

"It was a girl," I add helpfully.

"Still no better," he grumbles.

"Is that really what you're focusing on right now?" I ask, and he pouts at me, looking way too adorable. "Well, do you want to work together to catch a killer, baby? We could play detectives."

He groans, flopping back. "You're going to want nicknames and weird outfits, aren't you?"

"You know it." Standing, I tug on his arm to get him up. "Come on, we can start in the library. There must be news articles about what happened, and they have stored all the local newspapers."

"Fine, but I refuse to have code names," he snaps as he gets up, slinging our bags over his shoulder.

"Princess Cupcake, are you in?" I hiss into the phone.

His sigh is long and suffering. "I'm in."

"I'm sorry. I didn't hear that. Could you repeat, Princess Cupcake, since I don't know whom you are addressing?" There's a long silence where I'm sure he's debating murdering me.

"I said, I am in . . . Sprinkle Tits." It's low and growly, and I can't help but laugh as I hide in the back of the library. I have a student card, so I got in easily, but Alek not so much. Last time we came, it was nighttime and easy to slip inside, but not today. I distracted the security officer and receptionist while he snuck in and hid, but I wasn't sure if he made it.

Putting the phone down, I bite my lip to hold back my laughter as I wait, and two minutes later, he appears at the end of the row of shelves and heads my way, looking way too grumpy and sexy at the same time. I grab his hand and silently pull him toward the door. "The nice receptionist—"

"Whom you were flirting with."

I turn, my eyebrow raised. "She was like forty. Now, don't get me wrong, I get the whole cougar thing . . ." His eyes narrow in warning, and I grin. "But I'm more into the grumpy mechanic thing. It's the coveralls that do it for me."

"Fine."

"Anyway, she said this is the room we need. I booked it for the next few hours so we can look in peace. Apparently, they have physical copies, but they were also integrated into an online catalog. Let's go."

Putting in the code she gave me, I scan my ID and tug him into the dark room, then I shut and lock the door. His hand slides up my arm to my shoulder, and I hit the door.

His lips meet mine, his tongue tangling with mine as I groan and pull him closer, unable to resist. The darkness of the small room only makes it that much hotter, knowing we could be discovered at any moment. I pull away, my eyes wide as I try to see him, but it's too dark.

"Catching a killer, remember?"

"Hmm. Just one second. I need to remind us that you belong to me, otherwise I might go a little crazy with the way everyone has been flirting with you today."

My breath comes out in heavy pants as he slips down, his shadow crouching before me as he unfastens my jeans.

My eyes widen in shock at how brazen he is as he pulls my boxers down, his tattooed hand wrapping around my length. I groan, and his lips curve with a wicked smirk as he leans in and swipes his tongue along the head of my cock. My hips jerk as desire courses through me so hard, I can't catch my breath. Leaning back into the door for support, I reach down and slide my hand into his hair, needing an anchor.

Seeing Alek Anders on his knees for me is a godly experience.

"Is this how you like it, pretty boy?" he murmurs before sucking the head of my dick. The suction is so strong, my back bows as fire races down my spine. "Yours is the first cock I've ever sucked, so you might need to teach me."

His teasing tone drives me wild, but something about the idea of teaching him has me tightening my hand in his hair until he groans. Tugging him closer, I slide the wet tip of my length across his lips. "I'll teach you, princess. Open up." Obediently, he opens his mouth, his dark, wicked eyes glittering as he watches me above him.

Biting my bottom lip, I push my cock into his mouth, the warmth making me grunt as he closes it around me.

"That's it," I purr, my hips stuttering as I slide deeper into his mouth. His eyes tighten, and I groan. "Breathe through your nose," I order as he starts to gag. Pulling out, I let him recover before pushing back into his mouth. His other hand grips my thigh, and I start to pull back when I see tears gathering in his eyes, but he pushes his head farther down, taking all of my length to the back of his throat and holding himself there. His hot, wet mouth is wrapped around my length so tightly, my hips buck.

Gripping the dark strands of his hair, I tug him from my length and slam back in, unable to hold back. My head hits the door with a bang. "Please, baby," I beg, my chest heaving.

I groan his name, and it bounces around the dark room. His mouth goes wild on my length, sucking and licking as I drive into his throat over and over. My rhythm is faster than it should be, but I can't help it, and he doesn't protest—if anything, he drags me deeper, letting me use and abuse his throat and mouth. His watering eyes remain locked on me, drinking down my every reaction.

My free hand slides up my shirt, across my abs, and up my throat before hitting the door with a thump. My eyes want to roll back, but I keep them locked on him, not wanting to miss a single second of this.

Pulling back, he licks his raw lips. "You taste good, rich boy," he murmurs, licking the tip of my cock again as my hips jerk, my balls drawing up. "I want more of it. Fill my mouth with it until you're all I taste."

Fuck!

That thought is enough to have me tumbling over the edge, and he opens his lips wide as I slam into his mouth before pulling back, reaching down, and pumping my length for him.

"Stay like that," I demand breathlessly, working my cock hard and fast until I come.

Groaning deeply, I shoot ropes of cum into his open mouth, watching as it hits his tongue and slides down my hand. I massage his throat. "Swallow me," I order.

His mouth snaps shut as he swallows, letting me feel it, and then his tongue darts out to lick his lips. He catches every single drop of cum before he leans back to sit on his heels. "Well, is the teacher happy with my performance?"

All I can do is nod jerkily, my legs weak, and he grins.

Sliding up my body, he kisses me softly, letting me taste my release. It might have started with me playing with him, but we both know it ended with him getting what he wanted—me.

"Good boy," he purrs against my lips. "Next time someone looks at you, remember me on my knees for you, that you are mine, and this"—he grips my softening dick, making me gasp—"is mine."

I nod. "Yours."

"So what year should I start on?" I glance over, my mind still locked on what he just did to me. My eyes drop to his lips, and he smirks. "Focus, pretty boy."

Coughing, I rub my neck. "Maybe start five years ago? I think that's when her brother graduated."

"Got it."

I continue to stare as he searches through the boxes on the shelves, and he must feel my gaze because he turns and winks at me. "Keep looking at me like that and I'll bend you over that desk. You wanted to catch a killer, remember?"

Turning away before I order him to do just that, I wiggle the mouse and bring the computer to life. I plug in my ID and password and wait for the slow system to load. I hear him muttering as he searches. We decided to divide and conquer, with him on the physical papers and me on the system. It finally loads, and I almost groan at the system's organization. It's dated, but there isn't much more than that.

I click on the year I want and start to scroll, losing myself in each newspaper.

"Look at this," Alek calls, making me jump. Turning, I see him bent over the middle desk, newspapers spread out before him. Getting to my feet, I stretch and head his way, reading through the article he's pointing at.

SUICIDES ON CAMPUS SHAKE PINE VALLEY

It's a tiny article, almost hidden, and labels them as a suicides. I meet Alek's eyes, and he points at the box.

"The next few are missing, almost a month of articles just gone."

"How? Why?" I frown, looking back at the article. "Is someone still trying to cover up what happened?"

"Maybe. Why else would they get rid of them? You said this is the central storage for all news in Pine Valley. Aside from the journalists, no one else would really have them, right? Unless it made national news, but I don't remember seeing it."

"Me either," I murmur as I reread the article. "Maybe they didn't erase them from the online system." I hurry to the computer, hoping I'm right. We could use a lead.

"What's the date?" I call.

He reels it off, and I search for those around it and load them up.

"Okay, there are only two left," I tell him as I read through one. "Nothing in this one. It must have been before it happened. Wait—" I load the second, my eyes widening at the article hidden at the bottom. If you weren't looking for it, you wouldn't have a clue.

"A female student, Clarissa Wright, admitted that she was worried about walking on campus before the suspected murders even took place at Pine Valley, stating she felt unsafe, and there was a worrying pattern of stalking and abhorrent behavior," I read out loud. "This is before they called it suicide. It doesn't say much else, but it's something." Leaning back, I grab my phone.

"What are you doing?" Alek murmurs as he peers over my shoulder.

"We have a student and teacher directory, and alumni are included too. I'm searching for her." I type in her name and wait. There are only two people with that name, and one graduated ten years before. The other has a student ID but no alumni information.

"That's weird," I mutter.

"Why?" he asks.

"She should have graduated. This means she was a student but didn't . . . Maybe she dropped out?" I look up at him. "And I'm betting I know why."

"But how do we find her?" Alek asks.

"They don't list contact information or addresses." I have an idea and pull up Bones's information, hitting dial. He answers within seconds.

"You okay, Evan?" he asks. "I'm at home, but I can be at school in ten—"

"No, no, I just need a favor, if that's okay?" I reply.

"Of course, tell me," he murmurs. There is a voice in the background, and then the sound of a door shutting.

"I need you to find someone, and I know you have connections. Her name is Clarissa Wright. She left Pine Valley three years ago. She was a student," I explain.

I hear him typing. "Got it. Give me ten, and I'll call you back, okay?"

The fact that he doesn't even ask why makes me grin. "Thanks, Bones." I hang up and smile at Alek. "He'll find her, then we can speak to her and find out what really happened."

He nods and then tilts his head. "How do you know Bones?"

"You know Bones?" I gape.

He chuckles as he lifts me then sets me on his lap, wrapping his arms around me and tugging me closer. "Hmm." He nods. "He's teaching Alice self-defense. I met him at the gym."

"Ah, he goes here." I hate that I have to lie to him. "We met in a club."

"A club? I didn't know you were part of a club," he asks curiously, not suspiciously.

"Oh, you know how it is, so many clubs. I just wanted to try one." I cough and straddle his lap, sliding my hands up his chest to distract him. "Want to fool around while we wait?" I wiggle my eyebrows, and he laughs.

"You are insatiable," he remarks, but his hand slides down my back, gripping my ass and tugging me closer so we are pressed together.

Lowering my head, I place teasing kisses along his lips until he groans and yanks my head to his. I moan as he kisses me deeply, but my phone rings, interrupting us. Opening one eye, I grab it and hit speaker as I pull away. Alek keeps kissing down my neck, making me close my eyes in bliss as I bite back a moan.

"Hmm?" I answer.

"Evan?" Bones asks in confusion.

"I'm here." My voice is slightly breathless, but honestly, he's doing this thing with his tongue. I hiss as he bites me and push him away, then I narrow my eyes in warning. "Did you find her?"

Bones chuckles. "Am I interrupting something?"

"Nothing," I warn Alek with my eyes as he smirks.

"Okay, well, Clarissa Wright dropped out. She moved home, which is three hours away, but when her mother died, she moved in with her father just thirty minutes away. I'm texting you her address. She is still there, registered as his nurse and working at a local pet supply shop. Is everything okay?"

"Yep, just some research," I reply. I'll tell him later when Alek isn't here.

"Okay, well, good luck. Let me know if you need anything." He hangs up, and I swing my gaze back to Alek.

"You'll pay for that!" I growl as I lean in and bite his shoulder, making him yelp.

SHAW DRIVE
ANDERS AVE
ONE WAY
STOP
NO PARKING
ACTIVE DRIVEWAY
THE MOMENT
TOO
NO PARKING
SALE
SILENT ROSE
Pine Valley
EVER

FORTY-THREE

We eventually make it out of the library, and my neck still has a bruise from his teeth. It shouldn't make me happy, but it does. After checking on Alice and making sure she is in class, Evan skips his and we take the short drive to Clarissa Wright's address. We linger in the car, staring at the normal two-story house, wondering what answers we'll find. Evan was right—I need a purpose. I need to do something.

"Do not growl or glare, and don't scare her. We need her help," Evan reminds me.

"I do not growl." I frown, but he just arches his eyebrow. I slide into my seat, sulking. "Fine, I'll be quiet."

"Good boy. If you behave, I'll play with you later." He pats my thigh and gets out. Jumping out, I grab his hand and walk with him. He rings the doorbell as we stand on the welcome mat on the porch.

"Coming, one second!" a distinctively female voice calls. Two minutes later, a harried, smiling woman opens the door. Her smile fades, and she tilts her head as she looks at us. She's a few years older than us, with frizzy brown hair, pretty eyes, and a nice smile. She's small and seems to shrink before us, clearly anxious.

"Clarissa Wright?" Evan asks kindly, offering her a dazzling smile that makes her blink as she stares at him.

She looks between us in confusion. "Yes, who are you? I wasn't expecting visitors."

"We go to Pine Valley." All color drains from her face, and she goes to shut the door, but I wedge my foot in it.

"Please, just talk to us," Evan pleads as she continues to struggle to shut the door.

"I have nothing to say." She uses all her weight to try and close it.

"There have been two more murders," I tell her bluntly.

She freezes, her wide, shocked eyes landing on me.

"If you haven't seen anything yet, you will soon. They are saying it's suicide, but we know it isn't, and you know it too. We need to talk."

"I can't, please go," she begs, tears forming in her eyes. "If it's happening again—" She shakes her head, terror etched into her features.

"Clarissa, please," Evan implores, giving her his best sad puppy eyes. "Someone we care about is in danger, please."

She looks from me to him.

There's a gurgling noise in the background, and her head jerks around for a moment before she looks us over, her eyes lingering on Evan as if she's scared to look at me. She purses her lips.

"We aren't taking no for an answer," I tell her as kindly as I can.

Sighing, she glances over her shoulder again. "Don't worry, Dad, it's just some friends," she calls and opens the door. "Fine, come in." She wraps her arms around herself, and we step into the warm hall-way. There are family pictures on every wall, and it's clear it's a house full of love. To the right is a living room with a man in a bed facing a TV. He has an oxygen mask on his face, and he's skin and bones.

That same gurgling noise comes again, his eyes widening on us as he hits the remote for the TV.

"Don't worry, everything is fine," she tells him, forcing a smile and turning to us as he makes another noise, hitting the remote again.

"Come in here. I don't want to disturb my father. He's sick as it is. He doesn't need this."

She jerks her head, and we follow her down the hall, away from the living room and into a tiny kitchen with a ramp in it. She leans back against the counter, looking out of the sliding back door to a small, rear garden.

"I guess I knew this would happen." She sighs and looks at us then nods at the small round table. "Sit."

We do, our hands interlaced under the table.

"Do you want drinks?" she asks kindly.

"No, thank you, Clarissa. I'm sorry. I know it was a long time ago —" Evan starts.

"Not long enough. No number of years could make me forget what happened at Pine Valley," she says as she sits opposite us, her shoulders rounded.

"Clarissa, what happened?" Evan asks softly. "Why did you leave Pine Valley? Why did you say you didn't feel safe?"

"Because I didn't." She looks at her hands. "I left for that same reason. I knew if I stayed, I would have ended up dead." She sits back heavily, her eyes on us. "You said there were some deaths? Guys, right? Made to look like suicide?"

We share a look and nod.

"Then it's happening again. I guess I hoped it was over when I left. I should have known better." She laughs bitterly, rubbing her face.

"What's happening?" I ask.

She eyes me. "Your girlfriend?"

"Sister," I reply.

"Cute? Shy? Introvert without many friends?" We both nod, and she laughs. "Seems he still has a type. They were probably murdered for being near her."

"They attacked her."

"That will do it, but anyone who's close to her, a threat to him, will end up the same way. Don't rely on the cops. They won't do anything. They didn't for me." She purses her lips. "It wasn't about them. It's about your sister. At least that's how it was for me. The ones who were killed when I was there were my ex and someone I went on a date with. It didn't take me long to get the picture. I was terrified. Flowers would turn up with notes, and then it started to escalate. Someone broke into my dorm and slept in my bed, and one night, I swore someone watched me sleep, and then I started to feel them watching me all the time. It got really bad, and I was scared. I went to the police, and they listened to me at first and offered protection . . ."

"But?" I prompt.

"But he had money and connections and made it all go away. The murders were covered up as suicides, and even the police said I was making things up." Evan reaches over, covering her hand on the table, and she looks at him, her expression softening.

"My father . . . he doesn't know. No one believed me. No one wanted to after it was covered up. I was called a liar, a troublemaker. I ended up dropping out. I didn't feel safe or welcome."

"You are saying this person was obsessed with you, stalking you, and killing anyone who got too close to you, and no one did anything?" I snap.

"You don't understand," she hisses. "He's untouchable. He's like a god, comes from money and power. He's not someone you mess with if you want to live, and I wanted to live so I disappeared where he couldn't find me. I thought that would be the end. I'm so sorry. If it's him and he's taken an interest in your sister, then you don't stand a chance. Get her out of there fast. He won't stop, not until he has her."

"Who?" I ask. "Give me his name."

"No, I won't. I won't even speak it. If I do and you go after him, I'm dead. Don't you understand? He left me alone because I've been silent and his family made him, but if I speak, not only is my father dead, but so am I. His dad is covering my father's bills. It's hush money. I have no other choice. I can't. I wish I could, believe me, but he won't stop. He's only gotten meaner and older. He isn't afraid to kill someone to get what he wants. He knows he can't be touched, knows not even the police can stand in his way. Take your sister and leave before it's too late."

"And what about those who come after her? What about the ones he killed? We just let him?" I ask incredulously.

"You can't stop him." She stands. "Nobody can, not two boys from nowhere. It's better to run. You need to leave before he finds out you're here, please."

"Clarissa—" Evan starts.

"Please leave, now." We share a look and rise, but at the door, Evan looks back at her.

"Was it worth it? Running and hiding? You've lost your entire life. Don't you wish you fought?"

"I'm not strong enough. No one is," she admits. "No, it's better to lose everything. At least I'm still alive."

She shuts the door after us, and I grind my teeth. "We need that name. If she's right, he won't stop, and the police won't do anything. Maybe we should go?" I hate the idea, but if it's the only way to keep Alice safe, then I'll do it.

"I'm tired of running," Evan murmurs as he looks at me. "Besides, it won't stop, not even if we leave."

"I won't force you or her to give up your future, not for one wacko." I wrap my arms around him as we head to the car and get in, our eyes on her house. "We need to find who it was. We can look into who is paying for her father's care and talk to her old classmates. We'll find him before he finds us. I'll keep you both safe."

"You aren't alone in this," Evan says as I look at him, memorizing his beautiful face.

"I know. Thank you, pretty boy," I murmur as I kiss his hand, "for giving me something to do."

"Alice is my family now too," he says. "Besides, I want this idiot caught as much as you do. He got me detained, remember?"

"True, only I can put you in handcuffs."

"Exactly. Princess, you are getting bold, but I like your thinking." His smile fades. "If she is right, though, then we need more than just the two of us. We need to beat him at his own game. No one is untouchable."

"You have an idea?" Something in his eyes makes me frown.

"I do, but you aren't going to like it."

"You what?" I ask, gaping at him. "You are in a secret society, like for real, that isn't some movie bullshit?"

We are at my house, since he said we needed privacy, but this wasn't what I was expecting.

"It's a secret. I couldn't tell you." He sighs. "It's like a club. It's also how I met Bones. Each member is powerful, from important families, and we can use their help. We vowed to help each other, so if I ask, they will. They might be able to get us the information and force the police to do something."

"And what if they say no?" I snap.

"I don't think they will. I also think . . . I think he was a member. Autumn's brother was, and she mentioned one of them was blamed five years ago. I think it was the same guy and it was covered up, but they all suspected. It will narrow it down, and if we are going after a member of the Silent Rose, then we'll need all the help we can get. Clarissa is right. He was in this society for a reason. They are untouchable." He covers my hand. "Don't be mad, please. I couldn't tell you, plus when I was inducted, I didn't even really know you."

"Fine," I grumble. "At least tell me if it's just rich pricks sitting around?"

"Pretty much." He laughs. "It's mostly a brotherhood, a party, but they are actually really nice. That's why Bones got me out. They'll help."

He's so sure of it, I can't help but tug him closer. "Okay then, we will work with them. Will you get into trouble for telling me?"

"Maybe, but I don't care." He sighs, snuggling into my side. "What time do we need to go back for Alice? I could go and meet them—"

"She texted me saying she's coming home with Tommy and Lally later," I tell him. "I tried to tell her I would pick her up, but she insisted."

"She knows what she's doing. She isn't stupid, Alek." He sighs. "Plus, it's for the best. We were late getting back because of traffic. How about you cook for me, and I'll suck your dick?"

I almost fall from the couch, turning my head rapidly. "Jesus, Evan!"

"What?" he asks, fluttering his lashes innocently. "It's a good trade, right? I can't cook, but I can suck cock."

I just stare before jumping to my feet. "Deal." His laughter chases me into the kitchen.

FORTY-FOUR

"Princess, your phone is ringing," I shout from his couch as he cooks for me.

"Answer it!" he yells back.

Something about his response makes me grin, so I grab his phone and hit answer. "Hey, Alley cat, he's just cooking. What time are you coming back? We'll save you some—"

"Evan." The sob makes me sit upright.

"Alek!" I yell. "Alice, what's wrong?"

I hit speaker as Alek runs into the room with his frilly apron on, spatula in hand. "I'm sorry. I was so stupid. I lied to Alek. I'm not with Tommy or Lally."

"Where are you?" I demand.

"I went on a date." Alek and I share a look. "On the way back—" She hiccups, sobbing. "I was waiting for him outside of the restaurant since it was raining. He went to get the car. As he started to drive toward me, another car hit him. He's in the hospital. I'm in the waiting room. Can you come get me?"

"Which hospital?" Alek asks, ripping off his apron and grabbing his keys. "I'll be right there. Don't move!"

"Pinetree," she sobs. "Come quickly."

"We're coming." I hang up. "Breathe, Alek." I head into the kitchen and turn off the oven, moving everything away and grabbing his coat and bag. I find him at the door, waiting anxiously. "She's okay. She wasn't in the car."

"She's my sister, Evan," he snaps.

"I know." Taking his hand, I kiss the back of it. "Let's go get her."

We get there in record time, even with me driving since I didn't trust Alek to. I'm surprised he let me touch his baby, but he's worried about his sister, even though she told us ten times on the phone on the way here that she's fine.

It doesn't stop him from storming into the ER and scanning the space until he finds her. He rushes over and pulls her into a hug, and she bursts into more tears. I run my eyes over her, checking for injuries, but she seems okay, just upset and scared, which is understandable.

"Look at me," Alek demands, holding her at arm's length. "Are you hurt? Even a little?"

Leaving Alek to check Alice over, I head to the desk. "Hi, how is the boy who came in with Alice?" I point at her.

"I'm not supposed to tell." The nurse leans over. "But he's okay. Some bruises and bumps, a few broken ribs and a wrist, but he'll live. He's lucky."

"Thank you." I head back over to Alice and Alek just as Lally hurries into the emergency room, her eyes landing on Alice. She ignores us as she yanks her into a hug.

"I just got your text. Are you okay?"

Alek and I share a look. "Lally?"

She pulls away, sparing me a glance, but then focuses on Alice. "What happened?" she asks.

"Someone crashed into my date. The police think it was a deliberate hit-and-run. I've already spoken to them, but I wanted to stay so he wasn't alone." She sobs. "I was so scared." She melts into Lally's arms, who holds her and whispers to her as Alek and I share another look.

It has to be him. Clarissa was right—he's stepping it up. He tried to kill a boy who went on a date with Alice. It's obvious he thinks she's his, and he won't stop. If he's willing to murder two boys for even daring to go near her, then what else is he capable of?

Alice eventually calms down enough to talk to Alek, so I tug Lally to my side, knowing Alek needs this time with his sister.

"We'll go get some drinks." I drag Lally after me despite her protests.

"When did you two get so close?" I murmur, nudging Lally when we get to the vending machine outside.

She shrugs, looking over the drinks inside. "We are in the same school, and she knows you. I guess it just happened. When I found out she was going on a date, I texted her, and she just replied."

Hitting the buttons, I wait for the bottles to fall. I'm just bending over to get them when lights splash over us. Straightening, I cover my eyes, completely blinded. It's surprisingly quiet outside, I realize, as we turn to see a car pointed at us in the lot, its engine revving.

"Lally, go inside," I demand. "This must be the guy who hurt Alice's date."

"What? Why would you think that?"

"I'll tell you later, go," I hiss.

"What are you doing?" she asks as I step forward, intent on confronting him. "Evan." Lally grabs my arm. "Don't. If it's the guy, then that is some stupid horror movie bullshit to go after him."

I know she's right. Pulling my phone out, I take a picture of the license plate and grab Lally before I tug her inside, moving slowly. Whoever it is just watches, but I know it's a warning—a threat.

Back inside, I warn Lally with my eyes not to say anything, but when Alice talks to a nurse with Lally, I pull Alek aside. "Are you okay?" he asks with a frown.

"He was here," I murmur. Alek freezes, and I nod. "Outside,

warning us in his car. He's watching, probably stalking her. We need to be careful."

Our eyes go back to Alice.

"Do we tell her?" I ask softly.

"She needs to know," he admits. "Can you . . . Will you—"

"I'll be there. I'm not going anywhere," I promise.

SHAW DRIVE
NO PARKING
ACTIVE DRIVEWAY
THE MOMENT
ANDERS AVE
ONE WAY
STOP
TOO
CAR REPAIR
NO PARKING
SALE
SILENT ROSE
EVER
Pine Valley

FORTY-FIVE

ALEK

On the way back from the hospital, we stop at Evan's dorm so he can pack. We decided he will move in for a little while. I'll feel better having them both under one roof, and he wants to help protect Alice. We drop Lally off, and she has a whispered conversation with Alice.

When we get back, we sit her on the couch, both of us standing before her. "We need to talk, and you need to listen."

"I'm sorry for lying." She hangs her head.

"Not about that. That will be later," I warn her before softening my voice. "Alice, this is serious."

I know this is going to be hard, but she deserves to know. Keeping her in the dark won't help her at all.

Crouching, I take her hand. "The person who attacked you tonight, who sent those flowers, and who . . . who killed those boys—it's the same person."

"What do you mean?" she asks, scared.

We lay everything out, and I keep nothing from her. I won't lie to my sister, not about this. She needs to know. It's her life, and he is targeting her, so she needs to understand how serious this is.

After, she's pale as she stares at us. "He's targeting me . . . to kill me?"

I share a look with Evan, who sits at her side, and he takes her hand. "No, I don't think it's to kill you. I think he wants to . . . possess you. He thinks you are his. Has there been anyone like that in your life recently, Alice? Anything at all could help."

"No, no one, I swear." Tears fill her eyes and begin to flow down her face. "What if he hurts you two? What if he doesn't stop?" Her bottom lip begins to tremble. "I couldn't live if something happened to either of you."

"Hey." Evan tugs her into his arms. "That isn't going to happen, you know that. We can handle ourselves. We are more worried about you, you silly, kind girl. We will figure out who this is, and we will stop them, okay?"

"But to do that, I need to know you are safe. You will be with one of us at all times, is that understood? Apart from school, you won't go anywhere else," I warn, laying down the rules. "I mean it, Alice. I won't have you in danger, not even for your independence. I'd rather you hate me but be alive."

"Okay." She sighs, glancing between us. "I'll do as you say."

Evan and I share a look, silent messages passing between us.

We will do whatever it takes to keep her safe.

It's been suspiciously quiet for days, and it's putting me on edge as we wait for something to happen. I watch Alice like a hawk, and she is never alone. Both Evan and I escort her everywhere. It means I have no time for racing, and I've cut my hours at work, but I'd do much worse to keep her safe and happy. Her fear is starting to wear off and turn to annoyance, but it can't be helped. I'd rather she hate me than be dead.

We accompany her to visit her friend in the hospital, but he doesn't want to see her. I guess he's scared. I don't blame him. Evan said word has gotten around campus that some maniac is obsessed with her, and everyone is avoiding her apart from us.

We have been in the background, looking into the person behind Clarissa's father's care as quietly as we can, but we haven't gotten anywhere. I know Evan has approached his society about it, and they are also searching, so it's just a matter of time until we find this creep, but for a young girl, time goes slowly, especially with an overbearing brother.

It's Friday, and she wants to go out. She won't, but I can see it in her face. She's desperate to be normal and not miss out on college life. I might not understand that, but I can comprehend her wanting to be happy. I hate seeing her so downtrodden, and even Evan's sunshine can't seem to warm her.

I can't stand my sister's sadness, so I sigh deeply. "How about we have some friends over tonight?"

She perks up, looking hopeful. "Really?"

"Really. Evan can invite Lally and Tommy, and I'll ask Bones and Skylar to come over. We can watch movies and chill. We are safe here anyway. It can be like a mini party," I suggest reluctantly. At least if it's here, I can keep her safe. Besides, with us here, the creep wouldn't stand a chance.

She giggles. "You hate parties."

"I do, but I love you." I sigh as I glance at Evan, who's giving me a thumbs-up behind her back. "Both of you idiots."

"Aww, so sweet," Evan teases as he heads my way, grabbing my neck and tilting my head up as he places a soft kiss on my lips. Alice gags as Evan chuckles and grins down at me, his eyes sparkling. "Does that mean I get to see you dance?"

"Never," I vow vehemently.

FORTY-SIX

Alek is a liar. All it took was one pout and sad eyes, and now he's dancing.

I invited Tommy and Lally, and they jumped at the chance to hang out since I've been with Alice and Alek a lot recently. Alek said he'd invite Bones and Skylar, but so far, they are no-shows, but it's still early.

Pizza covers the table, along with beer and soda, and music fills the room. Alice dances happily with Tommy. He swings her around, dipping and twisting her until she laughs. That's one thing about Tommy—he can always sense when you need to be cheered up, and he will do anything to make it happen. He truly is an amazing friend, and from the glow on Alice's face, I know it's working.

I notice Lally watching them. More specifically, she's watching Alice, and my eyebrows rise before Alek turns me in his arms, moving slowly to the music. He doesn't match the tempo at all, but he doesn't seem to care, and neither do I. The next song comes on, a crooning indie rock melody, and we sway to the music.

His hands are on my hips, and mine are around his neck. I lay my head on his chest, listening to his racing heart, which makes me smile.

He always gets nervous around me regardless of how much time we spend together.

I hope that never changes. I hope he always gets this flustered with me because it's sweet.

We sway to the music, lost in our own world, as his arms wrap tighter around me. Suddenly, there is a knock at the door. He sighs and pulls away, striding over to answer it as Lally comes over and dances with me. I spin her in a circle as I keep watch. A grumpy, slightly wet Bones slaps Alek's shoulder before he heads inside, bags in tow. They go into the kitchen when there's another knock. I swing Lally to Alice, and Tommy collapses back on the couch, letting them dance.

Opening the door, I tilt my head at the man there. "Skylar?"

"The one and only." He grins, holding up a case of beer. "With goodies. Let me in, Alek's boy."

Shaking my head, I move aside, and he stomps toward the kitchen. "Yo, asshole, I parked out front to show off to all your neighbors. Well, hello . . ."

Leaving Alek to deal with his guests, I drop down next to Tommy, throwing my legs over his while Lally and Alice giggle, dancing to the music.

"You know, I think there's something between them," Tommy comments, looking at me.

"No shit." I bark out a laugh. "Tommy, you really are dumb."

Frowning, he glances at them. "You knew?"

"Even the hedges know," I tease, nudging him. "We just need to lock you down now."

Alek drags a grinning Skylar into the living room and throws him on the couch. "Stay and behave before Bones kills you."

"But he's pretty." Skylar pouts.

"If you like living, I suggest you don't call him that." Alek's eyes land on me and narrow. "Pretty boy."

Rolling my eyes, I lift my legs off Tommy, knowing Alek doesn't like it, and then I get up and lean into his side. "So Skylar—"

"You can call me Sky, Alek's boy." He toasts me with a beer.

Sitting next to him as Alek goes to find Bones, I turn to look at him. "Tell me all his dirty secrets."

"Only if you tell me about the tattooed asshole in the kitchen." I raise my eyebrow, and he grins. "I like them broody and tough, makes it that much sweeter when they give in and let me pin them down."

"In your fucking dreams," Bones snarls as he leans against the wall in the hallway, glaring at Skylar, who doesn't seem bothered by that at all.

"Oh, it definitely will be," Sky flirts, dragging his eyes along Bones's body. "You can bet on that. Tell me so I can make sure my imagination does my dreams justice, are your tattoos everywhere?"

Bones arches an eyebrow. "Skylar, was it?" Skylar nods eagerly as Bones leans in, and I bite my lip to hold back my smile when he's almost close enough to kiss. Skylar is wide-eyed as Bones places his mouth just above his. "You'll never find out."

He pulls away, and Skylar groans. "Mean, so mean and hot. You're perfect."

Bones smirks and hides it behind his cup.

Leaning into Alek, I look up into his happy eyes. "I bet you a blow job they end up fucking."

"Deal." He smirks, tugging me closer and dropping a kiss to my head. "Are you having a good night?"

I nod, leaning into him, my eyes on Alice. "I think she is too. It's just what we all needed, a break from the madness."

The music changes again, something upbeat, and I lose myself in Alek's dark eyes, but the lights suddenly cut out, plummeting us into darkness. There's a mix of screams, and when I turn my flashlight on, I find Tommy huddled behind us, still screaming loudly.

"Really?" I ask.

He coughs and closes his mouth but stays there. "Sorry, that freaked me out."

"Nope, this is some horror movie bullshit," Lally remarks.

"You are both idiots," Alek scoffs. "It's just the breaker. It's an older house."

"Alek," Alice calls.

"Hey, it's fine." I turn my flashlight to her. "We'll go turn it back on, okay? Just stay here."

She nods, sitting with Lally. Alek takes my hand, and we head outside to the breakers around back. It isn't the first time this has happened, so I'll act as his flashlight when he needs it, but when we get away from the windows, he pushes me against the wall of the house. His hand smacks against the wood as his dark eyes lock on me.

"Alek, the lights—"

"Can wait a minute. I've wanted to do this all night." His head lowers, and his lips crash onto mine. Groaning, I grip his shirt and haul him closer as he rubs against my body, his tongue tangling with mine.

His hand slides down, shoving into my jeans and stroking my length as I gasp, turning my head, but his lips press against my neck.

"Alek," I moan.

"That's it, pretty boy, moan my name. We all know you'll be screaming it later when I'm buried in your pretty ass."

Oh fuck. My eyes close as he strokes me, his teeth digging into my neck. "Please," I beg.

"You're mine, pretty boy. Say it," he demands as he tugs my jeans down and frees my cock. Shoving his pants down, he presses our lengths together as he slides his hands along me.

"I'm yours." My head hits the house hard as I thrust against him, desire flaming through me until I'm on the verge of coming from his touch. "And you're mine."

His lips tilt up against my neck. "I am yours, every inch of me, and you'll get every inch later to prove it, but for now, I want to feel you come. I want it on me when I go back in there so I can hold back while you grind against me like my own fucking porn star."

I laugh, but it ends in a moan when he squeezes my cock. Suddenly, there's a shout from inside. "Alek, hurry the fuck up. Tommy is being weird in the dark!"

We break apart, panting, and burst into laughter. "Come on, before they send out a search party." Reluctantly, I tuck my hard dick away, and he frowns, glaring through the house's wall before kissing me harder.

"Later," he promises.

He puts himself away then takes my hand once more, and we head into the back garden. He crouches down at the box as I shine the flashlight, and he quickly takes care of it before we go back inside hand in hand. We shut the door behind us, and I raise my eyebrow when I find Tommy twerking on a very amused Skylar.

"You know what? I'm not even going to ask."

Just then, the lights cut out again, and we all turn to the front door. I glance at Alek. "It shouldn't do that, right?"

"Maybe there's a problem," he mutters, but he's frowning. "Stay here."

"Like hell I will." I follow him back out, no funny business this time, and when I shine my flashlight on the box, we both freeze. It's damaged, the wires cut. Our eyes meet, and we both turn to the house.

"Alice!"

We start running just as a crash cuts through the air, followed by screams.

SHAW DRIVE
ANDERS AVE
ONE WAY
STOP
THE MOMENT
ACTIVE DRIVEWAY
NO PARKING
SALE
SILENT ROSE
EVER
Drive Valley

FORTY-SEVEN

ALEK

"What happened? Why are you screaming?" I ask as I hurry into the living room, searching Alice for injuries.

"The crash scared me, that's all." She looks upstairs where it came from.

"Stay here," I order everyone, grabbing a baseball bat from a closet. I ascend the stairs, turning when there's a creak to find a determined Evan right behind me.

"Downstairs," I hiss.

"No," he snaps.

I grit my teeth, knowing it's no good to fight with him. I search the bathroom then Alice's room before mine. The back window is smashed in, glass covering the bed, and there's a giant rock on the comforter. Picking it up one-handed, I turn it over to find writing on the back.

SHE'S MINE.

I show Evan, and he nods. "He's here. We should call the police."

"Go back downstairs, I want us all together."

I follow him down and lock the front door, checking the windows. Everyone is huddled together in the living room. "Don't panic, okay? He's here." Alice's eyes widen, and I pull her into my arms. "He's

349

trying to scare you. I'm going to call the police. The doors are locked. They'll come and get him, alright? You're safe. We are all here."

Just as I finish speaking, there's a crash from the back of the house —the kitchen. I share a look with Evan, who finished setting out candles. "Stay with her," I order. Gripping the bat tighter, I make my way down the hallway, but I feel Evan follow seconds later. When I glance back, Bones and Skylar are standing next to Alice, and they nod at me to let me know they have her.

I turn back to the hallway, peering at the dark kitchen, straining to see anything.

There's another crash, this time from the front of the house. I hesitate but keep moving, needing to check the back door.

"Well, that's clearly a trap, so nope, I'm not doing that. Not today, Mr. Serial Killer. You will have to do better. That's a basic bitch move right there," I hear Lally call as I move to the kitchen, Evan on my heels.

It's dark, but light from the back garden streams inside.

The back door is open, the lock on the floor. I search the empty space, my eyes landing on the knife block and the empty spot where the biggest knife should be. All the hair on my body rises as fear washes through me. This is serious. I need to get them out of here. It's no longer safe. "Evan, we can't wait here for the police. We'll drive to the station. Tell the others—" I turn just as something flashes in the dark.

A blur heads toward Evan, knife raised to plunge it into his body, the sharp tip glittering in the limited light.

Snarling, I push Evan aside, and he slams into the floor as I take the blade meant for him.

The sharp pain makes me grunt as I hit the wall, the knife sticking from my side before the shadow yanks it out and raises it again. My hands come up slowly to cover the wound when Evan yells and tackles the shadow, sending them sprawling across the room.

"Evan!" I yell, stumbling forward.

They grapple until Evan is above the masked assailant. The light shining in allows me to see a creepy mask over his face. Evan doesn't care. He slams his fist into the man's face over and over until he stops moving, then he grabs the knife and jumps to his feet. He turns to me, his eyes dropping to my side where I'm bleeding.

"Alek," he whispers before he grabs me and shoves me down the hallway to the others. Alice screams when she sees me.

Evan grabs my keys and looks at the others. "Go now! To the cars! Head to the station," he barks, shoving me to the front door as he glances back at the kitchen, the knife held in his hands as I grab him and pull him out after us, and we spill into the front garden. We all sprint to my car, squeezing in—Evan in the driver's seat, me in the passenger seat, and the others in the back, sitting on knees. As Evan turns on the engine and peels away, I turn back to see the masked man run from the house and dive into a car two doors down. The lights splash on the empty, quiet road, and then he's driving after us.

I look at Evan and find him gripping the wheel, glancing at the mirror over and over. "Ease up, baby," I warn. "Head to the station." Glancing down, I peel my hand away to see the bleeding wound. It's deep, but I don't think it hit anything vital or I would be bleeding more.

"What happened?" Bones asks from the back, where he's perched on Skylar's knee.

"Alice's stalker was there. He tried to gut Evan, but I stopped him."

"And got stabbed!" Evan yells hysterically, glancing at me with worried eyes. He looks at my side, where I'm holding the wound, and he gulps.

"Shh, it's okay, pretty boy, just a flesh wound," I promise, trying not to let my pain show.

"You let yourself get stabbed. Who lets themselves get stabbed nowadays?" Skylar scoffs.

Sighing, I glance back at him in disbelief. "I didn't let myself get stabbed. I got stabbed. There's a difference," I grumble.

"Who gets stabbed? What are we, in *Scream* or *Freddy vs. Jason*? Hell, even *Texas Chainsaw Massacre* or some *The Strangers* bullshit?" He just keeps rapidly listing horror movies, and we all turn, even Evan, to stare at him. He stops babbling and glances around nervously. "What?"

"You have a suspicious amount of knowledge about horror films," Bones deadpans as Sky's cheeks heat, making me grin.

"I watch them when I want to feel something, okay?" Sky counters, and despite the situation, I kind of want to laugh, which is probably why he did it.

"When this is over, I think we need to get you a therapist," I suggest with a grin.

"Or laid." Bones snorts, glancing back at Sky, who wiggles his eyebrows at the tattooed asshole.

"Are you offering, sexy?"

"Is this really the time?" Evan yells, glancing at me as I staunch the blood flow. His eyes are wide and wild, and he's holding the wheel like a lifeline.

"Right, serial killer on the loose and chasing us. Alek let himself get stabbed—"

"I didn't let myself get—you know what? Throw him out and let the stalker have him," I tell Bones and Evan.

"Then you wouldn't have any friends," Sky retorts.

"I have Bones," I argue.

"Nope, not your friend." Bones shrugs casually, even as we speed through the streets, heading toward the police station. I glance in the mirror but don't see any lights. Did we lose him?

"I'll be your friend," Evan says, throwing me a worried smile, knowing we are doing it to keep and me calm. My sister is practically hyperventilating. Lally has her arms around her, whispering to her quietly.

"Aww, that's so cute, I'm going to throw up," Bones grumbles.

Alice starts yelling then, which is better than crying. "What the hell is wrong with all of you?"

It goes silent, and Sky leans into Bones as I glance back at my sister. "I think she needs to get laid more or go to like a rage room or something. Why don't we get her drunk at a quiz or something?"

Alice turns and gapes at Sky as Evan focuses on driving, and I pull out some rags from the glove box. They are cleanish, thank fuck, so I bind my waist to stop as much bleeding as I can.

"I like quizzes," Lally says helpfully as Tommy nods, looking far too pale where he's squeezed between them.

"We should call our team Super Gays," Lally muses, following along to calm everyone down.

"I am not calling it Super Gays." I sigh then wince when it tugs on the wound.

"Right," she says. "Because Evan is bi."

"Seriously?" Alice yells, throwing her hands in the air before pointing at us. "Stop it. What the fuck is going on?"

Anger is better than fear, though, so it's working.

"Alice, it's okay," I tell her. "It didn't hit anything important. I'm stopping the bleeding, and we are heading to the station. I'll get seen, so sit back and calm down, alright?" I wait until she does that, huffing, but it's obvious she's worried. Glancing at Evan, I see him staring at the road as he presses down on the pedal, driving my car erratically, but I'm more worried about his grinding jaw.

Leaning over, I lay my hand on Evan's thigh. "Baby, slow down."

"I can't," he admits and lowers his voice. "He's following us."

I follow his eyes and see the lights hitting our back window. "He won't be able to follow us into the station. It will be okay."

"We have a problem with that." Evan nods his head, and I turn to see the road we need is closed, with flashing cones and signs blocking it. Groaning, I look back and turn to Evan. "Okay, we can just go around—" We are hit from behind. I slam my hand against the ceiling and my arm across the middle to stop them from flying through the windshield. Evan grits his teeth, controlling our spin as best as he can, jerking us back onto the road, but we are rammed again by the car. We fishtail, spinning, and luckily Evan stops us from flipping before we slide to a stop.

I look into the back. "Are you okay?" I ask them. They all nod, and I glance at Evan. "Evan?" I panic.

"Fine, I'm fine." He hits the steering wheel as the engine cuts out, and he turns the key, trying to restart it. "It won't fucking start."

"He might have hit something. I don't have time to fix it." The revving of the other car makes my eyes narrow, and I jerk around, looking at where we are. The familiar art buildings on campus catch my eye. "Come on, let's get out. We can hide in the school and call the police."

"That's what he wants—us on foot," Evan hisses.

"I know, pretty boy." I grip his hand and kiss him. "But it's all we have."

"This is fucked up," he snaps. "He planned all of this."

"I know." Gripping the bat, I hand him the knife and glance back. "There are tools under the seat."

Bones leans over, grabbing the box and handing out wrenches and screwdrivers. It's better than nothing.

"We'll run to your art building." I can't believe we are here, of all places. "We'll get inside, find a classroom, and block the door while we wait for the cops."

"It's an away game today," Bones adds unhelpfully. "No one will be around to help."

"Fucking great." Gripping the bat, I run my eyes over them. "Run fast."

"Alek." Alice shakes her head. "I can't. Please, let's just go to the cops—"

"Look at me," I order, and she does. "You can do this. I'll be right there, okay? He isn't getting anywhere near you. If we stay here, we're dead. We have to keep moving and find somewhere safe."

Bones nods. "I can take him. It's one fucking guy."

"With a car," I remind him. "If it comes to it, we can all take him, but not with him using a car. We would be sitting ducks. He's proven he's willing to kill."

"So am I," Bones replies seriously.

"Will you marry me?" Skylar teases.

I spare him a glare as the car revs. "Now!" I roar.

I kick open my door and climb out, ignoring my wound as much as I can. The back doors open, the others spilling out as I meet the eyes of the man in the car. Lights spread across us and the road, doors slam, and I turn away.

Throwing Alice at Lally, I push them forward as we start to run.

I grab Evan's hand and tug him after me as we burst into a sprint, heading toward the school. The car revs, and I glance back as we hit the path that leads past the parking lot, and the car suddenly rolls forward, heading straight for us. I stumble, but Evan pulls me upright, and we move faster. I can feel blood running down my side and jeans, but I ignore it, urging the others on.

"Keep going!" I yell as lights splash over us so brightly it burns, and I can nearly taste the metal of his bumper as he chases us. There's a groan, and I glance back to see him jumping the curb before he hits the path and barrels toward us, rocks spraying everywhere from his tires.

I push my body as fast as I can. The sound of Alice's panicked breathing reaches me from the front, where Lally holds her hand, pulling her along. Bones and Skylar reach the door first and yank it open, Tommy tumbling in after them. Racing up the steps after my sister, I push her inside and slam the door, turning as the car barrels into the stairs and stops, its engine smoking.

"Is there a lock?" I ask.

"No, not on the front door. It stays open for students working late," Evan mutters. "Come on, there's a lab on the second floor. It's keycard only."

Nodding, I keep my eyes on the car and the unmoving masked man inside before turning and following after them. Lally leads the way, holding onto Alice as we hit the stairs, taking them two at a time. I grit my teeth against the pain, not wanting to worry the others. Evan has his phone out, and I hear it ringing as we reach the second floor and hurry down the hallway, our feet squeaking on the tile.

"Hi, yes, we are at Pine Valley College. We have been attacked, and one of us has been stabbed. The assailant is still here. Please come quickly, we think it's the killer." He reels off more information as Tommy slides his card into the lock over and over until it glows green. We duck inside, shutting the door and turning on the lock. I push Alice under a desk with Lally while grabbing Evan and shoving him under another.

"Okay, they are coming. They said to hold on. Apparently, there was a big fire downtown," Evan whispers. "We are safe here. We just need to hide until they get here."

I hate hiding, but he's right. I'm injured, and I need to protect my sister. Who knows what this guy is capable of?

Sitting under the desk with a wince, I meet Evan's worried gaze. I open my arms and urge him to move closer. "I'm okay, pretty boy," I soothe.

He slides to my side as I meet Alice's worried gaze and smile. She gives me a shaky smile back, and I check on the others. Tommy is huddled under a tiny desk, and Skylar and Bones are under another one. I shake my head when Bones smacks Sky as he sneaks a hand down to his ass.

Sky isn't one to miss an opportunity.

"What does this psycho want?" Tommy mutters. "Is he seriously planning on killing us to get Alice? What the fuck?"

"He's insane," Evan replies. "He isn't thinking clearly, but if we play it safe and make it until the police get here, they'll get the bastard, and it will be over." He leans back, blowing out a breath, determination filling his gaze. "Okay, show me your wound, Alek, and let me see what I can do."

"Evan—"

"Now, Alek," he hisses. "Don't fight me on this."

I grin lazily. "You're hot when you're angry."

"Not the time, princess," he mutters, but he smiles like I wanted.

God, I love this boy.

I really fucking love him, and I hope I make it through the night to tell him that.

FORTY-EIGHT

Lifting Alek's ripped shirt, I press the blood-soaked material against his skin, trying to staunch the flow. Running probably didn't help, and I'm worried about how much he's losing. "Sorry, princess," I murmur as I lift the rags away, and they stick to the skin.

He groans. "It's okay. You can kiss it better later."

"Really? Right now?" Tommy mutters. "Not only am I being chased by a serial killer, but I'm feeling single as fuck. I might be single by choice because commitment scares me, and deep down I'm a whore who craves attention and love, but that's beside the point." I glance over to see him grabbing a pillow and tugging it closer.

Ignoring Tommy, I smile as I look back at the wound. "Hey, princess."

The edges are jagged and raw, and he'll need to go to a hospital soon, but he's right. It could have been worse. I think he must have turned when he was stabbed so it didn't go too deep or wide. Still, being stabbed isn't good.

"We need to fill the wound to stop the bleeding." Knowledge from past fights and TV fill my head, but I gnaw my lip as I look around before stopping on Alice, who is huddled against Lally, her bag still over her shoulder.

"Lally, check Alice's bag. Does she have a pad or anything?" I ask, my voice as loud as I dare. The police are coming, but that doesn't mean anything, and I'm not taking any risks.

Nodding, she takes Alice's bag and rifles through it, sliding it to me across the floor. "No pads, but there's a tampon. Will that work?"

I take it from her and push it from the applicator. "Maybe," I mutter, looking at the wound then Alek. "This will hurt, but we need to stop the bleeding, princess."

"Just do it," he mutters, eyeing the tampon.

"Hold him still," I order Lally, who presses against his side, holding him as I press the tampon into the wound. It absorbs the blood and expands, and when I'm done, Alek is panting, eyeing me and Lally as we high-five each other.

"Damn fruity friends," he mutters, making me grin.

Grabbing the bottom of my shirt, I tear off a strip and wrap it around his waist, leaning him forward to tie it at the back. "That's the best we can do. We are going to need to clean it, and you'll need to see a doctor, but you won't be dying anytime soon."

"Always great."

Wiping my hands on my jeans, I check on Alice, who is back in Lally's arms. Tommy rubs her back, while Skylar and Bones hit each other and whisper furiously.

Just then, a sound fills the air, making us all fall silent. I hold my breath, listening until I hear it again.

It's a door.

It isn't the police because they would have sirens, which means it's him.

There's another creak of a door—the stairs, shit. Sinking lower in the dark, I keep my eyes on the glass door into the lab. The desks shield us, but there are half windows along that wall, so if he looks closely, he will see us.

I check on Alek, whose face is grim as he reaches for the bat at his side. I grab the knife again, ready to protect him and everyone else if that's what it takes. Footsteps head our way, and we all freeze, barely breathing when he appears before the window.

He holds another knife in his hand, this one as long as a machete. The mask turns, the mouth tilted in a wicked smile and dripping blood, and I stare at him, certain he can see me. He stares at me for what feels like forever, and I don't move, then he turns and continues on, apparently not spotting me in the darkness. I slump, feeling relieved.

My phone starts to ring, the vibration smashing to the wood of the desk. With my heart leaping from my chest, I scramble to grab it, silencing it. I look back, waiting one beat then the next, and when he doesn't reappear, I slump.

Flipping my phone, I frown at the caller ID and quickly call back. "Evan?" Autumn says, sounding breathless.

"Hi," I whisper.

"I found out what you wanted. The name of the person who paid for the medical procedures for Mr. Wright was a Mr. Ford—Mr. Ellis Ford. His son is Stan Ford."

I frown, going cold all over, my eyes going to Alice. "The art teacher?" I whisper.

"Yeah, he was a member of Silent Rose. I looked. He's an alumnus, and he was in my brother's year. He was the one they suspected back then, but his father paid to cover it up and he got off. He's from money. It's him, Evan. He killed them. Where are you?"

Swallowing, I keep my eyes on Alice, who's staring at me worriedly. "At school," I croak. "The police are on the way. He's here."

"Get out of there now—" Her phone cuts off, and I drop mine as I stare at Alice.

"It's Mr. Ford. That's who is behind the mask."

"No, it can't be," she whispers. "He was always so nice to me. He genuinely cared—" She stops, realization coming over her as a shudder of horror rocks her body.

"But if he's a teacher," Alek starts, and I turn to see him, following his train of thought.

My eyes go to the door. "Then he has a card!"

Crawling across the floor to the door, I hold the handle, pressing my back against it. My eyes meet Alek's gaze as he kneels, his chest heaving. "Evan, get back here," he demands.

"No, we can't let him get in," I hiss. "The cops will be here soon—"

Glass shatters next to me, and I jerk, my arm coming up over my face before I drop it to see a chair on the floor. In the next second, he's up and through the window. I leap to my feet, wanting to smack myself, my eyes landing on my knife by Alek.

"Get out now!" I yell at the others, then I throw myself at him, hitting him while I have the element of surprise. We hit the wall hard, and I slam my hand into his arm, trying to get him to drop the knife, but he elbows me, and I stumble back and then jump to avoid his wild swing. Bringing my arm down across his, I grab his wrist and twist, trying to break it to get the blade, but he switches it to his other hand and stabs.

Stumbling back, I watch Lally drag Alice out, Bones and Skylar following, making sure they are safe. Alek and Tommy hesitate, gripping weapons to try and help as I avoid his desperate slashes.

He comes at me fast, and I leap across the desk, then he rolls over it, following me. I duck and weave, moving backwards before grabbing a chair to hold up as a shield.

"Hey, asshole!" Tommy throws a chair. "Leave my friend alone, you sick fuck!"

Alek leaps over the desk, bringing his bat down on Ford's back, and I thrust the chair out. It hits him, and I run him into the wall, pinning him with a grunt as I glance back at Alek and Tommy.

"Tommy, get him out of here now!"

"No!" Alek roars, but Tommy grabs him.

"Go! I'm fast, remember? I'll catch up to you!" I yell, struggling as he fights to get free of the chair, his mask knocking to the side to reveal a familiar face.

Autumn was right.

Alek lets Tommy grab him, but at the door, he pushes Tommy out, gripping the frame. "Get out here now!" he roars.

Knowing he won't leave me, I push the chair with all my strength to keep Mr. Ford there, and then I turn and sprint, grabbing Alek's outstretched hand as we slide into the hall and run to the stairs, where Tommy is waiting.

"Go, go, go!" I yell, and he hurries down the staircase, holding onto the rail as he slips. Alek and I are slower due to his wound, and I won't leave him, but when we hit the stairs, a hand grabs my hair, throwing me back against the wall as he kicks Alek.

I hit the wall, crumpling with a groan as Alek is thrown down the steps. Horror fills me as he hits every stair and then lands in a heap on the next landing.

"Alek!" I scream, but he doesn't move. Turning my head, I look up as Ford puts his mask back into place. "Fuck you," I spit at him as I struggle to sit up.

"No, I'm going to kill you. She's mine. You can't have her," he growls, his knife pointed at me. "I saw how you looked at her, how you touched her in the dining hall. You're always hanging on to her. You can't have her!"

I smirk as he lifts the blade. "Neither can you."

I roll to the side as he brings it down, hitting the stairs and falling down a few before I stop myself and flip him off.

"You're dead, you sick fuck! Nobody fucks with Team Super Gay!" Tommy yells and runs up the stairs, hitting him with a fire extinguisher.

"Tommy, let's go!" I yell as I hurry down the steps and grab Alek, shaking him. "Wake up, now!" I hiss. He groans, and I glance back to see Tommy struggling, but then he loses the extinguisher, and Ford hauls him up by the throat. His legs kick in the air, and then he flies down the stairs. Tommy hits the wall hard, and I stare at him.

"Tommy!" I beg.

"I'm okay. I have a thick head." He crawls over and shakes Alek. "We need to go. Can you lift him?"

Nodding, I help Alek to his feet and glance back to see Mr. Ford stomping slowly down the steps, taunting us. Grunting under Alek's weight, I drag him to the first floor, where we can see the others outside the front door, nervously looking at us. Their shouts reach us, urging us on, and I grit my teeth, dragging Alek as Tommy takes his other arm.

"Go!" I yell at them, but they refuse, waving us on, those mother-fuckers.

Something hits us from behind, and we go down hard. Scrambling back, I turn to see Mr. Ford waving with his blade. Fuck this. Looking at Tommy, I nod at Alek. "Get him out of here."

"No." Tommy climbs to his feet and searches for a weapon. Getting up, I rip off the rest of my torn shirt and wrap it around my knuckles, waving him on.

"Come on, you bastard." I move to the side, turning us around so Alek and Tommy have a clear shot at the door. "You're right, you know. I want Alice. She's so sweet. You should see her in the morning in these little shorts—"

He lunges at me with a roar.

Ducking under his rapid swings, I bring my knee up, and he stumbles back. "I'm not an easy kill, you sicko." I grin. "And you fucked with the wrong family. She's ours. You can't have her, but I'll give her your head as a present."

He leaps at me again. He's strong and fast, but he isn't as trained as I am and is clumsily relying on his weapon. I duck under his swing again, sliding to the side, and bring my leg up in a brutal kick. He hits the notice board, the glass cracking, and then spins to me, swinging. I jump back, but he cuts my side. Hissing, I ignore the blood I feel running from the wound and focus on the blade as he comes at me again.

I avoid it as much as I can, but he lands another blow across my cheek, opening it. I want to fight back, but all I can do is avoid his blows. I can't even afford to look away for a second, but Alek calls my name, a groan, pained sound, and I can't help myself—I turn to look at Alek, and it's the opening Mr. Ford needs.

I hear the blade heading my way, and when I jerk my head back, I know it's too late to avoid it. It is coming right for me—a killing blow.

"Evan!" The terrified bellow stops my heart. I hate that he'll see this, that Alek will be brokenhearted again, losing another person he loves.

He'll blame himself. This is all I can think about as the blade heads for me.

Suddenly, a body appears between me and the blade, and when it makes contact, we fall back into the wall. I catch Tommy as he gasps, my eyes wide as I stare down at him to see a huge, gaping wound in his chest. His eyes meet mine as we slide down the wall, his weight dragging us to the floor. "I've got your back," he whispers, his face pale as he blinks in shock.

"Tommy." I slide out from behind him and sit him up as best as I can, my hands covering the wound as he blinks at me, blood bubbling from his lips.

I hunch my back to protect him as a kick hits my side. Grunting, I stay in place, holding the wound. We need to keep the blood in. We need to staunch it. He'll be okay. The police will be here soon. My side is hit again and again. Mr. Ford is just beating me, punishing me, but I don't care.

My eyes are on Tommy as he blinks. "Sorry, Evvie," he rasps. "I should have been faster."

"Shh." I lean over him. "You're okay. You're going to be okay, I promise. You'll be okay."

"I love you, Evvie," he whispers. "Thank you for being my family when no one else wanted to be." His words are too calm, and blood pumps through my fingers, too much to stop.

Tears flow from my eyes as I stare at Tommy. His head is propped against the wall, his neck at a weird angle, and his wound is still bleeding, yet he smiles at me. "We're brothers, right?"

"Brothers." I nod, pressing my forehead to his. "Always."

Another kick hits me, and Alek calls my name. I lift my head to see him barreling our way.

Alek hits him with a roar, the force sending them down the hall as I sob, my hands over Tommy's wound. "Evan, go!" he roars, looking back at me.

I look at Tommy, but his eyes are staring past me. "Tommy," I call, shaking him with my hands on his chest. "Just hold on, okay? They'll be here, then when you're better, we'll go skate at that park you mentioned. I'll be your wingman. We'll go to your favorite BBQ place. Just hold on."

He doesn't respond, and something inside me cracks.

"Evan, go!" Alek roars from my right, grunting as he struggles with Ford.

"Tommy," I plead through my sobs. "Tommy, wake up." Blood coats my hands, still pumping despite him being motionless. "Wake up! Stop joking. Wake up!"

He doesn't.

He doesn't move, and the pool of blood circling us gets bigger. Tommy's eyes are open and unseeing, and his lips are covered in spit and blood.

"I love you. I love you, brother. I'm right here. You're not alone. I'm right here. It's going to be okay." The words tumble from my lips as I press firmly against the wound, as if that can save him.

Sirens fill the air, the bright lights flashing around us. There are shouts, and Alek is at my side, but I don't look away, even as police drop beside me and others race down the hall after Ford.

My eyes are on Tommy's open, unseeing gaze.

"Tommy," I croak, shaking him. "Stop it, wake up."

"Evan—" Alek reaches for me, but I push him away.

"Tommy, Tommy, wake up," I beg, leaning into him. "Please, please wake up. You're my best friend, my brother, please, please don't leave me. I have no other family, please wake up. It's not funny anymore."

"Oh god!" Lally screams, dropping to her knees at my other side. "Tommy!"

"Tommy, please, I can't do this without you," I whisper, but he doesn't reply.

He can't.

He's dead.

He died protecting me.

Turning away, I crumple into Lally's arms as we both sob, Tommy's blood covering us as we stare at him.

Our best friend.

Our third.

Our brother.

NO PARKING
ACTIVE DRIVEWAY
SHAW DRIVE
THE MOMENT
ANDERS AVE
ONE WAY
TOO
STOP
CAR REPAIR
NO PARKING
SALE
SILENT ROSE
EVER
Pine Valley

FORTY-NINE

"Thanks, I will." I nod at the paramedic after he finishes patching me up in the back of the ambulance, the back door open to show the school filled with police and parked ambulances Sky and the others flagged down.

Too fucking late.

They were too fucking late.

The older man sighs. "I mean it, kid, you need to go to the hospital."

Sitting up, I grunt in understanding and grab my ruined shirt, sliding it on over the wound before I climb from the back. I'll go later. Right now, I need my boy, and he needs me.

I find him sitting in the ambulance opposite me, a blanket over his shoulders. His blond hair is stained with blood, and he sits with his hands on his knees, palms up, staring at the crimson staining his skin. His wounds have already been treated, but he looks so lost and forlorn.

Alice and Lally hurry my way, and I kiss Alice's head, wrapping her in a hug. "Are you okay?" I ask.

"I'm okay." She sobs against my side, and I hold her, my eyes on Evan. He doesn't move, not even when an officer tries to talk to him.

They caught the bastard, and he's already been taken away in a police car in handcuffs, but it doesn't change what happened or who we lost.

Tugging Alice and Lally with me, leaving Bones and Sky to talk to the cops, I lay my hand on Evan's cheek. His head jerks up, his eyes finding mine, and his lower lip starts to tremble.

"I'm here, pretty boy," I murmur, tugging him into the shelter of my arms. "Shh, it's okay, I'm right here."

That's all I can offer. Nothing I say will make it better. Tonight was one big nightmare.

He cuddles into my side as I hold him and my sister.

There's a banging sound from the school and the squeak of a gurney being pushed.

I lift my head, Evan does as well, and our eyes track the gurney with the black bag on it as they move toward the third ambulance. Tommy is inside.

Lally bursts into tears, burying her face in Alice's neck, and my sister strokes her back. I glance down at Evan, tears sliding silently down his cheeks. He cries without a word, no doubt blaming himself.

I know it was because of me.

If I had been awake, if I had been faster and stronger, I could have saved us.

"We'll take you all to the station," a cop tells us softly.

I nod, holding them tighter, but Evan sniffles. "My friend . . . where will he go?"

"To the hospital," he answers, smiling sadly at Evan. "We will take good care of him."

Evan nods rapidly, looking back at the van. "Can you open the bag a little? He doesn't like the dark, and I don't want him to be scared."

The cop glances at me, and I lean down, turning Evan's face up. "They'll open it and keep all the lights on, okay? He won't be scared."

"But he'll be alone," he whispers so brokenly, I swear my heart shatters.

Swallowing my pain for him, I lean down and kiss his head. "He won't be for long, I promise. We'll go straight there, okay?"

He nods, and I wipe away his tears, hating them—each one is a blow to my heart, reminding me I failed him. "Come on, pretty boy, we'll go with them, then to the hospital, and then we'll go home after. You need to rest." Taking his hand, I help him to his feet, and we follow the cop to his car.

My eyes go back to the school, and I wonder if anything will ever be the same again.

The station is bustling, even at this hour, with more people than I've ever seen until some of the officers finally clear them out. Mr. Ford is in the back, so we are safe. It's over, but the emotional and mental pain still lingers.

I refuse to leave Evan and Alice, despite them wanting me to get checked over at the hospital. My family needs me, so I stay, helping them explain everything that happened tonight to the officers who, despite everything, are very nice. It's clear they feel guilty for suspecting Evan and not stopping this sooner.

Evan leans into me, his gaze far away as Alice sobs through her explanation again. His face is pale and tearstained, and he's cold. An untouched coffee sits before him, and he has a blanket draped over his shoulders, which I tuck around him before I bring him into my arms. He doesn't even blink.

I think he's in shock.

I'm worried, but the paramedics assured me he would be okay physically. It's his mental state that concerns me. Evan is my sunshine, he always has been, and I hate seeing him so . . . broken. I'd do anything to put a smile back on his face, but I know there's nothing I can do except be here for him.

Tommy was his best friend, his brother, and he's gone.

Not only that, but Evan is blaming himself.

Guilt will eat you alive if you let it.

"Okay, okay," Winchester says kindly. "Let's take a break. You have all been through a lot tonight."

"What will happen to him?" I nod my head to the holding cells in the back.

They share a look before answering me. "He'll be moved in the morning and then charged. We have enough evidence for murder, stalking, and property damage. He won't be bothering you anymore. You can trust that." They stand, Winchester wincing as he looks us over. "Let me call some officers to take you home, okay?"

I nod and watch them leave before checking on Alice. She's curled into Lally, still crying, and Lally looks torn, her own tears falling even as she tries to stay strong for my sister.

"Thank you," I mouth to her before pulling Evan's head from my shoulder, holding it up. "Pretty boy," I coo. He doesn't react at first, so I stroke his face. "Come on, baby, talk to me."

Nothing.

Worry fills me, and I swallow hard, searching his icy eyes. "Hey, rich fucker," I snap, my voice mean.

He blinks, his eyes flitting to me. "Alek?" he whispers.

"There you are, pretty boy. You were scaring me," I admit, rubbing his cheek. "We are going home, okay? Just hold on."

He blinks and stares at me, and when his voice comes, it's low and sad. "I need to call Tommy's parents. What do I tell them?"

"The police will do that, baby," I assure him.

He shakes his head, tears squeezing from the corners of his eyes, and his voice is raw when he speaks. "No, it should be me, not a stranger."

"Okay, pretty boy. I'll be right there with you, alright?" I murmur, stealing a soft kiss. "Then you need to rest and eat something. You are far too pale. Let me look after you, Evan."

He nods, glancing at Alice. "Are you okay, Alley cat?"

She sniffles, wiping her face. "I don't even know."

God, my heart breaks for them both. I wish I could do something, but my fists won't fix this. Instead, I tug my sister closer and wrap them in my arms, ignoring the lingering pain as I hold the two most important people in my world. "It's okay. It's going to be okay. I'll be right here, and no one will ever hurt you again. Just cry, scream, whatever you need to do. I'm right here. I can take it. Blame me if you need to blame someone."

"Alek." Alice pulls away. "It's not your fault. Don't do that. You did the same thing when Mom and Dad died. You won't bear this weight alone. What happened tonight was horrible, but it isn't on your shoulders, okay? You did everything you could to protect us. It isn't your fault, big brother."

Why do her words make me want to cry?

"When did you get so smart, kid?" I tease, ruffling her hair.

She smiles, if only slightly, before glancing at Evan and then looking back at me. "Look after him, alright? I can take care of myself, I promise."

Blinking, I stare at my sister, realizing for the first time just how grown up she is. She isn't the same little girl I gave up my life to raise and protect. She's a woman who's strong and kind, and she's giving me permission to let her go.

I don't think I'll ever be able to fully, but as she sits back and takes Lally's hand, I know I can a little. Evan is right. My life isn't Alice's.

It's mine and Evan's.

He's my reason for living, and he needs me right now.

I'll stay and take his pain, anger, and guilt. I'll do whatever it takes to help him heal from tonight.

I don't know what I should be feeling right now, but I'm a mess inside—cold and numb and feeling too much at once. It's almost like a dream, one I can't wake up from, like I can't take a breath deep enough to fight it off.

Tommy deserves this though. Alek is worried, wanting to go with me, and I know he wants to help, but this is something I need to do.

Taking my phone outside, I look up at the night sky for strength, my finger hesitating on the call button. I can't even imagine what they will feel when they get this call in the middle of the night.

Their son is dead.

He was murdered.

How do you recover from that?

You don't.

Glancing back through the glass doors, I see Alek waiting for me in the station. Alice leans into Lally's side, her eyes closed, and Skylar and Bones argue at another desk, which makes me smile for a second, but we are missing someone. We are missing our painter, and I know there will always be a hole where he belongs. All of us feel that, bonded over the trauma and horror we endured tonight.

Looking at my phone, I linger over the number, scared.

"Evan?"

My head snaps up at the soft, familiar, female voice, and I see a hesitant Clarissa standing there, her teeth digging into her lip nervously. "It is you, hi," she murmurs, glancing around.

My brows draw together as I meet her eyes. "Hi, what are you doing here?"

"A friend told me what happened tonight and that he's here." She looks scared, her eyes darting inside as she hesitates. "Is it true that he's been caught? For good this time?"

I nod, pushing away from the wall and pocketing my phone. If anyone understands trauma, it's her. "It's true. He was caught, and he won't be getting out for a long time. Do you want me to walk you inside?"

She bites her lip harder. "I don't know if I can go in just yet. Can you stay with me for a minute?" Her eyes widen. "I'm sorry. That's so selfish of me. I can't even begin to imagine what you have endured tonight."

I wave it away with a forced smile. "I need air anyway. I like the silence out here. My friends are worried, and it's kind of choking me."

"I bet. I used to hate the way everyone looked at me," she admits, wincing. "Pity mixed with—"

"Guilt and relief," I mutter, and she nods, moving closer.

"How about we take a little walk and then go in together? Just two survivors?" she suggests.

I nod, and we walk through the parking lot, taking in the night air. "How's your father? I don't know what will happen about his care now that he's in jail," I say.

She laughs bitterly. "Don't worry about it."

My eyebrows draw together again as we stop before a black Mercedes. "What do you mean?"

"He died last night," she replies. She looks distraught, but there's something in her eyes—something that puts me on edge.

"I'm sorry to hear that. He was very ill—"

"Death happens every day," she remarks, her voice strange as she steps closer. "You know that. You're like me."

"Like you how?" I frown as I step back. There is something inside me warning me that something is wrong.

"Determined to get what you want, strong, a survivor . . . smart. I like that. I knew you were the one." She smiles, and it's wicked, one I haven't seen on her face before.

"Look, Clarissa, I think I should go back—" I step past her, freaked out. I don't know what her problem is, but she isn't the same woman we met at her house, and I've had enough crazy for tonight.

Something sharp stabs into my neck, and I whirl, my eyes wide as I stumble back. There is a needle in her hand. I try to run, but my legs give out, and I hit the pavement.

"I knew you would be mine the moment I saw you." She grins. "You're perfect and just what I wanted. Tonight didn't go as planned, but that's okay." She leans down, rubbing my cheek.

I try to slap her away, but my body won't work.

It's too heavy.

"Shh, it's okay." She wipes away a tear I didn't even know I spilled. "I'm here now. Everything will be okay."

I stare up into her eyes, finally realizing what's wrong with them.

They are cold, empty, and dead.

The last thing I hear before whatever drug she gave me takes me is my name being called from far away.

Alek.

ALEK

"I can't find Evan." I pant as I burst back into the waiting room where everyone is. Our driver escorts are on the way. Most of them were diverted to the school and the fire.

"What do you mean?" Lally asks, standing. "He was right outside—"

"He isn't there." I know I'm panicking, my eyes wild, but something is wrong. I know it. I couldn't find a trace of him; he's just gone. He wouldn't do that to me or us, not after tonight.

A bitter laugh fills the air, and we all turn to the cell we have been studiously ignoring. Ford sits up from the bench, his hands cuffed together as he leans casually into the bars. His eyes linger on Alice for far longer than I like, so I step in front of her.

"She has him now. You're too late."

"What are you talking about?" I snap.

"Don't listen to him. He's fucking insane," Skylar interjects. "Come on, I'll help you find him."

His laugh comes again, chilling me to the bone, and the hair on the back of my neck rises. "If you want answers, then come here."

"Alek—" Sky tries to stop me, but I step closer, unafraid as I face him in his cell. He's just a man, nothing more.

"Who has him?" I demand as I grab him through the bars, ignoring the shouts as I slam his face into them. He hisses but grins. "Talk!"

"Do you really think I could do this all by myself or that I even wanted to? I had a job—not what I wanted in the long run, but I had a life until she came back into it. I'm betting she gave you the sob story, right? That I stalked and harassed her, even killed those boys when we were in class together."

"Who are you talking about?"

"Clarissa Wright." He spits the name as I go cold. "Don't you see? This was all her plan, not mine. She wanted him. I simply got what I wanted as well, freedom from her while keeping Alice safe and sound. The fire? She started it. The flowers and everything, she sent them all. She was in the car, not me. You played right into her hands. We all did."

I search his eyes, but all I see is the truth.

"She's the crazy one, not me. I took the fall for her all those years ago out of guilt. It was my father's suggestion since it was our fault her father got sick, and I might have flirted with her. I did everything they ordered. I smeared my name, ruining my future, and she dropped out and left us alone. That was the deal—until this year. She found out I liked a student. I don't know how, but she threatened to kill her. She must have seen Evan with her, and when she met him for real, she came to me. She wanted him. She will stop at nothing to get what she wants. I knew she would kill Alice for even being near him—fuck, she killed those students for daring to touch him—so I did what I had to so I could protect the woman I love."

"You're sick." I slam him into the bars and step back. "It's a lie—"

"No? Then where is he? She used me, used all of you—the fire, the school, me getting caught, I'm betting it was all her plan to get him alone and swoop in. She'll have him, and you're just the fool who was too slow to save your friend and boyfriend. You are just too fucking slow."

Bones grabs me, and he and Skylar drag me back as I lunge at him.

He's telling the truth. I can taste it.

He might be behind this, but he isn't the only one, and if what he's saying is true, then we walked right into her plan. We basically handed her what she wanted on a platter.

She has Evan.

"Alek, the officers aren't back," Alice whispers, and I glance over my shoulder, frowning. "They went to get their stuff from the back when you went outside. Why aren't they back?"

The lights turn off, and his laughter rings out in the dark.

"I guess she's keeping her end of the deal after all. She gets Evan, and I get Alice. It's time to end this once and for all."

We hear the buzz as the cell swings open.

He's free.

NO PARKING
ACTIVE DRIVEWAY
SHAW DRIVE
THE MOMENT
ANDERS AVE
ONE WAY
TOO
STOP
CAR REPAIR
NO PARKING
SALE
SILENT ROSE
Pine Valley
EVER

FIFTY-ONE

"Alek." Skylar tosses me something, and I catch it in the dark as red lights flicker on in the station. I grab Alice and start to back her to the front door, but something crashes there, so I turn, and we back toward the rear of the station, where the officers went.

"Anyone see him?" I hiss, keeping Lally and Alice behind me, but Lally darts away, using her phone's flashlight as she grabs a phone from a desk and holds it like a weapon, winking at Alice.

"I've got you."

Ignoring her for now, I strain my eyes, searching the darkness as his laughter comes again. "She's mine, not yours, never yours. While we have our fun here, she will be having hers. There will be nothing left of your precious Evan when she's through with him."

Gritting my teeth against my panic, I move us closer toward the door, counting each step. His voice echoes around in front of us, like he's trying to scare us. Alice whimpers, letting me know it's working, but I refuse to give in. Evan is tough, one of the strongest people I know, so he'll be okay.

He has to be okay. Right now, I need to focus on getting us out of here alive so I can rescue my boy.

"Ten steps," Bones whispers, letting me know how far we are from the door since I can't look back. Nodding in understanding, I startle when there's another loud bang in front of us.

"You won't survive this night. You know that, don't you? I can't let you. I can't lose everything for nothing. Before dawn, Alice will be mine, and you will all be a tragic story—nothing more, nothing less. For some of you, I'm doing the world a favor by getting rid of you. You're nothing," he sneers, his voice slightly manic.

Whatever Clarissa did to him, it royally fucked him up. Either he was crazy before her or she made him that way. Regardless, it doesn't matter. It's clear he's willing to do whatever it takes.

I can't afford to be weak or I'll lose someone else I care for.

"Five steps," Bones whispers. "Three."

"She is mine!" he yells.

Just as my hand touches the doorknob, two flashlight beams rush through the front of the station. "Hold your hands up!"

Police.

I hold mine up, but their lights fall on someone else—him. For one moment, he's framed in the flashlights, still wearing the same clothes but his mask gone.

"What the fuck?" one of the officers whispers. They hesitate, and it gives him the opening he needs. He ducks under their lights, then I hear grunts as their flashlights swing wildly, trying to track him, their guns raised.

It's the opening we need. Maybe it's cowardly, but I need to find Evan and keep Alice safe.

Still, I hesitate, watching the light beams and ignoring the others' urgings. If he dies here, I need to see it, to be sure. I duck when one of the officers fires, covering those behind me, but he simply laughs, and then there's a blood-curdling scream. One of the flashlights drops to the floor. I watch it roll until it turns to illuminate a horrific sight. One of the officers is hanging from the lighting above, a phone wire wrapped around his neck. He kicks and fights, his face turning purple.

I begin to step toward him to help, but Alice drags me back as the other officer backs toward him, lifting his legs to help him breathe, all while aiming his gun.

Gun . . . Where is the other officer's gun?

Just as I think that, there is a distinctive bang that has me crouching lower still. The officer holding up his partner jerks from the impact, a bloody hole appearing in his shoulder, and then there is another bang, this time hitting the officer in his side.

Ford's laughter fills the air, indicating he's taunting them.

He's killing police officers for fun.

They are going to lose.

Turning, I rip open the door and push Alice inside. "Go!" I roar as Lally follows, then I grab Bones and Skylar and throw them in. I turn to shut it just as a body hits the floor where I was just standing. Gulping, I stare down at the bleeding police officer, his eyes wide and blinking. He reaches for a gun that's no longer there.

Fuck! He's armed with two weapons now.

Reaching down despite my worry, I grab the officer and haul him in with us, kicking the metal, bulletproof door shut just as bullets rain across it.

Dragging the officer farther in, I lay him down then rush to the door, putting my ear against it. It's silent on the other side, which is concerning. "I don't think he can get in here," I mutter as I turn to the others.

"Jesus fucking Christ," Skylar growls. "This is some fucked-up shit. He's killing police officers now? He really won't stop, will he?"

"No, he won't," I answer, my eyes on Alice. "We need to get out of here. I don't know when more will come, but we can't depend on the police anymore."

"Five, six—" The officer on the floor coughs.

Hurrying over, I kneel at his side as he grabs my hand, and I see another hole in his chest. He's dying, and he knows it. The guys' flashlights land on us, letting me see the terror in his eyes.

"What did you say?" I ask.

"Five, six—" He coughs, his body shuddering. "Five, six, seven, eight. It's the code for the back door. Go out, your car is there, so are squad cars. My radio is gone. Use theirs to call for help." Blood bubbles on his lips as he coughs. "We are spread too thin. You need to go . . ." His words trail off as his body shudders with a rattling cough, and as I watch, the light extinguishes in his eyes and the hand holding mine turns limp.

Letting it go, I lean down and close his eyes. "Thank you," I whisper, knowing he just saved our lives. He died for his job, and I can't let that be in vain.

"Let's go," I order as I jump to my feet just as a door deeper into the station bursts open. The two officers, Winchester and his partner, hurry over wearing bulletproof vests, one holding a shotgun and the other with a pistol.

"What the fuck is happening?" Winchester asks. "We tried to put the system back on, but it's fried—shit, Henderson." He gapes down at the dead officer.

"Ford got out. He killed two of your officers," I tell him, worried they will think we are involved, but their faces cloud with anger as they glance at the door beyond. "He was in there. I don't know if he still is."

"We managed to reboot the doors and locked down the front, so he has to be," Winchester murmurs as he looks back at Henderson.

"He told us the back door code to get out," I say. "Will it work?"

They share a look before running their eyes over us, no doubt seeing a number of terrified but determined faces splattered with blood and dirt before coming to a decision.

"He's right. The back door works on a separate circuit in case of an emergency. Go, we called this in. We'll stop him, but you need to get out of here. Head to the hospital or the fire scene and stay there with the other officers," he orders as he stomps past us, both of them moving to each side of the door before looking at us.

"Go now!" Winchester commands.

I hesitate while the others hurry to the back door, and the officer nods at me. "Go, save your family. We'll stop him here and give you a chance."

Backing away, I nod my thanks before turning and following my friends and family. The back door is already open, the finger pad smeared with blood, and they are waiting outside, looking back at me. My car is parked behind some police cars, and I spy the keys inside as I hurry over before hesitating.

"Are we really going to hide at the other scene?"

I look over at Skylar. "What do you think?" I retort, one eyebrow arched.

He groans, sharing a look with Bones. "I think you're going to do something crazy and find Evan and stop a crazy serial killer."

"Then you're right." I open my door, nodding at Alice. "Get her to safety—"

"No, I'm going with you," she argues.

"Alice," I start, just as Skylar rolls his shoulders back.

"She's right. We are going with you," he states. "You aren't in this alone. Evan is our friend too. We won't let anyone else die tonight. Tell us your plan."

Just then, there's gunfire inside, and we all turn to look before sharing a worried expression. "I have a feeling they won't stop him," I admit. When I looked into their eyes, I saw that they knew it as well. They knew they were going to die, but they did it anyway. "Which means he will follow us. We need to find Evan." I rub my head, worried and stressed.

"He couldn't have gone far with her," Bones reasons. "The whole city is in lockdown. She would need to lie low until it lifts. The school. It has to be. It's close, and it's the last place they would think to look." He opens up his phone and snarls. "I knew it. She's in Rose Manor. We have an entry camera. It clocked her just twenty minutes ago. She must have stalked either Evan or Ford there before. She's using the Silent Rose hideaway as her own, and nobody would have a clue since it's a secret."

I nod. "So we go there."

"And him?" Sky gestures at the police station when there's more gunfire and screams from inside.

"We show him who he messed with. No one touches my family and gets away with it." I glance at Alice. "Are you sure about this?"

"Evan is my friend, and this is because of me. I won't run and hide. We are in this together."

I hate it, but looking into her eyes, I know I can't talk her out of it. She's just as stubborn as I am, and honestly, the best place for her right now is probably at my side. I can't keep her locked away forever. This is her life, her friends' lives. She deserves to be part of it. I won't take away her freedom.

I can't. There is a difference between love and control, and I never want to control her.

"Then I have a plan," I say as it becomes quiet inside. I know he killed them and will be coming after us. We don't have a lot of time, so I explain it quickly as they stare at me.

"It's totally batshit," Bones grumbles.

"I've always wanted to race in a cop car." Sky grins at me. "Let's show Ford how fast we really are."

Grinning, I nod at him. "Let's do this. We'll end this where we started, on the streets."

This has to work. It *has* to.

Bones is in the back, lying across the seat to hide, and Lally is in the back seat of the police car Skylar . . . borrowed and seemed far too happy about. We are parked next to each other, with Alice in my passenger seat.

"Are you sure you can do this?" I ask her, gripping the wheel.

"Trust me, Alek, please, just this once," she begs.

"I do," I admit, looking over at her. "I trust you more than anyone. Don't get hurt, okay?"

"Don't you get hurt either," she orders as she grips the handle.

We wait, and when I see the back door opening, Ford in the doorframe, I turn on my engine, Skylar doing the same, and then we share a look. I had just enough time to fix what was wrong with my car, but I sure as fuck hope it holds out. I wish I had my Skyline, but tonight, I'm racing in this. I rev, getting his attention so he sees Alice in my passenger seat, and then we peel away. As soon as we are around the corner and out of his sight, I slow, and Alice leaps from my car and into Skylar's. Our doors slam as I gun it to the left, and he speeds off to the right.

I hold my breath, hoping it works, and when headlights shine over my trunk as Ford swings out onto the road behind us, chasing me and where he thinks Alice is, I know I have him.

"I got you, you bastard." I smirk as I shift gears and slam my foot to the pedal.

I hit my speaker, and Sky's voice comes through with a whoop. "He bought it."

"Where are we going?" Lally asks through the phone.

"We are going to Evan. She has him, and we can't waste time," I reply.

"Um, and what about the crazy killer chasing us?"

I spin in the middle of the street and gun it as I grip the wheel, my face contorted with anger. "We follow the plan. It will work," I say, hoping I'm right.

I drift around the next corner, watching him try to keep up. "He's a fool." I smirk. "These streets are mine. Let's show him that."

"Outsmarting a serial killer, who would have thought?" Skylar laughs, feeling the high like we always do.

"He's fucking crazy," Bones mutters.

"Aren't we all, my pretty, tattooed boy," he flirts as Bones rolls his eyes and climbs into my passenger seat from the back.

"Anything?" I ask, his phone clutched in his hand.

"They are still inside. I called reinforcements." He grins. "We aren't just a secret society for parties, you know."

Nodding, I glance back to see the creep gaining on us, so I push my car to its limits, the engine revving.

"Let's see if you can keep up, old man," Skylar teases as I hear his sirens.

"Sky." Alice sighs, switching them off. "Drive safely, Alek. I know you race for money, but this is different—"

I glance down at my phone, even as I spin around the next corner. "You know?"

"Of course I know. I'm not an idiot. You're an adult. So as long as you come home in one piece, that's all that matters."

"You little brat," I snap.

"Not the time for this discussion," Skylar reminds us.

"Right. Serial killer. We'll finish this later," I mutter as I take the next corner faster than I should. Bones swears and grabs the handle, but he doesn't look away from the camera on his phone, keeping an eye on my man for me.

"Three streets out," Sky offers as I hear him gunning it.

"Five," I reply as I speed over a hump. We get some air and then land with a crash, racing forward. "He's still behind me."

"This better work," Bones mutters. "What about his gun?"

I don't have anything to say to that, and he groans as the road signs pass us.

"One street."

"I'm there," Sky warns.

I turn onto the flat, quiet road. It's a long stretch with a hill to the right and a cliff to the left, which is exactly what I need, and it's our usual racing strip, one we know better than our own hands.

I shoot forward before hitting the brakes and spinning the wheel. We turn, and he has no choice but to brake as I slide to a stop sideways across the road, blocking him.

Getting out, I pull the gun I stole from my waistband and aim it through the windshield. I fire once in warning, and he tries to back away, but Sky shoots out, blocking the road behind him.

He's trapped as they get out, and we surround the car.

Ford is armed, but it's now or never.

"Get out," I order, pointing the gun at the driver's side.

He gets out slowly, his own gun aimed at me. "You think you can shoot before me?" He grins. "Even if you do, I'll hit you too, and we'll both die tonight."

"It's a risk I'll take," I reply.

Alice steps in front of me, her arms spread wide. "If you shoot, you'll shoot me."

"Alice," I hiss.

She glances back at me briefly. "He won't do it, trust me." She meets his eyes. "Drop the gun or shoot me. You pick."

He snarls, his eyes hardening as he glares at Alice. "Move."

"No." She tilts her chin up defiantly, ignoring my urgings. "Shoot or drop it. Now!"

His chest heaves, his hand wavering on the gun, and it's the opening we need. Sky leaps over the roof and lands on him while I grab Alice and turn us. A gun goes off, and I look back. No one appears to be hurt, and Sky pins him while Lally kicks the gun away before heading to me. I pass Alice to her and put my own gun away, then I walk over and crouch next to him as he struggles.

"She's your weakness. You taught me that." I drive my fist into his face. He groans, spitting blood, so I do it again and again. I let my rage consume me until arms tug me back—Bones.

"You wanted him alive, remember?" Skylar hisses, but he doesn't stop me. In fact, he holds him down tighter.

"Let me go!" I roar, fighting to get to him.

"Kill him, I don't care," Sky says as Bones tugs me closer, "but what about Evan?"

He's right. Evan's name clears my bloodlust, and I stare at Ford's unmoving body. Pushing their arms off, I walk away. "I'm fine," I tell them as they watch me pace. "You're right. Tie him up and gag him. We still need him."

"Are you sure about this?" Sky mutters as he pulls out the tape and rope, throwing some to Bones.

"We need him," I say. "He's the only one who can stop her, who can get her attention. She let him free for a reason rather than just killing him. You don't become obsessed with someone and then just discard them, not like that."

Sky sighs as he starts to tie Ford's ankles while Bones binds his wrists. "You're good at that," Bones comments with a frown.

"You have no idea. I'll show you later if you're good." Sky winks.

Looking back at Alice, I see her and Lally together and nod. "This next part won't be easy."

"None of this has been," Alice scoffs.

I smile widely. "You did well, little sister."

"So did you." She grins. "Now let's go get Evan back. No one will ever put up with your shit like that guy does."

Rude, but true.

FIFTY-TWO

I keep my eyes closed as long as I can, knowing something is wrong. My brain is foggy, and my body feels sluggish and off. I attempt to force myself to relax as I try to remember what happened, but everything is obscured by smoke. Every time I think I have an answer, it's swallowed up by the darkness.

I'm breathing too loudly, and something is across my mouth. Slowly, my body starts to wake up, and I realize why it feels so wrong. My arms are bound behind me, and when I twist my wrist, something constricts them. Slowly, I test my legs and find each tied with something as well.

What the fuck is happening?

I know I need to look and find out, but fear fills me. Something inside me tells me not to, that I don't want to know.

"I know you're awake." The female voice echoes slightly. "You can't pretend. The drugs I gave you are short-lived, just enough to get you where I need you for now."

The voice is familiar, and it sets off alarms in my head, but I can't figure out why. I try to fight the fog when I hear footsteps treading closer, stopping before me, then warm breath wafts over my face.

"Open your eyes," she whispers seductively, but I ignore her, trying to push the drug out of my system faster.

"Open your eyes!" The slap makes my eyes open and clash with hers.

Clarissa.

Everything comes back, leaving me gasping and struggling.

"There you are." She grips my face, stopping my struggles as she perches on my knee where I'm tied to a chair, blocking everything else out. "Your eyes, they are so bright." She rubs her fingers under my eyes, making me jerk my head away in disgust. Bile crawls up my throat as I finally get a good look at the room we are in, and I frown in confusion.

This is Rose Manor. The living room is dark, but I would know it anywhere. The question is, how does she?

I meet her eyes as she tilts her head. Her gaze runs across my face obsessively, and I want to recoil from her, but there is nowhere to go. Alek and the others must know by now, right? They will be looking for me. Alek would never let me go. I just need to hold on or get out of here.

She's only one woman—a crazy one, but one woman.

"You are much prettier than him. I do like a pretty face," she whispers, and my eyes widen as she drags the sharp tip of a needle across my cheek. "Now behave or I'll knock you out again. I would much prefer to have you awake so we can speak. I don't want any lies between us."

Breathing heavily, I mumble behind the tape across my mouth, and her eyebrows rise.

"If I take this off, will you behave? If you don't, I will be very angry."

I jerk my head in a nod, playing along for now. She watches me for another minute before standing and putting the needle away. Leaning down, she rips off the tape, making me groan. "Aww, did that hurt? Let me make it better." She kisses me hard. I try to tug away, but her hand grabs my hair, keeping me in place. I keep my lips locked as bile and shame roll through me. Finally, she pulls away, licking my lips and then hers. "Soft like I knew they would be."

I want to gag, but I swallow it back, refusing to show weakness in front of her. She's crazy, so who knows what she will do if I piss her off. No, I need to play this smart.

"Why are we here?" I ask, my voice rough and throat scratchy.

"I needed a place for us to wait until sunrise, until all the police officers are too busy catching him to look for us. What a better place than where it all started?" I frown, and she laughs as she sits down on the sofa opposite me. "You don't know? I was a member too, a long time ago. Hell, he introduced me to it himself. He flirted and played with me. I didn't know then, but he did it with everyone. I thought I was special. I'll admit I became a little . . . obsessed and unhinged. When he turned me down, I thought if I could just get him to see me, he'd understand, but he was always surrounded by people, so I removed them so he would notice me, but he got mad. However, my dad was sick. He'd been working at one of Ellis Ford's factories when he fell ill. He felt so guilty, so I used it." She smirks.

"I used it to keep us attached, even after we made the deal. He would take all the blame, and I would leave him alone. The idiot felt so guilty for his friends' deaths, blaming himself for me, that he took all responsibility, ruining his future. It was good, and I would wait for him to come back to me, but then he started teaching here." She stands. "And he met her. The moment I saw the way he looked at her, I knew he wanted her. He tried to keep his distance so he could keep her safe, but I saw it." She stops before me then, tilting my head back.

"I was going to kill her, but then I saw you and I understood, but then you met me and you were so kind. I knew you felt the same way I did, but you were trapped, even though you couldn't admit it, so I made a deal with him. He could have her if I got you. In return, I'd let her live, but he had to get rid of everyone around you to free you." She straddles me again. "Don't you see? I freed you. I freed you from them so we could be together. I did it all for you."

"And Ford and Alice?" I whisper, fighting back my sickness.

"He can have her," she scoffs. "It won't be for long. The idiot didn't understand that he wouldn't get out of tonight alive or without being thrown in jail. He'll take the fall for everything just like he did in the past. This time, his daddy can't save him. No money can, and I'll be free to have you for the rest of our lives. I don't need him anymore." She strokes my cheek as she speaks, petting me like a dog. "I have you, and we'll be together forever."

"Your father—"

"Is dead," she reminds me. "A necessary evil. He started to suspect something was wrong with me and kept trying to warn people, even you. Honestly, he was a terrible father. He was always working and too busy to notice me. I think that's why he never realized what I was like. It was a shame he died of his illness—the one I made." I frown harder. "I needed an excuse to be tied to him, so I made him sick like some of the other workers, and I kept him sick, but he outlived his purpose just like everyone else."

Jesus Christ, she's utterly insane.

"Why me?" I ask, trying to keep her talking as I twist my hands, attempting to break the bindings while she speaks. I need to get out of here before she realizes I'm placating her and she drugs me again. I can't fight her when I'm drugged, and I have a horrible feeling I know what she will do to me.

She thinks I'm hers, just like he was.

"I watched you. At first, I thought you were dating Alice and that I could use you, but then I realized you were just friends. I let him think otherwise, though, to make him mad. But why you? You're pretty, so pretty, and you see this world for what it really is. You see the monsters in it, and you aren't scared to do what you need to do to get what you need and want, and when you touched my hand? I liked that. You hide everything behind a pretty smile, but there's a killer in you, Evan. I just need to push you hard enough, and then you'll be my perfect partner."

"You're wrong," I hiss.

"Am I? Tonight, you would have killed Stan if you had the chance." I shake my head in denial, and she grins. "Liar," she whispers into my ear before biting it as I jerk away. "You wanted to kill him, I saw it, especially when he killed your friend, the one always hanging onto you. What was his name? Tommy?"

I snarl, jerking against my restraints, and she falls from my lap from the force, the chair creaking. Laughing, she climbs to her feet as I swear. "Don't you fucking say his name."

"There you are," she purrs breathlessly. "So beautiful, that darkness you hide from everyone, born from pain, from surviving this world. We are the same side of a coin, Evan. Don't you realize that? I knew it the moment I saw you. I knew you belonged with me."

"Fuck you!" I scream, refusing to play along. I tug at my hands, feeling my wrists cut and bleed. "I'm nothing like you! Nothing, you sick bitch, and I will never be yours."

"You are mine!" she screams in my face, backhanding me, and I taste blood.

Laughing, I spit it at her. "No, I'm not. I won't ever be," I protest. "You make me sick."

"I will make you mine," she growls as she pulls at my jeans. My eyes widen, and my heart skips a beat.

"Get off me!" I yell, trying to push her away, tugging my legs and arms, but they are tied tightly. She manages to undo my button, and I start to truly panic. No, no, no, this can't be happening.

I struggle harder as she grins at me. "Let's see how much you protest after this—" I ram my head into hers, unable to do anything else to get her away from me. She stumbles back with a cry, clutching her nose, her eyes widening.

I panic at the fury I see in her gaze. She's crazy, and if I'm not useful to her, will she kill me?

"Evan," she warns.

"I want to know your plans," I tell her, hoping she believes it despite my outburst. "You're right. I've been hiding for so long. I can't just accept this."

She sighs, prodding her nose, and gives me a warning look. "I suppose I can accept that."

Jesus Christ.

A noise has her turning, and my eyes widen. I know that sound. It's the tunnel. Someone is coming.

It has to be Alek. He would never let me go. Worried she will attack him, I blurt out my next words.

"Kiss me, show me." She turns, distracted like I wanted, and despite feeling sick, I smile at her as seductively as I can. "Show me what it means to be yours."

God, even the words make me want to hurl, but I hold it back, and desire gleams in her eyes as she heads my way. She places her hands on my shoulders as I keep working my bleeding wrists, and she lowers herself onto my lap, grinding against me as her lips find mine. I have to fight not to throw up in her mouth as she gasps and kisses me.

My eyes are open, locked beyond her as I see the shadows move. There is more than just one person sneaking in behind her. They are all in robes, Silent Rose robes, and I frown in confusion, but when she goes to pull away, I open my mouth and let her deepen the kiss despite the sick feeling running through me.

One robed figure pushes his hood back, and Bones lifts his finger, pressing it against his lips, and I blink to let him know I understand as they hide.

Another robed figure is pushed from the tunnel, stumbling out. The sound makes her pull away.

I look past her and smile. "Looks like we have a visitor."

She turns, climbing from my lap to face the robed figure. The shape of them looks wrong, but I can't quite put my finger on why, and the robe conceals who it is.

Turning my head, I wipe my mouth on my shoulder as best as I can, feeling nauseous, and my eyes land on Alek, who's hiding in the dark. He winks at me and blows me a kiss, and I almost slump in relief, tears filling my eyes.

"I'm here, pretty boy," he mouths.

"Who are you?" she calls, and I turn forward to see her staring down the robed figure. I want to warn them, but Alek is asking me to trust him, as is Bones. I sit back, working my wrists harder, the blood making it easier, and I feel the binding loosen enough to start slipping my hands free.

The figure stumbles again, and the hood falls back, exposing Stan Ford's face. I just gape alongside her. "How did you get here?" she asks, hesitating, one hand clutching the needle she was going to use on me.

I need a distraction to get free. I need—an idea comes to mind, a bad one, but it's all I have. I don't know if this is what Alek planned, but it's too late to ask. "Kill him," I call. She glances back at me, and I smile. "He hurt me. If you love me, if you truly want me and say I belong to you, then kill him."

She turns back to him as he blinks, his lips twisting in a snarl, and I realize what's wrong—his arms are tied behind his back. "You," he hisses. "This is all your fault—"

"He wants to take me from you," I say, egging her on. His eyes jerk to me, and he frowns. "He wants to kill us and run off with Alice. You can't have that. He can't have anyone else, and he can't hurt me. Kill him and we can be together."

"Shut up," he orders me and then looks at her. "Where is she? Where is Alice?"

"Alice, Alice, Alice," she repeats. "I am so sick of that name." She lunges at him, and he falls backward as she stabs him. He screams, unable to protect himself. I watch as she brings the needle down into his chest and neck over and over. He chokes on his blood, his eyes wide as she kills him.

I keep my eyes on her as I finally get my hands free.

I lunge from my chair and into Alek's waiting arms in the darkness. He cups my face and kisses me swiftly. "I knew you would come for me."

"I've got you," he promises. "It isn't over yet."

Someone thrusts a robe at me, and I struggle into it, confused, Clarissa's screams still reaching me. "Trust us," Alek murmurs as he pulls his hood up, covering his handsome face.

"Follow my lead, pretty boy. It's time to end this."

"You are one of us. It's our duty to stop you," someone calls—

Autumn, I realize—as we climb to our feet and create a circle around Clarissa, who is panting, a bloody needle still clutched in her grip.

"You hurt one of ours and killed one of ours. Blood in, blood out," Bones calls. "It ends tonight."

She climbs to her feet, her eyes wild, then she lashes out. I gasp as Alek staggers back, the needle sticking from his chest. He plucks it free and tosses it away, but I know it had to hurt.

He's been chased, stabbed, and almost shot, and now he's bleeding again.

All for me, because of her.

Fury races through my blood, heating it as she stumbles backward, trying to find a way out. She might be a killer, but she isn't smarter than all of us, nor is she stronger. In the end, she's just a lonely, weak little girl.

I have an entire society.

Pushing my hood back, I step forward as I smirk at her in disgust. "You made a mistake," I say. "This is my house, this is my society, and that is my man."

I slam my fist into her face, knocking her to the floor as she gapes at me. "Evan—"

"I'm not yours!" I yell as I hit her again, breathing heavily. I have no qualms about hurting her. She's a fucking killer, a goddamn virus, and maybe if someone had looked beyond her gender to the truth of her before now, Tommy might be alive.

I hit her again, and she takes it, not even fighting back, just looking up at me before she smiles. "I told you that you're like me."

I silence her by slamming my fist into her face once more.

I am not like her.

I'm not.

"Evan." A hand catches my bloody fist, and I look up, meeting Alek's eyes. "It's over."

"She's still breathing. I won't let her hurt you again," I warn.

The smile he gives me heats my blood, even here. "She won't, but I won't let you become a killer, not even for me, pretty boy." He pulls me into his arms, wrapping one across my chest as I press against his body, his chin going to my shoulder as we look at her. "She's done. It's over."

I can't believe it.

It can't be . . .

Tonight has been one long nightmare, so I can't seem to relax, but when he turns me and presses his forehead to mine, I see the truth in his eyes.

"It's over, baby. I promise," he whispers. "You are safe, I'm safe, and Alice is safe. We are all okay. It's over. It really is."

I don't know why, but I start to cry, and before I know it, I'm sobbing in his arms as he holds me. More arms surround me, and I lift my head to see Alice, Lally, Bones, and Sky. They hold me as I cry until I pull back and wipe my face, looking at Clarissa just as dawn breaks through the glass window, illuminating the space.

"Now what?" I whisper.

"Now we go home." Alek kisses my cheek.

"He's right, go home," Autumn says. "We'll take care of everything."

I hesitate, and Bones nods. "The police are already on the way. We'll tell them everything. They'll want to speak to you, but our lawyers have already been contacted. Everything will go through them. This won't touch your future, and we'll control the stories that are released. We'll take care of everything; it's what we do. We are family. Now go home and rest."

"He's so hot when he's in control," Skylar whispers to me, making me choke and smile despite everything.

Alek picks my wrist up, frowning at the bleeding skin there. "Yes, and we'll get you cleaned up and treated."

"Me? You were stabbed twice tonight," I mutter as he leads me toward the tunnel.

"That's right." Sky slings his arm over Alek's other side as Alice and Lally shake their heads and walk in front of us. "Who gets stabbed twice? Seriously?"

"Not this again." Alek groans as I grin.

"Hey, Evan." I turn back to catch the phone Bones throws at me.

"That's yours. Don't let the dead control you. We survived, and that's all that matters. Leave everything else in the past." He turns away. "Let's sort this mess out. It started with a Silent Rose member, and it will end with us too."

Smiling, I clutch my phone. I know he's right.

Tonight was the most horrendous night of my life, but looking at those surrounding me, I know it would have been a lot worse without them. I am so thankful they are at my side and that they love me. No matter what happens now, I won't ever let them go.

NO PARKING
ACTIVE DRIVEWAY
SHAW DRIVE
THE MOMENT
ANDERS AVE
ONE WAY
STOP
TOO
NO PARKING
SALE
SILENT ROSE
EVER
Pine Valley

FIFTY-THREE

ALEK

I swing by the hospital at Evan's urging, and both of us get checked over. They want us to stay, but we refuse. I'm exhausted, and so is he. All I want is my bed and my boy in my arms where I know he's safe. When we get back, Alice and Lally crash on one couch, and Skylar stretches out on the other.

Evan's hand is in mine as we stare at them. "Come on, let's get some sleep." I tug him upstairs, knowing I have a lot of cleanup to do in the house, not to mention rebuilding my car, but I'm the best mechanic, so I can do it.

I can fix everything that's broken.

I tell Evan as much later, when he's in my arms after I clean the broken glass and cover the window, stroking his tired face. "I'll fix whatever is broken, pretty boy. My car, this house, your heart—I'll spend my life fixing everything. They don't get another second of you, do you hear me?"

"Tonight will change all of us," he admits.

"It should." I nod. "You don't survive something like that and come out as the same person. It should leave a mark, but we won't give them the satisfaction of taking another second of our time. We'll keep moving forward and keep living to spite them. We'll be happy and find new hope together—all of us."

"Almost all of us," he whispers. "I wonder if they have told his parents yet."

"If they haven't, you can call them in the morning," I tell him, kissing his head. "But you need to rest now, okay? Don't make me get all growly and order you around."

He grins, moving closer. "Why? We both know I like it when you do."

"Not tonight, pretty boy. Tomorrow, I'm going to spend hours ensuring myself you're alive and okay, but for now, we are sleeping, right here in our bed where you belong."

"Okay," he whispers. "Everything else can wait for tomorrow."

"Tomorrow," I agree.

I leave Evan sleeping. Like Bones and Silent Rose promised, no cops knock at our door. Instead, I have a text telling me our lawyers are waiting, and when we are ready to go to the station, they will go with us to give our statements. It seems like the police have enough to occupy them rather than chasing us for information and statements.

Social media is exploding with theories, but nothing else has been released as of yet, and my respect for Silent Rose's power only rises.

We are lucky we had them last night. We needed numbers and help, and they were there for him. I'm so glad he has a place like that, a home, with them and with me.

I look up when there's a noise and watch as Alice sits opposite me, her hair sticking up all over like when she was a kid. Reaching over, I take her hand, and she laces our fingers together.

I want to say something to make her feel better, to comfort her, but honestly, what can I say? Suddenly, she speaks, her voice soft so as not to wake the others. "Are you okay?"

"I should be asking you that," I murmur.

"No, we should ask each other. You're my older brother, Alek, not my father." I flinch, and she smiles to soften the blow. "Not in a bad way. I love you, but I want a brother, not a father. I want someone to talk to and play with, not someone to order me around and protect me. All this time, I let you do just that, depending on you more than I should and taking you for granted, and I almost lost you last night. We are family, Alek, but we should lean on each other. We should have our own lives, and you shouldn't live for me." She glances at the stairs.

"I'm glad you have Evan. Before him, you would have taken me and run last night, not caring about anyone else, but now, you let people in and gave yourself the chance to love and live. I'm so happy, and I'm so sorry, Alek, for depending on you so much and making you carry that weight alone. You were just a kid too, but it's time for you to live your life now. If last night has taught us anything, it's that life is too fucking short to have regrets. I know I don't want any. I refuse to be scared anymore, and I want you to do the same. I'm going to move out, and I want you to choose what makes you happy. I'm also going to get a job and pay for some of my tuition."

"Don't grow up too fast, okay? Don't take everything from me. I need you to rely on me a little," I admit, and she grins.

"That's because you like being needed, like having a purpose, but Evan needs you, Alek, and I will always need you. You will always be my family, the place I come home to, but it's time we find our own lives separate from each other. All I want is for you to be happy, big brother."

"And that's all I want for you," I murmur. "It was a price I willingly paid. I raised you well, sis. You've become one hell of a woman. I realized it last night when you were willing to take a bullet for me. You're all grown up. I'll stop treating you like a kid if I can."

She smiles. "And I'll stop treating you like a crutch."

"Everything is changing," I say, frightened.

Evan shuffles into the room, his eyes half closed. "Coffee," he demands like a zombie.

"Not everything." She laughs.

"Coffee?" Lally groans, stumbling into the room, just as much of a zombie as Evan.

"No wonder they are besties," I scoff just as Skylar groans from the living room.

"You're all so loud with your feelings. I was having a good dream about a certain tattooed asshole—"

He grunts when I throw a pillow at him, but it ends in a laugh that fills the house, and I can't help but smile.

Everything is changing, but it's for the best.

This house is a home now, filled with laughter and love, and no matter what happens, we'll face it together.

FIFTY-FOUR

I know Alek is worried about Alice and me. He shows it by hovering around and trying to take care of everything. It's sweet, but I can see Alice rolling her eyes. It seems they had a heart-to-heart this morning, which was needed. I'm glad Alice is realizing just how much her brother does for her and giving him some freedom from that. He needs to know it's okay to let her live her life and for him to live his.

By early afternoon, we are all restless, unsure what to do, so we contact the lawyers and head to the station. In the daylight, it's a much different sight than last night. There are police cars everywhere, and when we walk in, there are more officers here than I have ever seen. There aren't any bodies or blood, so they must have cleaned it up, but I know they must feel the loss.

Their officers died protecting us last night. It makes my steps heavy with guilt. However, none of them blame us or glare. They welcome us warmly and take us to a side room, and a burly man comes inside with an older man carrying a briefcase.

He's attractive, probably in his mid-forties, with a strong build. He's wearing a designer, tailor-made suit, a Rolex on one wrist, and a diamond ring on his left hand. His hair is artfully swept back, displaying strong features, and he seems familiar, but I can't place why. "I am Sergeant Rodgers, and this is my precinct. It's nice to finally meet you," the burly man says as he sits.

"I'm Declan Townsend, and I will be representing you in any matters." The man nods at us and sits. He has an elegant if slightly stiff aura about him—arrogance, the type that comes with power and money. I know that all too well because it surrounded my family.

"I tried to explain you don't need representation," Rodgers starts.

Declan simply smiles. "Then I'm here as a formality."

"I see." Rodgers eyes him and then turns to us. "Interesting how you sought the richest and most lethal lawyer in the vicinity."

"You flatter me." Declan smiles. It's sharklike and reminds me of Bones for a moment. Shit, is this Bones's dad?

I eye him again, noticing the resemblance once more. It has to be. He mentioned his dad owns a law firm. He hired his dad for us?

"Yes, well, I'll cut to the chase since we all know that we have our dead to see to," Rodgers says, his eyes haunted. "All I need are your statements on what happened last night. We have camera footage and witness statements, including ones from Officer Beckett, Winchester's partner."

"He survived?" I lean forward.

"He's in critical condition, but he's alive." Rodgers nods. "We know you have nothing to do with any of this, but you were here, and we need answers. I'm going to record it, if that's okay."

I look at Declan, who inclines his head and leans into us. "Look at me before speaking. You don't have to answer anything I say not to."

"Declan." Rodgers sighs. "I'm not trying to trick them—"

"William," Declan retorts, using the sergeant's first name since he did the same. "I will advise my clients as I see fit. You may record the interview, but they are free to ignore your questions or leave whenever they wish. You have already said they have no charges being pressed against them. Now, let us begin. My clients have been through a terrible ordeal and should be resting."

"We lost good officers last night," William snaps. "I just need to know how and why."

"A great loss." Declan nods. "But your anger is misplaced. Aim it at Miss Clarissa Wright, who you have in holding, not my clients. Now begin."

William looks tired, and I feel for him. These officers were probably colleagues and friends for many years. I know that loss well.

For the next two hours, we go over everything in detail. I leave nothing out, neither does Alek, and when it's over, Declan stands with us, but I hesitate.

"Has Tommy Mashou's parents been notified?" I ask, looking at William.

His eyes soften. He's a stern man, and it's obvious why he's in power, though I'm betting he's feeling that weight now, but he is also kind and never pushed us nor blamed us for anything. If anything, he went out of his way to make us feel better. "They were. I called them myself this morning. They will be coming down today to see their son. He's at the hospital if you wish to see him as well."

I roll my lips inwards. "I said my goodbye," I say. I don't think I could bear to see him again. "But thank you. He is—he was a good man."

"I know. I looked into him. I am sorry for your loss. I know you were close." He stands and holds out his hand. "I'm here if you need anything, Evan, and please be assured she won't be getting out for a very long time. You're safe. You all are."

"Thank you." I follow Declan outside, where he nods at us.

"I will wait here. Your friend, a Miss La—" He stumbles over her name, his brows furrowed.

"Lally." I grin.

"Yes, Lally." Declan coughs. "And Skylar Warren and Silas Townsend—or I suppose you know my son as Bones—will be speaking and giving statements soon. I mean it, though, go rest."

"Mr. Townsend," I call when he turns to go back inside. "Thank you."

He shrugs. "My son made a deal with me for my help. I don't need your thanks."

My eyebrows rise at his cold tone, and I wonder what Bones

offered his father for him to waste his time with us. Probably nothing good, but I have enough of my own worries, so I let it go.

The story breaks that night, and Alice, Alek, and I sit and watch the news. Just as Bones and the others promised, it's brief, mainly focusing on the great loss of everyone who perished last night. Our names are kept hidden, and for that, I'm grateful. I don't need to be reminded of what we endured and what we lost.

Alice sleeps here for what will be the last time. It seems she is taking her newfound independence seriously, and I'm proud of her. I know Alek is worried, but it's obvious he's trying to let her go and give her what she wants. I know it won't be easy for either of them, but it's a healthy move.

All I can do is be here for both of them as we heal together, and as I watch Alek sleep soundly at my side, his hand clutched in mine, I know I'll stay right here at his side, in his bed, and in his home.

I knew that Alek was my forever type of thing, but after what happened, it only made it that much clearer. He was willing to die for me, to kill for me, and he loves me. He will never let me go. I know if we can survive this, then we can survive anything that might arise in our lives.

Some might say we are too young, but I don't care. When you find the one you love and want to spend the rest of your life with, you hold on tight and don't let go.

I've spent my life ignoring others' opinions, and I won't start caring now.

Leaning down, I smooth the furrow between his brows and kiss his worries away. "I'm right here, princess. I'm not going anywhere," I murmur. "Thank you for coming for me. Thank you for saving me."

"Always," he whispers sleepily as he guides me down into his arms. "I'll always find you, pretty boy."

"Thug," I tease.

"Rich prick," he retorts, and something clicks in my heart, letting me know we will be okay.

The grief for what we have lost will go on, but I hope it will get easier. If I can have him waiting for me every night, it will be worth suffering through it all, and I'm excited for dawn and what it will bring.

NO PARKING
ACTIVE DRIVEWAY
SHAW DRIVE
THE MOMENT
ANDERS AVE
ONE WAY
STOP
TOO
SILENT ROSE
NO PARKING
SALE
EVER
Pine Valley

FIFTY-FIVE

I think it's too soon, but Evan insists it's time.

The school reopened two days ago after shutting down for the investigation and damage, and Evan and Alice haven't been back yet, but they insist on going today.

"Alek." Evan sighs as I block the door to the car I borrowed from Sky, since mine needs to be fixed. "It's time. I can't hide at home forever, and as much as we would both enjoy it—"

"Disgusting." Alice coughs, making us both smile. She moved out the other day, but like she promised, she came back for breakfast and let me look after her, just a little.

"It's time. This place doesn't scare me, and I refuse to let him ruin the happy memories I've made here. I need to get back to normal." He steps past me and takes my hand. "But how about you walk me to class?"

"Oh, walking the rich boy to class, I've never done that before. Fine." Shutting the door, I grab his bag and throw it over my shoulder, ignoring his sigh and pointed look at my side where I was stabbed. Honestly, it twinges every now and then, but it's a good kind of pain because it reminds me I'm still alive.

We walk toward the building, and everything looks like it's back to the way it was, like nothing happened, and I know Evan and Alice feel it as they stare up at the doors we ran through a week ago, scared and chased.

"It's all the same," Evan whispers before rolling his shoulders back. Pride fills me at his courage as he leads me up and inside to the very hallway where his friend died. His strength staggers me, and I know I need to be equally as strong for him. He lost someone important. You don't just get over that, and he might be acting unaffected, but I know he's hurting, and I'll be right here for him the entire time.

There's a crowd down the hallway, though, and Evan hesitates. "What?" He tugs me after him when I try to stop, but when I see Lally, I nod, and we push through.

Evan gasps, his eyes filling with tears as we stare at the wall. Tommy's blood and body are gone, but in their place is a permanent reminder—a good one.

His name is scrawled in graffiti, alongside skateboards, flowers, and paint splatter, with candles and flowers placed before it. I wasn't sure if it was going to be ready in time, but when Lally reached out about it, I knew I wanted to help in some way. I did the art, but she did everything else, and as I stare into Evan's eyes, I know it was worth sneaking out during the night.

"Do you like it? Lally told me his favorite colors—" I'm cut off as he jumps into my arms, and I catch him.

"I love it," he mumbles. "Thank you."

"I've got you, pretty boy. You aren't alone, remember? This way, when you come here, it will be a place to remember him, not just that night. We are turning the bad into good, aren't we?"

He nods as he pulls away, then he pulls Lally into a hug, all of us looking back at the memorial for the man who saved my love's life.

I pull the flowers from my bag and place them before the candles. "I didn't get to say thank you, Tommy, for saving him that night. I couldn't live without him. I would have died right alongside him. I know you did it because you loved Evan, but I wanted to thank you, and I promise I won't let him blame himself. I'll try to keep him in check as much as he lets anyone." I crack a smile as I straighten some of the candles and pictures. "Thank you for being his family."

Stepping back, I take Evan's hand, and a while after everyone else has headed to class, we stand there until I drop his bag at his feet, kiss his cheek, and retreat, letting him stand with Lally and talk to Tommy.

When he's done, I walk him to class. Ignoring the calls and whistles, I kiss him goodbye and promise to pick him up after.

It's hard to walk away and leave him alone, but I manage it.

I hate being away from him for this long. I've gotten used to being at his side twenty-four seven and knowing he's okay. Maybe I'm clingy, but I don't care. I check my phone for the tenth time in the last two minutes. He hasn't replied to my latest text, which might have been the twentieth this hour, but still.

"Will you chill out?" Sky calls, sprawled out on my couch, watching TV as I work on my car. I don't know why he followed me here. I have a sneaking suspicion Evan asked him to, but he's wearing out his welcome. I only like having Evan in my space.

"He didn't reply," I tell him.

"So whipped," he retorts. "He's fine. He's at school. Focus on fixing your baby so I can have my car back."

"Shouldn't you be practicing?" I counter as I wipe my hands. It will take me a couple of weeks to fix it up for good, but it will be better than new. I understand cars better than I ever understood people, but luckily my boyfriend doesn't seem to care, and neither does the little family I seem to have adopted—including this lazy asshole eating all my snacks.

He reaches for a packet, and I snatch it away as he raises his eyebrows. "They are Evan's favorite. Eat something else."

"Whipped." He nods. "What's the point in practicing? There aren't any good competitors."

I frown as he sighs and looks away. "I'm tired of street racing. I guess it lost its thrill after . . . Anyway, someone like me will never become a real racer. We both know that."

"So what, you're just giving up?" I scoff.

He shrugs. "Maybe, but I did put in a good word for you."

"What do you mean?" I ask.

"I saw some ads for experienced mechanics and submitted your information." My eyes widen, and he grins. "Before you get mad, Evan helped. He knew you wouldn't do it alone. Hell, even your boss, that scary—"

"Whistler," I add.

"Yeah, him, he helped. He actually said, 'Good, take the grumpy asshole. He's better than this stinking job anyway.'" He arches his eyebrow. "Evan seems to think that means he likes you. You wanted a garage of your own, and you'll get there someday, but for now . . ." He shrugs. "Something new can't hurt."

"Like anyone will want me. I have no qualifications," I mutter as I head over to my car.

"But would you try if you were offered something?" he asks.

"Maybe," I admit. "I guess I was a little stagnant before. I love racing and working at the garage, but something different might be good."

Then, as if fate intervenes, my phone rings. I grab it, expecting Evan, but it's a number I don't recognize, and Sky grins like he knows something I don't. Flipping him off, I answer with a gruff, "Yes?"

"Um, yes, hi, is this Alek Anders?"

"Who's asking?" I mutter as I stare into the engine. Something is out of place, but I can't figure out what.

"It's Noah from Starfire Racing. You submitted an application for the head of our garage last week. We would be thrilled to offer you an interview. We have seen your work, and after speaking to your boss and some connections in the industry, we think you would be a great fit."

"Me?" I gape, pulling my phone away. "Is this a joke?"

"Um, no?" Noah replies.

"I'm a brute," I say. "I have no qualifications—"

"So? Neither do I," Noah says, "yet here I am, running a racing team. Interview is tomorrow at eleven. I hope to see you. Qualifications or not, Alek Anders, we want you."

He hangs up, and I'm left staring at my phone in shock.

Interview? Me?

Starfire?

What the fuck?

"You've got this," Evan says, straightening my jacket. I refuse to wear a suit, but I did put on my clean boots and nice pants and shirt. I just happened to add my leather jacket. Either they hire me as I am or not at all. I'm not changing who I am for anyone, not even a job—even if it is with the most renowned racing team around.

They are at the top of the industry, which makes me that much more suspicious. Why would they want me? They could have their pick of mechanics.

Their base is a large, white-brick garage with two open doors, rock music blasting from inside. One of their smaller tracks is to my left, the bigger one spread out behind them just outside of Pine Valley.

It's the team Skylar always wanted to race for, and I hate that I'm here and he isn't, but he wished me luck this morning and told me not to be a total prick and to impress them. Alice cooked me breakfast, and Evan drove me here. All of them are supporting me, so even if I wanted to chicken out, I can't. I owe it to them to discover if I want it. It isn't something I had ever thought of before, but I can admit it's a great opportunity.

Being their mechanic would allow me to do what I love and be in charge of a garage. I try not to get my hopes up too much though.

Evan pats my chest, bringing my eyes back to him. "Knock them dead. Just try not to glare at everyone, okay?"

"I'll try," I reply before stealing a kiss. "Be back soon."

He nods, leaning back against my car as I head to the open door two minutes before eleven.

The inside of the garage is exactly what I expected. Race cars are everywhere, and there are even some of their older models and their champion car on display. Photos cover the walls, as does their logo. Mechanics and techs bustle between cars as I head through to the back where there's a partial wall. Around it, I find a table and chairs and doors beyond that lead to locker rooms and offices.

There aren't any racers about or anyone else, so I hesitate until a voice sounds behind me. "So you came." I turn to find a middle-aged man grinning at me. He is lithe, with blond hair and mismatched eyes. He's wearing overalls tied at his waist, revealing an oil-stained tank underneath. "You must be Alek, right? I'm—"

"Noah Fletcher," I finish for him, and he grins. "I used to watch you race when I was a kid."

"Ouch, now I feel old." He laughs, shaking my hand. "I'm in charge of the team now. Come, let me walk you through the garage." I fall into step at his side as he shows me around.

"That's Mackie's car." He nods at a vehicle on jacks, the engine roaring as they test it. "That's Whip's car. We do all our own tuning and tech here. We are a tight-knit family. Our old head of the garage left to help take care of his youngest daughter who's going through chemo. He was actually the one who suggested you. We like to keep our eye on talent, and it seems he did too."

I look around at the magnitude of the garage. "I'm used to working in a tiny garage filled with nude magazines," I admit. "I don't have qualifications for this, like I mentioned. I just like cars, that's all."

"We want talent. We want drive and attitude. I don't need qualifications. I can teach everything else," he murmurs. "Honestly, I saw you race a couple of times, and I would have hired you for that, but I have a feeling you prefer to be in front of the engine rather than driving it. Am I right?"

I nod, and he smiles. "The job is yours." My eyes widen, and he laughs. "Seeing you was a formality. I like to look a person in their eyes before I bring them on, but I knew it was going to be you anyway . . . if you want it?"

What do I want?

Evan's voice fills my head, daring me to dream.

"I want it."

"Good, then welcome to Starfire Racing, Alek Anders. I can't wait to see what you're capable of."

Neither can I.

FIFTY-SIX

"Surprise!" I yell alongside the others as we step into Alek's house. He was quiet the entire way home, but I can tell he's excited. He didn't expect to get the job, but I knew he would. Nobody deserves it more than he does, and I'm so proud of him for taking his dream and running with it.

A hastily handmade banner hangs above the living room with balloons spread about and pizza and beer on the table. Skylar, Bones, Lally, and Alice clap and yell as I grin and tug Alek inside.

"Congratulations!" Skylar whoops and pulls Alek into a hug. "Let's hope they put up with your grumpy ass."

Bones nods at him as Alice rushes to hug him. "I knew you could do it. I'm so proud of you, big brother."

"Evan." Alek sighs as I grin.

"I'm proud of you too." I grin as I kiss his cheek. "Now accept it, and let's celebrate. We could all use something good. Let us do that for tonight."

We drink and eat and celebrate Alek's future, our futures. We tell stories and talk, never once bringing up what happened. Tonight is for the future, not the past, and although Tommy's spot remains empty and open, I know he'd be happy we aren't wallowing forever.

As more and more liquor flows along with the music, I sneak upstairs, knowing Alek will find me. Less than ten minutes later, he steps into his room. I shut and lock the door, and he whirls to me.

"Pants off, Anders. It's time to celebrate." I wiggle my eyebrows at him.

"Wow, how can a man resist when you offer like that?" He smirks.

"Cock out, Anders. We have to make this quick before they come up here, and you know Sky will—" My sentence ends on a gasp as he kisses me, hard.

"Then let me unwrap my present for doing well," he murmurs.

Our lips meet in a sloppy, drunken kiss. Alcohol heats our systems, along with desire, as he undoes my pants and pushes them down. I step out of them as he shoves his hand into his jeans and pulls out his dick. He rubs his hard length against mine, and we both whimper into our kiss. Gripping us both, he slides our cocks together as I gasp, my back hitting the wall hard as I jerk into his hand. "I want to play with you all night," he murmurs, "but if Sky comes up and sees you like this, I might have to kill the only friend I have."

"Later," I promise. "Now fuck me."

Reluctantly, he releases the grip on our cocks before he backs me up. My ass and back hit the dresser, then he lifts me onto it, bending me over the wooden top as I moan into his mouth.

His hands span my thighs, pushing them apart so he can fit between them, and he pants into my mouth. "Open up, pretty boy. Let me have my gift."

My hands hit the dresser, curling over the edge as I lift my thighs for him. He blindly grabs a bottle, covering his cock in lube before pressing against my ass, teasing me as his lips meet mine in a bruising kiss.

He pulls my hips to the edge of the dresser and slams into me.

My eyes roll back from the pleasure and bite of pain. He's so big, stretching me, and he tilts my hips so he's sliding across my prostate with each quick thrust.

His palm hits the wall, the dresser rocking with each thrust, smacking into the wall.

Our lips clumsily meet, and we swallow each other's moans as he fucks me. My cock jerks against my stomach, the pleasure spiraling through me heightened by the alcohol buzzing in my system and the fact we could be caught at any minute.

"Evan." His teeth tug at my lip as he hammers into my ass. It's almost too much, too painful, but it also isn't enough at the same time. I love soft, sweet Alek, but brutal Alek? He makes me harder than ever, leaking on my stomach as I push to meet his thrusts, wanting more.

"Alek," I whisper, biting his lip until I taste blood, and he snarls, pummeling my ass so hard I can't hold back my cry.

"Close, I'm so close," I warn, pleasure building inside me like a tidal wave until it finally crests. I bite back on a yell as hot ropes of cum spill from my cock. Snarling, he fights my fluttering ass, yanking me on and off his dick until he yells into my lips, following me over the edge. He shoots his release so deep inside me, I know I'll never get him out.

Panting heavily, I open my eyes to see him inches away, our bodies locked together, and we both laugh. His lips find mine in a soft kiss. "Thank you, pretty boy, for believing in me . . . for loving me when I didn't love myself."

"Anytime," I murmur as I push him back and hop off, stumbling on weak legs. He catches me, making me grin, and I lean up to kiss him again. "I'm so proud of you, and you can play with your present all night when everyone leaves." I wiggle my brows as his grin widens.

"Deal."

We quickly dress and clean up as best as we can so they don't send out a search party.

Heading downstairs hand in hand, we both stop at the bottom, Alek's cheeks heating while I grin when we see them all gathered at the bottom step with knowing looks on every face.

"Bravo." Lally claps.

Alice covers her eyes, shaking her head, but she's smiling.

"Big ending. Eight out of ten," Sky says, nudging Bones. "Don't worry, I can do better—"

Bones simply smacks the back of his head and turns away, Sky following after him like a puppy.

"Come on, love birds, let's celebrate!" Alice calls.

We rejoin our friends, all of us looking toward the future.

Leaning back in my lab chair, I sigh as I stretch. It's been a busy few weeks. We had Tommy's funeral, which wrecked me, and there was also a memorial held in the city for everything that was lost. Alek started at his new job, and I'm so proud of him, but it means he's busy, so I use that time to focus on my work. The end of the semester is coming up, and I really need to crack down. I won't waste the opportunities I was given, not because of what happened.

Speaking of, I heard yesterday that Clarissa is being sentenced soon. Luckily, they don't seem to want or need our contribution, which I'm happy about. It truly is over.

Lally snores on her desk next to me, and I smile. The computer to my right is empty, as everyone knows to leave it like that for Tommy. It's where he would always sit, and it remains like that. We will never replace him.

I haven't been able to go back to my dorm as of yet. I can't face it, but I know I will have to one day unless I take Alek's offer and just move in with him. He's been hinting at it since the attack, and I have to admit, it appeals to me. I don't want to go back to an empty room filled with ghosts, even good ones. I don't want to wake up in pain every day. I want to wake up happy like Tommy would want.

My eyes go back to my screen and what I'm working on.

If he asks again, I'll say yes.

I'll race toward my future with him, like I know I deserve.

A few hours later, I wake Lally up, and she heads off to who knows where. She's been distant lately, and I know it's her way of dealing with grief. When she needs me, she'll tell me. Instead, I turn toward

Alek, who is leaning against his car, newly fixed and shiny as ever—my name printed on his passenger seat.

He grins as he takes my bag and helps me inside, and when we are back at his place, he takes my hand and leads me upstairs. "I'm tired, maybe later," I whine as he opens his door. "Fine, just a quickie—"

I stop, gaping at his room which is now filled with suitcases and boxes, his drawers open and filled with my clothes. "I don't have many, so I gave them all to you." He turns to me as I stare. "Alice is gone, so I figured I could either keep hinting or could make it happen. We were never good at doing things the normal way, so I just moved you in. I paid off your dorm so they will keep it empty for now in case you want it, especially for Tommy. I heard his parents cleaned out his room, but you never know."

"You moved me into your house?" I can't help but smile. "You are such an asshole."

"You know it, rich boy. Now, about that quickie—" I back away with a laugh as he lifts me into his arms and throws me onto our bed.

My boxes are spread around us, ready to be unpacked, but the message is clear—I'm here to stay, and I'm more than okay with that.

NO PARKING
ACTIVE
DRIVEWAY
SHAW DRIVE
THE
MOMENT
ANDERS AVE
ONE WAY
TOO
STOP
SILENT ROSE
NO
PARKING
SALE
Pine Valley
EVER

FIFTY-SEVEN

ALEK

"Your boy sure is pretty," Mackie teases from his position opposite my desk, his boots propped up on it. As the head driver, he's a cocky fucker, but surprisingly, we get along well.

Noah laughs, taking the framed photo from him with a grin. I snatch it back without looking and place it on my desk, unable to stop my smile.

"Look at that smile. He's the only one who gets the big bastard to grin. Have you noticed that?" Noah teases, and I simply roll my eyes. In the few weeks since I started working here, I've realized I fit in far too easily. They might be a famous, multimillion-dollar racing team, but at heart, they are all car junkies, and we get each other. Besides, we have a lot in common. It's nice, and I really like working here. They were right, I fit, and everyone welcomed me, which was amazing. I still have a lot to learn, but I'm excited for it and the possibilities it holds.

"It's your boy's show tonight, isn't it?" Noah asks conversationally. I don't know why they insist on eating lunch in here when we have a kitchen, but they always seem to. Evan thinks it's because I never join them and they are trying to include me. He's been here a few times, enough to meet everyone and for me to warn them away from him. I'm not the least bit ashamed of that, and I know my smile turns goofy and proud when I meet Noah's eyes.

"Yep, five." I look at the clock, counting the hours. I need to shower and dress up before then—he's the only person I will dress up for. "He's going to kill it."

"Look how proud he is." Mackie laughs. "I don't blame you. If I had someone like that in my life, I'd brag too. You're a lucky man, Anders."

Noah shoots him a glare he doesn't seem to notice.

"I know it," I admit. "Now either get out or share your food. I need to place an order before I go," I mutter, making them both laugh.

Yes, I fit in here. I'll admit I miss my old garage sometimes, and I still join the odd race every now and again, but my future is bright, and Evan was right. I deserve to dream, and Starfire Racing is the place to do that.

By the time I shower and dress, I run to the showcase so I'm not late.

Luckily, the venue is the school, and I make it there to find a line to get in. It might only be a student showcase, but the recent attacks have everyone's eyes on this school, and before that, it was one of the only high-profile colleges to continually pump out the best of the best. Evan explained that even scouts for magazines and agents come to check out future acquisitions and keep their eye on students, so it's an honor to be involved.

Previously, I scoffed at the showcase out of fear, but now, I proudly stand in line. I see Lally waving me to the door. Some people eye me in confusion and others in anger because I'm getting in before them, but I hurry through the open door as she links her arm with mine. "Come on, he's freaking out. He needs you." She leads me through the glossy reception area, past the ticket sales table, and to the gallery beyond. "You look amazing by the way. He is going to freak."

"What's wrong?" I ask worriedly as I hurry through the gallery, barely seeing any of the other students' submissions. My eyes land on Evan, who is pacing at the very end where a huge rectangle of the room has been cordoned off. Everything else fades, and all I see is him. Even Lally's voice disappears into the background until I know I'm just staring. "Huh?" I ask, blinking as I look down at Lally.

She snorts and pushes me his way. "Go on, Romeo, you'll figure it out." Nodding in thanks, I quicken my steps so I'm practically running to him, slipping past the rope to reach him.

He must hear me because he turns, and I get the full Evan Shaw effect. I actually stumble. His hair is wavy, with two pieces hanging down in front as usual, and his ears are exposed, stacked with piercings. His lips are rosy like his cheeks, his eyes darkened with liner, but his outfit blows me away.

He looks like a prince in an old-school fairy-tale book.

He's wearing loose, flowing white pants with a gold belt, a sheer shirt with open buttons, exposing his tan chest nearly all the way to his navel, and an oversized blazer. He looks like a goddamn knight in shining armor.

A frost prince.

If he's the white knight, the prince, then I'm the goddamn villain coming to claim his soul.

I'm dressed head to toe in black. Even my shoes are black, formal, and shiny. My suit pants are ironed, paired with a black, long-sleeved, button-up shirt. I couldn't bring myself to add a tie or coat, but my hair is styled.

I cleaned up as best as I could, wanting to impress him, and when his eyes drop to me and widen, I know I succeeded. "Jesus, Anders. You should wear that every day. I mean *every* day."

"Don't get ahead of yourself." I smirk as I pull him closer and lean down to steal a kiss. "Though I might make some exceptions if you dress like this." I bring my lips to his ear. "You look good enough to eat. In fact, I just might."

He smacks my chest with a bright laugh, his eyes twinkling with genuine happiness, and my heart is so full, it feels like it might burst.

Cupping his handsome face, I stare into his eyes. "I love you, Evan Shaw," I declare, pushing everything I can into those words.

I'm not good with words like him, or able to capture a moment through a lens, but I want to seize every moment with him. I want to give him the words to make him understand the depths of my devotion and my love for him.

"Is that right?" Taking my hand, he steps back and gestures around us. "Then figure out how I feel for yourself."

My eyes widen as I look around at the photographs.

"I know you were worried how people would react, but they aren't tasteless. I really love them," he starts to ramble.

"Evan," I say, and he stops speaking as I bring my astonished gaze back to him. "I love them." I mean it. You can feel the need, love, and obsession pouring from every frame. Yes, I'm shirtless and posing, but it's more than that. I don't even understand photography, but it's the angles and the way he shot me. I can actually feel him through his work.

I walk around, looking at them, and he silently walks by my side as I stop at the last one. "You really love me," I murmur into the silence. His barked laugh makes me grin. Uncaring who is watching, I pull him into my arms and kiss him deeply.

"I love you, Alek Anders," he says brightly, and I swear I have never been so happy. Hearing those words heals something inside me.

Evan Shaw heals me every day.

"They are amazing. Everyone is going to love them."

"Do you think so?" he asks, looking at me for reassurance.

"If not, then they are morons, and I'll hit them for you. Evan, they are so good. You are a goddamn rock star. They'll see it," I promise as I take his hand. The last one along the back wall is large, the first and last photograph you see.

It's not me—well not just me, and I smile when I realize where it's from.

It's us, our little family, from the night of the attack before everything went to shit. We are smiling at the camera, and in the center, smiling goofily, is Tommy.

"I figured everyone could remember him for the way he was. I know it's probably not a good thing right now, but when I look at this, I remember how happy we were, and I wanted to replace the last image I have of him with this—his smile and his love for us all."

"It's perfection. The perfect tribute," I assure him as we stand before it, staring up at our smiling faces, red from alcohol and laughter.

"I miss him," Evan admits. "I wish he were here."

"He is," I reply, lifting his hand to kiss the back, "and he would be so proud." I turn to him and encourage him to look at me. "I am so proud of you. Screw your parents." He jerks, and I know I hit the nail on the head. He invited them, I know he did, but they didn't even bother to respond. I want to throttle them for that and for missing out on this. "It's their loss. They are missing out on seeing your talent and meeting the incredible man you have grown to be. Fuck them, pretty boy, you don't need them. You have us." I turn him to see Lally, Alice, Sky, and Bones, who are waiting on the other side. When we glance their way, they wave, and Evan smiles so broadly I know he's going to be okay.

"Fuck them," he whispers as he looks at me. "Blood isn't family, this is."

"So true, pretty boy, now let's go meet your fans."

This is Evan's night, and I'm happy to be at his side, watching him dazzle the room like he dazzled me. He works his way into their lives, stealing their smiles and laughter. It's what he's best at, and he does it so well. He's so genuine, loving, and passionate, you can't do anything but adore him.

I answer some questions, but mostly, I just stand proudly at his side as he talks to everyone and shows off me and his photos. How could I ever think this would be something bad? Seeing his pride and love as he explains them steals my soul one inch at a time, and there's something about the acceptance in everyone's faces that just makes me happy.

It's the way he introduces me. "Yep, that's Alek, my boyfriend, and these are our friends—" He speaks as if presenting me as his boyfriend isn't a big deal, as if us being gay isn't a spectacle like I thought it would be. It's not a conversation, just a fact.

I couldn't love this man more.

"How are you doing, pretty boy?" I ask, handing him a glass of water when there's a lull. Everyone is amazed by his photos, so I steal him for a moment, blocking people so he can breathe.

His smile is so wide, it must hurt as he looks at me. "They like them. They really like them."

"When are you going to stop doubting yourself?" I grin. "Of course they love them. They are of me."

He laughs as he smacks my side, and then someone clears their throat. "Mr. Shaw?" We both turn to see a man wearing thick-rimmed glasses smiling at us. It's a kind smile, the type that makes you want to smile back. Wearing loose, camel-colored pants and a sweater, he looks sophisticated and rich, the watch on his wrist screaming money. "I'm—"

"You're Conan, *the* Conan White," Evan exclaims, staring at him in shock. "You won the Arbel Photography Prize recently, and you worked with nearly every publication."

Conan laughs. "I guess you know me." He seems almost embarrassed. "I apologize for being late tonight. I was on a shoot, but when I heard of the rising star of Pine Valley, I had to come. I went to this school, you see, and I know us Pine Valley boys are the best." He looks around before grinning at Evan and handing over a card. "You have real potential, Evan. I mean it. It's been a long time since I've seen talent like this. Give me a call tomorrow. I'd love to speak to you more. For now, enjoy your night. You deserve it." He nods and wanders away to another group, and Evan just stares down at the card like it's the holy grail.

"That's good, right?" I ask nervously.

"Good?" He looks up at me, whispering in awe. "He makes

careers. You don't become a photographer without his stamp of approval. He's a recluse, a total genius—"

Laughing, I kiss his cheek. "And he likes your work. I told you, pretty boy, you're so fucking talented. He's right, though. Enjoy your night. Want me to look after the card?" He tends to drop things after all.

He nods, handing it over carefully, and I add it to my wallet next to his picture so it doesn't get lost, knowing how important this is to him.

Eventually, he gets over his shock, and Lally drags him into a group to discuss his work. I find myself standing before one of the photos of me, a rare one where I'm smiling for him. Suddenly, I feel a presence at my side, and I glance over to find Conan there, looking at the photo.

"He has the rare ability to capture people's souls. That's not something you can teach," he murmurs.

"You think? You can see my soul?" I ask, not doubting Evan's talent but the sincerity of my soul.

"I can, and it's beautiful," he tells me with a smile. "I see why he loves you and you him. I can feel the love through these photos. He will go far, so be prepared because it won't be easy."

"We have handled worse," I say truthfully. "But how do I support him? I don't know all the ins and outs of the photography world—"

"Just be there. Listen to him, hold him, and trust him. That's all he needs." We both glance over at Evan as his laughter reaches us. "Don't let anyone steal that spark. It isn't something you get back, trust me."

I regard him carefully, sensing the truth between his words. "I won't. I'll protect him no matter what."

"Good, he's lucky to have you." He claps my shoulder. "I would offer to photograph you, since you have the perfect face for it, but I have a feeling you are exclusive to him, no?" He smiles, putting me at ease, and I know he meant no harm.

"Definitely."

"Good. Had to check." He winks as he waves at Evan and looks back at the photo. "Love, it's a magnificent thing, isn't it?" He wanders away.

I can see why he's a recluse, but when I look at the photo again, I understand what he means. Evan captured something in my eyes, something even I didn't see but he did.

He always saw it in me, and he waited for me to see it too.

I watch my boy, and I know I will love this man until the day we are entombed together, the earth taking us back.

FIFTY-EIGHT

I can't believe how many people came and saw my work tonight. Even now, I'm shocked as I stare at the empty gallery and my images still hanging on the wall. When I agreed to the showcase, I didn't know how it would go, but I'm so glad I did it.

Alek was supportive all night, singing my praises, and I swear I fell in love with him all over again.

Moving through my portraits, I stop before the one I never intended to put on display. It's a happy memory, even if I know what came after, but it's the last image I have of Tommy. We all look so happy and untouched by the violence this world offers, but we've all changed since that night, even in little ways.

Alice struggles to sleep with the lights off.

Lally is scared of loud noises, thinking it's gunfire even if she won't admit it.

Alek worries continually about all of us and is still healing.

Skylar . . . well, he won't admit it, but I found him placing flowers at Tommy's memorial, and Bones? Bones is Bones. He keeps it all inside, but we've become a lot closer.

As for me? I have nightmares, ones I don't tell Alek about, but he knows, and he never demands I speak. He simply holds me through them. Last night, when he pinned my hands behind me while we were playing, I freaked out so badly I cried.

Yes, we all have our shit now, and we will never be as free as we were in this photo, but we are alive and we have to keep living.

I can't dishonor Tommy and his sacrifice for me by not. It's hard, and sometimes I feel so much guilt for him dying to protect me that I can't breathe, but I'm trying.

I want to make him proud, so when we meet each other again, he'll give me that wicked Tommy smile and welcome me into his arms.

I never thought I'd have to live without him, but I am, and I know I would give anything for one more minute with him. He was so fucking young, but that is life. We take what we are given, and we find happiness between then and the end.

I smile through the pain as my eyes rove over his handsome face.

"You ready, pretty boy?" Alek calls, and I turn to see him standing with his hand out, waiting for me.

I turn forward, my eyes lingering on Tommy's face, and I smile softly. "You'll live on in all of us and through our art, I promise," I murmur before I take Alek's hand and let him lead me to the gallery exit. Once there, I look back at the image and reach out to turn off the light.

"Take me home," I tell Alek.

"Gladly." We head toward his car and our home.

Toward my future with him.

We barely make it through the front door before I grab him and throw him into a wall. I hear something crash, but neither of us care as our lips meet in a desperate, wicked kiss, our tongues tangling as he tries to strip my jacket off with a mumbled growl of impatience.

Grinning against his lips, I tug his shirt out of his pants and slip my hands inside the deep, gaping material, caressing his chest. He moans, his head falling back against the wall as I slide my mouth down his throat and across his pecs.

"Pretty boy," he begs.

Smirking, I slide lower until I'm on my knees, and I meet his gaze.

"Fuck," he whispers. "You look like a goddamn angel right now on your knees for me. You make me feel like a fucking devil about to defile you."

"Hmm, really?" I ask as I undo his belt and slowly tug his pants down, exposing his tight black boxers and his huge, hard length underneath. The sight makes my mouth dry as my dick jerks. I want to feel him inside me. "I think it's more like I'm about to defile you," I retort with a grin.

"Too fucking true. You've tempted me since we first met," he growls, sliding his hand into my hair as I place a kiss on his cock. Gliding my mouth up his body, I press my lips to his once more.

"Then let me tempt you again," I whisper wickedly. "I know what I want as a prize for being a good boy and keeping my hands to myself all night." We've talked about it before.

He smirks. "You felt me up in the bathroom."

"Doesn't count." I nip his lips. "I want your ass. I want to be inside you while I stare into your eyes."

I pull back slightly, watching him gulp. I know it's a big step for him, and I can wait, but it's what I want. I've been imagining it for so long. "Evan," he whispers.

"I'll be gentle," I promise, kissing him softly. Sliding my hand down, I grip his cock and rub him through his boxers. "Don't you want that? Me inside of you? Claiming all of you?"

"Yes." He pushes himself into my hand.

Stepping back, I release him as I take off my jacket and toss it aside, kicking off my shoes, then I head to the stairs. "Then come on, big guy, let me make you feel good."

He stumbles after me, swearing as he shoves his pants off and slips his arms around me from behind as we hurry up stairs. He grabs my pecs before slamming me into the hallway wall, yanking my pants down and ripping at my shirt until I hear buttons ping away as he strips it from me.

His lips slide down my back before he bites the globe of my ass, making me moan. Desire hammers through me so hard I can barely think.

My cock weeps, desperate to be inside him, my abs clenching in want.

"Alek," I warn as he slides up, his hands hitting the wall on either side of my head as he presses against my back, rubbing his hard cock along my ass.

"You want me, pretty boy? Then you better fight for it," he whispers darkly, and I grin.

I knew he wouldn't make it easy, and it's exactly what I want. I spin in his arms and leap. He catches me as I wrap my legs around his waist, both of us grunting as we hit the other wall. His palm grips my ass, and he turns and stalks to his room, carrying me easily, and once there, he throws me onto his bed. I slide and twist, landing on top of him, pressing my mouth to his ear.

"You're mine, Alek Anders, just accept it."

He tries to push me off, and I lift up enough for him to roll, his dark eyes watching me hungrily as I tangle our legs together, rubbing my body against his. "You're mine too, pretty boy," he says, placing his hand on my shoulders then sliding it down to grip my ass. "But show me how much I'm yours. I need you."

The old Alek never would have dared to utter those words, so in reward, I lean down and kiss him until he's panting, rolling his hips against me.

Reaching over to the bedside table, I uncork the bottle and rub the cold lube over my dick before kissing him again. "Lift your legs, baby."

He does as I ask, hooking his hands behind his knees and lifting them as I continue to kiss him, circling his hole with two lubed fingers until he pushes onto them like we've been playing with. Sliding them inside him, I work them deep as he moans against my lips, his whole body jerking. "Does that feel good, baby?"

He hums, licking my lips as I work them deeper before pulling them out. "Then imagine how good I'll feel," I tell him as I twine our hands and hold them above his head while I press my dick against his hole.

Leaning down, I kiss him once more before leaning up.

He looks up at me, his eyes wide. "Have you ever . . ." He trails off, but I know what he's asking.

I claim his lips in a promising kiss. "No, this is my first time doing this, and I'm glad it's with you."

When he relaxes, I slowly press inside him, letting him adjust as I work myself into his tight, warm ass. Feeling him wrapping around me as his plush lips part on a moan is addictive, and I know we'll be doing this over and over if he lets me just so I can capture that expression again.

"Evan," he groans, pushing down to take me deeper.

"That's it, let me make you feel good," I murmur as I work myself as deep as I can, and then I lean down and kiss him as he adjusts to me being inside him. He feels so fucking good, so fucking tight and hot, that I can barely hold back, but I do. I finally get why he's like an animal when he fucks me.

"God, move, please."

Keeping our hands together, I slide my lips across every inch of his body I can reach as I pull out and thrust back in, claiming his ass with slow, rolling thrusts that have us both groaning.

"Fuck, fuck, fuck." He releases my hands to grip the bedding, ripping at it before they slide up my thighs.

Smirking, I tilt his hips so I hit his prostate with each thrust, making him cry out below me. His dark eyes open in shock, his breath leaving him in a woosh. "Oh fuck, there, right there—"

"I've got you, princess." I lick my lips and run my eyes over his tattooed, muscular body. I love how he looks below me and hearing the pleas on his lips.

I pull out and slam back in, speeding up. I need to watch him bounce on my cock, need to be as deep as I can. His tight, hot ass grips me like a fucking vise, already making me want to blow.

He moans loudly, the sound so fucking hot I can't take it. I bite his nipple, making him yelp, and then I sooth it with my tongue while I fuck his ass. His hands grip my hips, urging me on.

"Evan, I can't—it feels too good."

I bottom out in his clinging ass, fighting my own pleasure as I watch him. "Shh, baby, I've got you. Hold out a bit longer, I don't want to come just yet. I want to feel and see you like this all night."

His nails dig into my skin, cutting it, his jaw jumping as he grits his teeth, fighting his release as I stroke inside him. Sweat drips down our bodies as we fight off the inevitable pleasure so we can be locked like this forever.

"Please, pretty boy," he whimpers. "I can't . . . You feel too good—I—oh fuck!"

I watch as his cock jerks and swells before shooting ropes of cum all over his chest as he gasps and shudders below me, his thighs shaking against my body from the force.

Seeing him come like that pushes me into madness. I can't take it either.

My lips meet his once more, swallowing his grunt of pleasure, and then I follow him, filling his pretty ass with my cum. I slump into him, our bodies still locked. His arms come around me as he kisses the top of my head, and I kiss over his racing heart.

"I love you, Alek Anders, every single inch of you, even that cruel, mocking mouth."

"I love you too, pretty boy, even if you act like a rich prick."

I can't help but smile. Everything feels right in the world when we are like this.

NO PARKING
ACTIVE
DRIVEWAY
SHAW DRIVE
THE MOMENT
ANDERS AVE
ONE WAY
TOO
STOP
CAR REPAIR
NO PARKING
SALE
SILENT ROSE
Pine Valley
EVER

FIFTY-NINE

ALEK

"Yes, Alice, I had dinner." I sigh into my phone as I lean against the car I'm working on. I nod at Mackie as he heads to his car to let him know I finished working on it. "Yes, I remembered to go for my checkup. Who's the oldest here?" I tell her, but I smile at her worry. Over the last few months, the dynamic between us has changed a lot.

She's grown up dramatically, and although I miss the days when she needed me, I really like this new relationship we have. We are so much closer, like actual siblings. She worries for me, I worry for her, we hang with friends, and we are just together as a family.

"Okay, okay," I respond with a sigh. "How are your classes going?" I ask instead, changing the subject.

I listen along, but it's more of a rant than her needing my input, and when she finally says goodbye, I rub my head and the ache blooming there.

"Yo, Anders!" Noah calls.

"Here," I reply, pushing from the car and heading through the garage to find him and the others all gathering around a brand-new race car. "Damn, is that for the newbie?"

We took on a new racer recently. He's supposed to be the best, but he demanded a whole brand-new car, which Noah obliged, but as I stare at it, I whistle. It's boring as hell. Is that how he wanted it?

"You paint, right?" Noah asks as I join them. I don't speak, and he rolls his eyes. "I know you do. He didn't like any of the designs they could do, so it's up to you." He slaps a booklet against my chest with a grin, and I know he did it on purpose. He ordered it plain so I could paint it. I mentioned how I enjoyed it and wanted to try more once or twice, and here he is, giving me the opportunity.

That's one thing about Noah: he cultivated his family here. He gives them what they need while making it seem like we are doing him a favor, and I'm forever grateful for the day he took me on.

I never knew this is where my life would be, but I couldn't be happier.

As they scatter back into the garage, I pull out my phone and turn, snapping a selfie before the car.

Alek: Look what I get to paint.

Pretty Boy: Is it my ass later?

Pretty Boy: Damn, I can't wait to see what you do with it. I told you Noah loves you. I'm so proud of you, baby.

EVAN

LOML: I'll do both ;)

Laughing, I put my phone away and hurry over to the camera. Conan is waiting with a welcoming smile. He might be odd, but damn is he talented, and when I called him after my show, he offered me work experience with him this summer. It means I had to quit my part-time job, but they were more than happy to see me go, and they even threw me a congratulations party. I truly am blessed.

I work around my degree and help him with shoots, and he even put my name on one of them. It appeared in a magazine and every-thing, and Alek had it framed and hung above our bed, the loser.

He grins. "Are you ready, Evan?"

"Ready." I nod rapidly.

I hold Alek's hand as we walk under the cherry blossoms, my camera bouncing on my chest. I can't help but smile. "Remember how we met here before?"

It's become our place, where we met, argued, reconciled, and now come to be together when both of our lives are super busy. When it's a person you love, though, you make time to spend with them no matter how busy you are. I came straight from the shoot, and he took a break from painting so we could spend some time together.

We wander down the path, my eyes lifting to the trees as I breathe in deeply, letting it relax my soul.

"Evan?" Alek tugs me to a stop, and I blink, glancing at him. His cheeks are red, and he looks shy as he pulls a box from his pocket. "I got you something. Well, us something really." He rubs his neck, a sure sign he's worried, which is so fucking adorable.

"What is that?" I murmur, staring at the deep purple box.

"It's a ring. I got us both one. It isn't a proposal, not yet, but a promise that one day, this ring will be a proposal when you're ready," he admits as he opens it to show two black rings inside. The middles glitter with something, as if filled, and they are stunning.

I lift my eyes to his, shocked and so happy I want to cry. "And when that day comes, I'll say yes," I tell him without hesitation as I pluck a ring from the box and grab his hand, sliding it onto his index finger. He grins and grabs the other one, sliding it on mine, and we hold our hands up, watching them glitter together.

"This way, wherever we are, we are together," he murmurs, kissing my finger before pressing his forehead to mine, wrapping his arms around me. "Always joined. I'll always have you with me, just like I want, and when the time comes, I'll replace it with a diamond—"

"A big one," I tease, and he grins.

"A big one, such a rich prick," he jokes.

Kissing him, I taste the love on his lips as our ringed hands twine, locking together. "I love it, and I love you."

"I love you," he murmurs, "from the very bottom of my heart, the one you make race every single day."

"Cheese ball," I tease, but I can't contain my smile.

Under the blossoming trees, I let go of my past and worries, and I hand them over to him to keep safe.

Instead, I let myself be happy.

We found love in an unexpected place. It wasn't easy, but it's so worth it, and I'll fight for it every day of our lives because my racing heart is his too.

EPILOGUE

"Fuck, fuck, fuck! Fuck that little prick. I should have known he would do this. He had so many demands! I should beat some manners into him," Noah rants as I wipe my hands on a rag and join the others watching him.

"What's wrong, boss?" I call despite the others gesturing for me not to interrupt.

Noah turns toward me, looking more flustered than I have ever seen him. "I'll tell you what, that new fucking racer we hired? He joined another team. We have one week until the qualifiers for the championship, and we have to enter two racers, and I only have one!" he yells, his chest heaving.

My eyebrows rise. I've spent weeks painting that car for the little brat, and he left? Shit, did he get a better offer? That's so fucked up. Starfire Racing is the best, so why would he ruin his shot like that? If anyone is reaching that title, it's us, and he knew it, which is why he came on board. I suppose it doesn't matter now, but I think Noah might explode if he gets any more worked up.

"I know someone," I tell him, trying to hide my smile. "He's one hell of a racer. A bit of an ass, but he'll fit right in, and he's been dying for a chance to race for this team."

He's been down lately, distant and worried about his future. Some might call me a good friend, but I'm just sick of him turning up drunk at my door. This might give him purpose again and stop him from interrupting my and Evan's date nights.

"Call him," Noah demands, striding over.

Grabbing my phone, I hit his number. "Skylar?" I say when there's a groan.

"I didn't vomit in your bushes. That was Evan," he mutters, his voice thick.

"Are you hung over? Never mind. I have an opportunity for you. Starfire needs a racer. Do you want in?"

There's silence for a moment, and then I hear heavy breathing. "Are you fucking with me?"

"Nope. You get one shot. Don't fuck it up. Give it your all and be here tomorrow." Hanging up, I smile at Noah. "He's in. You got your-self a new racer. Just don't say I didn't warn you."

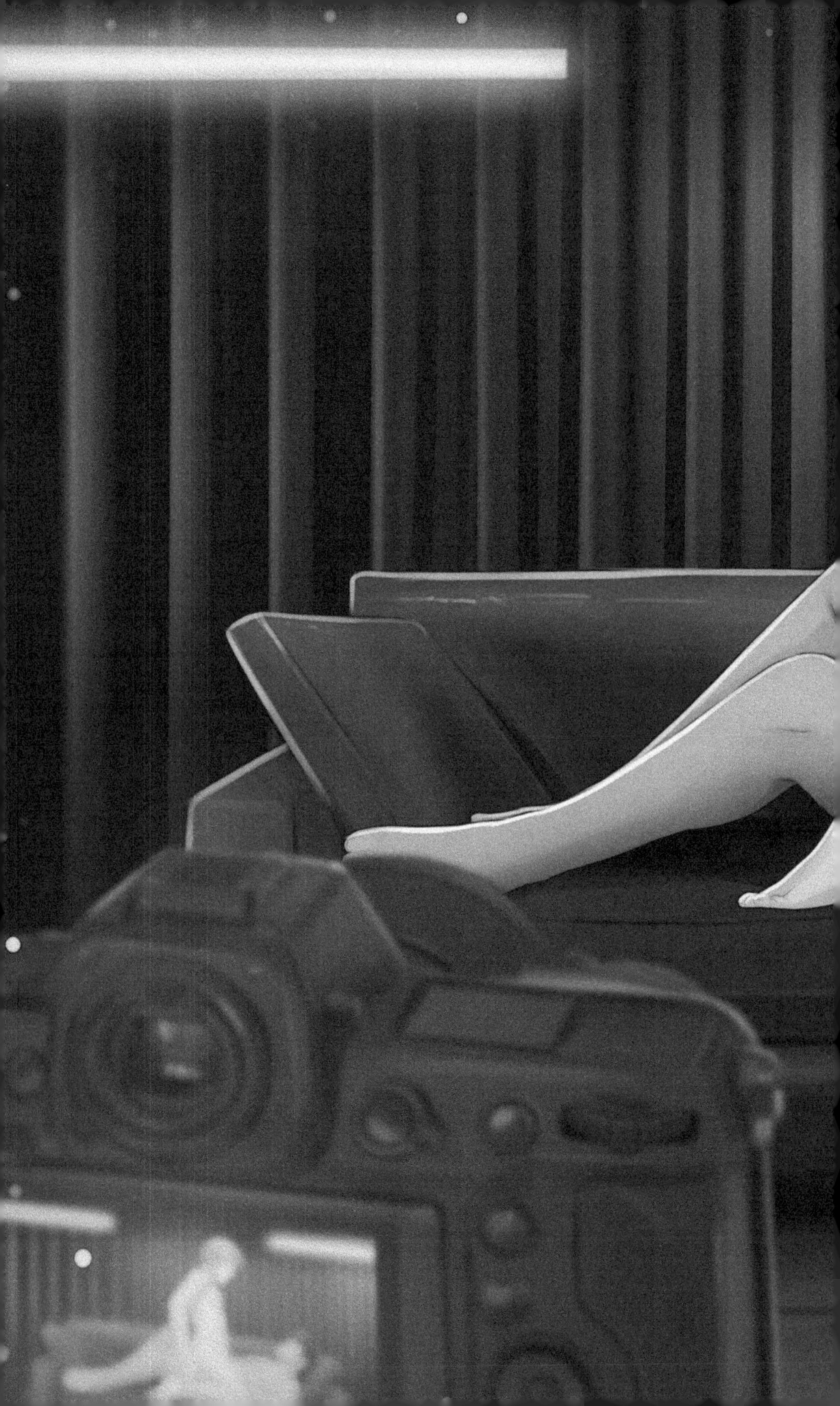

ABOUT K.A. KNIGHT

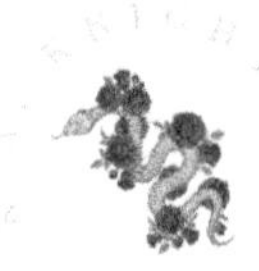

K.A Knight is an USA Today bestselling indie author trying to get all of the stories and characters out of her head, writing the monsters that you love to hate. She loves reading and devours every book she can get her hands on, and she also has a worrying caffeine addiction.

She leads her double life in a sleepy English town, where she spends her days writing like a crazy person.

Read more at K.A Knight's website or join her Facebook Reader Group.
Sign up for exclusive content and my newsletter here
http://eepurl.com/drLLoj

OTHER BOOKS BY K.A. KNIGHT

CONTEMPORARY

LEGENDS AND LOVE *CONTEMPORARY RH*

Revolt

Rebel

Riot - coming soon..

PRETTY LIARS *CONTEMPORARY RH*

Unstoppable

Unbreakable

PINE VALLEY COLLEGE *CONTEMPORARY*

Racing Hearts

DEN OF VIPERS UNIVERSE STANDALONES

Scarlett Limerence *CONTEMPORARY*

Nadia's Salvation *CONTEMPORARY*

Alena's Revenge *CONTEMPORARY*

Den of Vipers *CONTEMPORARY RH*

Gangsters and Guns (Co-Write with Loxley Savage) *CONTEMPORARY RH*

FORBIDDEN READS *(STANDALONES)*

Daddy's Angel *CONTEMPORARY*

Stepbrothers' Darling *CONTEMPORARY RH*

STANDALONES

The Standby *CONTEMPORARY*

Diver's Heart *CONTEMPORARY RH*

DYSTOPIAN

THEIR CHAMPION SERIES *Dystopian RH*

The Wasteland

The Summit

The Cities

The Nations

Their Champion Coloring Book

Their Champion - the omnibus

The Forgotten

The Lost

The Damned

Their Champion Companion - the omnibus

PARANORMAL

THE LOST COVEN SERIES *PNR RH*

Aurora's Coven

Aurora's Betrayal

HER MONSTERS SERIES *PNR RH*

Rage

Hate

Book 3 - *coming soon..*

COURTS AND KINGS *PNR RH*

Court of Nightmares

Court of Death

Court of Beasts

Court of Heathens - coming soon..

THE FALLEN GODS SERIES *PNR*

Pretty Painful

Pretty Bloody

Pretty Stormy

Pretty Wild

Pretty Hot

Pretty Faces

Pretty Spelled

Fallen Gods - the omnibus 1

Fallen Gods - the omnibus 2

FORGOTTEN CITY *PNR*

Monstrous Lies

Monstrous Truths

Monstrous Ends

SCIENCE FICTION

DAWNBREAKER SERIES *SCI FI RH*

Voyage to Ayama

Dreaming of Ayama

STANDALONES

Crown of Stars *SCI FI RH*

SHARED WORLD PROJECTS

Blade of Iris - Mafia Wars *CONTEMPORARY RH*

CO-WRITES

CO-AUTHOR PROJECTS - *Erin O'Kane*

HER FREAKS SERIES *PNR Dystopian RH*

Circus Save Me

Taming The Ringmaster

Walking the Tightrope

Her Freaks Series - the omnibus

STANDALONES

The Hero Complex *PNR RH*

Dark Temptations *Collection of Short Stories, ft. One Night Only & Circus Saves Christmas*

THE WILD BOYS SERIES *CONTEMPORARY RH*

The Wild Interview

The Wild Tour

The Wild Finale

The Wild Boys - the omnibus

CO-AUTHOR PROJECTS - *Ivy Fox*

Deadly Love Series *CONTEMPORARY*

Deadly Affair

Deadly Match

Deadly Encounter

CO-AUTHOR PROJECTS - *Kendra Moreno*

STANDALONES

Stolen Trophy *CONTEMPORARY RH*

Fractured Shadows *PNR RH*

Shadowed Heart

Burn Me *PNR*

Cirque Obscurum *PNR RH*

CO-AUTHOR PROJECTS - *Loxley Savage*

THE FORSAKEN SERIES *SCI FI RH*

Capturing Carmen

Stealing Shiloh

Harboring Harlow

STANDALONES

Gangsters and Guns *CONTEMPORARY*, IN DEN OF VIPERS' UNIVERSE

OTHER CO-WRITES

Shipwreck Souls *(with Kendra Moreno & Poppy Woods)*

The Horror Emporium *(with Kendra Moreno & Poppy Woods)*

AUDIOBOOKS

The Wasteland

The Summit

The Cities

The Nations - *coming soon*

Rage

Hate

Den of Vipers *(From Podium Audio)*

Gangsters and Guns *(From Podium Audio)*

Daddy's Angel *(From Podium Audio)*

Stepbrothers' Darling *(From Podium Audio)*

Blade of Iris *(From Podium Audio)*

Deadly Affair *(From Podium Audio)*

Deadly Match *(From Podium Audio)*

Deadly Encounter *(From Podium Audio)*

Stolen Trophy *(From Podium Audio)*

Crown of Stars *(From Podium Audio)*

Monstrous Lies *(From Podium Audio)*

Monstrous Truth *(From Podium Audio)*

Monstrous Ends *(From Podium Audio)*

Court of Nightmares *(From Podium Audio)*

Court of Death *(From Podium Audio)*

Unstoppable *(From Podium Audio)*

Unbreakable *(From Podium Audio)*

Fractured Shadows *(From Podium Audio)*

Shadowed Heart *(From Podium Audio)*

Revolt *(From Podium Audio)*

Rebel *(From Podium Audio) - coming soon*

FIND AN ERROR?

Please email this information to thenuttyformatter1@gmail.com:

- *the author name*
- *title of the book*
- *screenshot of the error*
- *suggested correction*

www.ingramcontent.com/pod-product-compliance
Lightning Source LLC
Chambersburg PA
CBHW051125300726
48981CB00023B/550/J